What the Heart Wants

AUDREY CARLAN

What the Heart Wants

HQN

ISBN-13: 978-1-335-66889-9

What the Heart Wants

HQN
22 Adelaide St. West, 40th Floor
Toronto, Ontario M5H 4E3, Canada
www.Harlequin.com

Printed in U.S.A.

To Jeananna Goodall...

*Thank you for sharing your mother's essence with me.
I'd like to believe the real Suda Kaye Ross
would be thrilled with the outcome of this book.
May her beauty live on through you,
your children and the generations to come.
She left us all such a beautiful gift in you.
I, for one, am grateful to her.*

What
the
Heart
Wants

PROLOGUE

My eighteenth birthday

Fly Free.

I trace the two words, written in black ink by a hand more beloved than my own. The color is stark against the pale pink of the parchment paper it's scrolled on. This was so her. Something she always did. Write letters. Mostly to my sister, Evie, and me over the years during her times away. Sometimes it would be a postcard from one of the faraway places her wandering soul would take her. Other times, it was a quickly scribbled note on a bar napkin enclosed with a ticket stub from a concert she'd seen on her adventure.

Once she sent us these incredible jeweled necklaces from a German glassworker that were blown glass and hand painted. Every time the mailman came to the reservation where we stayed with our grandfather, I'd pray there was a message or package from Mom.

From the time I could speak and understand, I'd hang on every word of the fantastical stories she'd tell us upon her return. Her stories took us everywhere from Istanbul to Iceland and all the way to a Burning Man festival in the California desert. That time, she gave us tiny finger cymbals that belly dancers used. After that gift, Mother signed us up for our first round of belly dancing lessons, something Evie and I still love doing together.

The reality in our home was that our mother, Catori Ross, went where the wind blew her.

I adored my mother and envied the life she lived. Still do, even after she left us for her final journey. Her one last adventure, she liked to call it. One she promised Evie and me would make her happy for eternity.

Never worry about me, beautiful girls, she whispered, each of her hands outstretched, my hand in one, Evie's in the other. Her body sunken in, nothing but skin and bones, in the bed she'd not left in months. She smiled and shifted her dark gaze first to Evie and then to me. *I've never been anywhere there wasn't beauty.* With a squeeze of our hands, she closed her eyes, exhaled, and was gone.

It was the last thing she said to us. What's amazing, though? I believed her. Death would be Mom's final stop whether or not she wanted it to be. Even then, I knew in my whole heart that she'd find beauty wherever her soul flew. It was her way.

The one saving grace in all this sorrow was that Mom truly *lived*. She never settled. Always kept one foot outside the door, hands tightly gripping the wheel of life. With every breath she took, she exhaled freedom, spirit, and love. Wanderlust oozed out of every pore. Nothing could hold her back. Not her military-driven husband or her two daughters. A fact that has hurt Evie deeply.

Me, I've always understood. I'm just like my mother. My feet are constantly itching to dance, to run, to fly. Which is why, scanning the last paragraph of my mother's words to me on this, my eighteenth birthday, I've come to the revelation that I, too, can't settle. I won't be held back by obligation, responsibility, or even...love.

I shuffle through the stacks of sealed pink envelopes beside the satin ribbon that held them together when my grandfather handed these letters to us after my mother died six months ago. Each envelope carries a date or specific event in our lives indicating when we are to open them.

Evie and I share the same birthday, so she opened her first letter marked with the same date as my own. Today's date. Her twentieth birthday, my eighteenth.

Evie sniffles from the papasan chair she's snuggled into and folds her letter into thirds before stuffing it back into the envelope. She presses the flat of her hand along the front and lifts it to her nose.

"Smells like her." Evie clears her throat as a tear slides down her cheek.

I sniff my letter and note the subtle hints of citrus and earth, maybe even patchouli. "Mom always said if you're going to smell like anything, let it be natural. Fruit and spice."

"And everything nice!" Evie chuckles, then lets out a long sigh. "I miss her. Sometimes I pretend she's just gone off on another one of her adventures, you know? Then I can be pissed off and plan out all the catty things I'm going to say to her when she finally returns with a suitcase full of dirty clothes and presents to smooth over the hurt of her absence."

My throat tightens, and I suck in a harsh breath. "Evie, she didn't want to leave..."

"Not this time, Kaye, but what about all the other times? Years and years of time lost. And for what?" She huffs and stands up to pace, clutching her letters to her chest. "Fun. Wild experiences. Adventures!" Her irritation grows along with her volume. "It killed her. This need to see the greener things on the other side." She points at me with a mighty scowl and indignation seeping from her. "Well, that won't be me. No way. No how. I've got my feet firmly planted on terra firma. I'm going to finish school, get my bachelor's in finance, then my master's and make something of myself. And I'm going to be happy!"

I watch my sister's golden-blond hair swish back and forth down her back in a tumble of beachy waves. Her blue eyes are blazing with determination when she tosses her letters to the chair and flings herself on the bed next to me in a dramatic heap.

My sister is light everywhere I am dark. Mom never said much about my real father other than that his name was Ian and I look exactly like him. Coffee-brown hair and amber-colored eyes. Evie and I both got our mother's Native American bone structure, including the high rounded cheekbones, thick hair, long bodies, dark golden skin tone, and warm hearts.

Unfortunately, we didn't get her or our grandfather's awesome, pitch-black, pin-straight hair or super-dark espresso eye color. Our eyes are the same almond shape, which I've always thought was one of our most attractive features. Although we have different biological dads, our shared genes still make us look very much alike.

Slowly, I stroke my sister's hair until she turns over.

"What did your letter say?" she asks.

I lick my lips, wondering if I should share. It's hard when my sister and I have never kept secrets from one another. Ever. It's always been Evie and Suda Kaye against all odds. Knowing I can't hide from her, I hand her my letter.

"'Suda Kaye, my little *huutsuu*.'" She covers her mouth and closes her eyes. "Little bird," she croaks at the endearment Mom always called me.

I smile. "Always and forever, *taabe*," I use my mother's nickname for her, Comanche for *sun*.

Evie quickly reads the letter, her hands shaking as she passes it back to me, her face a mask of worry. "You're not going to do it, are you?"

I bite down on the inside of my cheek and nod.

"Kaye…you can't do that. What about Camden? He won't understand. A guy like that. The life he wants to give you. No way. You just…" She lets out a breath, grabs my hands, and squeezes them. "What are you going to do?"

My heart pounds inside my chest, and I stare into my sister's eyes, my soul readying for the challenge ahead. "I'm going to fly free."

"Suda Kaye, baby, are you sure? We can wait." Camden hovers over me, his face so close to mine I can taste the peppermint on his breath. He moves one of his hands along my bare shoulder and down my arm where he laces our fingers together. He lifts and holds my hand up by my head against the blanket we're cuddling naked underneath. We're in the loft of the old barn on his family's farm.

I shake my head and lift up until my lips touch his. He kisses me slowly, nibbling on my bottom lip before dipping his tongue into my mouth. We kiss until my jaw hurts and I can't breathe. I pull my head away, gasping for air while staring into his handsome face. I've never in my life met a more beautiful boy. Wavy, dark blond hair, sexy hazel eyes that burn with lust.

"It has to be tonight. Now," I urge, lifting my hips up and glorying in the naked ridge of his length along my thigh.

He takes a deep breath before nodding and shifting his hips until they fall between my thighs. The first contact of his manhood and my center is electric. Arousal and excitement rush through my nerve endings, and a fierce need throbs inside of me.

"Please..." I whisper against his cheek near his ear.

Camden is breathing heavily against my neck. "I don't want to hurt you."

I smile and kiss his cheek. "Evie swears it only hurts for a minute, and then it's nothing but bliss. For us both. Now, please, make love to me, Cam."

His arms are trembling as he lifts his big body over mine and reaches for his jeans, the ones we discarded in our haste to make out. Only tonight, I planned to take it all the way and wanted to surprise him.

The blanket falls to his hips and I look down my body at his muscular form kneeling above me. The long hours he's worked this past year in his father's steel company, learning the job from the ground up, have sculpted his body into a work of art. I trace his box-shaped abs until he lets out a pained groan when I wrap my hand around his length and give it a healthy stroke. His penis is long and thick and glistening at the tip with his excitement. I lick my lips, wanting to put him in my mouth.

This is not the first time I've seen him naked. We've been together for four years, since I was fourteen and a freshman in high school, and he was a sophomore. The first day of school, he picked me out of a crowd in the cafeteria and asked if he could eat with me. I looked into those hazel eyes and fell in love. Right there. Back then, it was puppy love. Four years later, it is the kind of love to build a life on.

Cam's hands shake as he rolls on the condom and strokes

his length once again. I moan and lift my hips, wanting him to do something, *anything* to make the need stop. It's our final step sexually, and I'm more than ready for it.

He eases his hand between my thighs and sighs when he encounters my flesh.

"Wet," he whispers, rubbing his fingers back and forth.

"Yes." I moan when he presses one long digit inside and uses his thumb to circle the bundle of nerves that makes me lose my mind every single time. Over the years, he's perfected this move. Only now, it's not enough. "Cam…please," I beg again, needing him, wanting this one last connection to the man of my dreams.

Cam removes his fingers and centers himself between my thighs. He leans over so that his body is hovering over mine. "You know I love you, right?" His words are guttural, as if they've surfaced straight from his soul.

"Yeah." I nod frantically, lifting my hips until the head presses inside.

He firms his jaw and speaks through clenched teeth. "You know I'm going to marry you someday?"

I grin and grip his hips. "Do it. Come inside."

He gives me an inch more while I open my legs wider, making entry easier. Instantly, I feel a pressure I can't explain. It's tight and hot and hard. So much bigger than two of his fingers.

"Tell me you love me?" He presses his forehead to mine. "Tell me you'll always love me, Suda Kaye," he demands, on the brink of losing it.

I swallow as tears prick the backs of my eyes, knowing what I'm about to do and how utterly selfish it's going to seem. But I can't move forward without this. Without having experienced Cam's love to its fullest, just this one time.

"I'll always love you, Camden. No matter what happens."
Which is the truth, just not the whole truth.

He smiles, presses his lips to mine and thrusts all the way
inside. I cry into his mouth, into his kiss where he holds steady
as the piercing pain shimmers through my body and steals
my breath. He holds me, staying perfectly still until my body
adjusts and the tension slowly ebbs away, leaving a burning,
needy sensation between my thighs.

He lifts his head and peppers kisses along my cheeks, forehead, and eyes. "You okay? Want me to stop?"

I swallow down the bite of pain between my legs and shake
my head. "No. I'm perfect. You're perfect," I assure him.

"God, so are you." He kisses me, eases out slowly, and
thrusts back in. This time it feels warm, not hot. The pain
has receded and the wetness between my legs has grown, eas-
ing his way in and out more smoothly. Cam picks up a slow
rhythm, and I wonder why the hell we've never done this
before. It feels too amazing to describe.

Cam tucks his hand at the nape of my neck, the other
around my shoulder while he leverages his hips in a faster,
more erratic rhythm. My body is alive with sensation and
tingling ripples of pleasure as our bodies mist with sweat.
A buzzing feeling warms throughout my limbs and fires up
from my core to my chest. I wrap my arms and legs around
Cam in a fierce grip as he starts to slam his hips against mine.

He's holding on to me so tight, his muscles and body rigid
with the control he's holding on to. "It's so good, sweets. Baby,
it's so good," he grinds out through clenched teeth. He presses
in and holds for a long moment. "Never thought it could be
this good. I love you. I love you," he declares into my ear as
he picks up his momentum.

My entire body goes electric and fills with the need to

burst, to explode, to *something*, and then it happens. He slips a hand between our bodies and spins firm circles around my clit with two fingers. I lose all focus as I skyrocket into pure nirvana, stars flickering behind my closed eyelids and my body on a never-ending loop of ecstasy.

Three more thrusts and Cam mashes our lips and hips together as his body goes tight as a drum, every muscle I touch straining and bulging as he groans in relief at what I hope is one of the most memorable moments of his life.

It has to be. It has to last a lifetime.

I hold on to him like my life depends on it, wanting to never let go. Only I know that's not how our story ends.

No, once Cam snuggles against my side, he pulls off of me and loops his arm around my waist. "I'm going to love you forever, Suda Kaye Ross," he promises, then kisses the back of my neck, sighing contentedly. He removes the condom and stashes it in a paper towel nearby before coming back to cuddle next to my cooling flesh.

I wait a good twenty minutes, lying there, memorizing the feel of his arm around me, the ache between my thighs, the fullness of my heart, until I know he's asleep. That's when I remember what I have to do, and my heart cracks and breaks open, spilling all the love we have out into the air around us. I leave it all there, in the place where Camden Bryant made love to me inside the barn loft, the giant window all the way open so we could stargaze.

It was the best experience of my life.

Swallowing down the heartache and sadness, I quietly remove myself from his arms and slip back into my dress and panties, noting the tinge of blood smeared on my thighs. I grab my flip-flops and clench them in my hand, not wanting to make a sound. I grab my phone, lift it up, and take a single photo of my sleeping love because it's the last I'll ever get.

On my hand, the moonlight reflects off the small gold-and-diamond promise ring he gave me last month when I graduated high school, and he promised me a good, solid life where he'd take care of me. At the time, I wasn't sure where my life would lead, so I accepted the ring. That was before I read my mother's letter—the letter that changed everything.

I slip the ring off my finger and set it on top of his phone along with the small pink note I wrote him before I came over tonight. It's only a few words, but he'll understand their meaning.

Be happy. Love another.
Fly free,
Suda Kaye

With one last look back at the man I'll love until the day I die, I step down the ladder, letting him go one rung at a time. By the time I've left the barn and made it to the car my mother's inheritance bought me, I've already put the love for a life I wasn't meant to live behind me. With every mile I drive, that life disappears, and new opportunities present themselves. My half of the money Mom left Evie and me will last a long time and I plan to use it to live my life to the fullest.

No settling. No laying down roots.

I'm living for the moment, not for the future.

I have to see for myself if Mom was right.

The grass may not be greener on the other side, but if you look hard enough, you can always find beauty.

1

Present day

Wanderlust. A word for some, a lifestyle for others. Wanderlust is not something that's easy to ignore. It lives and breathes inside you. A yearning that's hard to describe. Once you know it's there, alive, calling out to you, enchanting your thoughts with grand adventures and discoveries, you are driven to make one of two choices: accept its siren call or banish it forever.

Like my mother, I felt the empty hole in my gut that urged me to move on. To go. To flee. To fly. It still lives inside me, sometimes satisfied but never full, always yearning for something more.

From place to place I went. For a decade, I lived the life of a true wanderer. Slept on the couches of people I met at a concert, caravanned with other nomads, performed with a belly dancing crew all over Europe, and enjoyed all types of pleasures.

Sumptuous foods around the world.

Sensual clothing that flirted and aroused.

Visited exotic locales most people could only imagine in their wildest dreams.

Though the men I met, tasted, bedded, and experienced incredible pleasures of the flesh with, never, not once, compared with the single night I had with my first love.

Oh, don't get me wrong. In every place my wandering soul took me, I worked hard at starting anew, leaving behind my life in Colorado. And for brief moments, I succeeded. Until that gnawing, twisting feeling in my gut would start again, and I'd have to go. Off to the next adventure, always attempting to fill that emptiness.

I've driven the Autobahn in Germany. Spent a month in an ashram in India, learning the art of yoga and self-love. Kissed a Frenchman under the Eiffel Tower. Eaten pasta with a stunning Italian in a small seaside town at the tip of the boot in Italy. I've ridden a camel through the desert and touched the pyramids of Giza. Prayed for clarity at the foot of the Christ the Redeemer statue in Brazil. Worn a fuzzy Cossack hat in Russia while twirling in circles in the snow. Ridden a bicycle in Copenhagen. Sailed the fjords in Norway. Watched the ball drop in Times Square on New Year's Eve on my twenty-fifth birthday. Evie flew out for that one, and she was my first kiss that year.

Despite all of these wonders, this incredible life I've been blessed to live, the night I gave my heart and body to Camden Bryant is one I've never topped. It's my most cherished memory. I hold it close, never speak of it, not to anyone. Even Evie. She knows that I lost my virginity to Cam and left town the same night, but she has never—not once—dug for more information. Somehow, maybe through our sisterly connection, she knew I couldn't talk about it.

For years, I've given myself to the wind the same way my mother did, and I don't regret it. The grass is definitely greener on the other side, only because it's a new experience.

All new things tend to come with that breath of whimsy, that moment of awe. But what I've come to learn is that nothing, not the Great Wall of China, not Machu Picchu, the Taj Mahal, the Hawaiian Islands, or any of the other extraordinary places I've visited, the incredible things I've done, come close to the feeling of being home.

In recent years, I've come to understand why Mother always came back. It wasn't just Evie and me or our grandfather Tahsuda, the reservation back in Oklahoma, or even Colorado where we ended up. It was all of it. The entire kit and caboodle. It was the green grass of familiarity. A beauty Mom already knew existed, not one she had to search for.

I clutch Mom's letter while the plane makes its final descent into Denver International Airport.

With shaking fingers, I open the letter and take a full breath, remembering where I was just eighteen hours ago.

Australia. My twenty-eighth birthday.

I celebrated my birthday yesterday in Sydney, but once I read Mom's words, I packed up my things, kissed my current fling, Brody—an Australian surfer with golden skin and a bright white smile—a quick goodbye and wished him well. I had to go home for the first time in ten years. Had to. It was my destiny.

Brody, being the total hippie, Mother-Nature-loving, pleasure-giving sweetheart that he is, understood. He didn't even question me. He knew the score. Every man I spent any time with over the past decade knew the score.

Suda Kaye Ross went where the wind took her.

It was in writing. Written on pink parchment paper in words left to me by one of the two most important women in the world.

Since I left Pueblo, Colorado, a decade ago, I experienced

everything my mother suggested with a flourish and desire for life that couldn't be quenched. This last letter, though, threw all of her other teachings into the fire. It was a complete one-eighty from the letters that came before.

The letter on my twentieth birthday had told me to go to Europe and see a man named Marco in Calabria, Italy. She gave me an address and a phone number. When I showed up, Marco knew immediately who I was and welcomed me with open arms. His son, on the other hand, was even more welcoming, warming my bed and getting me over my Camden slump. We spent months in bed and working in his family's Italian restaurant by the sea, until my feet started to itch and the pit in my gut twisted in warning. After six months, I left and headed to France, meeting up with another of my mother's contacts.

Along with the letter Mom wrote for my twenty-first birthday, she'd given me a thin book, filled with names, numbers, and addresses alongside the following note:

Suda Kaye, my huutsuu,
Open this book, point to a page, and go where the wind takes
you. Do it every time the urge to spread your wings comes upon
you. Fly free, my little bird. Live life to the fullest. Always be
honest with your intentions toward others. Never let them ex-
pect your feet to stay on the ground.
Have no regrets, my darling.
All my love,
Mom

I've been pointing and flying for years. Sending Evie postcards and presents from my travels but never going back home. Even the thought of being in the same place where I'd lost my mother and left the love of my life was too painful. Until now. Until my mother's two words spirited me into immediate action.

I sigh and unfold the letter, looking at her beautiful handwriting for the hundredth time since boarding this flight.

Suda Kaye, my huutsuu,

You've had your adventures. Hopefully you have heeded my words and spread your wings across the globe using the money I've left you.

If there is one thing I could take back in the life I lived, it would be that I never had the time to share in the adventures I wanted to have with my girls. You will understand one day. Wanderlust may be inside of us, but we decide when to set it free.

Today, and for the foreseeable future, I want you to be brave, to be strong, to be everything I was never able to be.

Settled.

Fully at peace with your lot in life.

You have the ability to make that happen for you, my darling. Now is the time to set me free alongside that need inside of you to fly. Don't clip your wings, for you'll need them one day.

A solid friend.

A true wife.

A responsible mother.

A committed sister.

Be there for Evie. For our family. Plant the seed. Make roots. Ground yourself to somewhere and something that fills your soul with a different desire. The desire to be needed. Wanted. Loved. Present.

Go home.

Wherever home is to you, go there now.

With all the love the world has to give,

Mom

Go home.

After years of celebrating life, all the beauty that the world has to offer, my mother's words spill into my mind like a warm ball of light. The thought of Evie, making a life near her feels...right. She's the closest thing to home I've ever had.

It's time I make peace with all that I left behind. Time that I ground myself, turn my life into something solid. Stable.

A joy I haven't felt in ten years seeps into my bones, warming me from the inside out as the plane's wheels touch down. I look out the window and smile at the Colorado sky.

I'm home.

The second I step foot outside of the Denver airport, I see a sleek, black Porsche Cayenne idling at the curb. Only that's not what takes my breath away. It's the stunning goddess leaning nonchalantly against it, arms crossed over her chest, long blond locks hanging over her shoulder like bushels of wavy spun gold. She's rocking black aviators with a sweet chrome trim, a pair of tapered midnight-colored dress slacks, a silky, flowy white blouse, a sexy-as-fuck pair of black stilettos, and a black leather blazer to top it all off. My sister looks hot and *expensive.* It's like she just stepped off the cover of *Business Badass,* the smokin' female edition.

Her pink-tinted lips curve into a simple smirk.

"Took you long enough." She tips her chin up before her smirk turns into a full-fledged beaming white smile as she opens her arms and pushes off the car.

"Sissy!" I squeal and take off in my cork wedge sandals, my maxi dress flying all around me, one arm holding my floppy wide-brimmed sun hat in place as I run.

We collide, giggling like schoolgirls instead of a woman

in her late twenties and one having just knocked on the door of thirty.

"Happy birthday!" I lean back and kiss her cheeks, then her forehead, and then her lips in a quick touch.

"Right back atcha, sis!" Evie grins before turning and looping her arm around my waist and leading me to her fancy SUV.

"Nice ride." I chuckle.

"Better than the rickety old baby blue Beetle I was driving last time you were here, eh?"

I laugh and lug my gigantic suitcase into the back of her car with a resounding thud. My entire life is in that case, and for a moment, I send up a thank-you to my wandering mom's juju that she must've passed down in her genetics since I've never lost the case in all my travels.

"Absolutely!" I slam the hatch down and we both jump in the car.

Once we're on the road, I take off my hat and unceremoniously toss it in the back before digging through my giant hobo bag-slash-purse, looking for some lip balm. That plane ride dried me out.

"So, you still in Colorado Springs? Last we spoke, you mentioned the possibility of moving back to Pueblo." I cross my fingers at my thigh in the hope that we're not going back to Pueblo where Mom had her long battle with cancer. At the time, she wanted us to have a "regular" high school experience instead of the years of study we had on the reservation when we lived with our grandfather.

Evie pushes her long hair back behind her ear while focusing on the road for our almost two-hour drive.

"Yeah, but I visit my Pueblo office often since it's only

forty minutes away. Once or twice a week I drive into Denver to do meetings with headquarters." She crinkles her nose.

"Bet you love that." I smile and lay my hand over hers where it rests on the console.

She squeezes my hand and the sensation of sister solidarity shoots like lightning through my palm, up my arm, and fills my heart with a warmth I have only been able to experience with my older sister. "You know me well," she says.

"I know that you've never liked to drive. I'd offer, but honestly, I love you too much, and I'm too tired. I'd crash into a girder or go down in a ditch. That flight was brutal."

Evie laughs. "Remind me, how long were you in Australia? Sometimes your adventures bleed into one another for me."

I shrug. "Hmm, I think three months. I was in New Zealand before that. Rode around with the rugby team there."

Evie's eyebrow rises over her glasses, and she turns her head, dipping her chin to give me a peek at her icy-blue eyes. "A rugby team? Kaye, don't tell me you banged an entire rugby team."

I open my mouth half in shock and playfully smack her arm. "No way. I only bedded two…but it was at the same time, so it didn't really count as more than one fling."

"Seriously?" She raps on the steering wheel, sounding half scandalized and half jealous. She shakes her head. "Some life you live. Who'd've thought my baby sis would travel the world and fly by the seat of her pants?"

"Mom did," I say softly, thinking about the reason I'm back.

Evie's shoulders slump, and she sighs heavily. "Yeah, you're right." She clears her throat as a thick fog of sadness fills the interior of the car, both of us likely thinking about Mom.

"Well," she says, breaking the silence, "tell me a little bit about Brady, the Australian surfer?"

I smile, recalling Brody's messy long hair down to his shoulders, his big blue eyes and svelte body. "Brody. And he was great. A true gentleman."

"Really? A gentleman?" Evie counters in disbelief.

I snort. "No, not really. He's a peace-love dove, pot-smoking hippie who fucks like a god and surfs as though his legs were made for the sea."

Evie smiles and chuckles. "And he was totally fine with you leaving?"

"It's part of the deal. They want a piece of me, they take what they can get. No more, no less." I run my fingers through my long brown hair, trying to work out the knots from sleeping on the plane.

"Isn't that hard? Spending intimate moments, sharing a bed, months at a time with all of these different people, and then just walking away when the mood strikes? I don't know how you do it, Kaye. I've never known. I especially didn't understand it when Mom left us, month after month, returning for a brief couple of weeks, until she'd be off again. Stars in her eyes and the wind beneath her wings."

Her words hammer into my chest, and that pit in my stomach twists.

Evie pulls off her glasses and looks at me, her wounded gaze piercing straight through to my soul. "We were never enough for her. And then she got sick..."

I swallow down the bile that scratches at my throat. "Evie... she just couldn't stop. It wasn't inside her at the time, and when she finally did—"

"It was too late."

"At least we had those years with her. We should be thankful for that."

Evie huffs, not seeming at all thankful. More like she'd

rather scream her frustration at the top of her lungs, but she's too cool a cucumber to explode. Too reserved. Proper. Put together.

As I watch the simmering anger cool in the silence between us, I vow to help my sister bring those emotions she's suppressing to the surface. No one should live their life holding any piece of themselves back. Putting on a mask to hide the sorrow underneath. It's not healthy.

I'm smart enough to know this is not the time for that. Not when I've just made it back home after a decade.

Evie sucks in a full breath and offers a pitiful, fake smile that I see right through. "So, how long are you staying? When's the next big adventure and where is it taking you?"

I grab my sister's hand, bring it to my lips, and kiss the top. "I don't know. My heart and soul brought me home."

"Oh yeah? Does that mean I may get you for two weeks? A month? Three? Like sexy surfer Brady?"

I giggle and hold her hand. "It's *Brody*, and no, I'm not putting a time frame on it."

"Well, you know you always have a home with me. No matter when or for how long."

I smile. "Good. I'm counting on it."

Evie hums a long "hmmmmmm" so that it extends for a full breath.

"No *hmm*, just home. I felt the need to be home," I insist with a finality I'm trying to believe myself.

"Yeah? What did Mom's letter to you say about that? Have you opened it yet? Last one told you to jump off a cliff in New Zealand, which is how you first met sexy surfer, the one who saved your ass from drowning, if I remember correctly."

I touch my lips and shrug. "Totally true, but that's not what Mom's letter to me said this time."

"Oh yeah? What did it say?"

Biting into my bottom lip, I turn sideways so that I can look right at her. She turns her head to glance my way and then back at the road.

"Am I going to hate this? Every letter Mom writes stresses me out even though I can hardly wait to read the next one in the stack," Evie confides.

I know the feeling. It's like Christmas, New Year's, and every fun holiday rolled into one every time the date of the next letter comes around.

"She told me to spend some time at home. With you."

She narrows her brow, her lips twisting into a pout. "So, you just dropped everything and got on a plane back home. After ten years of being away?"

"Yep. Exactly."

"Kaye, do you realize how freaking crazy that sounds? Are you listening to yourself? I appreciate having Mom's words, too, especially after losing her, but..." She blows out a breath harshly and then pushes her long swooping bangs over to the side of her face. "*Huutsuu*, they are not the be-all, end-all. You need to live for you. Do what you want with your life, not what our mother said you should do."

"And where would I be right now if I did that?"

She shakes her head. "I don't know. Married to a great man, probably Cam, with a couple of towheaded babies on your hip and a truckload of money in your bank account from his steel empire?"

Hearing Camden's name steals my breath. I run my hands down my neck and quickly tap the button on the car door to lower the window for some fresh air. "Not cool, Evie. Not cool."

She sighs and reaches across to rub along my arm. "I know, I'm sorry. But honestly, I don't even know why talking about Camden is off-limits since you're the one that left. You never even told me what happened between you. All I can remember is him showing up at our house brokenhearted and you being long gone."

I hold up my hand. "Just stop. I can't talk about him. It's ancient history. Just know that I'm here now with no plans to leave."

"I'm sorry if I don't believe you, Kaye." Evie's tone is tortured. "I just can't get my hopes up."

"What will it take for you to believe I'm staying? A promise? I'll promise you. I'm staying."

"For a year. No, two!" she fires off, but it's the desperation in her words that slithers around my heart and squeezes tight. She needs me.

Evie continues undaunted. "The Ross sisters have been apart for too long. I don't want to have to hop on a plane to see my sister in some random location. Traveling is not my thing and you know that."

"Oh boy, do I know it."

"Then promise me. Two years. Give staying in one place a shot. For me. For us. We need this." She grips right above my knee. "I need this. I need to not worry about you dying on some mountain in China or in a shady biker bar. Give me some peace of mind. Give me your time."

"On one condition."

"Name it," she offers instantly.

"You'll help me figure out what the hell to do with my time for the next freakin' two years." I beam and cover her hand, giving it a squeeze.

Evie smiles so huge it's as if the clouds have parted, the sun started shining brighter, and the heaviness in the car lifted, filling the space with happiness and love.

"Deal."

2

Two months later

"Wake up, sleepyhead!" My body is shifted from side to side as I open my eyes to see nothing but pure icy blue.

"You mumbled something about having an appointment today," Evie says. "And why are you sleeping on the couch when I have a perfectly good guest room? You hang your clothes in there, why not lay your body down on the comfy bed?" She palms my cheek as she presses her booty into the curve where my waist dips and my knees are cuddled up as I sleep on my side.

"I love your face." I smile up at the most beautiful woman I know.

She taps my nose and gives me a saucy wink. "And I love yours. Now what's all of this?" She spreads one arm out at all the mess I have cluttering the room. There are mismatched fabric swatches draped all over the table. Lying on the floor are other boxes of various knickknacks I brought with me from all over the world. I was sorting through and evaluating them to see what might work as merchandise for the idea I've had swirling around in my head the last two months. Sitting on top of the fabrics from Istanbul are import/export catalogs that have brightly colored tabs poking out in every direction, marking products I've got my eye on.

I lick my lips and bite down on my bottom one.

Evie narrows her gaze to mine. "Oh no, nuh-uh. I know that look." She stands up in a rush. "You're getting ready for your next adventure. I know that look, Suda Kaye. Mom trained us from an early age to be leery of that look. You promised!" Her voice hangs on the last word with a major dose of disappointment lacing each letter. I'm surprised she didn't stomp her foot.

Pushing up into a sitting position, I shake my head. "No. Nothing like that. Just planning. I have an idea, something I wanted to talk to you about but...um..." I glance over at the clock and realize I'm going to be late if I don't get my ass in gear. "Later. We'll talk later. Tomorrow maybe, when I have more put together."

"Tomorrow is Saturday, and we swore we'd visit Tahsuda at the reservation. It's a long drive, but you are not avoiding our grandfather any longer." She purses her lips defiantly.

I let out a groan and stand up in nothing but a cami and a pair of lacy panties. "I won't bail. He'd probably put the smackdown on me with the elders and they'd conjure up the *Pia Mupitsi* to whip me into shape."

We both shiver at the mention of the Big Cannibal Owl monster that our grandfather used to scare us with as children in order to keep us in line. He never took a hand to us, but he'd sure scare us straight.

"You don't want to risk pissing off *Toko*. He's already annoyed you've been gone so long," Evie warns.

I feel my shoulders slump and guilt rears its ugly head that I haven't kept in better touch with our only living relative on my mother's side, our grandfather Tahsuda, or *Toko*, maternal grandfather in Comanche. Of course, there's our absentee father, Adam Ross. Technically my stepdad, Evie's real father, but we were never close. I wonder where in the world he is right now. I'm sure Evie knows. She was always better at keeping up with his military position and stations.

"You're right." I make my way toward the coffee machine, pop in a pod, position my mug, and press the start button. "What do you have going on today?"

"Business meeting in town. You want to do dinner tonight?"

"Sure. Sounds good. You know, sissy," I tut like any good sister would, "I've been here two months and you have yet to go out on one date."

Evie picks up her purse and pulls it over her shoulder. "And?"

I frown. "And how are you getting your lady business tended to if you're not ever seeing anyone or at least picking up a guy at a bar?"

Evie lifts her head to the sky and sighs.

"How long has it been? A few months?" I ask softly.

Evie's lips compress into a flat thin line.

"Six months? A year?" My mouth drops open. "More than a year?" Her face doesn't change one iota. I gasp. "Holy shit, Evie!"

"Shut up. Not everyone is a wild child like you. I don't have the time to meet men. After I broke it off with Stan Ludley..."

"You mean Dudley," I mumble and grab the coffee mug. I take it with me to the fridge where I pull out the pumpkin creamer and pour in a huge dose. Pumpkin flavor all year long, I say. The creamer people should never take this off the shelves. And until the day they do, pumpkin bliss every day.

"Oh, come on, Kaye. Stan wasn't that bad."

I spin around, bringing the cup up to my face. "No. Stan Ludley was as boring as his name. I mean, who names their kid that? Boring parents, that's who. Set that poor guy up for a life of boredom."

"Oh, I wouldn't know what that's like... SUDA KAYE!" She enunciates my name loudly.

"Exactly. Eeev-ieeeeeeee. My point exactly. You need someone named Rico or Javier." I grin.

She crosses her arms over her chest. "And what about you? It's been two whole months since you've gotten laid by surfer boy."

I set down my cup and smack the counter with my other hand dramatically. "I know! Two months too long! In my defense, I've been focused on figuring out what the hell to do with my life and getting to know Colorado Springs and poking around back in Pueblo." I tap my bottom lip with my index finger. "I've got it. We need to get out there and hook ourselves some hotties. Have a little fun. I'm feeling a girls' night out on the town is in order."

"No. No way. You'll force me to get all dolled up, drunk, and I'll end up underneath some stranger and wake up hungover, doing the walk of shame."

"God willing." I clap, grinning ear to ear.

She shakes her head. "I'm not like you, Kaye. I can't just sleep around."

"You calling me easy?" I purse my lips.

"Are you implying you're not?"

I bite the inside of my cheek and shake my head. "Not exactly."

"How do you do that so often and not feel anything?" Her tone comes off snide and judgmental.

A wave of fire hits my chest as though she's struck me. "Wow, Evie, that was harsh. I feel deeply for the men I share my body with. Just because I'm not in love with a man I spend some physical time with does not mean I don't care, appreciate, and respect him. And vice versa. I'm just open-minded about sharing an experience. As long as you're safe, it's consensual, and you're not in a committed relationship, why wouldn't you want to feel something beautiful with a person you feel connected to, even if it's only for a night? I'd much prefer that than be alone and untouched."

Evie drops her arms and runs her hands down the front of her shirt, straightening the already perfect hem of her silk blouse. Today she's paired a red silk blouse with a pair of black cigarette-style pants and a red peep-toe. Her hair is pulled back in a tight chignon, and she looks business-executive-hot from top to toe.

"I'm sorry. It's not any of my business."

"Everything about me is your business, Ev."

She smiles softly.

"Just maybe—I don't know—try to be a little more open-minded once in a while," I say. "Step outside of the box. Color outside of the lines now and again. Let go."

Evie sucks in a huge breath and sighs. "Maybe I don't know how."

I smile and sip my coffee. "Then I came home just in time because I'm an expert at this."

She closes her eyes and offers me a sad grin I don't know how to interpret. "See you later. Maybe tonight you could put some pajama pants on before bed?" She turns and grabs the handle of the door.

"Maybe. Not likely." I shimmy and shake my hips from

side to side. "You're lucky I'm wearing clothes at all. I usually sleep naked."

Evie shakes her head and chuckles. "Miss me," she says.

"Miss me more."

"Always," she whispers and shuts the door.

I close my eyes and lean against the counter, remembering all the times Mom said that to us before she headed off on one of her adventures. The one thing she never did was leave without her version of "goodbye" or "miss me." Until her final goodbye.

"And how much did you say the monthly rent would be for the entire place?"

"Four thousand. If you're planning on renting the top studio, too, I can definitely get you a deal, probably around thirty-eight hundred. Providing, of course, you have the six months' rent for both in full and in advance. Meaning approximately twenty-two thousand eight hundred dollars. I know the building owner pretty well and he wants to get this place rented out," the property manager states.

I look around the wide-open space, noting the exposed brick walls and all the charm. "First of all, the top studio does not have a separate entrance from the store. It's separated by a door leading upstairs, but that door is inside. Meaning, if he tried to rent that space separately, the person would have to have access to my boutique to enter their home. Not happening. That alone should knock quite a bit off the total price. Get him down to thirty-six per month, otherwise, I walk."

Anxiety swirls in my stomach when I turn, my silky skirt swishing against my ankles as I give the property manager a few minutes to figure out what she can do. I walk over to the front of the big, open space. It will need a lot of work. I run my hand down a random wooden beam that breaks up the center of the room. I'm not sure if it's load bearing, but it doesn't look like it. I'll have to find a really good contractor to help on the cheap if I'm going to have any hope in hell of making this place workable. As it is, I'm going to have to ask Evie for a loan. A mighty big one.

I turn and watch as people pass by the almost floor-to-ceiling window front, carrying their purchases from other businesses. Paper covers the bottom half of the window, but the top is bare, which allows me to see through to the busy coffeehouse across the way and the high-end jewelry store next to it. Directly across the street in my line of vision is a cycling and ski shop. Next to that, a bookstore. Sharing a wall with this place is a candy store and a shoe store. Down the way, a high-end purse boutique. This location is absolutely perfect for me to set up my shop.

It has taken me the entire two months to finally decide what I want to do, how I plan to make my mark. To settle down. And it came to me by looking through my pictures and trinkets from all over the world: I want to bring bits and pieces of the world right here to Colorado. And even though I would have rather set up shop in Colorado Springs and avoided Pueblo at all costs, the main strip is the perfect location. The rent is semi-kinda affordable, especially since I'll be living here, too. The other small businesses on the strip are doing really well, or at least walking through them and conversing with the local owners has given me reason to believe so.

"The owner wants to know what you plan to do with the place renovation-wise before he commits to the lowered rent. He needs confirmation that you're not going to junk up the building or give him some problems to deal with from the other business owners he rents to in the area," the property manager says as she holds her phone against her chest.

"I'm going to make it into a boutique selling clothes, jewelry, candles, crystals, gifts, and more."

The woman repeats what I say into the phone.

"And you're going to live on the top floor. Do you have any children or pets?"

I shake my head. "I'm not opposed to having a cat." The words fly out of my mouth and even I can't believe them. I have never wanted or desired a pet in my life. I mean, animals are cool. Who doesn't love animals? It's what they represent that's scary.

Pets mean stability. They also mean you can't just get up and leave on a whim. With a cat, you can blow out of town for two or three days, leaving them a big bowl of food, water, and a clean litter box. But overall, they still hold you down to a place.

"No kids. No animals at this time. Maybe a cat in the future," she speaks into the phone. "Owner says it's not a good idea to have a cat in a business since people can be allergic."

I blink but don't say anything. *What the hell does he care?*

"But it's not a deal breaker. He agrees to your terms. Thirty-six hundred per month but only if you pay the full six months in advance. He's not paying any of the renovation costs aside from the building inspections required for a new renter, and he's only willing to do that because you're paying reno costs."

I smile. "Tell him I'll get back to him early next week once I've talked to my business partner."

Now I just need to convince Evie to pony up a hundred grand and invest in my new business.

Piece of cake.

★ ★ ★

"Absolutely not. No way. Are you certifiable?" Evie snort-laughs from the passenger seat of her swank Porsche the next day. We're headed toward the Native American reservation where *Toko* lives, which is a solid three-hour drive away.

My palms are sweaty as I grip the wheel and try to focus on the road ahead, worried about seeing my grandfather for the first time in a decade, not to mention the fact that my sister is not buying into my new business plan.

"No, I'm not crazy, Ev. I'm being realistic. Responsible. *Grounded.*" I accentuate the last word.

"Grounded. Like my bank account will be if I piss away a hundred thousand of my inheritance on your latest crazy idea."

I jut my chin out. "Crazy idea? When have I ever had a crazy idea?"

She twists in her chair. "You're kidding, right? For the last decade you've been spending your inheritance from Mom on traveling the world like a bum, not settling down, not committing to anything. That in itself is the definition of insanity."

"No, the definition of insanity is doing the same thing over and over and expecting different results. Besides, aren't you the one who told me to find something I love and do that, so I wouldn't ever be working a day in my life but making money doing what I love?"

She opens her mouth and blows out a frustrated breath. "Kaye, you're twisting my words."

I shake my head. "No. I'm actually *listening* very intently, and I'm hearing that you want me to set up a life. One that includes committing to something for a long time."

"What's a long time to you? A month? A year?"

"That's not fair, and you know it. I had to go, Evie. Mom knew it and gave me the means to do so. I've traveled the world—"

"And all of a sudden you think you're ready to settle down. Long-term. Meaning no future plans outside of this store and what it's going to bring to your life for the next several years."

I shrug. "I don't know, and I can't promise you anything except that I want this. I really want this, and it's a great idea. My whole heart and soul believes in this. Now I just need you to."

She firms her jaw and looks out the window, thumb and finger to her forehead as though she's getting a headache. "How much do you have left of your inheritance? I'm assuming you're coming to the table with something? You can't just expect me to bankroll your business."

I squirm in my chair. "Not completely, no. I have around forty-six thousand left that will just about cover the rent for a year. That's including the studio on top that I'll be living in. And of course, I'll be manning the store twenty-four seven, so I'll probably only need a part-time employee to help out here and there, once it takes off and we get super busy."

Evie runs her hands over her knees in what I know to be one of her self-soothing gestures. "And you still have to renovate. Have you even thought about that?"

I clench my teeth. "Yeah, sissy, I have. It's going to cost about fifty thousand in renovations, another fifty in product costs, utilities, and equipment like the computer and accounting systems."

"And what about you? How are you going to get paid? Buy a bed, furniture, food, a freakin' car? It's a lot to take on, Kaye. More than you've ever committed to in your life."

"This is true." I hit the blinker and check the rearview mirror as I head out on the next highway. "However, you are a financial guru. As a partner, financial and otherwise, your experience, expertise, and know-how will set me up. I have total faith in you." I reach for her thigh to give it a squeeze.

She huffs. "Sissy, I cannot run another business. My own is growing like wildfire, and I have to answer to my corporate clients in Denver all the time and—"

"Please. I need to start somewhere, and you promised you'd help me get settled and figure out what I'm supposed to do."

Evie sucks in a quick breath. "Yeah, but I didn't know that meant you were going to be asking for wads of cash to do it. Money to get a car, maybe, but a hundred thousand? Besides, you're going to need more than that. More like a hundred and fifty in order to get set up, have some cash in reserves, and be able to pay yourself in order to live. On top of that, it usually takes years to get a business off the ground and super successful to the point where you're actually making profit. I just don't know if this is the right route to go."

"But—"

"Maybe you should take classes on business management first or try going back to college. Figure out what type of career calls to you?"

I laugh out loud. "Going back? You know as well as I do, Ev, that I've never stepped foot into a college class a day in my life, and I don't plan on making that a life goal. School is not for me. You are the brainiac in the family, not me."

Evie shakes her head.

"Look, I've got deals across the globe for really cool product that's new and hip and exactly what that touristy town needs," I continue. "I stood in the window yesterday for ten minutes and watched at least fifty people walk past. It's a prime spot for customers. The businesses surrounding it have been profit bearing since year one, not year three. I got the rent several hundred cheaper per month than he wanted to charge, and I'm going to live there, so bonus and tax write-off!"

"Technically you're supposed to only write off the square footage of the business, not the living quarters," she mumbles.

"See, now you're thinking like my big sister who's amazingly smart, beautiful, rich, and ridiculously generous and supportive of her baby sister." I grin and bat my eyelashes.

Evie scrunches up her face and glares at me. "Not cool."

"Hey, I'll do whatever it takes to make Gypsy Soul successful, including guilting you."

"Gypsy Soul." Evie's voice catches, and I smile at hearing the emotion in those two words.

"You always said Mom and I had the souls of a gypsy. What else would I name a kick-ass store that's going to have wares from around the world, beautiful clothing, much of which I will design and make myself so they are one-of-a-kind pieces? Jewelry, crystals, art, knickknacks, unique cultural items from all over. I want to share everything I experienced in my travels. Fill the entire store with nothing but...well, me."

Evie twists her lips and pats them with two fingers. "It's a lot of money to commit and you don't have a lot to contribute, but I'll tell you what, I'll gift you half. Seventy-five thousand."

"Oh, my word. No way. No gift! Partners."

She shakes her head. "Wait a minute, you haven't heard the rest."

My heart hammers inside of my chest so hard I almost want to pull over and take a minute. Instead, I take a few deep breaths and get myself under control. With Evie, you gotta be a smooth operator, just like her. She's the queen of cool, and I have to prove to her I can handle anything that comes my way. "Okay, go ahead. What's the rest?"

Evie grins. "I'll gift you the seventy-five thousand from Mom's inheritance—"

"That's your money, Ev, not for you to bail me out."

"Mom would have given it to you in a heartbeat if she was here."

I reach out and take hold of Evie's hand and try not to let the emotions overwhelm me. Instead, I focus on the road and what she's going to say next.

"All you have to do is get another company or person to invest the other half. You need someone watching your back and committing to this thing in order to ensure it won't fall to the wayside if you get one of your wild hairs—"

I open my mouth to fire off a pissy retort when she continues.

"Remember I said *if*, not *when*. I'm trying to give you the benefit of the doubt here, Kaye. If you truly want to be in business, you have to be willing to put yourself on the line. I'm gifting you the money because lending between friends and family is a recipe for disaster. I want to love you and support you your whole life, the same way I know you love and support me. I do not want to suddenly despise you because you blew out of town and left me hanging with a business to run. Trust goes both ways. I'm giving you this money because I trust you will do the right thing."

She takes a deep breath. "I want to believe in your idea because it's a good one. Except, Kaye, you don't have a great track record with staying in one place. Until I see otherwise, I cannot throw my own hat into the ring fully. I'd rather cheer from the sidelines, whether you win or lose in this venture. Does that make sense?"

She squeezes my hand so tight it hurts. I mull over her concerns and realize she's doing this to not only protect our relationship but to help me by forcing me to make this happen on my own. She's giving me some of the tools and resources by offering half the money I need. Now it's up to me to make the rest happen.

I nod. "It does, and I don't know how to thank you for such a generous gift."

"Want to know what my letter said?" Evie blurts cryptically.

"Yeah." I swallow, trying not to let the next round of emotions take me down for the count.

"My letter told me to do whatever it took to help you settle into your new life but not in lieu of my own happiness and stability. She said something like, 'Evie baby, don't clip your sister's wings, but help her see the beauty in her own backyard. Show her the way of building a life in one place, but don't do it for her. Lead by example not by force.'"

The sweet pitch of her voice as she tries to mimic the way Mom spoke fills my heart with immense joy. "Smart lady."

"She was that," Evie agrees.

"Now I just need to figure out how the hell I'm going to get a seventy-five-thousand-dollar loan."

Evie grins conspiratorially. "I may have an idea for that, too."

3

We pull into the small reservation about three and a half hours outside of Colorado Springs, on the edge of the New Mexico and Colorado border. This particular reservation has an unusual reputation. Over the years, it's become a mixed community of Native Americans, regardless of their tribal beginnings. The community is primarily focused on continuing Native American traditions.

Evie and I spent our early years learning about our Comanche and Wichita heritage as much as the Navajo, Cheyenne, Shawnee, Apache, and so many others here on this reservation. Our mother called this home the melting pot for American Indians of the Great Plains.

As we round our way down the dirt roads to the primary hub of activity, we're waved through a set of gates that is monitored by the locals. They take turns manning the gate to ensure that their private land isn't accessed by just anyone. They must know Evie's car and/or Evie since she's waving at the man in the guard booth as I roll through. He waves back.

"Friend of yours?" I ask.

She narrows her gaze. "That's Biyen. You remember. We

went to school with him. He still lives here, only he's married Aylen."

"Oh, Peter." I use the name he used when we were children versus the Native American name Evie used now. I scrunch up my nose. "He married Aylen? She was so mean!"

Evie laughs. "Yeah, she's grown up a lot since our school years. Does most of the cooking for the elders and other members of the community who need assistance."

"Wow. Times have definitely changed." I stare out through the windshield at the mountains beyond the plains. A shiver of recognition rolls through my body and with it a sense of comfort and anxiety at being back where so many of my childhood memories originated.

"You'd know if you had come to visit once or twice over the years."

I clench my teeth together. "Is this going to be a thing with you? Ongoing and relentless?"

Evie shrugs. "I don't know. Maybe I'm still a little miffed."

"You are not keeping it a secret, that's for sure." I sigh and pull up to the terra-cotta home situated not far from the community area and park the SUV.

I lift my head and see him standing there like a dark knight, only he's aged. There's definitely some silver streaking through his long black hair, which is untied and flowing free in the breeze. He's wearing a red woven poncho with a white stripe down the center that has black arrows running through it.

I get out of the car without saying a word. Not to Evie. Not to anyone. All sound disappears. The only thing I can see or feel is the tether around my waist pulling me toward the only *real* father I have ever known.

Tahsuda stands at the edge of the covered porch, a wrought-iron sun hanging on the wall at his back next to the sturdy dark wooden door.

I make my way over to him and bow my head. Tears form and spill down my cheeks, and my shoulders quake while my knees feel like they are going to crumble to the earth. Two calloused, warm hands fall to my shoulders. I close my eyes at the first touch I've received from my grandfather in ten years. Heat presses into my skin as ribbons of love and joy wrap themselves around my heart.

"*Huutsuu,*" he says in the deep melodic voice I know better than my very own. "You have come home." He speaks in Comanche, but I remember the language as if I've spoken it every day since I left.

I nod but don't dare lift my head until he requests it of me. I'm the one who has disrespected him with my long absence. It is up to him how he will receive me.

"*Huutsuu,* look at me. Give me your eyes."

I lift my head and stare into the coal-black eyes and weathered face I've adored my whole life. Tears fall unchecked, but I don't care. He's the most beautiful thing I've seen in a decade, aside from my sister.

"Did you find what you sought?" His voice is a low rumble, like thunder before a storm.

"I'm still deciding that," I whisper and swallow down the thick wave of emotion that threatens to drown me.

He nods and firms his lips. "You have been gone many moons. Are your wings weary?"

"Yeah, *Toko.* I'll be staying a long while."

A speck of a smile flits across his lips but is gone before I can be certain it was ever there.

"Ah, so your journey has brought you back."

"I missed you. So much. And I'm... I'm sorry, *Toko*, for being gone so long."

This time he cups my neck and uses his thumbs to bring my head toward his where he presses his lips to my forehead. "If you are gone a day, a week, a year, or ten, I will miss you the same. My love for you has no clock, no condition. It is as the sun and moon. Always is and always will be."

I fling my arms around my grandfather, and he pulls me tight against his barreled chest. "My little birds have returned to the nest. This makes *me* happy." He smiles and kisses my hair and does something over my shoulder to my sister because from what I can hear she's laughing softly.

The tears turn into laughter as he hugs me tight. I allow the moment to imprint on my soul.

"I love you, *Toko*."

"And I you, *huutsuu*. Now come in and sit with me. Tell me of your adventures." He opens his arm and Evie cuddles in. "My whole world." He kisses Evie's head, then mine once more.

For hours I tell my grandfather about my travels and what I did in each locale, leaving out the parts that seemed risky and moving on to the concept for my shop.

"And you are planning to help your sister with this business?" *Toko* asks Evie over a steaming bowl of beef-and-vegetable soup and fry bread. The bread is soft on the inside, a bit firmer on the outside. *Toko* serves it warm with the perfect chewy texture that reminds me of home on the rez. The bread is circular and dense enough to dip into the soup and sop up some of the steaming broth.

Evie nods, tearing a piece of bread. "Well, you know Mom left us her life insurance policy when she passed. Kaye still has quite a bit of hers, and I invested what was left of mine after paying college tuition and setting up my own business, so I still have most of it. If Mom were here, she'd be behind the counter working it with Kaye. The least I can do is help put up some of the capital."

I run my hand down Evie's forearm soothingly. "And your baby sis loves you for it and will be paying you back when I'm making a profit."

Evie shakes her head. "Not part of the plan, Kaye. You do what you have to do. This is a gift. No strings. I already told you that."

Toko crosses his arms over one another and focuses his gaze on Evie. "You do not give a gift of this magnitude and not expect a token in return. What is your token, *taabe*?" I love when he calls her his sun just like Mom did. Though my guess is she got our nicknames from Tahsuda.

I frown, realizing how huge a point our grandfather has made. Regardless of the whole "neither a borrower nor a lender be" idea, no one just gives a person seventy-five grand for nothing.

Evie stands up abruptly and grabs her glass. "Have any more of that Kuleto wine? Always thought it was cool how you do all you can to support Native Americans, even down to the wine you drink being made by them," she prattles on, pouring herself a huge glass.

I sit back in my chair and watch Evie ignore *Toko*'s question, but I'm not letting her get off that easy. No way. "Evie, what are you getting out of this?" I say with a little more force to my tone.

She groans. "Nothing. I already told you. Just leave it be." She sets down the bottle of wine with too firm a hand and it clatters on the counter. She jumps at the noise, but thankfully, the bottle is sturdy and doesn't break.

"*Taabe*, come sit," *Toko* demands.

Evie sucks in a breath and lets it out before putting on her calm face and a fake smile. It takes every effort I have not to roll my eyes. She's not pulling a fast one on me or our grandfather. Knowing *Toko* is never going to let this fly, I sit back in my chair, cross my arms, and wait for the show.

"Yes, *Toko*?" Evie says softly, batting her eyelashes and pouting her pretty pink lips like she did when we were kids and she was trying to get her way. What she obviously does not realize is that she's a grown woman and there is no way that shit can work at thirty like it did when she was three or even thirteen.

He cups Evie's cheek and says nothing, just stares into her eyes for a long time.

She starts to squirm before she breaks eye contact and her shoulders slump, her words coming out in a rush of truth. "If I give Suda Kaye the money, maybe she'll feel beholden to me."

"And?" *Toko* encourages.

Her gaze flits to me, then to *Toko*, and back to me. "Then maybe she'll stay."

I close my eyes at the real reason my sister is dumping this wad of cash on me. Collateral.

"Ah, now I see your token. You want your sister in your life, and this is your way to ensure that," *Toko* surmises.

Evie licks her lips as a tear slips down the side of her face. That single tear rips a hole through my heart so big I'm not sure I'm ever going to be able to sew it back together.

"Evie…" I whisper, not able to form the words or express what I'm feeling.

"I want you in my life, Kaye. *Toko* lives way out here.

Mom's gone. Dad is off in Poland doing something with the military that's all very hush-hush." She waves a hand in the air. "And you, my best friend in the entire world, are gallivanting your way across the globe. I worry every night I'm going to lose you, too. Find out you've died in one of your crazy excursions. Cliff jumping! Jesus, Kaye, if that surfer hadn't been there, you could have drowned."

"But I didn't."

"And what about when that moped hit you in Italy and you broke your arm?"

"If you remember correctly, I had a very lovely nursemaid named Alfonzo that kissed that arm and made it all better in no time." I grin.

"And when you slept in a tent in the Swiss Alps for weeks with that forestry guy?"

"Mmm, Elias. He was one of the manliest men I've ever met in my life. I watched him fish bare-handed in a river." I smile, remembering.

Evie's voice is strained when she says, "You could have died out in the wilderness. Eaten by a bear or a coyote. Heck, you didn't even know this Elias very well."

"Uh, I would beg to differ." I drop my voice, making the innuendo implicit but not exactly tawdry in front of my grandfather. "We got to know one another very well."

Evie pushes her hands through her hair. "Kaye, I need you. Don't you understand that? I need you alive. I need you where I can look at your face. See you are healthy and happy."

I shake my head and reach for her hand. "Ev, I'm fine. I'm healthy and very happy. There've been very few times in my life when I've been unhappy. Mom always taught us to find happiness in every day. In the little things. I've lived my life by that motto. You don't need to watch over me."

"No. But I *need* my sister." She pounds a hand on her chest. "I need you, Kaye. I'm giving you that money because I know you well enough to know you will do anything to make this store successful in order to make sure you didn't hurt me by wasting that money. And to me, Kaye, it's only money. You—" she grabs my hand and squeezes it "—you in my life, that's what makes *me* happy."

Crap. The tears are back as I stand up and yank on my sister's hand until she stands and wraps her arms around me.

Evie pulls back and cups my face, tears running down her cheeks as she wipes mine away. "I love your face, Kaye. I want to see it. Every day. All the time. If that makes me selfish, then so be it. I'm selfish."

I smile and rub my cheek into her hand. "No, sissy, it doesn't make you selfish. It makes you human. I missed you, too, you know. A couple times a year and a weekly phone call was never enough. I always wanted more but..."

She closes her eyes and runs her hands the length of my hair. "I know. You had to do it."

I nod and wipe her tears away. "But I'm here now."

She bites into her bottom lip and asks the one thing I don't know. The one thing I can never give her for fear of hurting her. "Yeah, but for how long?"

"Ev..."

She pulls me to her side where she hooks an arm around my waist. "Whatever it is, I'll take it."

Tahsuda watches us with a serenity I don't feel right now. Then again, the old man is wise well beyond any man I've ever met.

"Calm down and eat. *Taabe, huutsuu,* I am happy you are around my table. I will pray with the elders that both of you find the solace you need. All will be as it should be," he says as if it's law. And to him, it probably is.

"Thanks, *Toko*." Evie sits and smiles, picking up her spoon to dig into her still-steaming soup.

I grin and take my seat. "When you say pray, does that mean you're going to smoke your peace pipe, because I could *so* go for experiencing that." I plunge my spoon into my bowl and scoop up some meat and veggies.

Evie smacks my arm. "Kaye!" She chuckles.

"Well, I could!" I say around the soup and dunk my fry bread, then take a huge bite. The flavors slide over my taste buds as familiar as buttered toast. Fry bread and soup has always been a staple in *Toko*'s home. Absolutely delicious!

"You are not old enough," *Toko* says flatly, then opens his mouth and takes a spoonful of the meaty veggie goodness.

I stop mid-chew and Evie snorts around her bite, trying not to laugh.

"*Toko*, I'm twenty-eight years old," I protest.

"Exactly. Not old enough. Come to me when you are older."

"How old do you have to be to smoke with the elders?"

He smirks. "Old."

"Great, then I'm never going to smoke with you."

"Exactly."

"Some things never change," I grumble.

Evie reaches out a hand to me and *Toko*. "You're right, some things never do change," she says with the biggest smile on her face.

I shake her off. "Shut up and eat your soup, brat! You're on his side!"

She shrugs. "Always respect your elders, you know that."

★ ★ ★

The next morning, I'm sitting on my grandfather's porch taking in one of the most beautiful views. Vast, open land. Trees, hills, the plains. Animals graze to my right in the open flat space. A few houses way off in the distance dot the horizon, close to the community but still maintaining the residents' privacy. I inhale the scent of the earth, allowing the musky smell of the dirt and the surrounding trees to fill me with comforting nostalgia.

Holding a cup of coffee, Evie bumbles out in a sundress. It's the most relaxed look I've seen on her since I came back. The peach color makes her look soft and welcoming. Being here has given my sister what looks to be a sense of peace. Her shoulders are relaxed and loose, her back isn't so ramrod straight, and she's rocking a carefree smile.

I love this Evie.

Seeing Evie at peace is rare. The woman has always had the weight of the world on her shoulders. Helping to take care of me when we stayed with Tahsuda growing up or with Mom when we lived in Pueblo and she got sick. She made sure I got to and from school, packed my lunch, made breakfast every morning and dinner every night. Even after Mom died, Evie went to college and still made sure I had everything I needed for the last six months of school.

Those were the hardest six months of my life, having to finish high school with no mother and living in the small two-bedroom apartment with my nineteen-year-old sister. I could have railed against her, not done what she said, but I wasn't the only one who was struggling to keep going after Mom died. Yet, like always, Evie held it all together.

Evie sits down next to me and crosses her bare legs. "Beautiful, isn't it?"

I sip my own coffee. "It's home. Kinda. For me, though, *you're* home. Wherever you are is the best place in the world."

Her blue gaze flits to mine, and there's a seriousness there I've not seen in a long time. "Do you mean that?"

I don't look away, not for a second. I hold her stare and try to put my intention into my gaze. "Yes. I do."

"I'm counting on it," she says cryptically and breaks the contact, her brow furrowing as she looks off into the distance. "Who's this?"

A huge, shiny black Ford truck rolls up and parks next to Evie's SUV. A dark-haired figure opens the door and glides out. When he makes his way around the car door, I can see his entire body in its full glory.

"Oh shit. This is about to get interesting." I grin, holding my cup near my face with both of my hands as my sister sits up straight as a ruler.

"Not a word!" Evie growls under her breath and stands up.

The man stops in front of the two of us. His eyes take me in briefly, so I offer a finger wave around my mug before his gaze goes to Evie.

"Milo, I had no idea you were going to be here. It's...uh, wow. It's good to see you." Evie opens her arms and walks toward the hulking hot guy. And when I say hot, I mean *insanely* good-looking. He's tall, at least six foot four. His chest is broad, covered in a red dress shirt. At his neck is a silver bolo necktie with a turquoise right in the center at the dip in his throat. The tie's long black woven leather strings hang down his chest almost like an arrow pointing to his fine-fitting black dress slacks.

His long black hair is tied back with a series of matching bands down to the middle of his back. But it's those high cheekbones, that perfect brown toasted skin, and the fire in his gaze as he takes in Evie that makes me grin.

He pulls Evie into his arms and holds her for what to me seems like an overly long time. "Evie, *nizhóní*, how long has it been?"

Nizhóní, beautiful in Navajo. Very nice. I grin around my cup as Evie pulls back her upper body, her hands remaining on Milo's sizable biceps.

"Um, in person, several years, I think. Though we've kept in touch on social media." She moves her hands to play with the edges of her sundress that falls mid-thigh.

A pair of dark eyes meet mine. "And Suda Kaye is back. It's good to see you."

I smile. "Always good to see you, Milo. Right, Ev?"

My sister turns her head so fast in my direction I worry she might hurt her neck. "Of course. Always good to see someone familiar from when we were kids."

"I'm here to talk to some of the people here about their finances," he says. "Thought I'd check in on elder Tahsuda Tahsuda, see if he needed anything tended to while I was here." He says our grandfather's name twice, because legally his name is Tahsuda Tahsuda. Back in the day, in order to get a birth certificate, Native Americans had to give first and last names. My grandfather only had one name, like many others. Instead of choosing one of the English settlers' surnames like Jones or Smith, he rallied against the law and gave them his name twice. So now he's officially Tahsuda Tahsuda. My grandfather the rebel.

"Wow. That's so sweet. Caring about our people like that. Isn't he amazing, Evie?" I layer on the sugar, loving every second of my sister's discomfort. Milo is the boy she's been in love with her entire life. The one guy that never looked at my sister as though the sun and moon rose and set with her. Back in school and on the reservation, guys would fall all over themselves to talk to Evie, circle around her, waiting for morsels of her attention. When the only guy Evie ever had eyes for was totally off-limits, a few years older than her, hulking Milo Chavis.

"It is very kind of you to check on our grandfather," Evie says. "And actually, I was going to email you, so it's amazing that you're here. The timing couldn't be more perfect. I need a favor."

Milo smiles, looking down at my sister. "Anything for my *nizhóní*, Evie." He places a hand on her shoulder and squeezes.

I swear I can visibly see my sister sway toward him at his touch. Damn, these two need to hook up. I wonder if he's available. Last time Evie mentioned him, she was twenty-four and he was twenty-eight. He was introducing his serious girlfriend to his family. Bringing her home for the holidays. That was the last time I ever heard Evie talk about Milo. Now he's got to be thirty-four. A lot could have happened in six years.

"Actually, it's for my sister, Kaye." She hooks a thumb over her shoulder, and I stand up to get closer to the conversation.

Milo waits for Evie to continue while I make my way to their little huddle.

"Tahsuda told me a few years ago that you were working on a project for one of your clients here on the reservation—" Evie begins.

"I'll stop you right there. I don't talk about my clients' finances with anyone." His voice is a low, deep rumble of hotness.

She waves her hand in front of his chest. "No, no. What Tahsuda told me was that you were working with a member here and another company that takes on small business projects. Helps finance them, get them up and running in the Pueblo-Colorado Springs-Denver area. Does that sound familiar?"

He nods and crosses his arms over his massive chest. Uh, yummy. My sister gapes at the size of those guns. Okay, good. At least she's not dead. Evie licks her lips and I watch as Milo catches the move and a heat no one could deny blazes in his eyes.

This just got *way* more interesting. He's totally into her.

"Anyway, Kaye is going to open up a boutique in Pueblo," Evie goes on. "She's got a solid seventy-five thousand to contribute right out the gate, but what she needs is an investor to go in with another seventy-five to a hundred thousand as well as help her start her business. Teach her the ropes. The reason I remember this situation is because Tahsuda went on and on about how great it was that you were helping a member of our extended family get his business off the ground which, in turn, helps all of the Native American people."

Milo chuckles, and it sounds deep and full. Yummy again.

Once more, Evie notices, this time, biting her bottom lip and gazing up at Milo in that dreamy way that is not playing it cool even one iota. To help her out, I nudge Evie's shoulder, breaking her out of her dream sequence that likely included Milo biting her lip.

"That sounds super cool. Does that company still work with new startups?" I ask.

Milo doesn't respond; his focus is one hundred percent on my sister's face.

Awesome.

He shakes his head as if clearing his mind. "Uh, yeah. Actually, it's the little brother of an old friend from college. Bigwig in that area. Has a committee that meets once a month to go over prospective projects to invest in, but I'm sure I could get you a meeting. You'll need to pull it all together. Profit and loss estimates. Budget and cost centers. Business plan for one, three, and five years. Location. Costs. All of it laid out in black-and-white. No hidden agendas. They are all about full disclosure, and they get in deep with the owner."

The things he mentions are all things I've heard Evie say but a lot of it is foreign to me. I've spent the last decade of my life jumping from couch to couch, working when I needed to. Profit and loss estimates and business plans all sound very complicated.

Evie grins. "You just get us the meeting and we'll be ready. You have my email, right?"

He smiles softly. "I definitely do."

"Then email me when you find out anything. In the meantime, we'll be doing our homework, right, Kaye?"

"Absolutely. Thank you, Milo."

"Ladies." He dips his chin at the both of us and winks at Evie as he heads into our grandfather's home.

The moment he's out of earshot, I squeal and jump up and down. Evie does, too, and wraps her arms around me. We both speak at the same time.

"You're going to get a meeting!" she says at the same time I say, "He's totally into you!"

"Wait, what?" we both say over one another.

"Milo, he couldn't keep his eyes off you," I say. "I'm telling you, girl, you were a cool drink of water on a hot day, and he was *thirsty*!"

Evie plants her forehead into her palm. "Kaye, focus. He just told us he's going to get you a meeting with his friend's brother. The one that helped a guy open up his own successful business. He's going to vouch for you!"

I shake my head. "No, he's going to vouch for me because of you. If you think that one email is going to be the end of Milo Chavis, you've got another thing coming! Mark my words. There is one thing I know better than anything and that's when a man has his eye on a woman. And that man's eyes were glued to you, dear sister."

"Whatever you say. I'm just happy he can get us a meeting. Besides, the last time I saw him, he had a serious girlfriend. He's probably married to her by now."

"And have you seen him post his status as Married on any of the social platforms you stalk him on? I sure as hell didn't see a ring on his finger."

Her gaze narrows. "I do not stalk him."

I pout. "No, you probably don't. You're too damn classy for that. Looks like we have our homework for tonight."

"Yeah, get started on your business plan," Evie says at the same time I say, "Look up Milo Chavis online."

Evie stops where she stands and leans closer. "You're not going to let this go, are you?"

"Not a chance in hell." I hook my elbow with hers so we can go have breakfast with *Toko* and catch another eyeful of Muscular Milo.

"Lord deliver me."

I snort. "Right into Milo's bed." I elbow her in the side.

"Kill me now," Evie murmurs woefully while I tip my head back and laugh until my belly aches.

"I love coming home!"

4

"Good morning, Suda Kaye," says a deep rumbling voice.

I lift my head from where I was scanning my proposal for the hundredth time. "Milo!" I stand up and wrap my arms around his large torso in a tight hug. "Thank God, you're here. Evie got stuck in traffic in Denver and couldn't make it. I was freaking out!" I squeeze his strong shoulders.

Milo smiles softly and rubs a hand up and down my arm. "That is why I am here. Your sister called me. I was home in Colorado Springs and able to adjust a few things on my schedule."

I lean back and grin. "You live in Colorado Springs?"

He tilts his head to the side. "Yes."

It's impossible to hide the big smile that automatically takes over my face. "You know Evie lives in C-Springs, too?"

His head tips as if he's curious. "Really? I thought she lived in Denver."

I shake my head. "Nope. She travels there a couple times a week for work. You know how it is...the finance world is all abuzz."

His lips twitch into a smirk. "I'm happy to be here to help."

"Let's be real. You're happy to be here so that my sister owes you a favor." I prop a hand on my hip and stare him down.

"It never hurts to have a beautiful woman owe you a favor. This is true."

"You married?" I ask, going right for the bull's-eye.

At that exact moment, the receptionist calls out to us. "They're ready for you."

I pout and Milo smiles, holding a hand out toward the conference room door.

"Shall we?" He leads the way and opens the door.

As I follow him in, I see there is a long conference table with five men and two women sitting around it. I scan each face and stop at the last one. My entire body goes completely still for about two normal heartbeats. And then all hell breaks loose. My palms start to sweat, my vision sways, and butterflies take flight in my stomach.

Milo is speaking and pointing at each person as he introduces them, but I hear none of what he says. My focus is lasered on one man.

Dirty blond hair, longer than I remember, just barely touching the collar of his pitch-black suit. A beard and mustache combo that does nothing to distract from his handsome features, rather adding to them. He's older. A full ten years will definitely show on a person, only all ten of those years have added to his appeal. His hazel eyes are gleaming a mossy green reflected from the olive-colored shirt he's wearing under his jacket. No tie. Top two buttons opened at the collar show a swatch of tanned skin.

He stands and I swear the room gets smaller. His muscular form fills the space. Standing right in front of me, he seems taller than I remember. Almost as tall as Milo, maybe six foot two or three. Definitely much taller than my five foot eight.

His hand comes out and I place my now cold one into his warm palm. Pinpricks of electricity zap me, and I almost pull away, but he holds fast, covering the top of my hand with his other one so that mine is encased between both of his.

"It's like seeing a ghost," he whispers.

I swallow, not capable of speaking through the desert that's now my throat, but I don't need to because Camden takes charge.

Stepping toward me, bringing our hands flat between us, he dips his head down to my cheek where I feel the slightest warmth of his breath against my ear. My knees wobble at his nearness, and the familiar crisp clean scent of lemongrass and musk fills my nose. I reach out with my opposite hand and grip his arm, fingers digging in, to not only hold myself up but to press closer.

"It's good to see you, Suda Kaye." His voice causes a frisson of excitement down my spine along with instant recall of all the times he spoke in that rough voice against my ear.

I hold onto his arm as my knees quake. "Camden..." I say breathlessly.

He kisses my cheek, and as quickly as he entered my space, he is gone. Nothing but cold air chilling the entire front of my body. I blink stupidly and reach for the satchel over my shoulder so I have something to hold on to until I feel a warm hand at my lower back.

Milo maneuvers himself in front of me, blocking my view of the man I walked away from all those years ago. "You okay?" he asks softly.

I lick my suddenly very dry lips. "Not even close," I admit and his brow furrows as I continue, "But I'll get through this. Don't worry."

With a smile on my face, I allow Milo to lead me to the chair that's directly across the table from Camden.

"Everyone, this is Suda Kaye Ross. I'm Milo Chavis, as most of you know. Thank you for seeing us today so that Suda Kaye can present her business concept for consideration. Go ahead, Suda Kaye."

I riffle through my satchel and bring out the pristinely typed business plan and supporting documents that Evie helped me put together. Thank God we went over it so many times, because the moment I turn to the first page it's like turning on a prerecorded message. I am able to go through each page sounding as though I know what I am talking about because I do. For the most part.

As I continue, I find if I don't look Cam in the face, I'm able to push on. Blessedly, throughout the entire hour, he doesn't ask a single question, until I smile and look up at every person, my gaze finally landing on his gorgeous face.

"Are you prepared, Ms. Ross, to stick it out through lean business times? Sometimes an owner will have to work for years to reach a point where they are experiencing consistent monthly profit. That's quite the commitment. Do you consider yourself a woman who commits?" One of his dark blond eyebrows rises.

I lick my lips and bite down on my bottom lip, and I swear his eyes spark before going flat once more, hiding my effect on him.

Doing the best I can not to squirm in my chair, I place my hands in my lap, straighten my spine, and stare him down. "I'm prepared to stick it out as long as I need to. I'm investing a very large sum of my own money, and I'm prepared to put down a deposit and sign a two-year lease for a storefront on Main Street, as my proposal mentions. Two years is a long time…" I start to say.

"Not in a business startup. Two years can be considered a drop in the bucket. Many won't even profit on something they've put their blood, sweat, and tears into for the first few years. And that's if it's a success. Some aren't so lucky."

His reference to a few years feels like putting my head into a guillotine and chopping it off on the basis of spite alone. There's a hint of anger in his tone that I imagine has everything to do with my leaving and nothing to do with my desire to seek funding and business assistance.

"I'm committed to doing whatever it takes to see my dream come true," I hedge, looking at the other investors as if they'd have a way out of these shark-infested waters.

"I distinctly remember a time when I had a dream so real I thought I could make it my very own, worked myself to the bone, gave all of myself and it wasn't enough." His gaze blazes straight through to my heart like a laser beam.

He always used to call me his dream come true. Said he couldn't believe he'd found the only woman he'd ever want to be with so young. I fed into that dream for four years… and then I ran away.

I lick my lips and let out a slow breath. "I understand that the business world can be tricky. Failure isn't an option. I won't let it be." I methodically look at every pair of eyes at the table, including Milo's. He gives me a small tilt of his lips in what I hope is pride.

Cam taps his fingers across the top of the table, clears his throat, and sits back in his chair, looking like the king of the castle. "Excellent. I believe we'll be able to discuss your request and give you an answer before you leave today."

"Okay." I lace my fingers together in my lap and squeeze, waiting for him to slam me with another shot from our past.

"I'm not sure if Milo explained how we do business. If we agree to help you with your small business startup, giving you the requested money, that is not where our involvement ends."

"No, I appreciate the committee will want regular updates and—"

Cam shakes his head, a lock of hair falling down around his right cheek. "One of the committee members will be assigned to you. That means day-to-day or week-to-week, you will have a member of our team in your store, working alongside of you. Not for all hours of the day or a full forty-hour week, of course, but regularly. One of us will work by your side and ensure that not only is our investment being used according to plan, but you are utilizing the best approach to success."

I tilt my head and glance around the room. "Uh, okay."

He continues, his gaze not leaving mine. "We take a hands-on approach. Financially and *physically*. We're there every step of the way the first year you're in business. Put simply, we're experts in business. Each of us has started or been a part of a business that's just beginning to grow. We know what it takes to make a business successful, and in Pueblo, we want all businesses to be successful. It's our home. Where we all live. We don't just give you the capital and walk away hoping you'll do well. For the first year, we make sure of it."

"Yes, that sounds reasonable." I push a lock of hair behind my ear.

But Cam isn't finished. "And the foundation has a stake in your company. Once our contribution is paid back in full, the foundation we represent owns ten percent of your company until you can afford to buy us out. This helps put money in our coffers for future business startups as well as keeps our community and economy ripe with money-making and tax-paying companies."

"Ten percent?" My voice rises with this new bit of information. I thought once I paid back the loan I would be done. But I understand why they need to make something out of it. Otherwise, why would they do it?

He nods. "If you can agree to those terms, we'll discuss your proposal and come to a decision while you sit in the waiting room."

Milo reaches out his hand and covers mine, squeezing it. Camden sees the move and scowls before looking away.

"It's a good deal, Suda Kaye. Your sister would approve as well." Milo leans his head toward me as he whispers.

"You think?"

"I'm in finance and this is an excellent offer," he confirms.

I swallow down the fear and take a deep breath. "Your terms are acceptable."

My stomach twists and turns, and I swear if I think too much about the double whammy of seeing Camden after ten years on top of going into business for the first time in my life, I might throw up all over the pristine waiting room floor.

"This will go only one of two ways," Milo declares. "Yes or no."

I close my eyes and lean my head back against the wall. Without warning, flashes of Camden and me together back when we were teenagers rushes through my mind like a spinning wheel of fortune. So much love and laughter. And the smiles. My goodness, when the man smiled, my entire body warmed with light. Until I put that light out.

After I left, I only allowed myself that first year to regret the decision I made to leave Camden and Evie. It was easier with Evie because I knew I'd see and talk to her again. When I walked out on Camden and disappeared, I hadn't planned on ever seeing him again.

I'd spent a full year telling myself that leaving him was the right choice. The only choice. I had to see the world, live life free, and he had to stay here, go to college, and work in his family's steel empire. It was all planned out. There was no wiggle room. He wanted a woman who would keep his home, make his dinner, and raise his children to be the next line of steel-empire-running men and women. I wanted to travel, take risks and chances on things I'd only every dreamed of.

We weren't meant to be. No matter how much love we had, my mother was right. She knew what I needed before I did. Until now. Being here is so far outside of my comfort zone, I'm nowhere in the vicinity of feeling at peace with the decision I made all those years ago or the one I made recently by coming back.

Seeing him again brings it right to the surface. The hope and excitement about the future we shared. It took my mother dying and her letters for me to accept my fate, to have the courage to walk away. And here I am, standing in front of the only man I've ever loved, asking him to commit to my future when I wouldn't do the same for him ten years ago.

"This is horrible." My hands start to shake, and I grip the chair arms so tight my knuckles turn white.

"How so? Unless you're referring to the energy pouring off you and Camden in there. Judging by his familiar greeting as well as the way he couldn't take his eyes off of you, I'm assuming you have a history. Want to fill me in?"

I shake my head. "Not really."

Milo's gaze pierces mine.

"We uh, we knew each other when we were teenagers."

"Knew, meaning…dated?"

I nod. "Yeah. For four years."

The dark slashes that are his eyebrows rise up toward his hairline. "Long time."

"Mmm-hmm."

"Guessing it didn't exactly end well?"

"That would be an understatement."

Milo is about to say something else when the door to the conference room opens and Camden strides into the waiting area.

"Ms. Ross, may I speak to you over here privately?" Camden gestures to another door down the hall.

I stand up, my hands still shaking. Shit. The last thing I want is private time with Camden Bryant. "Um, sure. Can you watch my things, Milo?"

He nods but his gaze is firm and set on Camden.

Camden opens the door to a much smaller room with a round table and four chairs around it. The moment I'm in the room, I hear the door shut, and then my wrist is snagged, and I'm spun around with my back against the door. Camden presses his body a scant inch from mine, arms at the sides of my shoulders, caging me in. He's so close I can feel his warmth hovering over me.

"Why are you back? Why are you here?" he hisses.

I shake my head. "Cam, I had no idea you ran this foundation or were a part of it. Milo was my contact. Apparently, your group helped one of his clients."

"And who is he to you? Your boyfriend?"

"Milo? What on earth? No." I blink rapidly, trying to figure out where this conversation is going.

"Did you plan to come into my company, looking like a million fucking bucks, your hair styled in a way *you know* used to drive me crazy, to what? Show me what I lost out on when you left? Huh, Suda Kaye? You trying to torture me? Trying to drive a stake into my heart?" His tone is raw and angry.

"No! My God, you know me better than that!"

He huffs and I can smell mint and the hint of coffee on his breath. "Do I? Do I really? Maybe ten years ago I would have said so. Though I would have been wrong. Because the woman I loved, wanted to spend my life with, the woman I'd gotten the first damn taste of left the same night I took her innocence," he says crudely.

"C-Camden—" I stutter, desperation lacing the single word. It feels like a thousand bees are stinging me over and over as waves of hurt barrel through me.

He continues undaunted. "The girl I knew, she never would have left me to wonder what I did wrong. If I'd hurt her that night. If she hated me for what we did. That girl would have *stayed*. This girl—" his gaze runs up and down my body "—this girl, I've never met. So you tell me—why are you here?"

"I—I—"

"Spit it out, Suda Kaye. You've got three seconds before I walk out the door and my foundation's money with me."

"Cam..."

"Three," he says stiffly, his eyes blazing white-hot fire. "Two."

"I just needed an investor for my store. I swear!"

"That's it?" He clenches his jaw and I can see a muscle jumping in his cheek. "No other reason?" He brings his head closer.

I close my eyes and without knowing what the heck I'm doing, I place my hands on his waist. "Camden... I'm..."

He brings his nose close to my neck, and I tremble as the hair from his short-cropped beard grates along my tender skin. While he makes his way up toward my ear, he turns my sadness into something quite different. Hotter. More electric. "Tell me why you're here? The real reason. You have one second left," he whispers almost soothingly.

"I need an investor. I had no idea you'd be here."

"I don't believe you," he says as he dips his head closer to mine and inhales. He closes his eyes before speaking through clenched teeth. "You still smell like cherries." His jaw is tight when his gaze meets mine, but he steps back, making me cold yet relieved at the same time.

I stand there silently, nothing but the air in my lungs sawing in and out of my body. I feel as if I've been on a treadmill at a dead run for the last fifteen minutes, not losing my mind while standing quietly in front of the only man I ever loved.

He shakes his head. "You're not going to tell me the real reason you're here, are you?"

I open and close my mouth, lost in his gaze. The blanket of sadness fills the room and covers us both with its melancholy.

Cam purses his lips, places his hands on his hips while his hazel eyes stare at me. They're filled with that sense of familiarity and something I would have never expected...

Grief.

Loss.

Heartbreak.

After so many years, it's still there, simmering beneath the surface of this beautiful man's gaze. And I'm the reason it's there.

"One," he says cryptically before stepping past me and opening the door, leaving me breathless and speechless. As he retreats, I watch him run his hand through his hair and growl. "Christ...still screwing with my head, even after all these years."

Once he is farther from me and closer to the waiting area, I finally find my footing and follow him stiffly. I'm still not exactly sure what happened in those moments before he walked out.

As Camden reaches Milo, he turns around to look at me. "We've agreed to invest in your business. The money will be transferred later today into the account you provided in the proposal. Your committee mentor will be assigned and show up at your new building sometime in the next week or two. Start your renovations, and we'll be in touch."

I stand there, staring at Cam, probably looking like I've just been taken for a ride through the rinse cycle of a washing machine. It's definitely how I feel at the moment.

"Uh, that's wonderful news. Though, Cam, I'm guessing we should probably talk..." I hook my thumb over my shoulder pointing to the room we just spent the last few minutes in. The last thing I want to do is go into detail about our past or the new feelings that have just risen due to seeing one another again, but perhaps it's the most logical plan if we're going to be working together.

Camden doesn't respond, just stares at me. While we have our stare-off, a woman enters the waiting area.

"Hi, sugar plum! I'm so glad I caught you!" A leggy, gorgeous woman wearing carnation pink from head to stilettos wraps her arms around Camden's waist, nuzzling against his side. Her dress is formfitting, revealing that she's got the body of a Playboy Bunny, with the platinum-blond hair to match.

Camden blinks and looks down at the woman at his side. A flash of annoyance flits across his gaze, and he closes his eyes before taking a breath. He puts his arm around her waist and glances at me, making a point to bring the woman as close to him as possible. "Hey, uh, cookie, what are you doing here?"

Cookie?

The brown-eyed woman smiles a beaming white, beauty-pageant smile up at Camden. "Hoping my sugar lumpkins can step away and take his best girl to lunch. I haven't seen you much all week! I miss you."

Holy hell.

At this point, Milo clears his throat, and the woman finally realizes that she has company. "Oh, wow. Aren't you a big fella?" she says and beams up at Milo. "Clients of yours, sugar plum?" She glances back to Cam before her gaze falls on me and she takes me in. She looks me up and down, and her lips twist into a little smirk as though she finds me lacking.

There's nothing to say. I just spent the last few minutes in an emotionally charged meeting with her man. My heart hammers in my chest and my entire body feels hot. I bite back the emotions rising to the surface and promise myself I'll hold them back until I can get back to the safety of my sister's house. Then I'll cry my eyes out and drink copious amounts of tequila until Camden Bryant and his beauty pageant girlfriend are nothing but a stain on an otherwise great day—in which I got everything I wanted.

As in, money for my business…not the man I've been pining for most of my life.

I'm a Ross; the last thing I'll do is let him see my weakness. "Yep, that's what I am. Brand-new client of Mr. Bryant's." I wave. "Suda Kaye Ross," I say and know she recognizes my name. Her smile fades, and her mouth compresses into a flat thin line, her brows pinching together. "Your boyfriend just agreed to fund my business. Isn't that awesome?"

"Brittney Cooperland of the Cooperland Sporting Goods chain." She must be a trust fund baby. Only rich people immediately mention their lineage.

Brittney runs her hand up and down Cam's chest territorially. "My *fiancé* is a giver." She wiggles the fingers of her left hand, showing off the huge diamond on her third finger. "He gives and gives, in all the best ways—part of the reason why I love him so much." She snuggles more fully against him and lays a sloppy kiss on his jaw.

I want to gag.

Milo moves to my side and wraps his arm around my shoulders in what feels like brotherly support. Man, he's such a good guy.

Camden watches the hold Milo has on me, and his mouth tightens. "We'll be in touch. And, Ms. Ross...always a pleasure."

Ms. Ross. I close my eyes as the tears threaten. Milo hands me my bag, and I pull it over my shoulder while he leads me out of the office. I don't look back. I can't.

It shouldn't feel like I'm leaving the love of my life all over again, but it does. I'm the reason why he's in that woman's arms, living the life he was meant to live. It's my fault and this is part of my penance.

With a heavy heart, I put one foot in front of the other.

Just like my mother taught me, there is no going back, only forward.

5

"Tell me again why you aren't having Mr. Fix It paint your studio?" Evie complains while rolling eggplant-purple paint over the wall I already primed. Her long blond ponytail swishes from side to side as she reaches up as high as she can go with the extension rod.

I grin and dip my brush into the dark orange paint bucket near my feet. I'm inside the small bathroom in my place that's separated from the open studio by square glass bricks, a small L-shaped wall, a door, and nothing else. Basically, if the lights in the bathroom are on, you can see the silhouette of the person moving around inside. It's weird, but I'm warming to the quirkiness. Especially since I'm the only one living here.

"They have enough work down at the store," I say. "I told you. Ev, I'm trying to push to have the grand opening be a week earlier. The faster the store is open, the faster I'll be bringing money in and paying off Camden's foundation." I scowl and slap a brushstroke of paint along the corner of the wall to get the corners first.

I hear her footsteps before I see her reflection in the mirror in front of me. She crosses her arms and leans against the doorframe. "You know, you don't have to rush any of this.

Just because that asshat is running the company that invested in the business doesn't mean you have to prove something other than what you're proving to yourself. That you are an amazing, talented woman with a great idea and the guts to put her all into making it successful."

With a flourish, I dump the paintbrush I was using into the bucket. A little slops over the side and spills on the concrete floor below. I frown and then shake it off. "Mr. Fix It is going to do the tile in here anyway. What's a little paint gonna hurt?"

Evie grins. "That's my girl. Now, are you ready to talk about the fact that Cam almost kissed you last week?"

My eye twitches at her question and the scowl comes back. "He did not almost kiss me. There's no reason to even talk about him. He's history. Besides, he's engaged. Seeing him may have brought up a million old feelings and but that's natural after not having seen one another in ten years, and I'll repeat...he's *engaged* to a woman that looks like she could be Miss Colorado. So no, I'm not talking about Cam. It's over and done with. I've already forgotten about it. Camden who?" I blurt and spin the brush around in the paint bucket unnecessarily.

"Mmm-hmm. How's lying to yourself working for you?"

I glare at my sister. "And how's avoiding Muscular Milo working for you?"

"You have got to drop this, Kaye. Milo is a friend. Nothing more." She blows her long side bangs out of her face.

I roll my eyes and go back to painting, this time around the edge of the vanity mirror, being careful not to get any on the funky wooden frame surrounding it. Whoever owned this place had a wild sense of design and decor, but I'm loving the strangeness and going with the flow.

"Look, I don't want to talk about Cam, and you don't want to talk about Milo," I continue. "Which I'll end by saying is *weird* since it's not like you ever dated him, he came back into your world, gave you a bunch of money, and then pranced his fiancée in front of you."

Evie sighs and her shoulders drop. "That's a good point. I'll leave it if you will. For now."

"Deal."

A banging sound below startles the both of us. I slap my chest with the orange paintbrush and look down at my now orange-splattered yellow tank with a groan. "Seriously! He's at it again."

"Who?" Evie asks as I drop the paintbrush in the bucket. I push her aside and storm toward the stairs that lead to my shop.

"That damn contractor!" I growl in frustration. I've told him before I prefer to know when he's here and starting work instead of being surprised.

Evie follows close behind me. "What in the world?" she says as the sound of a saw whirs to life.

I come to a screeching halt at the bottom of the stairs when I see a mountain of a man standing behind the guy that's been working on the renovation and driving me bonkers. Except this new guy is nothing but muscles on top of long, sinewy beautiful muscles, not at all hidden under a stark, bright white, tight-fitting T-shirt.

"Jesus..." Evie chokes out, running into me from behind at the same time I blurt, "Holy hotness."

Hot White T-shirt gifts us both with a devil-may-care smirk and adjusts his tool belt on his perfectly trim hips.

Let me say that again. *Adjusts his tool belt.*

I can actually feel the heat between my sister and me as we both follow that move with laser beams for eyes.

Hot White T-shirt grins full-out this time. "Hello, ladies."

For a moment, I just stare at his long, denim-clad legs, tool belt, white T-shirt, thick-looking dark brown hair that's a little long, maybe only by a week or two. There's a healthy dose of scruff around his square chin as if he couldn't be bothered with shaving today, and frankly, why would he when he's got a face like Henry Cavill, with the piercing blue eyes to match?

"I came to introduce myself." He holds out a hand toward me and I place mine in his on autopilot. "Kyson Turner, owner of Turner Brothers Construction." He shakes my hand.

"I'm, uh, Suda Kaye. Who are you again?"

Evie snickers from behind me and bumps my shoulder. "He just introduced himself, wipe off the drool and get with the program. I'm Evie Ross."

Hot White T-shirt lets go of my hand to shake Evie's, and I miss the warmth instantly. Even though he shakes my sister's hand, his eyes stay on me.

"You've met my brother, Lincoln." He nods in the direction of the grumpy-ass guy I know very well. The one who always shows up without saying he's here and just gets to work hammering and sawing away. I never complain because at least he isn't wasting my time or screwing around. His work ethic is top-notch, and he's absolute eye candy, but I wouldn't mind a little hello and how-do-you-do when he arrives so he doesn't scare the bejesus out of me.

"I'm the owner and obviously, the one you spoke to over the phone the first time. I believe you called originally for a Mr. Fix It?" He smirks, and I'm pretty sure my panties just got a little damp.

My cheeks heat and I cover them with my hands. "Um,

yeah. Sorry about that. I can be a little sassy when I'm over-whelmed."

His lips twitch as he looks at my mouth. "I'll be sure not to overwhelm you...much." He winks.

Winked. Hot White T-shirt Kyson Turner just winked at me. At least I think he did. It happened so fast I'm not sure I didn't imagine it.

"Well, now that we've met," Kyson continues, "I'm going to go through what Lincoln has already started work on this week and see if we can't make some serious progress on your renovation. How does that sound, brown eyes?"

Evie chuckles behind her hand and turns her head toward me, mouthing, "Brown eyes," and smiling like a lunatic.

"Sounds like a dream come true, Mr. Fix It." I pucker my lips and dip my head not quite shyly, just enough so he knows I like what he said and welcome his flirting.

"A dream come true. I'll take that as a challenge I need to best." He smiles, showing off a pristine set of straight, pearly white teeth.

God, I love a good smile. Melts my panties in seconds.

I offer him my sexiest return grin and turn around, loop-ing my arm with Evie's. Her shoulders are quaking, and she's failing at keeping her giggles under wraps. The second we hit the stairs back up to my place, she lets it all loose, cracking up and barely making it up the narrow hallway.

"Really, Ev? This is why you haven't gotten laid in a mil-lion years. You can't even keep a straight face around a hot construction worker."

She pulls herself up to full height, clutching at her stom-ach. "I couldn't help it. You two were shooting off fireworks like a mating signal. Is that how it always is with you? Jeez Louise. All hot guys beware!"

I shrug a shoulder. "Not gonna lie. That guy is insanely good-looking. However, it's all just harmless fun. I'm not going to bang my contractor." I roll my eyes dramatically.

Evie stares me down with her best "you're full of crap" look.

"Okay, I'm definitely not going to bang him *while* he's my contractor. Maybe when the job is done." I grin and the two of us burst into peals of laughter.

Once we get ourselves under control, we pull out a bottle of pinot grigio Evie brought over and a couple of coffee cups.

"I'll get you some real wineglasses," Evie says while filling the mugs I bought at the café across the street. She hands me the deep-handled, blue, ceramic, bowl-like mug while she takes its bright sunshiny-yellow twin.

"Wine is wine to me, whether it is out of a mug, a cup, or a fancy stemmed glass." I swallow down my first sip of the fruity flavor. "Mmm, it's good. Thank you."

Evie extends her glass toward me for a toast. "To possibilities and new grounded adventures."

I smile and click my mug with hers. "And smokin' hotties in tight white T-shirts and Native American hot guys with broad shoulders, hair prettier than mine, and giant hands!" I waggle my eyebrows at her suggestively and sip the wine.

"You are relentless," she says and sips her own drink.

"In everything I do, sister. Get used to it because this is your new life."

Her gaze focuses on mine, and her tone is drop-dead serious when she responds. "I've never wanted anything more."

"Sissy..." I whisper, the emotion of her words clogging my throat.

She inhales deeply, lifts her shoulders, and drops them down. "Time to get to work and get you settled. I know I'll feel better when it's all done, and you're set. Safe and sound and back home." She walks over to her pan of paint, sets her mug on the floor, and picks up her roller, dipping it into the dark purple paint.

"Settled," I whisper. A word I would have never associated with my life but I'm suddenly starting to understand its weight and value.

A week later, I'm hovering over a man-made sawhorse with a huge four-by-eight-foot sheet of plywood and a giant, unrolled set of blueprints flattened on top. Kyson leans against my side, the warmth of his body permeating my senses while I study his design.

He points to the section of space in the store where the checkout and jewelry displays will go. "And here you can add a hanging feature where you can dangle some of your more exotic pieces like art instead of just with floor stands." Kyson runs a finger along a section in the blueprints.

The sound of a door opening distracts him. He looks up and lifts his chin but goes back to pointing and tapping the layout.

I'm still stuck on the hanging-art concept. I press my hand on his thick biceps. "Kyson, that idea is incredible," I say breathlessly, the possibilities jumping around my brain in a kaleidoscope of color and light. "Do you think we can do something like that around the edges of the room so we can display different clothing and handmade items?"

The smile on my face is gigantic—as if he's just told me he could bring back Jimi Hendrix and Bob Marley and they were going to play for my grand opening in a duo of epicness, the likes of which the world has never seen.

Kyson lays a hand on my hip and curls his fingers in, bringing my body a few inches closer as he dips his head down.

"Brown eyes, you keep looking at me like that and you can have anything you want, and I mean *anything.*" His lips twist into a sexy smile and my throat goes dry.

"Excuse me?" A deep, familiar, irritated voice shakes me out of my sexy-Mr.-Fix-It stupor and I turn my head to the newcomer.

Camden freaking Bryant is standing there in a pair of perfectly fitted dress slacks, a blue button-down dress shirt cuffed at the elbows and showing off a pair of muscular forearms. A tribal tattoo disappears up his arm under the shirt. He's not wearing a tie, and his suit coat dangles from a finger over his shoulder. His hair is falling in waves around his face and brushing just past his bearded jaw. He looks like he just took a break from a photo shoot selling high-end menswear.

"Cam." I push away from Kyson as though I've been burned. I'll have to run over that moment in my head, oh, about a hundred times to figure out why I responded like I was doing something wrong when I most certainly was not. I'm a free agent. Free. Absolutely one hundred percent free to do what I want, when I want. That's always been my way. I'm just not so sure it's the right way anymore.

Kyson frowns at me, then folds both of his massive arms over his chest and turns toward Camden, taking in all that is the new man in the picture. "You are?"

"Investor, partner, longtime...*friend.*" He says the last word on a wince, as if it pains him to do so. "I gather you're the contractor?" He holds out a hand and takes a few steps toward Kyson.

Kyson shakes his hand. "Kyson Turner, owner of Turner Brothers Construction."

Camden looks around the room, which is in various stages of renovation but mostly in complete disarray. Shelving units lie against one brick wall next to stacks of wood that will be used for additional cases. The molded front-window box display is half finished, completely open at the back even though it's easy to see how cool it will be when it's done. Dangling wires and wire boxes are strung haphazardly along the high ceiling where we'll set up the lighting and put in a drop ceiling or bolts of fabric running across to make the space a bit more comforting and feel less like a warehouse.

"Seems like you've been hard at work. Judging from the plans Suda Kaye shared with us, it's going to be beautiful. Looking forward to seeing the end result. If it's as good as your plans, my company will start having you bid on our jobs."

Kyson clenches his jaw and tilts his head, then runs his hand along the back of his neck. "And what is your company? You said you were an investor?"

Cam sets his jacket over one forearm. "My foundation is the investor on this project and many other startups in the area. We're always looking for an honest, high-quality contractor to work on renovations and new projects, but in my day job, I'm the CEO of Coltrane & Sons Steel."

Kyson's eyes widen. "Shit, man, I thought you looked familiar. I saw you in the paper not long ago getting an award or something for opening that new plant that brought ten thousand more jobs to the area. Said you're the richest man in Colorado."

Camden chuckles. "Maybe that's true, but not where I focus my attention. My father built a company from the ground up and offered a resource to the people of our good nation. I'm continuing the legacy he built."

"Good man." Kyson pats Cam on the arm a few times, his entire demeanor changing to one of respect and gratitude. "One of my uncles and a couple of my cousins work at one of your plants. It's hard work, but they get paid well and have good benefits. They never complain."

"Great to hear," Camden responds cordially, as if he hears this type of thing all the time.

My heart is pounding a mile a minute, imagining how many people Camden employs. How many families are living, bringing children into the world, and retiring off something he's keeping alive and well on their behalf and vice versa. None of this ever occurred to me when we were teenagers. I just knew he'd be working with his father and brothers. I had no idea he'd be taking over the helm, leading the entire company.

"How many people do you employ at Coltrane now?" I ask softly but in no way disguising the awe in my tone.

"A couple hundred thousand across the country."

My mouth drops open; there's no way I can stop it. It's automatic. "That's amazing," I gasp, staring into his mossy-green gaze. "I always knew you'd be incredible at whatever you put your mind to, but, Cam, wow…it's unbelievable."

Camden gets closer to me and reaches out, swiping a lock of hair out of my face and behind my ear. "I guess we all wish we could have known back then what we know now, huh?" His soft gaze turns hard and the shutters close down on the windows of his soul. It leaves me feeling bereft and alone, and a cold chill seeps into my bones. My gut twists and I wrap an arm around my abdomen to ward off the tension.

"Cam." I reach my hand out toward him to say something, I don't know what, I don't know if there is anything I can say at this moment; my emotions are confused and bouncing all over the place.

He saves me by shaking his head and maneuvering to the

side to look at the blueprints. I drop my hand and scratch at my thigh instead.

"Why don't you show me what's in the plans and what's on the docket for this week?" he says. "I can see if there's anything I can assist with. Which reminds me, have you set up a meeting with the mayor regarding the grand opening?"

I frown. "Should I have?"

He smiles softly.

Kyson butts in by placing a hand on the back of my neck and squeezing. I turn away from Cam's enchanting gaze and look into Kyson's deep blue one.

"I'll just get to working on that section we discussed," he says, "if you're good with the layout of the primary checkout. We're shooting for a tavern-like feel with the L shape and saloon doors separating the space for customers to pay and staff to package up the product, yeah?"

I nod. "Yeah. Your vision is perfect."

"My vision for a lot of things is perfect, if given half the chance." Kyson's gaze runs down my tight-fitting electric-blue camisole. I left my pink lacy bra straps exposed for a little funky flare, and five beaded necklaces hang over my top for a layered effect. All of that is paired with my super dark, almost black denim skinny jeans that fit like a glove, making my ass look like it was molded by the heavens. And last, but absolutely not least, the super spunky, smokin' hot, pink canvas platform wedges show off the pale, shimmery pink nail polish I put on my toes last night.

My entire body gets hot, and a rush of heat flames across my cheeks, so much so that I have to lift my hands to ward off the fire. Kyson offers me a sexy wink that would make any woman lose her mind with lust and turns to walk away. Without even realizing it, I'm following him, this hot hunk of a man, to the front of the shop, until a tight grip curls around my upper arm and spins me around.

The spin is so fast I trip over my platform wedge and slam into the utterly delicious chest of the only man on earth I truly want to be plastered against.

"Nice show. You with him now?" Camden lifts his chin toward Kyson before looking down at me. "I thought you were with the big guy with the long black hair."

My mind scrambles from the proximity of being in Camden's arms for the second time in two weeks. I place my hands against the planes of his chest and notice it's hard as a rock and far more muscular than when he was nineteen.

"Um…huh?" I mumble as his intoxicating scent filters into my nose. I breathe the lemongrass and musk in fully, not wanting to miss a second of that smell. So familiar, like a distant, beautiful memory of us riding along in his truck, holding hands without a care in the world.

He runs his hand down my back, not pushing me away or bringing me closer, much to my dismay. "Milo Chavis?"

I rub my fingers back and forth across the sumptuous blue fabric of his dress shirt, noting how buttery soft it feels, and I want to rub my cheek against its silkiness, until his words seep into my brain. "Milo?" I jerk my head back and cringe. "Ew. No way."

Camden frowns. "Ew? Seriously? I've met the guy several times and women swoon everywhere he goes."

I sigh and roll my neck from side to side. "I mean he's a total hottie, as in most women would want to have his children within two point five seconds of meeting him, but no way. My sister has been in love with him her entire life. He's like family to me, and one day, I hope to actually be able to legally say that. So yeah. Ew."

Camden stares down into my face as I stare into his. A wide smile crosses his lips. "I missed this. Having cute and sassy in my life."

I close my eyes and realize where I'm standing. In Camden's arms, his warmth seeping into my palms and fingertips and even my chest, but it's not right. None of this is right. In fact, it's all wrong. "Cam...don't say things like that."

"Why not?" He dips his head and pulls me closer, his face dipping near my neck. He inhales deep and lets out a breath I can feel across the upper swells of my breasts. Gooseflesh covers my skin and I shiver.

"Cam..." I warn, really not wanting to but knowing I have to.

"Yeah?" he whispers, ignoring me and rubbing his nose along my cheek. I close my eyes, allowing myself a single moment to soak in his nearness.

"Cam, you're engaged."

His entire body goes rigid in my arms but he doesn't move aside. His chest rises and falls with his breath.

"Engaged *to be married*," I say more clearly with grit in my tone as we both push away, stepping back.

His hands fall to his sides, one of them now clutching his jacket in a white-knuckled death grip.

He clears his throat and looks away, his jaw clenched so tight he could probably chew through leather in one bite. "You're right. I apologize. I've, uh, had some time to think about you being back, and regardless of what happened toward the end...you were my best friend, Suda Kaye. I'd like to have that back. Especially while we work to make this business a success."

I'm pretty sure my heart stops and I've died a tiny death, all within the span of a single minute. I lick my lips and swallow while gathering my thoughts. "Let me get this straight, you want to…" I shake my head, hardly able to form the words. "You want to be my friend? You and me. Friends."

A muscle in his jaw ticks and his Adam's apple bobs while I wait for him to form the words I can't believe he's saying. "It's the right thing to do," he manages at last. "We need to be able to work together, regardless of what happened between us in the past."

I scratch the side of my neck and lay my hand over my chest, trying to remind myself to breathe and my heart to beat. "Camden and Suda Kaye, friends." The words continue to roll around in my head like marbles on concrete, going every direction and never stopping in one place.

"That's the plan, for now." He's asking for friendship, but I can hear the distrust and hint of resentment in his tone and the tightness in his body language. There is still so much unsaid between us. I can only imagine what he truly wants to say to me. Eventually we're going to have to address it, even though I'd rather walk across hot coals than have that conversation.

My realistic side responds before my professional side can. "Cam, we've never been friends. We've always been an *us*. I fell in love with you the first day we met," I blurt, and want to kick myself for spilling the truth unintentionally.

His shoulders tense and his gaze blazes white-hot fire. "I know. I was there."

His words are a force of nature pushing to the surface memories of better, happier times, when we were an us and the entire world was ours for the taking.

I shake off the memories. "You couldn't possibly think we can be friends and run a business together with our shared history." I rub at my chest, forcing myself to breathe in and out. "You have to assign another mentor. This isn't healthy for either of us." I reach out and grab his hand.

He squeezes mine in a viselike grip, as though he'll never let me go. "There is no one else available. Besides, I'm a risk taker," he states flatly.

I fire back the only shot I can think of. "Since when?"

"I'll admit, back then I wasn't. The man you knew did what he was told and went after the life set in front of him, carved out through years of family legacy. Now I do things my way. I've found a happy medium. A compromise between obligation and freedom."

Obligation and freedom. Sounds exactly like where I'm smack-dab in the middle of myself.

"I'm glad to hear you're happy, Cam. It's all I ever wanted." I grind my teeth together and lift my chin, praying I don't let the tears that want to surface spill out and destroy our level playing field.

"What about you?"

"What about me?" I say in a scratchy, emotion-coated voice.

"Are you happy?" The three words dig into my soul with a monster-size shovel.

"I always find some form of beauty," I say automatically.

"That's not what I asked." He takes a step toward me. His mossy-green eyes have turned a swirly dark green, exposing the torment he's trying to hide. "Did you ever find your happy, in the years that you were gone?"

I tell him the God's-honest truth. "I found a lot of things that made me happy."

His head drops forward and then he lifts it, those eyes blasting me with so much unshared emotion I can barely breathe through the thickness surrounding us. "Then why are you back?" He takes a step closer and runs his fingers down the side of my face, cupping my cheek delicately as if he doesn't even realize he's doing it.

For a brief moment I close my eyes and nuzzle into his touch before opening them again and letting my heart break wide-open.

"Because none of them held a candle to the happiness I felt when I was home."

The spell breaks as what I said seeps through the moment and he drops his hand and nods. "Keep up the good work. I'll, uh, be back to check in soon."

This time Camden is leaving me, walking out the door but not out of my life. It's a smidge of what he may have felt all those years ago, and it breaks my heart in two.

What in the world did it do to him?

6

"He said *what*? After practically holding you in his arms and interrupting you with Kyson?" Sitting on top of her kitchen counter, Evie crosses her legs, a bulbous glass of red wine in her hand.

I slice into a cucumber, creating uniformly thick circles for our salad. "Friends. He wants to be friends."

"Hmm." Evie sips her wine and extends her hand to snatch up a cucumber slice. "And what do you want?"

I shrug, setting down the knife and grabbing my wine. As I take a huge gulp of the zinfandel my sister poured, I let the hints of blackberry and currant coat my senses. A sigh slips from my chest while I lean my ass against the counter. "Honestly, I don't know. It's odd and perfectly familiar being around him at the same time. It seems we've both changed so much, yet there's this invisible force that brings us closer. You know what I mean? I'm sure you have a little of that with Milo."

"Milo?" My sister shakes her head. "No. Not even close. We were friendly as kids, mostly me crushing on him from afar, then we've been acquaintances online. All of a sudden, though, it's like he's popping up everywhere."

She frowns and I smile.

"Divine intervention." I spin back around to put the cucumbers in the already full salad bowl.

Evie hops off the counter. "You could say the same about you and Cam, too."

I purse my lips and tilt my head from left to right, letting her comment sink in. "Maybe. And then, of course, there's White T-shirt Hottie Mr. Fix It." I lick my lips. "Yummo."

"That guy is fine. There's something closed off about him, though. Like he's a player but not."

I laugh and take a sip of my wine, then point at my sister when the thought hits. "Yeah, actually, he's probably more like me than I realized. A good time for now but no promises of forever."

Evie picks up the salad bowl and brings it to the small kitchenette. "Don't you get tired of that lifestyle? A new man whenever the mood strikes?"

I grab the container holding the pasta she made, making sure to keep the potholder on the bottom so it doesn't burn my hand or the table. "It's not exactly like that, Ev. It's more that when I meet a guy I know I can have fun with, we just keep it simple. No strings. No commitments. We have our fun, then over the course of time, if one or the both of us starts to either get more serious or fade away, we usually mutually agree to move on."

Evie nods and takes her seat. I follow suit.

"I want more for you." She reaches for my hand on top of the table and gives it a squeeze.

I hold her hand and look into her beautiful blues. "And I want the entire world on a silver platter for you. I want you to live like there's no tomorrow. Fly until your wings get tired and your feet itch to be on the ground."

"Is that how it is for you? You feel something inside?" Evie asks conversationally, but I know it's more than that. She wants to know why I left and didn't return until now.

I scoop some salad onto Evie's plate and then onto mine. "In a way, yeah. There's definitely a sensation, a twisting feeling in my gut that hits me at random. I've always considered it my intuition leading me to my next destination or journey."

Evie licks her lips and bites down on the bottom one. "Do you think that's what Mom felt?"

I smile softly and remember the times when Mom would swing us girls around the living room, dancing, singing at the top of her lungs, clapping. Those moments would lead into her telling us that she'd gotten the bug. The itchiness in her soul to go on an adventure. For a while, we thought it was funny. We'd laugh with her and dance without a care in the world. Then, a few days later, with my stepfather always on deployment, she'd pack up her suitcase and drop us off at the reservation with Tahsuda, not to be seen or heard from for weeks at a time.

"Yeah, in a way something called to her and she answered."

Evie winces and her lips flatten into a white line. "Wish she would have answered the call of raising her daughters."

I reach out and grab her hand as she's about to lift the lid off the pasta. "*Taabe*...you know Mom loved us and missed us when she was gone," I attempt in a soft voice.

My sister shakes off my hand, grabs the spoon, and serves a couple scoops to me and then to herself. "There's a lot I believe about our mother. Did she love us? Yes, I know she did. Did she love us enough?" She huffs. "We'll never know now, will we?"

I close my eyes and let her fire burn through my chest. "Evie..." I whisper.

She flails her hands in the air, cutting off the conversation. "I don't want to talk about Mom. I want to talk about you and Camden and what you're going to do about the fact that he's going to be your mentor."

Allowing my shoulders and back to slump into my chair, I pick up my wine and take a sip, letting it sit on my tongue for a few moments before swallowing. "The only thing I can do."

Evie pokes a noodle and holds it in front of her face. "Which is what?"

"Wing it."

My sister smiles around her mouthful of pasta and shakes her head. "Of course. I wish I was a bit more like you and Mom."

At this comment, I perk up and stab a few pieces of pasta with my fork, my appetite renewed. "Yeah? How so?" I shovel the creamy fettucine into my mouth and moan around it. Evie was always an excellent cook. From the time she was ten, she made most of the meals, unless Tahsuda cooked a traditional meal or Mom called for takeout.

"Sometimes I wish I was fearless. Mom never worried, never concerned herself with things she couldn't control, and since she didn't think she could control much, she was genuinely happy. You're just like her. Traveling the world. Soaking up as much as you could in the shortest amount of time. Never a care in the world."

"That isn't true. I worry." I clear my throat and blink back the emotion that is starting to make me teary.

She chuckles and swishes her wine in a circular motion. A winemaker in Italy told me that helps the wine breathe better. Guess Evie knew that instinctually or likely read it in a book or learned it at some swanky restaurant.

"Oh, this should be good. What does my free-spirited, life-living sister worry about?" Evie smiles around a bite of pasta.

"I worry about you."

Her head jerks back. "Me? I'm the most solid person you know. I have two degrees, a successful business I own, plenty of money in my retirement accounts, own this condo and my car, and I'm in excellent health. What could you possibly have to worry about with me?"

"All of that. Everything you said. It worries the heck out of me. Don't you see?"

Evie shakes her head.

"You don't live. From the moment you turned ten, you've been taking on the role of provider. For me. For Mom. You worked yourself to the bone in college, graduating early with a bachelor's degree and then a master's. Opened up your own business for which you now have multiple offices, and you still work like a dog. You have had super boring boyfriends, and the only times you've ever traveled have been when you came to see me. And most of those times, you brought your laptop and worked in the hotel or by the pool and beach. I've never seen you drunk. I've never seen you let loose..."

Evie picks up her wine and holds it to her chest.

"You're one to talk. You've never worked a full six months in any one job in your entire life. You've given your body to more men than you have fingers and maybe even toes, and you believe every person you meet is good, honest, and kind, which in and of itself is crazy. Most people are freaks. Yet you act like the world is your oyster and dance through it without worrying when your next paycheck is coming in. Or who is going to take care of you when you're old. Or what happens if you get sick like Mom. Then what? Come back to Steady Evie to take care of you?"

"Evie…" I say. The emotion is sitting like a ball of cotton on my larynx.

She stands up, pushing her chair back so hard it almost tips over, and points a finger at me. "Grow up, Suda Kaye. You are twenty-eight years old and have just pledged yourself to opening a business. Your money, the money I gave you, and the money the foundation gave you is on the line. I am freaked out that one of these days you're going to realize that staying in one place is hard work. Running a business is a commitment. And eventually, you'll just drop everything and bail, leaving me and Cam to clean up all the pieces."

Tears prick at my eyes, but I fight them back. "Please, sit down. Talk to me. Don't run away." I voice the one thing I know my sister would never do. She doesn't run away from her problems. Ever.

Evie leans against the back of her chair, sucks in a deep breath, nods, and sits back down. "I'm sorry. I didn't mean to go off on you. I know you're doing your best."

I grab her hand, and she turns toward me and holds both of mine with hers.

"This time is different," I say.

"Why?" She sniffs and clears her throat.

"I can't put my finger on it, Ev. I just don't have that feeling in my gut. That gnawing, twisting feeling that kept me moving from place to place. And my feet don't itch to keep moving for the first time in my entire life. Something about being here now, opening this store, having you in my life every day, it's right. Feels right."

"And what happens when you get that feeling again?" She lifts her head and pierces me with her sad eyes.

"Then I'll go on vacation. Maybe drag my workaholic sister with me and show her a bit of what she's missing out on. No work involved. Just fun."

She smiles and nods. "You think that will be enough?"

"Right now, I can only tell you what I'm feeling and what I see on the horizon. You. Me. Gypsy Soul. Tahsuda. Colorado. That's it. Sissy, I'm happy. For the first time in a really long time, I'm happy."

Evie's voice falters when she says, "Really?"

I lift a hand and cup her cheek. "Yeah, really. Now eat your dinner because, girl, it is awesome."

"Like that, eh?" She smiles softly and picks up her fork.

"Yep. As usual, your ability in the kitchen is a gift. Though I've learned a few things in my travels that will blow your mind. Dinner tomorrow, on me."

Evie's expression is a mix of doubt and surprise. "You've learned to cook? I distinctly remember you burning water and toast when you were eighteen."

I grin and sip my wine. "Yeah, well, when you've bedded a French chef and an Italian who worked a restaurant, you pick up a few things." I wink at her and we both bust up laughing.

"I'll bet you picked up a few things, but were any of them food-related?" She cackles and I throw my napkin at her.

"Brat!"

She shrugs her shoulders, pokes a cucumber with her fork, and pops it into her mouth with a crunch. "Takes one to know one."

I roll my eyes. "Whatever." I smile and continue eating dinner with my sister, enjoying the fact that this is what normal is. Sharing a delicious meal with the one you love. Having a heart-to-heart with your sister. Working through real issues so they don't become thorns in your relationship. Trying to make one another laugh. Letting go of a long day. Spending quality time together.

Turns out, I'm starting to realize normal is beautiful, too.

Banging on my door startles me from a deep sleep. I sit up and stare at the door all the way across the entire loft from where my bed is facing the opposite wall. The knocking starts up again, and the distinct sound of a saw starts up, though that sound is separate from the knocking.

I swear, fling the covers off the bed and stand naked as the day I was born, pushing my hair out of my face and rubbing my eyes. The knocking gets louder.

"If you don't open this door, Suda Kaye, I'm using my key!" Camden's voice filters through the door.

Key?

"Crapola!" I reach for the purple satin-and-silk robe I have lying on the edge of my bed. It only goes to mid-thigh, but it will have to do. "Coming! Hold your horses already!" I yell and the knocking stops.

With ire on my heels and flames of irritation burning through me, I unbolt the lock and open the door with a flourish. "What the heck, Cam! It's like...the crack of dawn!" I snap through clenched teeth.

Cam's eyebrows rise up at my appearance and then his gaze does a full-body scan of my form. "Jesus!" he says harshly, putting a hand behind his neck and turning his face to look down the stairwell.

I glance down at myself and realize the robe is gaping open, giving a whopping view of my bare breasts, though not the whole shebang. Instantly, I grip the lapels and hold them together at my chest. "What are you doing here so early?"

"Sweets, it's ten o'clock."

Sweets.

I lose my ability to breathe. I haven't heard that word uttered in ten years. He called me sweets before he ever learned my name. He called me sweets in so many different ways. With laughter, frustration, happiness, in a sexy growl, against my lips as he kissed me. I had more "sweets" than I had kisses from the man. Something about him saying it now brings so much of that time back. Like I'm wading in a pool of memories, some more difficult to push through than others, some, like this one, sticking me to the spot unable to move past it.

"And?" I mutter and try to hide my mini freak-out with a yawn. I stare at his face as a smirk flits over his lips.

God, how I loved that smirk. Camden Bryant has always been good-looking, as a boy, and even more now as a grown man. When he smiles or smirks, it ratchets up his sexiness a hundred times and makes him swoon-worthy. My knees wobble, and I feel my nipples tighten into hard little peaks against the silky fabric. I lean against the door, trying to play it cool and ignore his scent wafting over me. The hints of lemongrass soap and musky man are turning me on.

He chuckles deep in his throat, and I have to refrain from sighing at the sound. "You always did like your sleep."

"Let's go back to the part about what you're doing here," I mumble. I try to push my wild bedhead back off my face so at the very least I have something to do with my suddenly shaky hands.

Cam watches me, his lips twitching. "Work. I'm here all day."

"Uh...what?"

"Mentor, remember? I had my secretary schedule me out a couple days a week so I can be here from the ground up. Want to help where it's needed, show you the ropes, and get things moving. There's a lot to do before the grand opening in four weeks. Chop-chop!" He claps his hands together.

I blink at him, not fully comprehending everything he's saying in my sleep-muddled mind.

"Coffee." He pushes on my stomach with his knuckles, and I step aside so he can enter. He looks around, then heads to the kitchen. "Not much here."

I scan my space and try to see it through his eyes. A queen-size bed with the headboard against the far wall. Two end tables on each side of it, one with a lamp and a clock, the other with a stack of books my sister swore I just had to read. And since I have been trying to focus on the store and making up for lost time with my sister, I haven't been going out and hitting the town. I'm finding I like to read at night before I fall asleep. Gives me something nice to drift off to instead of allowing my mind to wash, rinse, and repeat all the things I still need to get done in the store.

Across from the bed is a giant wardrobe. Since there are no closets, I had to make do with a piece of furniture to hold all my clothes. Except this one is sweet. It's a solid white oak antique, and I bought it for a song from a widowed lady who was off-loading her entire estate to move to Florida. She said I reminded her of herself in her early years and practically gave me the beautiful wardrobe. I forced her to take a hundred bucks and promised if she was ever in the area, she could score a huge deal on anything in my store. She took me up on my offer, wished me well, and even had two of her grandsons deliver it and bring the massive thing up the stairs.

So, my bedroom space is looking more lived-in. The living room section is sparse. I still have to get a lot in order to get my life together and make the space something I want to spend time in, but for now, it works.

"Yeah, working on that. As you can see, I have most of the bedroom set up but still need to fill the living room and kitchen." I glance to the area I've planned to put a table, the space now occupied with the table and folding chairs Evie gave me to use until I find a permanent set.

Camden opens the cabinet above the coffeepot and finds the coffee, filters, and cups. "How old is this?" He glares down at the ancient coffeepot I scored at a garage sale last weekend.

"Not sure, but the lady at the garage sale swore it worked like magic and it does. It didn't go with the motif in her kitchen."

"And it goes in yours?"

I gesture around the place. "Not a lot here. Starting over isn't easy or cheap. As a matter of fact, it's expensive."

"Is that what you're doing?" He puts a filter in the pot, pours in some coffee grounds, then takes the decanter to the sink. "Starting over?"

"Kinda."

"After ten years?"

"Um...yeah."

Cam bites down on his bottom lip, then fills the pot, sets it back on the hot plate, and presses Start. The coffeepot springs to life, making gurgling and sputtering noises.

To my surprise, Cam turns around, his suit coat flaring out, sexily showing off his trim waist before he leans against the counter. "What have you been doing? All these years?"

I turn around and leave him in the open kitchen and head to my wardrobe. "I need to get dressed."

"Suda Kaye, you can't avoid me or this conversation forever. At some point we need to talk about it."

"I don't." I shrug, acting nonchalant when inside I'm a tornado of contradicting emotions.

"That's rich. Every time I get near you, you shake like a leaf. You left *me*, remember? A day didn't go by that I didn't wonder where you were, what you were doing, if you were okay, whether or not you missed me, missed us?"

With a deep breath, I open the wardrobe and swallow back the hurt in my soul. I'm not ready to do this. It's too soon, but I have to give him something. With a heavy hand, I push aside my warmer weather clothes, pull out a tank top, then grab the first pair of jeans stacked on the bottom shelf.

"You need to dress in something more appropriate."

I spin around, toss the clothes on my bed, and place my hands on my hips. "Do not attempt to tell me what to wear or what to do."

He holds up his hands. "I'm sorry. I only meant that you need to wear something more professional than jeans and a tank top."

I scan his outfit. Dark navy suit, shiny brown leather shoes and belt, a pale yellow dress shirt that brings out the gold in his dark blond waves. I fight back a sigh, and it takes everything I have not to jump him. I mean it's hard not jumping him on a normal day, but right now when I'm naked, he's grumpy hot and I'm grumpy turned on, wearing nothing but silk, it feels like the entire universe is against me. "Why?" I finally ask.

"We have a lunch meeting with the mayor today." He looks down at his watch. "In an hour and a half to be exact."

Without speaking, I turn around and dig through to the far right of my closet where Evie put two of her best business outfits for me. I've already worn one of them to the first meeting with Camden, so that one is out. I grab the red sheath dress and black blazer with the tiny red piping along the lapel and pockets that matches the color of the dress.

I hold up the dress and jacket for Cam. He looks at the outfit and swallows slowly, his eyes turning that dark forest green I know means he really likes something. "That...uh... that'll do."

"Great," I say dryly and toss it on the bed. "And not that I want to talk about this right now, or ever, I uh..." I grab the clothes on the bed and shuffle around it, past where he's standing in the middle of the room toward the bathroom. "Just, well..." I stop and turn around when I'm standing in the door.

"I missed you every day." The admission leaves my lips unchecked and unfiltered. He takes a step toward me, and I hold up a hand, palm facing out. "Don't." The word is a plea.

"Sweets." He says the endearment as if it has been physically ripped from his throat.

I shake my head curtly. "Enough. Have some coffee. I'll take a shower and be out soon."

He puts his hands in his pockets, rocks back and forth on his heels while looking down at the ground. "Okay, Suda Kaye. Have it your way." He lifts his head, and his gaze is so sharp, so telling, I know he's hiding something behind those mossy orbs. If I were still the same woman I was ten years ago, I'd have a clue. In this moment, I'm floundering in a sea of uncertainty with no life raft in sight.

"For now," he adds, his tone low and serious. "I'm letting this go, for now." His voice is filled with promise.

I close my eyes and nod before shutting the door on him and the past in a single action.

That is...*for now.*

7

"Explain to me again why we need to have a meeting with the mayor?" I exit the bathroom fully dressed, sans heels and hair in wild curls down my back. Just because I have to wear a monkey suit doesn't mean I'm not going to have rock and roll hair. Makes me feel like I'm throwing up the middle finger to societal norms in my own secret way.

Cam's gaze lifts to meet mine as he holds the bright yellow mug up near his face about to take a drink. He's leaning against the bar, one ankle crossed over the other, perfectly at ease in his giant form. Which reminds me—I really need to get some barstools.

"I like your bathroom," is his cryptic reply, ignoring my question altogether.

I narrow my gaze and move to the section under the bed where I grab one of the drawer handles and pull out a long drawer filled to the brim with shoes. Finding the black stilettos Evie gave me, I spin around and set my booty on the bed, crossing one leg over the other so I can put on the shoe. "What do you mean? You haven't been in my bathroom."

He grins a cat-that-drank-all-the-cream smile. "I meant I like your bathroom wall. Made entirely of glass blocks. Genius design. Have you ever been on this side while someone's taken a shower in there?" He lifts his chin toward the glass block wall.

My entire face heats as the image of me naked in the shower flashes across my mind. "No..."

His grin was equal parts sly and lascivious. "Oh yeah. Hottest show I've seen in a long time."

"You're a pig." I stand abruptly after putting on the second shoe and wobble a little unsteadily until I get my bearings, which is a challenge, seeing as I'm beyond embarrassed.

"I'm only human." He says this as if it's reason enough for him to be gawking at me while I showered. "Besides, it's not like I haven't seen it all before."

I narrow my gaze and attempt to glare a hole straight through him. "I hate you."

Cam lets out a full belly laugh and sets his cup on the counter. "No, you don't, but I'll let it slide this time." He gestures to my Starbucks travel mug. "I've made you coffee to go. Pumpkin creamer, as sweet as you are, unless something's changed in the last ten years?"

I shake my head and take the mug from his outstretched hand. "Thank you."

He smiles softly and tilts his head. "Don't worry, sweets. I couldn't see anything but a sexy silhouette." Cam pushes a lock of hair behind my ear and caresses my face with one finger from ear to jaw where he cups my cheek and dips his face close to mine. I can feel his breath against my lips when he whispers, "My imagination had to fill in the rest." He gives me a sexy-as-sin smile/wink combo that heats my body from the inside out.

My mouth drops open, and I'm about to chastise him when

he lets me go, turns, and grabs his keys off the counter. "We need to hit the road. You ready?"

"Yeah. Just keep your filthy imagination to yourself." I follow his long, broad form as he opens my door. "And how do you have a key anyway?"

Cam holds open the door for me to walk through first. "Requested them from the building owner after providing proof I own a portion of your business. The key to the front of the store is the same as this door."

I frown but focus my attention on taking the stairs one at a time in the sky-high heels. How Evie teeters on these things all day I'll never know. I prefer a wedge any day of the week.

"And you used to love my dirty mind." His words seem to bounce and echo off the walls of the narrow hallway.

I lose my footing at his comment, but an arm comes around my waist and slams me back against him, holding me steady. Without meaning to, I lean back into his warm hold. His chin touches my neck, sending a shiver straight through my body. "I've got you, Suda Kaye."

With everything in me, I firm my resolve, straighten my spine, and move out of his protective hold. "No, you don't."

You've got Brittney is what I want to say but keep it to myself.

On my parting jab, I take the stairs far faster than I normally would, gripping the handrail for dear life but making it to the bottom in one piece.

At least physically.

My heart, however, can't take another emotional fall.

"Good to see you again, Mayor Browning." Camden smiles and rests his hand on my lower back. "This is the woman I wanted you to meet. The primary owner and shareholder of what we hope to be the trendiest new boutique on Main Street, Suda Kaye Ross."

I extend my hand over the table to shake the mayor's hand. She's a small, curvy woman, dressed in a simple skirt-and-sweater combo with a genuine smile and a no-nonsense glint in her blue eyes as she assesses me. "Nice to meet you, Ms. Ross. Our town is looking forward to your store going in. Please, let's all have a seat." She gestures to the table already set with plates and stemware.

Cam reaches for my chair and pulls it out until I take a seat. He helps push the chair back in. A move he must have practiced in the years after our time together. Cam was always a gentleman. Back then we were teenagers and very casual, he'd open the door for me, but I don't recall him ever holding the chair and settling me in my seat first.

He waits until the mayor is seated and then takes his own. "I wanted to connect with you because my foundation is contributing to the opening of Gypsy Soul, and we'd like to ask for a favor." He smiles at the mayor.

The woman nods, her dark hair not moving a speck from the perfectly stiff bun at the nape of her neck. "I figured as much. A Bryant only comes calling if they need a building permit, a favor, or are planning a donation to something for the city. I was hoping for the latter." She dips her head, piercing Cam with a pointed gaze.

Cam chuckles as the waiter comes over to take our drink order. Since the mayor and Cam both order nonalcoholic drinks, I settle on some iced tea.

For a few minutes, Mayor Browning and Cam talk general city business, how the steel workers union is getting on, the new plant Coltrane & Sons Steel put in, and the troubles the mayor is seeing in some of the younger teens as it pertains to vandalism and graffiti.

"Maybe they're just bored," I offer.

The mayor's gaze cuts to me. "How long have you lived in Pueblo, Ms. Ross? I haven't seen you at any of the city's chamber of commerce meetings or town halls."

Cam sits back in his chair and reaches out an arm, resting his hand on the back of my chair while turning more toward me, bringing me into their conversation.

"I used to live here as a teenager," I say. "My sister, Evie, and I both went to high school here—"

"Evie Ross?" Mayor Browning reaches for a roll, rips it apart, and dunks it in the olive oil she poured on her plate.

I nod. "Yeah, she's my sister."

"Evie is a gem. Her financial company is very generous with donations to the local causes and sponsoring kids sporting teams. She's a kindhearted soul. A true Coloradan, that one." She beams.

A sense of pride lifts my spirits as the waiter comes to take our orders.

"I'll have the Cobb salad with blue cheese dressing on the side please." I hand the waiter my menu.

"No carrots or onions," Camden says to the waiter, and I frown at him. "Suda Kaye, that salad comes with carrots and probably onions."

"Oh!" I lift my hand. "No carrots or onions." The waiter nods and takes Camden's and Mayor Browning's orders. When he steps away, I turn my body toward Cam. "You remembered I don't like carrots?"

He nods and reaches for his drink. "Or onions."

I let out a small breath of shock and turn toward the mayor.

"So, you two know each other well then?" she asks.

"Um..." I respond at the same time that Camden says, "Yes."

The mayor smiles and sits back in her chair, wiping her mouth and fingers from the bread and oil. "Interesting. You said you went to high school here?"

"Yeah. After I graduated, I...uh...did some traveling." Cam clears his throat, and I look down at the napkin in my lap and then away. "A lot of traveling, actually."

"Really? Where'd you go?"

I take a deep breath and avoid making eye contact with Cam. This is not something we've talked about, but it's not a secret what I did with my time since I've been gone. "The better question would probably be where have I not been?" I chuckle.

"Fascinating. I've been to Mexico on vacation and took a trip to England with my husband on our tenth anniversary. Have you been to either of those places?"

"England is lovely. I especially loved seeing Windsor Castle and Stonehenge. Even visited Bath, which was absolutely beautiful. Mexico has some of the best food in the world."

"Ain't that the truth!" She knocks her knuckles on the white tablecloth. "Where else have you been?"

I chance a glance at Cam. He's leaned to the side, and his focus is entirely on me, though his expression has gone blank. He's either masking his emotions or doesn't much care for where this conversation is going.

"Uh, I've been all through Europe. Spent time in most countries. Did a little traveling through India, South America, and Australia and New Zealand. But enough about me. I'm sure my itchy feet syndrome is boring."

"Not at all," the mayor says and looks at Cam. "Right, Camden?"

"Absolutely. I'd love to hear more."

"Yeah, fun talk first, business after we eat. Now tell me, which country is your favorite?" she asks.

I burst out laughing at the question. "Asking a traveler to name their favorite country or place is the same as asking a bookworm what their favorite book is. A true traveler finds beauty in all things. However, I will say one of the cities I appreciated the most and tend to visit more regularly is Paris. My sister, Evie, loves that city and had no problem meeting me there during my time away."

"I'd love to go to Paris," the mayor sighs.

"There's something uniquely special and romantic about that city that you won't find anywhere else in the world. Now if you're talking about natural beauty, I recall absolutely losing my breath where the Oslo Winter Olympics were held in Norway. The view from there shows multiple mountains with fjords running through. It's utterly magical." I look out the window behind the mayor and imagine I'm still on that mountain looking out over the vast horizon as if I am seeing the natural wonder for the first time again.

"Wow, you've lived some life. And for someone so young."

"My mother taught me from a young age to always spread my wings and fly free. I took that advice to heart in all things." I've said the words before I realize how they might affect the man sitting next to me.

Cam stands abruptly and buttons his suit coat. "Excuse me for a moment, ladies."

I close my eyes and hold my breath until he walks away at a rather fast clip toward the restroom.

Crapola! I chastise myself and play with my straw, picking it up and dropping it back into my iced tea, pulverizing the wedge of lemon in the process.

"I'm guessing you two were an item at one point before you left town?" The mayor leans over her plate, her large chest practically resting on the tabletop.

I mirror her pose and place my forearms on the table and lean over so she can say whatever she needs to say.

"It's obvious there's still something between you two," she goes on. "You should go for it. That man is a hot ticket, girlie. You do not want to let someone like Cam slip through your fingers."

I reach my hand out across the table and pat the top of hers. "Thank you for your concern, but it's far more complicated than that."

"It always is when the heart is involved." She squeezes my hand and the hairs on the back of my neck stand up as I feel him return before I see him.

"Getting along rather nicely without me, I see. Shall I go?" Cam jokes, but his tone is more guarded than it was when we started the lunch.

The mayor looks at Cam, looks at me, and smiles softly before she and I let one another go and sit back in our chairs.

Our food arrives right as Cam takes his seat. I swear it's that get-up-and-go-to-the-bathroom trick. Works every time.

When I notice he has a side salad, I request the salt and pepper from the mayor and promptly hand them to him. "Here you go." I lift my chin toward his salad when his expression contorts into one of confusion. "Salad." I bug my eyes out like a loon.

He chuckles and takes the salt and pepper, adding some to the leafy greens.

"Seems like the two of you didn't miss a beat. You remember what she doesn't like to eat. She remembers how you season your salad, of all things. How long were you gone?" The mayor digs for info, a questioning eyebrow rising.

"Ten long years," Camden says and shakes his head, poking at his salad so hard I can hear the fork tines grating on the porcelain plate.

Me, I'm a wuss. I leave it at that and keep my big mouth shut.

For the next twenty minutes, I let Cam lead the conversation as they discuss the issue of the teenagers. They both agree with my assumption that it's likely a lack of things to do in the town. The three of us brainstorm ideas on what the town, local businesses, and the schools can possibly do to help work through the problem.

Once we finish dessert, Camden sets down his napkin and gets to the point of our lunch meeting. "The reason I asked you here today is because we'd like to have you hold a ribbon cutting ceremony for the grand opening of Gypsy Soul."

"That's it? The entire favor you want?"

He chuckles and sits back in his chair, propping one ankle over the opposite knee, getting comfortable. "Well, yeah."

"Done." The mayor laughs. "You are far different than your father, young man."

"Am I?" he prompts.

"Definitely. He's a great man, too. Supports the town, provides the most jobs in the area, and is an all-around good guy. However, whenever his office would call in the past, it was usually to get me to sway another businessman to his side of thinking about a project, get my support on an issue needing the townsfolk approval, and the like. Heck, he even begged a few times for a speedy city permit—not that he ever got it, mind you."

She fixes her gaze on us, her expression all business. "He

most certainly never called to get me to participate in a rib-bon cutting. I'm happy to take part and will do you one bet-ter. I'll make sure the local paper does a write-up and brings their photographers. How about that?"

I beam and bounce out of my chair, almost toppling over on my heels until I realize Cam's there with an arm to hold me up. I shake him off and hug the mayor, probably making quite the scene in the swanky little restaurant.

She pats my arm. "Now, now, this is not an unusual re-quest, so don't think I'm playing favorites. I often attend rib-bon cuttings, and after having met you, I look forward to seeing your store. Just let my office know when the opening is, and we'll get it on the calendar."

"Thank you!" I clap wildly and smile at Cam, realizing he hasn't said a word.

When I turn around, he's bent at the waist, his hands grip-ping the back of the chair, one of his hands going to his neck. His face is a tortured shade of white, and he is straining with exertion.

I rush to his side and place my hand on his back. I dip my head to get a better look at him. "What's the matter? Are you okay?"

His voice is scratchy as he shakes his head and grips his throat. "Can't breathe. Th-th-throat swoll…" is all he gets out before his body slumps over and he falls to the floor in a heap.

"Oh my god! Someone call an ambulance." I turn Cam over on his back and assess his eyes. The green depths are murky and swirling with fear. I open his mouth and look in-side to see if he's choking but there's nothing there. I can't see past the fiery-red, swollen tissue at the back of his throat.

No. "No, no, no. What was in that tart?" I screech out while patting his cheeks. "Just breathe through your nose if you can. Super slow, try to get any air in there, sweetheart. It's okay."

I can hear sirens blaring way off in the distance, nowhere near as close as I want them to be. Cam is gasping for air and I can tell not much is getting in. His eyes roll back into his head and I try to smack his cheeks.

"No, baby, stay with me. Stay with me. The paramedics are almost here. Don't leave me!" I put my face right in front of his and his gaze seems to stay glued to mine as he clutches at his neck.

In the background, I can hear someone reciting the ingredients of the fruit tart. When he says pineapple puree, I close my eyes. A slithery dose of fear ripples along my spine and digs a scaly hand with razor-sharp claws around my heart and squeezes tight.

"He needs an EpiPen! Does anyone have one?" I holler out into the open room and the patrons standing around, watching the show like a twisted automobile accident. Fortunately, that's when I notice the two individuals in blue medical uniforms pushing a stretcher through the crowd.

I squeeze Cam's hand as I speak to the paramedics. "He's allergic to pineapple. Goes into anaphylactic shock. His neck and throat are almost completely shut. Please help him!"

"Please step back, ma'am. We've got him now."

I shake my head and move out of the way enough that I can still rub his shoulder and cheek. The paramedics administer some kind of shot, start an IV, and hook him up to a monitor of some sort while adding an oxygen mask.

I answer their questions as best I can, but it feels like an eternity is passing in slow motion until they are ready to put him on the stretcher. Their movements are quick and efficient as they secure Cam, who is barely awake but seems to be breathing easier. They raise the head of the stretcher and allow me to hold his hand and follow alongside, the mayor close behind.

She hands me my purse. "You go with him. I'll get in touch with his family."

I nod abruptly and follow the paramedics, making sure not to let go of Camden's hand the entire way through the restaurant and into the ambulance.

He seems out of it, but I reach for his hand and hold it in both of mine. In a moment of true beauty, he turns his head to the side and his gaze locks with mine.

The paramedics do their thing the entire way to the hospital, but I've only got eyes for this man.

Silently I'm praying over and over, chanting out my prayer to whoever will listen.

Keep him safe. Don't let him die.

Keep him safe. Don't let him die.

Keep him safe. Don't let him die.

Eventually, we reach the hospital, and he's whisked into the emergency department, our connection broken at the last moment when they push his stretcher through a series of double doors and a medical aide holds me back. His eyes close and his body goes limp before the doors shut, and I step up to one of the square windows and watch until they're out of sight.

Keep him safe. Don't let him die.

8

His hand is cold in mine. Too cold. I swipe my thumb over top of his hand over and over. I'm not sure if I'm trying to soothe him or me. Either is up for debate.

Camden groans and turns his head to the side; a chunk of dark blond hair falls into his face. I push the strands back and cup his cheek. His hazel eyes are a brilliant green as he smiles a crooked grin. "What happened?" he says, his voice mimicking the sound of crumpling newspaper.

The emotion that held its tight grip around my chest, stealing my ability to take a deep breath, comes out in a rush of relief. I press my forehead to Cam's and let the tears fall. "My goodness, you scared me."

A warm hand slides along the side of my neck and cups the back of my head. "I'm sorry."

"It was…uh…the pineapple. It wasn't listed in the ingredients on the menu since it's such a small amount. The restaurant manager is beside himself."

"And you?"

I don't move but an inch away, our noses almost touching as I stare intently into his eyes. "What about me?"

"Suda Kaye, the last thing I remember is you begging me not to leave you."

I narrow my gaze and swallow down the turmoil that's been lodged in my chest, the space now filling with annoyance. "That's not fair. You were dying!" I attempt to push away but he nuzzles close to my face and lays a kiss on my cheek.

His breath is warm against my skin as he speaks against my ear. "Thank you for saving my life."

Not wanting to give too much power to his words and needing to get as far away from this emotional landmine as possible, I push away from the bed since I'm hovering over his form. At the same time, two loud sets of footfalls barrel into the room.

"Son!" The older gentleman calls out. Coltrane Bryant. Camden's father.

Right on his heels is his mother, Patty. Man, I can't win today.

Two people I have loved almost as much as their son enter the room. I move out of the way as Patty falls over her son's chest, kissing his face, tears falling down her cheeks. "My sweet, sweet boy. You're okay. Oh my, thank the good Lord above."

Coltrane places a hand on his son's shoulder and squeezes; his voice is rough when he speaks. "Son, you had your mother and I worried. When the mayor called and said you'd collapsed at the restaurant—" he clears his throat "—well, I just... We're glad to see you're okay. Now, what in the world happened?"

With the two newcomers focused solely on their son, I try to tiptoe my way along the sidewall to the door a scant few feet away. Escape is nearly in my grasp.

Just as I curl my fingers around the doorframe, a small hand cups the ball of my shoulder. "Suda Kaye, is that you?"

I close my eyes at the shaken voice of the only other woman in the world I'd ever put up on high alongside my own mother and sister. Patty Bryant.

I plaster on a smile that turns genuine the moment I spin around and meet the face of the woman I've loved so dearly. The butterflies of excitement match the anxiety fluttering in my belly. "Hi, Patty. It's good to see you. Only...well, not under these circumstances."

Patty lifts a hand to her face as her mouth falls open. "My goodness! Two miracles. My boy is alive and safe, and my dear Suda Kaye has come home!" Tears form in her eyes as she opens her arms and pulls me against her chest. She rubs her hands up and down my back and squeezes me so hard I can't breathe until she releases her viselike grip.

"Well, my, my, let me get a good look at you." Patty's hands move up and down my arms, and she pats them soothingly. "You were always the most beautiful girl I'd ever laid eyes on. 'Course you had your mama to thank for that. Col, dear, look here! It's our Suda Kaye in the flesh!"

Coltrane looks me up and down, and for a moment, his jaw seems to lock until he closes his eyes and lets his shoulders fall. "Thought I could stay mad. Seeing you is a breath of fresh air, darlin' girl. Come here and give an old man a hug."

He tugs my arm and pulls me against his chest. One of his arms wraps completely around my entire body, holding me tight; the other hand is pressed against the back of my head. His cheek presses to mine in much the same way his son's did earlier. "Missed you, darlin' girl. But not nearly as much as my boy did."

My breath hitches, and I can't help the tears that form behind my eyelids.

"Dad, you're suffocating her…" Cam calls out on a low, gravel-filled chuckle.

"Shoot. Sorry, darlin'." His dad pats my arm the same way his mom did. His green gaze seems to scan my entire face. "You look good girl, but you always did. Prettiest girl I've ever seen aside from my Patty! Still true all these years later."

"Thank you. I missed you, too, and—"

"Oh. My. God! Camden! Sugar lumpkins!" I hear the screech along with clacking on granite until a bubble of pink flies through the room, blond hair bouncing in its wake. A pink snowball of a woman plows in between Coltrane and me, knocking me back against the wall and forcing Cam's father to brace on the chair next to him so he doesn't fall.

My elbow hits the wall, a shot of pain bursting from the funny bone. Instantly, I pull my arm in front of me to rub at the sore spot.

"Camden, sugar plum, I just heard. Are you okay? Is anything broken? Oh my god. I was getting my nails done… see!" Miss Colorado Barbie flails her cotton candy–colored nails in front of Cam's face.

He cringes and pushes his head back into the pillow.

"I was five minutes away from a full dry when your brother called me. I pulled right out of that dryer and ran out. Now look, I smudged two of them." Brittney pouts, pressing her giant silicone-filled bottom lip out while showing Cam one of her hands.

"Stinks, Brittney." He coughs and turns his head. She stands up fully and puts her hands to her hips.

"Well, excuse me, Mr. Grumpy Pants. I just wanted to make sure I always look good for you. What would people think if my nails were all chipped? They'd think I couldn't take care of myself or you, and you know I always want to make a good impression for you."

Camden groans and reaches out a hand, encircling Brittney's wrist. "Sorry, Brittney—" he starts but is cut off.

"Brittney? What happened to cookie? You know I love it when you call me your cookie." She leans over Cam and rubs her nose against his.

He closes his eyes, not as though he's enjoying the moment but trying to distance himself from it. Weird. Either way, that's my cue to get out of here.

I place a hand on Coltrane's shoulder and whisper, "It's good to see you. I'll be going now."

He pulls me into his arms for another hug. "Don't be a stranger."

Patty takes her turn and hugs me again. "Are you back for good, dear?" she asks.

"Yeah, I'm opening a business on Main Street. Camden's foundation is helping fund the startup."

Patty places her hand over her chest and smiles. "What an incredible coincidence. Fate bringing the two of you back together after all this time."

"Uh, well, I wouldn't call it fate so much as…luck perhaps?" *Bad luck more like it*, although I keep those thoughts to myself. I smile softly and back up a few steps.

"Suda Kaye," Cam calls out, and his parents step aside.

Brittney is holding Cam's hand and leaning against the side of the bed, staring daggers at me.

"Yeah?" I say, stopping at the door.

"Thank you, for today. If you hadn't figured out that it was my allergy to pineapple… I could have suffocated right then and there. You stayed calm and helped me through it. I can't…" He coughs and sighs. "Thank you."

I smile and nod. "You'd do the same for me."

"That I would."

"Get some rest." I tap the door. "We'll catch up when you're back at work. I'll talk to the mayor and let her know you're okay."

He nods and leans his head back against the pillow, his eyes still on me.

I bite my tongue, not allowing myself to say anything more. He's okay. He'll live to see another day.

When I make it a few feet from Cam's door, I can hear Barbie Brittney's whining voice announce, "You're allergic to pineapples? I love pineapples. They're so good for you."

I pick up the pace until I'm power walking to the elevator to get as far away from that woman as possible.

"Brown eyes, get your ass out of that chair, your eyes off that catalogue, and check this out," Kyson bellows from the front of the store.

It's two days after Cam's accident. I broke down and texted him yesterday to ask how he was. He responded that his throat still felt scratchy; otherwise, he was given a clean bill of health.

Now, I'm sitting in what will be my stockroom where Kyson crafted a large wooden work desk. At the moment, it's loaded to the gills with fabric, trinkets, catalogues, pictures, and other stuff I'm wading through to make sure I have all the product I need. To the right of the desk, he built me a shelving unit where I am able to load up all my beads, leather, and fabric rolls for all the things I'm making by hand and selling in my One of a Kind section of the store. Turns out I'm really good at making clothing, purses, scarfs, and other decorative accessories. I mean, I always knew I had a knack for crafts and making things, but I never thought I could use this talent and earn a living doing it. Definitely makes the store concept even more exciting and fun.

"Suda Kaye!" Kyson yells again.

I grind my teeth, set my catalogue down, and put a sticky note where I left off before I stomp out to where he's standing facing the open window. The vision that greets me makes my mouth dry. Muscular legs set wide apart, white T-shirt stretched across his broad back. I lick my lips and give myself a second to appreciate Kyson's body.

Kyson Turner is a woman's fantasy man. Tall, strong, works with his hands. Fills out a pair of jeans as though they were crafted solely for his body. Big chunky work boots that say, *I'm not only cool, I fix things.* Many woman dream of having a man who can not only hammer her good and hard in the bedroom but also knows how to use a hammer around the house. Kyson is a double whammy, and the woman who locks him down as her own is going to be a happy camper. I'm sure of it.

I cock a hip and prop my hand on it. "You bellowed."

Kyson turns around. "Took you long enough." He swings his arm wide and takes a few steps back so that I can see the front display area. "Check this out! It's done."

The wooden display fits along the window wall at about knee height. It's a solid dark cherry mixed with black so that the knots in the wood stand out strikingly. It's shiny, as though he's already lacquered it so it won't get scuffed up easily.

"Wow. It's beautiful."

He grins and holds up a finger. "Not done yet. Check out this idea. I know I didn't run it past you, but I had a feeling it would look awesome, and I wanted to surprise you with it. Plus, it fell within the budget."

He moves to the wall and I see a series of switches and buttons that weren't there this morning. He presses one of the switches, and a pair of heavy hooks suspended by wire ease down from the ceiling. "When you want to hang things, like tapestry or a piece of clothing or art, maybe some of your glass pieces, you can do so from these. Just use these switches up or down to get the height you want, and they can each hold over a hundred pounds. They've been tested."

"Wha...what? That is incredible!" I cover my mouth and touch one of the hooks.

"That's not all." His dark facial hair halos around his full lips and bright white smile. He presses a button above each of the switches, and a bright light shines over the hooked area, separate from the normal store lighting. "This will allow you to light up your pieces at night. Spotlight certain things to grab prospective customers' attention."

I jump up and down, not believing what I'm seeing. It's all coming together. "Kyson!" I fling my arms around him. He grunts as our chests flatten against one another and I hug him tight. He wraps his arms around me and squeezes, dipping his face where my neck and shoulder meet.

"Damn, brown eyes, if I'd known I'd get this reaction I would've added some more surprises to the job sooner." He chuckles and holds me tighter. He inhales deeply, the scruff of his chin abrading along my sensitive skin, making me sigh in his arms. "Mmm, you smell like cherries. Anyone ever tell you that?"

My entire body instantly goes completely still.

Yeah, one person has told me that. Only one.

I escape his arms quickly and fluff my hair back into place with shaking fingers. "Uh, I'm sorry. That wasn't exactly professional of me."

He hooks his thumbs into pockets. "Professional? Yeah, nothing about that hug said professional, brown eyes, but I don't look gift horses in the mouth. Now we've been dancing around an attraction between the two of us since I started on the job. Except I see that attraction changes the minute your, um—what did he call it—*old friend* comes to help out. You two seeing each other?"

I'm pretty certain my eyes bulge out of my head. "Cam? No. We, uh, dated a long time ago." Not that I wouldn't take a wild ride on that train a second time. It's just not in the cards.

He's getting married. Married, Suda. M-A-R-R-I-E-D.

In seconds I have my emotions back in check, and I focus on Kyson.

"High school sweethearts?" he surmises accurately.

"You can say that. Didn't end well, but we're, uh, friends now." I roll the word *friends* around in my mouth and find it tastes like dirt.

"Friends?" Kyson chuckles, and his gaze scans me from top to toe. "The man is not blind. And he doesn't want to be friends. He wants to get in there again. Question is...are you going to let him?"

A wave of intense frustration swallows my entire body in a fiery heat. I tip my head back and groan. "Why me, God? Why me?"

He laughs hard this time.

I cross my arms over my chest and glare at him. "You don't know anything about Cam and me. We're just friends."

Blech. There's that word again. Tastes even nastier the second time I say it.

"Friends don't look at one another as though they want to get in each other's pants."

I open my mouth and close it again, remembering the one

night I truly got into Cam's pants. It was heavenly. And ten years ago. Everything has changed.

"He's engaged," I supply flippantly.

"So?" Kyson shrugs.

"To be married. To a woman who looks like a beauty queen." I might have sneered when I said that last part even though it's the truth. Regardless of whatever work Brittney has definitely had done, she's every man's wet dream.

"Maybe he doesn't want plastic pretty when he can have tall, dark, and scalding hot in his bed."

I shake my head and tunnel my fingers through my long hair. "This is insane. One moment you and I are flirting, the next, you're telling me that someone else wants me? I don't get it. What does it matter to you?"

He takes a few steps forward and stands so close to me that I can feel the heat from his body. He cups my jaw and lifts my face toward his. "Just want to know the score, brown eyes. I don't play in another man's sandbox. You feel me?" He smiles but cups my head in his hand, his blue gaze intense. The smell of wood and earth hits my senses, and I place my hands on his waist, gripping the fabric of his T-shirt.

"Yeah." My voice sounds breathy and needy even to my ears.

He grins. "No, you don't. But you're gonna." And that's when he presses his lips to mine.

The kiss is slow at first. Easy. Just a gentle touch of lips to lips. Until he wraps an arm around me, bringing our bodies flush against one another, tilts my head to the side, and opens his mouth over mine.

When his tongue slides along my bottom lip, I open to him. He tastes of the citrus-flavored gum I know he chews obsessively and burning-hot male goodness. I hum in the back of my throat and wrap my arms around his neck, bringing us even closer, but the kiss still lacks that intensity of a first kiss with someone you're wild for. Our tongues tangle while our lips attempt to learn one another, giving and taking, neither winning the battle over the other.

Right as he runs his hand down between my shoulder blades along the upper swell of my butt and grips my ass, the front door opens, the small bell Kyson installed dinging loudly. The noise breaks me out of my stupor, and we both turn just our heads toward the door, still in one another's arms.

"Didn't mean to intrude," Camden states flatly, his face a blank mask I'm not able to interpret.

I push off of Kyson instantly and bring my hand to my mouth, wiping off the evidence of our kiss. Kyson licks his lips and then reaches out a hand and removes what I'm guessing is a smudge of my lipstick near my mouth. "I'm going to get back to work. We'll talk later."

I nod and rub my hands up and down my arms.

Once Kyson enters the back room, I stare at Camden. "That wasn't what it looks like."

Camden's eyebrows rise. "That looked like you were kissing your contractor."

"Okay, maybe that is what it looks like. But, um, it shouldn't have happened." I frown, wondering why in the world I'm telling him this. I don't owe him an explanation even if the kiss didn't flip my switch.

Cam sucks in a huge breath and lets it out slowly, as though he was a fire-breathing dragon calming himself down. "It's not my place to say anything."

I close my eyes and look away. Of course it isn't. He doesn't want me. He wants Miss Colorado. *His fiancée.*

His fiancée.

His fiancée.

Now that I've reminded myself of that important fact three more times, I put my hands in my back pockets and turn around, pushing the kiss with Kyson to the back burner. That issue is going to need a gallon of wine, a box of chocolates, and my sister.

"What's on for today?" I ask, plastering on a fake smile.

"Now that I'm back in business, I thought we could go over some of the product you've bought and your plans for the rest of the store stock."

"That's what I was doing before you got here," I offer helpfully, happy that he's going right to work and letting the Kyson kiss go.

He grins and saunters to me, looping an arm around my shoulders in what could be considered a rather friendly, still technically platonic gesture. "Yeah, that's what you were doing. We'll go with that."

I groan and tip my head to look at him and give him my best glare. "I was."

"Uh-huh. I believe you." He taps my nose with his finger. "Show me what you got, sweets."

Sweets.

Just that nickname sets fire to my libido far hotter than that kiss with Kyson. I'm doomed. Doomed to forever want what I can't have, what I let go of so many years ago.

"Grrr. Men are so infuriating," I mutter and move out of his hold.

"Oh, and Mom and Dad want you at their dinner table this Sunday." He tosses out the request as though it's yesterday's old news.

I stop at my desk and press my hands to the firm surface,

allowing it to hold me up as much as cool my jets. "Your parents...what?"

He leans against the wooden shelf, crosses his ankles over one another and his arms over his chest. God, he looks good enough to eat, dressed in a mouthwatering suit that fits his muscular form to perfection.

That's it. I need to get laid. First, I'm kissing Kyson, rubbing all over that hunky man, and then I'm drooling over my business partner and former love of my life. I need my head examined. Right after I get laid.

"They miss you. You can't possibly breeze into town, plant your roots, and not see them." Camden runs a finger along my chin before making a fist and locking his arm by his side. "I'm sorry." He glances to the side as if he's searching for something and lets out a long breath. "They love you and haven't seen you in ten years. They want you at family dinner. You know how they are. Once Mom gets an idea—"

"There's no stopping her." I groan. "Cam, it is not a good idea. I already saw how Brittney looked at me at the hospital. She knows we were an item in the past. I'm back in town. It has to rile her up, and frankly, I don't need to experience any more of that being thrown my way. I have enough going on trying to get my life in order."

"She won't be there."

I frown and crinkle my nose as though I'm smelling something fishy. "Sunday is family dinner night. Mandatory. The four years we were a couple we never missed even one."

He licks his lips and bites at the inside of his cheek. "Yeah, well, she's not been invited to one."

I gasp and sit on my desk, a catalogue pressing uncomfortably into the fleshy part of my bum.

"My parents haven't exactly accepted Brittney into the fold."

I shake my head. "No way. Now it's even worse. If she finds out that I went to dinner and she didn't? What is that going to say?"

"That my family is having an old friend over for dinner. Nothing more, nothing less." He tries to downplay what we both know is a bogus attempt at lightening the situation.

"Why don't your parents accept your fiancée?" I have to know. It's that little witch inside me that wants to be liked, wanted, needed.

"Say you'll come to dinner, and I'll answer the question."

"Men are certifiable," I whisper to myself.

"What's that?" he asks.

I clench my teeth and cross my arms over my chest. "Fine. I'll come to dinner. As an old friend. But I'm bringing Evie."

"Deal. Now show me what you've got in the works." He reaches for a stack of the fabric and flips through the swatches, nodding.

"No way, no sir. You didn't answer my question. Why haven't your parents accepted Brittney? She's perfect in every way. Maybe a little self-centered…" I let that last part fall away as I wait for him to respond.

Camden puts his hands in his pockets, looks up at the sky, shakes his head, and smiles before looking down at me. "She isn't you."

"She isn't me?"

"She isn't you," he reiterates and shrugs nonchalantly as if the words have no effect whatsoever. But for me, they're like a tidal wave engulfing my entire body and pulling me down into the dark depths of a past life I can't escape.

Worse, I'm not even sure I want to.

9

"You are something else, *huutsuu*." Evie shakes her head while holding a beautiful royal blue dress against her athletic form. Where I got Mom's boobs and booty, Evie got her insanely long legs and strength of character. Evie's not quite a member of the itty-bitty-titty committee; she's probably a full B cup to my overly full C cup. Those legs, though, I would kill to be that statuesque.

"Why? Because we're going to dinner to spend time with some people we've always cared for and loved? People that helped take care of us when Mom died?" I narrow my gaze at Evie while she assesses the dress in front of her before lifting her gaze to meet mine in the mirror's reflection. "Don't forget how Patty came to our house twice a week with dinner for us, or the times she made us eat at their table so we wouldn't feel alone. I sure haven't forgotten that."

Evie's shoulders slump, and she lets the dress hang by her side. "No, you're right. I just think it's an incredibly complicated situation. You already have to deal with Cam at work every day. Now you're going to spend your free time with his family...doing what? Rehashing the past? You won't even talk about it all with me."

"Ev," I warn.

She points her finger at me. "See. That right there is exactly why I think you're crazy for agreeing to this dinner."

I grab the next two items off their hangers and hand one to her. "Here, let's try on these." She glances at the flowery print and long flowing fabric that would hit her ankles. Evie's nose scrunches up into a cute little cringe. "For me?" I plead.

My sister rolls her eyes and grabs the dress. "Fine. For you, but you know I'd never wear something like this. It's all boho chic. You're boho chic. I'm not. I prefer my clothes to be tailored and formfitting, not blowing in the breeze."

I snicker and reach for the curtain to close us both in. I knew she wouldn't like the dress—it's actually one I'm considering buying—but I love messing with her. If she can make me wear business suits and find my professional side, I'll get her in some free-spirited clothing if it kills me.

Just as I'm about to close us in, I see Miss Colorado herself prancing toward the dressing room, one arm locked with another perfect woman's arm. A tired-looking sales associate holding a massive amount of clothes in her arms trails behind the duo.

"Now you're sure these are the most expensive dresses in the store?" I hear Brittney announce to the associate as I shut the curtain and spin around to Evie.

"Ka—" My sister moves to show me the dress she's thrown on, but I still her movements by placing a hand over her mouth and mimicking the shushing sound. Her expression flashes from surprise to curiosity in a split second.

I point to the curtain.

"You know I only wear the best," Brittney declares.

"Yes, Ms. Cooperland, I know," says a soft voice.

Brittney laughs, and I peek out the slip of space between

the curtain and the wall. Evie goes to the other side of the curtain to do the same.

"Soon I won't have to be charging all of these dresses and racking up my credit cards. Daddy's monthly allowance is pitiful, really. But when I'm Mrs. Camden Bryant, he'll be footing the bill." She laughs haughtily.

Her friend chuckles and flops down on a chair to watch Brittney look at herself in the mirror. "That man is fine, girl. I can't believe you're playing him. I mean, I can. Like I said, he's fine. But what does Alejandro think about it?"

Alejandro? I look at my sister and her eyes bulge while her mouth drops open in shock.

Brittney fluffs her hair in the mirror and blows herself a kiss. "Obviously he doesn't like it, but he's in love with me."

The brunette pulls out a compact from her purse and checks her face. Nothing is out of place. It's likely airbrushed and then sealed on. She snaps the compact closed. "You told me you were in love with him, too."

Oh no. This is bad. So bad. Heat starts to flood my body and pinpricks of anger and anxiety blanket across my nerve endings. I grip the curtain so hard my fingers turn white.

Evie's hand lands on my back and rubs up and down in a soothing gesture. I close my eyes and continue to listen.

"I am, but can you imagine? Me! Brittney Cooperland, the heir to the Cooperland fortune, marrying a landscaper?" She shakes her head. "Nope. Daddy would have been furious and cut me out of the will for sure. I have to protect my family's legacy, as you know."

Her friend yawns and nods. "So, you're screwing them both?"

Brittney chuckles. "I only had to seal that deal with Cam once."

Once? What is she talking about? I look at Evie, and she shrugs and shakes her head, but neither of us stops eavesdropping.

"You never did tell me how you hooked Camden Bryant a few months ago. How did you score that?"

A few months? He's only been with Brittney *a few months*, and they're already engaged?

The sales associate hands Brittney a dress. "As requested. The most expensive dress in the store in a size two."

Size two? Ugh. I like tacos way too much for that. My size eight to ten fits me perfectly. Besides, men don't seem to have a problem with my curves.

"Really? It was so easy. He was in that bar his brother owns, getting totally smashed. I sidled up to him and took advantage of his inebriated state. We drank together, and I brought him back to my room. He was a little sloppy in the sack, due to being totally smashed out of his mind, but I got the job done."

"When was this?"

"Back in August. Maybe around the fifteenth. He mentioned something about the date being significant, but I wasn't really paying attention. Apparently, he gets totally shit-faced on the same day every year. It may have been over some woman. I don't really recall since I was eye-fucking the bartender the whole time." Brittney chuckles.

August 15. That was only five months ago and our anniversary. We used to celebrate the first day we met at school my freshman year. I take a step back and press my hands against the wall. This woman took advantage of Cam. Planned it. Is still taking advantage while wearing his freakin' ring. Why the heck would he propose to her?

"Girl, you are cold," the friend admonishes.

She snorts. "Not according to Alejandro. Last night, he was all over me."

"Where was Camden?"

"Oh, we don't live together, and we haven't slept together since that first time. I've made sure of that. He's not my type at all."

"Wait. What?"

I want to say the same thing. How can she be engaged to a man she isn't intimate with?

Brittney walks over to her friend and sits primly down next to her. "Girl, give me a little more credit than that. After we slept together, he brushed me off. For a month. Then I found him at work, made a scene, and he took me into his office. I told him I was pregnant, and he would have to marry me or our fathers would lose their minds. Heck, I picked out the ring and told him which one I wanted. Didn't really give him much of a choice."

"You didn't!" the brunette says, absolutely scandalized. I give her credit for that minute amount of humanity but not much. I'm about ready to beat down Miss Colorado in the middle of a swanky store in Colorado Springs. What are the odds that Brittney would even be shopping this far from Pueblo anyway?

I suck in a deep breath. My sister wraps an arm around my shoulders and holds me there, shaking her head.

"I can't believe you got pregnant. Where are you hiding it?"

My heart sinks. She's having his baby? Of course, he'd marry the disgusting witch. The Camden I know would never forsake the mother of his child, regardless of what he wanted. He'd do the right thing. Family is everything to Cam.

"Oh, I never was pregnant. I just told Camden that to seal the deal. Then of course, last month, I conveniently had a miscarriage. Then I went on and on, crying about how he was going to leave me now that I wasn't carrying his child, and get this…he went for it! Honorable loser!" She bursts out laughing, cackling like a hyena.

My sister's hold tightens around my body as I move to enter the fray, consequences be damned. I'm taking this ho down!

Evie's mouth moves to my ear and she whispers, "Let the evil woman finish, and we'll deal with this after. Don't go off on her right now. There's more at stake."

Evie holds up her phone and shows me the red button indicating she's recording everything being said. I nod and grind my teeth so hard they may turn to dust. It's taking everything I have within me not to lay this chick out. Teach her what it's like to hurt the way she's hurting Cam.

"And Alejandro?"

"Will be my hunky man on the side. Everything is working out perfectly. Daddy will be happy. I'll have an endless supply of money, a great legacy, and my man on the side. Sure, I'll have to open my legs for Camden once a month when we're married. He's good-looking—it won't exactly be a hardship."

"And Alejandro? What does he have to say in all this?"

She huffs. "If he wants to keep me in his life, he'll have to be okay with being my secret. That's the way life goes. Sometimes you get what you want in every way you want it, and other times you have to make it work for you, no matter what. That's what I'm doing. Making it work for everyone involved."

"Except for Camden," the brunette wisely surmises.

"Um, hello? I'm a perfect catch and will be the best arm candy he's ever seen. The Cooperlands and the Bryants. It's like a royal match. It will be a fairy-tale wedding. I'm sure all the papers will want to cover it." She gazes off to the side dreamily, lost in some messed-up vision of the world she's created.

"And how are you keeping him from taking you to bed? You said you only had sex that one time."

She pats her friend's leg. "Have a little faith. In the beginning, I pretended to be too morning sick. Then, after I told him we lost the baby, I added that it hurt down there." She swirls a hand over her pelvic region. "And now I've got him believing it would be romantic if we both consummated our relationship for the first time sober on our wedding night."

"And he bought that?"

"Totally! He's so naive and a complete gentleman." Brittney grins wickedly.

"I gotta hand it to you girl, you are a stone-cold bitch." The brunette shakes her head.

Brittney laughs. "Takes one to know one!"

Evie and I wait for the devilish duo to leave the store before we escape the dressing room and the mall to head back to her house.

"What are you going to do?" Evie asks, her voice low and concerned, gaze on the road ahead.

"You mean besides open up a can of whoop ass on that bitch Brittney?" I growl.

"Uh…yeah. That? We're supposed to go to the Bryants' house for dinner tonight."

"I gotta tell him, but how?" I shake my head. "How do you tell someone that their fiancée is not only cheating on them but lied to them about being pregnant, lied about miscarrying a baby they never had in the first place, and is only marrying them for the social status and trust fund?"

Tears prick the backs of my eyes, and I squeeze them closed

and lift my fists to my eye sockets. I try my damnedest to hold back the tears and block out the vile things she said playing back in my mind. He got drunk and slept with her because of me. I mean, I can only guess that's the case. August is when we celebrated our anniversary, but that was a decade ago. And what about the things her friend mentioned? He never took a woman home more than once? Could he still be carrying a torch for me all these years later?

Yes. He could. Because I'm still carrying a torch for him. My one true love. Not that I'm capable of admitting it out loud, but I've never stopped loving Camden or missing the relationship we had. When I was with Cam, life was easy. Everything just seemed to fall into place. I never worried. Never once considered I was being held back, but I did want for things. Big things. Things I knew we didn't have in common.

I yearned to travel the world. I needed to experience everything my mom did. I wanted those twinkly stars to be in my eyes when I spoke of the places I'd traveled to, just like hers did when she'd tell Evie and me about her experiences.

By the time my mother died, I'd been nowhere outside of Colorado and the reservation. That's the one thing Mom didn't do. Strangely, she didn't take us anywhere. When she came home from her travels, she was tired and wanted to live her days being with her girls and her husband when he had leave. Doing mom-type things like baking cakes, driving us to and from school, attending art classes, taking belly dancing classes, teaching us about life and boys and how, eventually, they will always break your heart, but we'll love them anyway. And then she'd claim her feet were itching to go. And within a couple weeks of saying it, she'd be gone again, and we'd be at the reservation with *Toko*, wishing on stars just like she taught us to do.

I remember it so clearly when she taught us to wish on stars.

★ ★ ★

"*Huutsuu, taabe*, come here, my beautiful loves," Mom said while holding out her hands. We'd taken a walk together at sunset along the hills near the reservation. Usually she'd get us together right before she left on one of her adventures.

That time, she sat on the crest of a hill, the sun having set, the lights from the path giving off enough glow for us to see. I remember Evie and I had been picking bushels of wildflowers to place on *Toko*'s table. He didn't like that we took from the earth so carelessly, but since we were children, he looked the other way and let us have our fun. Still, he reminded us to thank the flowers every day they graced our table with their beauty before they wilted and died.

"Come, girls," Mom called, and we both rushed up the hill. It was harder for me since my legs were shorter than Evie's. At nine and eleven, we were both growing fast, but she was always so tall, and I couldn't wait to catch up to her glorious height.

Mom guided us to sit right at each of her sides, her arms around our backs, holding us close. "Look up at the sky. You see all the stars?"

Evie and I both looked up and nodded.

"Those are all the wishes of the world, waiting to come true."

I stared, overwhelmed by the millions of stars. "Really?"

"Yes, *huutsuu*. I'm going to teach you to wish on a star, but you must remember to not be greedy. Be thoughtful about your wish, for you only get one until it comes true. Then you can wish for another. But it could take what seems like forever for your wish to come true."

"Wow." I gasped in awe at everyone's wishes, glowing brightly in the open sky.

"How do you pick one?" Evie asked.

"One will call to you, *taabe*. Just like the sun calls to you, my golden girl." She kissed Evie's blond hair at the crown of her head before turning toward me. "And you, my *huutsuu*. Let the wind help you choose."

Evie and I sat there for a long time, staring at the stars and thinking about what to wish for. I remember so clearly feeling a subtle breeze brush my skin as I found a blinky little star next to Orion's belt that I believed held all the answers in the universe. It was my star; I just knew it.

"Did you pick one, my loves?"

Both Evie and I nodded, staring up.

"Okay now, repeat after me while looking at your star."

Evie and I both stared hard at the sky.

"I wish I may..."

We repeated it, our small voices filled with wonder.

"I wish I might..."

"Have this wish..."

"I wish tonight," Mom finished, and we repeated the last phrase.

"Now make a wish on your star but don't ever tell anyone what your wish is, or it will never come true."

That night, I wished to be just like my mother. A world traveler. I wanted to see everything there was to see until I was all filled up with adventure. I got my wish but lost the love of my life in the process.

Was this my second chance?

"Kaye. Kaye! Are you even listening to me?"

I shake off the memory and focus on my sister, who's getting out of the car.

"We need to get ready for dinner, and you need to figure

out how you're going to tell Camden about what we over-heard."

My gut sours, and it feels like the floor is going to fall away beneath my feet. "I know I need to tell him, but I don't want to break his heart. I've already done that once in this lifetime, and it would be better if I didn't do it a second time."

Evie opens the door to her condo and ushers me in. "Look, I don't know everything that went down..."

Something in me breaks, spilling out the truth I've held locked inside my soul for ten long years. "Ev, I left him. I left him the night I gave him my virginity. The same night I turned eighteen and read Mom's first letter."

"Oh, Kaye, how could you?" Her voice is filled with sorrow because she knows how much I loved him. More, she knows how much Camden Bryant loved me. Everyone knew. It was always Cam and me. Everyone who knew us thought we'd spend our lives together.

"I had to go. Had to. If I didn't leave then, I never would have, and I just..." Guilt swallows me whole and dries out my throat.

"You just left. I get it. Mom did, too. It's what you and Mom did best." Evie sighs.

"Evie, that's just mean." I clear my throat and focus on her icy gaze.

Evie nods, stares at me, and drops her arms to her sides, both hands in fists. "I know what Cam felt that night and the next day and the year after and more. We were the ones who were left behind. We weren't enough for you to stay. And you and I were never enough for Mom to stay, either."

"That's just not true!" I yell, stopping just short of stomping my foot. She must know that's bonkers. She's the most im-portant woman in my life. Always has been, always will be.

"Isn't it? You left the same way Mom did. After everything we went through as kids, only having one another through Mom's abandonment and again when she left us forever."

"Abandonment? Jeez, Evie. Mom *died*. I didn't die! And I kept in touch." I scowl and clench my jaw, trying to hold back the anger and self-loathing she's bringing to the surface.

Evie runs her hand through her hair and bites down on her bottom lip. "No, you didn't die, but for ten years, to Cam, to me, *Toko*, to everyone that loved you, you may as well have. You called and I made an effort to visit you a few times, but Suda Kaye, you left for ten years! Ten!"

"Yes, I did, and I don't regret it," I fire off dramatically, wanting to hurt her the same way she's hurting me.

She huffs and shakes her head, walking to her door. "Of course, you don't. Mom never did, either. You know what I regret—"

"No, I couldn't possibly fathom what you regret since you don't live in the first place," I sneer.

She ignores my jab and continues undaunted. "I regret being the one waiting for you to come back. Wanting you in my life so badly. Wanting you to *want* to be in my life…"

Her words hit my shield of armor in a blast so large I step back against the hit. "But I do! I am. I've always been in your life. And I'm here now."

She nods. "Yeah, you say that, and I want more than anything to believe it. I also don't want to be the schmuck always left behind. I imagine that's what Cam feels, too. Torn between loving you and protecting his heart. Something he and I have in common, I guess."

I stare at my sister with all the love and compassion I have inside of me, hoping against all things that she can feel my words deep within. "Evie, things are different this time. I'm staying. I've got the store. I'm committed to it. To you. To being part of your life."

"Okay," she says, but it doesn't sound like she believes me.

"I'll make you believe. Wishes do come true, Ev. My wish did, even though I had to lose something to get it."

"Yeah?"

I nod. "Mom was right. That night we wished on stars with her, do you remember that time?"

Evie leans against the doorjamb and crosses her arms protectively over her chest, rubbing her biceps. "I guess," she mumbles.

I can't stifle my grin. She remembers. My sister has an excellent memory. It's how she's so amazing with numbers. Why she graduated college with the highest honors.

"When we wished on those stars, I wished to be just like Mom," I say. "To travel the world and experience every adventure I could possibly wrap my arms around."

Evie closes her eyes and licks her lips, her features marred by sadness etching its way across her unlined face. Her voice cracks with emotion. "You're not supposed to tell anyone your wish."

"Don't you see?" I walk over to her and pull her into my arms. She wraps hers around me and tucks her face into the crook of my neck. "My wish already came true. I've traveled the world. Visited more of Mom's places than I ever imagined. Now, I'm home. I'm putting down roots. I want to live my life here, sharing it with the most amazing woman I've ever known. My big sister. My Evie."

Evie trembles against my body, her tears wetting the bare skin of my shoulder. "I missed you so much," she murmurs against my form. "So much. Please don't leave me again. You're all I have in this world."

This time, I let the tears fall. "You're all I have, too." I lean back, cup her cheeks, and hold her gaze with my own. "And, Evie, you're enough. My love for you, your love for me, our sisterly bond, it's enough. It will always be enough."

We stare at one another a long time before she pulls me back into a hug. We hold one another and let this thing between us, the worry, the anxiety of all the lost time, all of it just fall away into a dark abyss, hopefully never to be heard from again. Though I'm not so naive to think our issues and the chasm that developed between us during my absence won't come up again. The next time, I'll be ready for it.

"We're moving on," I whisper into her hair.

"Moving on. Together."

"Absolutely." I smile and take a deep breath.

"Now we need to clean our faces and deal with what we heard today." She wipes the tears from under her eyes.

I groan and drop my head back. "Ugh. Don't remind me."

"Kaye, I'm not letting you get out of this. If you don't tell him, I will, but he deserves to hear it from you. Still, I'll be there. Right at your back when you need me."

"Aren't you always?"

"Yep. It's my lot in life. My job as your big sis." She offers a small smile.

"I love you, sissy," I whisper, unable to hold onto the lightness the words intend.

She pushes me toward the spare bathroom and pats my booty. "Go. Get cleaned up. I'll have shots of Patron and some oranges ready for when you're done."

I flick my hair over my shoulder and waggle my eyebrows at her. "Ohhh, my sissy knows what I like."

"No. I know what you like to avoid, and tequila helps when

you've got to face something difficult. And… I love you, too, Kaye. So much. Now go."

"Aye aye, Captain!" I call over my shoulder and enter the bathroom. Time to get ready to tell the most loving, beautiful, compassionate man I know that the woman he thinks he's going to marry is a lying, cheating gold digger.

10

The Bryants' house is exactly as I remember. A beautiful, two-story, ranch-style home with a large wraparound porch on a massive amount of land. The breeze carries the scent of hay and farm life along with a chill that seeps deep into my bones. I pull my denim jacket tighter around myself, trying to ward off the cold. In the distance, I can hear the sounds of animals moving around. Pigs snorting, probably eating their late-night meal. Chickens clucking and horses getting settled for the evening.

It's all so familiar, the memories of what felt like endless nights walking this farm, Camden's large hand holding mine, rush over me in a blanket of happier times. Everything is practically the same, yet it still seems as if my time here happened in a dream a lifetime ago.

I've grown so much. Changed. I'm a different person than I was then. I'm not the naive young teenager in love with her high school sweetheart anymore. I've traveled the world. Experienced more in the last ten years than most ever will in ten lifetimes.

Still, I miss this quiet. The calm. Being in one place for longer than a moment. Knowing that where I am is where

I'm meant to be. I've never—not ever—felt that anywhere but here. The one night I spent with Camden making love in the barn loft was the only time in my life that I ever felt like I could stay there forever.

Fly free.

My mother's words echo through my mind as I take in the familiar surroundings. I don't regret the ten years I traveled the world. I soaked up every moment as if it would be my last, but now...here? I'm different. Experiencing something through eyes ten years older, a soul aged through experience, makes me see what I never saw before.

You *can* come home. It feels exactly the same and different all at once. Like an old quilt. Warm, familiar, yet softer with each washing. More comfortable.

"There you are. I was beginning to think you weren't going to come," a low voice calls out from the top steps of the porch.

I spin around from taking in the view of this beloved ranch and look up at the man leaning casually against the porch beam. Camden is wearing tight-fitting jeans, a pair of beat-up old motorcycle boots, a long-sleeved dark gray shirt, and a smile. His dark blond chin-length waves are pulled back away from his angular face and wrapped in a small bun at the back of his head.

My goodness, this man is handsome. He's stolen my breath as I take in the sharpness of his gaze, the strength in his corded neck and tight jaw. He purses his lips and gives a chin lift. "Evie. It's been too long, sunshine."

Evie takes the steps at a quick pace and throws herself into Cam's arms the way I want to but would never have the courage to do. It's not like that between us anymore. I lost the easy affection when I walked out on him ten years ago.

A pang hits my stomach as I watch him sway Evie from side to side the way a big brother who misses his sister would do.

She kisses his cheek and places both of her hands on his face. "You've always been a looker, Cam. Only gotten better with age, I see." She pats his cheek.

"I could say the same to you as well." He smiles, and I wince, jealous of my own sister that she gets the easy carefree man I once knew, and I get the tension-filled businessman who looks at me like I'm a stranger he's never met but still finds attractive.

"Go on in," he says. "Mom's cooked a feast as usual."

"With four men under her roof, I imagine that is commonplace." I smile and walk up the steps slowly, feeling as if every step is leading me down an unknown path I'm not sure I want to take.

Cam dips his head, his gaze running up my form from my red cowboy boots and blue jeans to my flowy, white, eyelet lace, off-the-shoulder top and jacket. I pulled my hair back into a simple ponytail while rocking a dangly pair of peacock-inspired feather earrings. I know Cam loved my hair down in the past, which is why I wore it this way. Back in the day, whenever we were together, he'd always pull my rubber band out of my hair and toss it aside like a piece of garbage. He used to say he loved being able to run his fingers through my hair whenever he wanted. Maybe I wanted to see if he'd accept the secret challenge.

"Like a diamond," Cam whispers, and I close my eyes and dip my head.

"Don't." I barely get the word out.

A warm hand curls around my neck, the other at my hip as he brings me forward against his body, his cropped beard brushing the sensitive skin of my cheek when he kisses my temple. A shiver runs down my spine. It should feel like an everyday greeting, but with Cam, with *this man*, it's so much more.

I pull him into a hug and hold on, wanting his comfort more than anything I've experienced in the last ten years.

"No matter what you wear, whether it's pajamas, a business suit, jeans, makeup or bare, you've always sparkled as bright as a diamond, sweets. Most beautiful woman I've ever known."

I close my eyes and let his words fill up that empty hole inside of me that missed him, missed his kindness and compassion. The ease with which he can turn any dark day bright just by being there, simply offering me a hug and a compliment has been sorely missed.

Doing my best, I remove myself from his hold. "What's on the menu this evening?" I ask, my voice husky and deep.

He guides me in the house with his hand at the small of my back. "Your favorite, of course. Mama's pork chops and peppers."

My mouth starts watering at the aroma that surrounds me the moment we get closer to the kitchen. Inside the open area is the huge kitchen on the right, all stainless steel appliances with whitewashed cabinets from floor to ceiling. To the left is the largest sectional I've ever seen. Four men sit around the TV, beers in their hands and a game on the big screen over the wide, rock fireplace.

"Oh, my darling Suda Kaye, come in, come in, and take a seat next to Evie." Patty waves me over. Evie is sitting at the long island, nibbling on a carrot stick. Patty is on the other side of the island, slicing green peppers.

"Mrs. B was just updating me on all the Pueblo gossip," Evie remarks. "I didn't realize how much I missed living in C-Springs the last several years."

Patty nods as I make my way over to her. She pulls me into a tight, motherly hug. After, when she holds me at arm's length, I note her eyes are teary. "Missed you so much, my dear. You and Evie both."

I squeeze her arms. "I missed you, too, but I'm back for the foreseeable future. You'll have to come to the store when it's open in a couple weeks."

She nods several times. "Definitely. Told my boy that the moment it opens, his father and I will be the first ones standing at the door to celebrate."

I smile so wide my cheeks hurt.

"Hi, Suda Kaye. Long time, no see." CJ, short for Coltrane Junior, the oldest of the Bryant brothers, says from behind me. CJ is about an inch taller than Cam, muscular, and the opposite of what I remember.

Ten years ago, he was all about riding horses and working the ranch when he wasn't hitting the books to finish up his master's in finance. Now he's beyond put together, wearing dress slacks, a silk shirt, and expensive shoes. His sandy brown hair is swept back and neatly cropped in a fashionable style you'd see on any smartly dressed businessman in the city. Instead of hugging me as he did in the past, he holds out his hand.

I look down at it and frown, realizing the gesture is a lot less welcoming, but knowing I shouldn't expect anything more from the Bryant brothers. They're fiercely loyal of one another, and I broke their brother's heart. I place my hand into his and he shakes it curtly before putting his hands in his pockets.

That reaction does not affect Preston, however. "Incoming!" he yells. Swinging his legs up and over the back of the couch as though he was doing an Olympic vault move, he bum-rushes me. Preston lifts me up with his beefy forearms under my butt and spins me around before setting me down on my feet where he catches me in a bear hug. When I say bear hug, I mean it. The man is huge!

"Holy muscles, Pres! You're squeezing the air out of me." I laugh myself silly.

"Can't help it, sister! I missed you so much." He snuggles against my neck, making growling sounds and kissing my neck, then both of my cheeks. He holds my face. "Let me get a good look at you."

"I think you've had your fill, brother," Camden says low in his throat, a warning if I've ever heard one.

"Hold your jockeys, bro. This is Suda Kaye! My girl." He grins and winks at me, knowing exactly how he's yanking his brother's chain. This is the welcome I would expect from all the Bryant brothers if things had been different.

"Technically, she was *my* girl..." he mumbles through his teeth.

Preston claps my cheeks anyway, ignoring his brother. "You're even more beautiful now than you were when you were eighteen. Damn!" He spins me sideways and takes a look at my booty. He whistles outlandishly. "Bro..." He points a finger toward my bum, which I know looks pretty good in these jeans because Evie told me so before we left the house. "You work out? I own a gym now. Free membership for hot chicks." He grins, and I laugh out loud.

Camden pushes his brother back and leads him toward the other side of the kitchen. "That's enough."

"But did you see how smokin' hot she is? Yowzer!"

"Ignore him," a voice says from behind me as I feel my ponytail being tugged twice.

I spin around and see the dark eyes of Cam's second older brother, Porter.

"Port." I lose my voice as I take in his handsome face. He's maybe an inch shorter than Cam at six foot one, but his features give him that tall, dark, and handsome vibe the others don't have. He looks more like what his father probably looked like in his youth. Brown hair, espresso-colored eyes, and just enough scruff on his jaw to make him look ruggedly sexy. If I hadn't met and fallen in love with Cam, I would have chased after Porter like all the young girls did.

Porter pulls me into his arms, and I get a good whiff of a light earthy cologne with a small dose of Irish Spring soap. "We missed you, Suda Kaye, but not nearly as much as Cam did. He won't admit it, but he's been lost without you. Never the same after you left."

A cotton-ball-size lump forms in my throat. "It wasn't easy, but it was what I had to do at the time," I say so low only he can hear me.

Porter pulls away, and his dark gaze meets mine. "You're really back?"

I lick my lips and think about his question, wondering if he means *back in the area* or *back in Camden's life*, in all of their lives. "I live in Pueblo now, yeah."

He smirks. "Not what I was asking but I'll take it for now."

"What have you been up to?" I ask, trying to change the subject.

"I own Bryant Brews a couple streets off Main. You and Evie should come down, have some drinks. On me, of course." His gaze goes to my sister, and those eyes seem to travel up and down her form appreciatively. He always did have a bit of a crush on Evie, though she'd never go for it. I think my sister's hot-guy-ometer is broken or severely off point.

"We'll do that, won't we, Ev?"

Her cheeks pink up, and she bites into a celery stick this time. "Yeah, sure."

"I'll look forward to it." Porter quirks an eyebrow.

"I'll bet you will." Cam shakes his head as he places his hand at the small of my back once again and guides me to a chair.

"Whoop! Looks like the gang's all here." Coltrane comes into the room from a door off the kitchen that I know leads to the wine-and-beer cellar. He's carrying a couple bottles of wine. He sets them down, comes around the island, kisses my cheek, and runs a thumb over my shoulder. "Darlin' girl. Good to see you, sweetheart." He repeats the gestures with Evie, and I take a full breath for the first time.

All is right in the world.

For now.

Out of nowhere, Evie shoves her elbow against my rib cage. We're sitting on the couch, stuffed to the gills from the juiciest, most delicious dinner I've had in a long time. Patty has always been an incredible cook, and this meal was stellar.

"Ouch." I nudge her back, the warm feeling of a full belly and two glasses of scrumptious wine and great company lulling me into complacency.

Evie dips her chin toward me. "You have to tell him."

I slump deeper into the couch.

"Tell me what?" Camden holds out another glass of wine for Evie and a glass of water for me. I'm driving, so two drinks along with a belly full of food is my drinking limit.

"He deserves to know, *huutsuu.*"

Cam narrows his gaze at Evie, likely knowing if she's using

my Native American nickname from our mother to encourage me, it means that what I have to say is not going to be good.

"This oughta be good." CJ enters the space unannounced, stands behind the leather couch, and crosses his arms. His face is a mask of distrust. All through dinner I'd catch him looking at me with an uncertain expression marring his features.

Preston's giant muscular form bounds into the living room and plops down right next to Evie, pulling her against his side playfully. "What should be good?"

I groan. "Um, Cam, do you think we could go somewhere and talk privately?"

"Now that's a very good idea." Evie lifts up her wine in a celebratory gesture before taking a sip.

Camden shakes his head. "No. Anything you have to say to me can be said in front of my brothers. Just spit it out. Does this have to do with the store? Are you backing out?" He jerks his head to the side and shifts a foot away from me on the couch. The distance might as well have been a mile for how much his words hurt my heart.

"I wouldn't do that." My voice is full of indignation.

"Wouldn't you? I seem to recall someone disappearing after some pretty heavy commitments ten years ago."

"Cam, this isn't about the past, it's about the present. Your present and your future actually." I lick my lips and take a deep breath, trying to gain as much courage as possible.

He huffs and waves a hand in the air. "Then, by all means, lay it out."

Fine. If he wants it out in the open, I'll give it to him. "Today Evie and I were shopping in Colorado Springs, and we…uh…overheard something upsetting." I frown, taking a sip of the water he gave me, stalling as much as possible before setting the glass on the coffee table in front of us.

"Okay. And?"

"It was…um…well, you know, your…uh…fiancée. Well, she…" I try to get the words out, but they feel heavy and bitter on my tongue.

"Brittney what?" he demands.

"Ugh. Brittney. God, she is an ugly person," Preston sneers.

Evie, Cam, and I both shift our focus to Preston, horrified expressions on our faces.

"What? She is. There is nothing real on that woman. I still can't believe you're marrying her." Preston's face contorts into a sour expression.

Cam stands up, anger sizzling in the space around him. "She is none of your business, Pres. Or yours, Suda Kaye."

"I know that, and I'm sorry. But she was talking to her friend about money and how you're going to be paying for everything soon—"

Camden starts to pace the room. He curls his hand around his neck and looks down. "I knew this was a bad idea. Dinner with the family like old times. I fuckin' knew it."

I stand up and put my hands out. "There's more. Cam, she was never pregnant. She lied to you. She used you."

Patty, plating dessert in the kitchen, wheezes, "Pregnant?" Her hand flies to her chest.

All I want right now is to be swallowed by the ocean and washed up along an opposite shore. Far away from this moment. Preferably Tahiti. I've always wanted to go there anyway. Now is as good a time as any.

Camden stops in his tracks and glares at me. "How can you say that? What do you think you know? You don't know a thing about Brittney and me and the baby we lost."

"There was no baby, Cam. I swear I can prove—"

He cuts me off. "No!" He makes a chopping gesture with

his hand, cutting me to the quick. "Brittney is sugary sweet and, yeah, maybe a bit made up and a little spoiled, but her heart is pure. I can't believe you'd do this to me. Try to drive a bigger wedge into my future than you already have by showing up out of nowhere!"

"Bro, just listen," Preston urges. "Hear her out, man."

Cam lifts his head back and laughs at the sky. "Fuckin' hell. You're so eager to toss Brittney aside because you don't like that she's a trust fund baby. Well, look in the mirror, big bro. You are, too! We all are. At least CJ and I are working for the company to earn ours. You hide behind your gym, bulk up your muscles, and shit on Dad's legacy!"

"Hey now, that's uncalled for," Coltrane pipes up while holding on to his wife's shoulders. "I'm proud of all four of you for what you're doing with your lives."

Preston stands up, and it's like a volcano bursting. "She. Is. A. Gold. Digger. Open up your eyes!" He holds two fingers in front of his face, making his own eyes wide. "She's not good enough for you! And I used the trust to open my own business and left the rest for my future kids. I'm building on Dad's legacy and brand. Don't try to piss on me because you got your feelings hurt. You gonna say the same to Porter for opening Bryant Brews instead of working the steel empire like you and CJ? Huh? Not what you said when you were knocking them back last week, fretting over the fact that Suda Kaye was home and you didn't know what the hell you were going to do about it! Don't put your shit on me, bro. Man up."

Camden huffs and squeezes his neck. "One day back with my family, and you've already made a mess of everything," he grates out between clenched teeth. His normally light eyes are pitch-black with fury as he glares at me.

A flare of white-hot anger flows through me. "I didn't want

to come. Sure, I love your family, that's always going to be the case. You made me come!" I point at his chest.

"Well, that was a bad idea. I don't want you here," he growls.

Before I can run out the door, a new voice singsongs through the room. "Yoohoo! Anyone home? Sugar lumpkins?" Brittney's sickeningly sweet, lying self enters the living room, a puffball of pink. "Oh, well, I see you have company." Her eyes go to me and Evie.

Evie grabs my hand and stands up.

"Sugar, why is your ex-girlfriend at your parents' home for family dinner night? I've never even been invited, and I'm your fiancée." She pouts, her overly full lips puffing up as if on cue.

Camden closes his eyes, and his shoulders slump. Every ounce of anger his body once held is gone, leaving a man who looks nothing but lost. He opens his eyes and stares at me.

"I'm sorry," I offer weakly.

"You're wrong," he says flatly and opens his arm to Brittney. "Come here, cookie."

Cookie. I hate her even more now. She doesn't deserve sweet nicknames because she's a lying slug.

"Come on, Ev, let's go. It's over." I pull Evie's hand.

Evie shakes her head and remains stiff. "I can't. It's not right." And before I can tell her to stop, she lifts her phone and presses a button.

Brittney's voice can be heard through the phone. "Soon I won't have to be charging all of these dresses and racking up my credit cards. Daddy's monthly allowance is pitiful, really. But when I'm Mrs. Camden Bryant, he'll be footing the bill." Her laughter fills the air through the phone's speaker.

"See, bro! I told you she was after your money!" Preston points at the blonde clinging to Camden's side.

She frowns. "Sugar, that's not true. I don't know who these women think they are, but they are wrong!"

The recording continues to play, this time with the voice of Brittney's brunette friend: "That man is fine, girl. I can't believe you're playing him. I mean, I can. Like I said, he's fine. But what does Alejandro think about it?"

Camden's brow furrows. "Who is Alejandro? Brittney?"

Brittney bites her lip, and tears fill her eyes.

In the recording, the brunette goes on to confirm that Brittney is in fact in love with Alejandro. Camden drops his arm from around Brittney while shaking his head.

Her lies unfold for everyone to hear: how she's in it solely to save her reputation and family legacy, how she purposely took advantage of his drunken state.

"Brittney..." Camden begins.

"Cam, I love you. You know that. Don't listen to any more of this filth. It's not real. I don't even know who that voice is."

The recorded conversation divulges how she had sex with Alejandro recently, how Cam's not her type, how Cam brushed her off and she went to his work to confront him and then lied about being pregnant.

Brittney's worst transgression crackles through the phone, adding the final nails in her coffin:

"Oh, I never was pregnant. I just told Camden that to seal the deal. Then, of course, last month I conveniently had a miscarriage. Then I went on and on, crying about how he was going to leave me now that I wasn't carrying his child, and get this...he went for it! Honorable loser!"

The room goes completely dead silent. I'm sure Brittney's

laughter at her deceit can be heard from a mile away even if it was only playing through my sister's small speaker.

"Get out of my house!" Patty struts over and grabs Brittney by the upper arm. "Get out of my house, and get the hell out of my son's life. You are not welcome anywhere near the Bryants. You might as well leave town because the moment I discuss this situation with your mother and father, you will wish you'd never set eyes on any one of my children."

"No, no, please, Mrs. Bryant. My daddy will cut me off. I don't have a job. I don't have any money!" she cries, black streaks of mascara running down her face. "I'll leave. I'll never bother any of you again. Just don't tell my parents. Please!" she shrieks as Patty and Coltrane lead her out of the room and out of the house.

Preston, CJ, and Porter gather around their brother, each one planting a hand on him in solidarity.

Camden looks like a man who has just lost everything. Maybe I had it all wrong? He wasn't pining for me. Sure, the attraction between us is there, but that's chemical. He didn't *believe* me. Thought I was trying to screw up his life. Ruining a good thing for him. When, in reality, all I was trying to do was save him from living a lie.

And the real truth is...he'll never trust me again.

Tonight proved it all in black-and-white. The hope of ever having Camden in my life, having this family as part of my world again is dashed within a single evening. I might not have loaded the gun that ruined his relationship with his fiancée, but I definitely pulled the trigger.

"Come on, Ev, let's go."

Evie and I skirt around the brothers' circle of comfort around Camden.

Cam reaches out and grabs my hand tight. "Suda Kaye..." His eyes look torn, but his entire form has been shredded.

"I'll see you at work." I tug on my hand until he finally lets me go.

"Please..." he calls out, a desperation in his tone I can only define as intense loss. I don't know how to give him what he needs right now, and as much as I hate it, I'm definitely not the one that should be trying. I lost that right a long time ago.

With heavier feet than when I left him lying naked and sleeping in the barn, I put one foot in front of the other, leaving him and his family to work through their grief alone.

Cam's words play in my head on an endless loop.

One day back with my family and you've already made a mess of everything.

11

The next day, I'm lying in bed, Mom's letters scattered around me as I reread her words, trying to find some hidden advice. Usually going through her letters heals any wounds or heartache I feel at the time. Right now, I have zero energy to get up and work on the store, but that doesn't mean that Kyson isn't making headway on the renovation alongside his grumpy brother.

It's already early afternoon and I just can't find it in me to deal with the light of day. My heart hurts and my body is sluggish. Visions of last night's carnage run on a rampant waterwheel through my mind.

Closing my eyes, I finger one of Mom's letters and speak softly to her like I've done so many times since her passing.

"Mom, I need your help. Your guidance. I've hurt Cam again. Irreparably. I didn't mean to this time. I swear. It…just happened. And I should be sorry. Really sorry, but something inside me broke open when that monster of a woman started spouting her evil. Mom, I lost it. I couldn't let him marry that snake, knowing she wasn't in it for love. Cam deserves so much more than that. He deserves the best."

I sigh and open my eyes while holding up one of Mom's

letters. It's dated my twenty-fifth birthday. It was the letter where she admitted her extramarital affair with my biological father Ian. She never gave me his last name or any identifying information. Every time I asked, she'd tell me I had a dad in Adam Ross, my sister's biological father and Mom's husband, and to leave well enough alone. Eventually, I stopped asking.

I know instantly why the universe or Mom herself put this particular letter in my hand at this moment in time.

Because it speaks of her regret. Most of her letters show her excitement, her never-ending search for new experiences, the same traits she saw in me. Not this one.

My dearest huutsuu,

Today I'm sad. Lost. Trying desperately to write as many meaningful words to you and your sister so that when I'm gone, you'll know you were loved every second of your life. I may not have been the best mother. In fact, I know I wasn't. I hope you know I tried the best I knew how, and when I was with you and Evie, I endeavored to give you all of me.

Ever since I was a little girl, the itching inside, the need to go, has always overpowered anything in my life. I can't explain it exactly, but my dear Suda Kaye, I think you understand and feel that emptiness inside of you. That thirst to be filled by all the things life has to offer. Though sometimes I wish I'd been more stable. Normal. A Betty Crocker–type mom, a perfect housewife to Adam...

Just thinking about Adam makes my heart ache. He's such a good man. Forgiving me for my transgression with Ian all those years ago, taking you under his wing as his own daughter. I'm not sure I could ever forgive myself for that betrayal. However, without that experience in my life, I wouldn't have you. And you, my huutsuu, are everything.

Beautiful. Effervescent. Wild. Compassionate.

I believe you'll be able to fly free without hurting others the way I did. Disappearing at the drop of the hat. You're smarter. Wiser. And hopefully, my letters and experiences can lead you down the right path. Whatever that may be.

Just promise me one thing, my darling…open your eyes. See the world for what it is. Beauty personified. Every living thing is a gift. Every stone you step on is a path of opportunity. Take it all in. One day, there will come a moment in time where contentment will find you. And it will be just as beautiful as all the experiences combined.

Unfortunately, I found my contentment with you girls and our lives in Pueblo too late. Don't make that same mistake. During your time traveling the world, keep your eyes open. Find your place. Your heart will lead you there. Until then, continue to fly, my little bird.

With all my love,

Mom

Tears track down my face in rivulets. This letter has always plagued me. It's as if she knew that eventually I would need to stop spreading my wings. And for the first time in a decade, my feet feel rooted to the ground.

To my sister.

To Colorado.

To my store.

To… Camden.

"Ugh." I kick my feet and legs out from under the covers and wipe the tears off my face. "This is useless. I have to figure out what I'm going to do for Cam to make it right. If there is anything I can do at all."

Leaning over my bed, I gather up Mom's letters, fold them

all carefully, and tuck them each in their corresponding envelope before grabbing the stack and setting them in my nightstand drawer for safekeeping before hoofing it out of bed.

I place my hands on my hips and survey the rather empty
apartment. I've made progress, but an empty living room does
not say "settled," and if what Mom was trying to tell me in
that letter is true, I need to commit to the place I'm supposed
to be. Fully commit. That means get back to the things I love.
Not just setting up the store.

A thought blasts through my mind, and I smile. I reach
for my cell phone, tug it off the charging cable, and press the
numbers I need.

In two rings, my sister picks up. "Are you okay after last
night? I was gonna come over and bring dinner if you didn't
call me first."

"Sissy, I have a better idea." I move around my bed toward
my armoire to get some yoga pants, a tank, and a hoodie.

"Why does it feel like I'm going to regret this?" she mumbles.

"Because I'm unpredictable, which is also something you
love about me."

"I wouldn't call that love. More like fear." She chuckles.

"Be that as it may, I'm in a funk, and I want to get out of it.
You're my sister, and it's your job to play along. Then, when
you're in a funk, I'll back you up."

Evie groans. "Okay, what do you have in mind?"

I grin wide. "Just put on some yoga gear and come pick
me up."

"Yoga? We're going to do yoga?"

"Or something like that." I snort. "Just get ready and come
and get me. I'd come to you, but I don't have a car yet."

"Speaking of…that should have been one of the first things
you did," Evie states with a hint of sisterly chastisement.

I groan dramatically. "Not helping my mood."

"Fine, fine. You win. This time. I'm taking off early today. I'll get home, change, and be there in an hour."

"Can't wait! Miss me."

"Miss me more," she fires off.

"Always!" I giggle and disconnect. Instantly, I pull up Google to search for what I need. Within minutes I've scored exactly what I'm looking for.

"Thanks for the nudge, Mom," I call out to the empty room while I shimmy the few feet to my bathroom to shower.

"You have got to be kidding me." Evie looks around the room of half-dressed women as I pull off my hoodie and shirt until I'm left in only my hot pink sports bra and gray yoga pants.

"I know it's probably taking you back to our roots, but I never left the practice. Though I'm rusty since I haven't found a new group to dance with."

Evie's shoulders drop as she glances around at the women in the room. Some are in flowing maxi skirts with belly chains and crop tops, others are in full workout gear, and a lot are dressed like I am. Free of too much clothing but still with the important bits covered.

"All right, ladies, pick a spot on the floor and let's get moving!" a beautiful, curvy, dark-haired woman calls out over the chatter.

Evie removes her sweatshirt but doesn't take off her tank and follows me to a spot off to the side where we can still see the teacher but not be fully called out.

I chuckle under my breath as Evie places her hands on her hips and waits for instruction. Like she needs it. Evie and I may be rusty, her more so than me, but we've been belly dancing since we were children. Mom taught us the Turkish method using finger symbols as well as the more fluid Egyptian variation. I spent almost a year touring across Europe with a group of belly dancers that had a wild array of styles and variations on the dance.

All the women in the room take a spot in the open space while the teacher steps up onto a platform and turns on a Middle Eastern tune I recognize from one of my last dance group's performances.

"Since this is the intermediate class, we're going to get right into the percussive movements and hip drops. I'll show you the sequence, and you can pick it up at your own pace."

Evie sends a virtual dagger through her glare at me and mouths, "Intermediate."

I grin wide and shrug.

She rolls her eyes and focuses on the teacher's movements. Within minutes, Evie and I are dialed in to the staccato vertical hip drops and outward punctuations that move into isolated hip rolls. I start to get into the movement, swaying my arms with the beat in a way I feel most symbolizes the music. Without even realizing it, Evie's movements mirror mine, and an easy smile spreads across her face.

For an hour, we rock our hips from side to side, spin in calculated but fluid circles and work our abdominal muscles as our mother taught us. Before long, we're so into it we don't immediately realize when the teacher steps off her podium and comes to stand with us. She picks up our well-rehearsed movements and follows along.

The entire room starts doing our moves as the teacher calls out each gyration or change in a sequence. It is one of the most unique and epic moments I've had with my sister.

Evie eventually opens her eyes and realizes that we've got

the crowd dancing with us. Peals of laughter fall from her lips as her hands rise into the air and she really gets into twirling and spinning around to the music. She's beautiful and beyond ethereal in her dance. She has the gift. I learned the dance and did it well. Evie, she lived and breathed the movements straight from her soul, though her icy demeanor would never lead anyone to believe she could be this carefree.

I know different. Mom knew different.

Perhaps it's my role to break her out of the perfectly square box she's put herself and her life into. Find ways to break her free from her own chains.

Eventually, the teacher goes back to the podium and turns off the music once the song comes to an end. Sweat is dripping down our faces, our bellies, and along our spines. We're a complete and utter soggy mess, and I've never felt better.

Evie, lost to the moment, opens her arms and pulls me into a sweaty, sisterly hug and kisses my cheek. "I forgot how much I loved to dance! It's been so long, but I swear it came back like I never lost a beat."

I push her hair off her face and tuck it behind her ear. Her cheeks are rosy, eyes a warm Caribbean blue, and her lips pink and full.

"You look happy, sissy."

She smiles wide. "I am. I have you back. What more could I ever want?" She tilts her head and stares into my eyes, and I could swear that look, packed with her honesty, fills one of the empty holes in my gut with pure joy.

I hook my sister around the shoulders as the teacher pops off the podium and rushes over to us.

"Hey, ladies, you both were amazing! Very advanced in your dancing. You totally inspired me and this entire class.

You simply must come back!" She holds up her hands in a prayer position in front of her ample bosom.

"Oh, we will." I nudge my sister's hips with my own and squeeze her shoulders. "Right, Evie?"

She laughs dryly. "Yeah, I'd be willing to come back to a class or two a month."

"Well, here's my card. I'm part of a belly dancing group. We do corporate gigs, shows, festivals, and the like when our day jobs allow. There are enough of us that we come and go as our schedules permit. I know for a fact the manager of the group would be over the moon to have two advanced dancers to add to the troupe."

"Right on!" I take the card and tuck it into the mini pocket in my yoga pants. "I'll definitely call. I used to dance with a group when I was living abroad but haven't found a new one since moving home."

"We'd love to have you. Looking forward to seeing you at a future practice." The teacher dips her head and moves back to pack up her stuff.

"You can count on it!" I holler, then smile as Evie leads me to where we dropped our things.

"Aren't you pretty busy with the store, Kaye?" Evie grabs her sweater and places her purse strap over her shoulder.

I nod. "Yeah, but I need to make sure I'm not consumed with Gypsy Soul to the point that I neglect all of the things that make me *me*. You know?"

Evie frowns and nods her head, but I don't believe she actually agrees with me. She likely doesn't want to dig further or share her own thoughts.

"What's next?" she asks as we make our way out of the facility and to her SUV.

"What else? Food and drink, baby." I grin and dance to the driver's side.

When I'm with Evie, she prefers me to drive. Always has. Even if it's her car. I'm pretty sure it goes back to when Dad was teaching her to drive, and she got into an accident. He smacked his head against the passenger-side window, which resulted in a series of stitches. He also suffered a broken forearm when the airbag deployed and smashed against his arm that he'd instinctively put across my sister's chest to prevent her from getting hurt. All of this took him out of work for a couple months.

Ever since, she's been a super wuss about driving. Only drives when she's alone. Probably part of why she never goes anywhere. Definitely something to think about when I'm helping her break out of her perfect little box.

On the way toward Pueblo, we find a cool little sports bar. With our hair pulled into messy buns and still rocking our yoga gear, it feels like the right type of locale for our mood and attire. I should have gone home and changed, because the moment we walk in, my gaze locks on the wide smile that splits across Kyson's unshaven face.

He stands up and his ever-present white T-shirt is stretched magically across his broad chest. He tugs up his jeans a little as he circles around his brother, Lincoln, and walks our way.

"Hey, ladies, what are you doing here? Didn't take you two for the sports bar types." He glances from our comfy Ugg boots to our painted-on yoga pants and hoodies.

"We're not," Evie quips. "We are the fried-food-and-beer-loving types."

He beams a megawatt smile that would make most women drool with the desire to kiss that smile right off his perfectly rugged face.

"Imagine that." Kyson runs his thumb over his bottom lip,

assessing me fully. "I'm that type of man. How about you two join me and Linc for some food and brews?"

As Evie is about to decline, I step in front of her and blurt, "We'd love to."

Evie tugs on my elbow and brings me closer to her side so she can whisper in my ear. "You are playing with fire, Kaye. This man is all about good times and nothing more."

I lick my lips and take in all that is before me. Perhaps he's the one who can take away all the twisted, ugly feelings I have inside about last night's confrontation with Camden and his family and the fact that I've probably lost him forever.

"And who says that's not exactly what I'm looking for?" I purse my lips and stare down my sister.

Her expression contorts into one of irritation. "It's not a good idea."

"Hey, hey, this doesn't require deep contemplation, ladies. I'm just offering you some company, some laughs, a basket of the best boneless wings on the planet, and a pitcher full of cold beer. Nothing else," Kyson declares as he holds his hands up in a submissive gesture.

Evie narrows her gaze. "That better be all you're offering, Mr. Fix It, or I'll be taking my sister to that empty table over there." She points to a random, lonely-looking spot right next to the bathroom.

"Ew, gross, Ev. I don't want to listen to people pee or smell anything funky when I'm trying to get my drink and eats on." I frown and give her a pretty-please puppy face.

She inhales long and full, letting it out in a dramatic huff. "Lead the way." She gestures with her hand to Kyson.

He grins and cocks his head to the side. "Right over there. Let me order up another pitcher of beer and some wings."

"Thank you," I offer in my sweetest voice.

As he moves away and we start toward his high-top table, Evie bumps my shoulder. "You better know what you're doing."

"Oh, I don't even have the first clue. All I know is I haven't gotten laid in months. Kyson's as hot as a habanero, built to ride a woman hard, he's kind and offering no strings." I shrug.

She stops me before we make it to the table. "Are you honestly thinking about wooing him into your bed?"

I snort-laugh. "Ev, relax. Besides, no one says *wooing* anymore, and I'm a very big girl. I can handle myself."

She shakes her head. "Obviously not, if you think jumping into bed with Mr. Right *Now* is going to fix the pain and hurt of messing up with Mr. Right Last Night."

I turn to my sister and cup her neck and touch my forehead to hers. "I'll be careful. Don't worry about me. I haven't made any decisions. I just know what I feel, and when I'm hurting, there are a variety of ways to ease that hurt. One being spending an awesome day with your sister. Another is chowing down on some awesome wings and chugging back ice-cold beer. And last, a fantastic night in the sack with a nice guy whose only aim is to please me in all the ways that matter."

Evie's eyes turn a fiery white-blue like the very bottom of an open gas flame. "Be smart, Kaye. Don't go there with your renovator. Don't go there when you're hurting from wanting what you don't think you can have with Cam. It's not fair to you, and more important, it's not fair to Cam," she whispers stridently.

I grind my teeth. "Girl, I got this. It's all good."

A whistle sounds and we turn our heads to where Kyson and his brother are sitting. Kyson is wearing a come-hither smile and holding up a fresh pitcher of beer.

"It really is all good." I wink and saunter over to the boys.

"This is going to end badly, I just know it," Evie mumbles but follows me to the table anyway.

12

"Easy, brown eyes, easy," Kyson warns as I trip up the second stair to my apartment. Behind me, my sister howls with laughter, which acts like a trigger, causing me to slump against the wall as I cackle like a hyena.

"Jesus, I did not sign up for this level of crazy." Kyson chuckles as he hooks an arm around Evie's waist and my own and practically drags us up the small flight of stairs.

At the top, Evie leans heavily against his side, her drunken self looking up at Kyson in complete and utter awe. "Wow, you're really pretty," she says, beer goggles firmly in place, her tone full of nothing but admiration.

He kisses the top of her forehead. "Is that right, beautiful?"

"Oh yeah," she says, nodding what seems like a hundred times.

I pet Kyson's bulging biceps. "You are *so* strong. I'll bet you can do a lot with those muscles. A lot, a lot, a lot." I offer him what I think is a sultry smile, which likely comes off as a drunken Elvis-style lip curl.

"Hell. If I was a different kind of man, I'd have you both in my bed begging for more and calling out to God. Since I'm not an asshole douchebag, how about you open that door, brown eyes, and I'll get you both safely inside so you can hit the sack?"

"Hitting the sack?" I grin wide and plaster myself to his side. "That sounds awwwesooome." I draw out the last word to denote my extreme excitement.

Kyson shakes his head. "Open the door, Suda Kaye," he demands gruffly.

I pout and dig through my huge bag. When I hook the key ring, I hold it up like a winning trophy. "Woo-hoo! Score!"

My sister high-fives me sloppily.

Kyson takes the keys from my hand, and I frown. Feels like he stole my win. I huff and cross my arms, letting my indignation at his alpha maleness put me into a grumpy mood all of a sudden.

Evie, on the other hand, has no such concerns. She's plastered to his side and rubbing her cheek along his arm. I get it. It's an awesome arm and looks super comfy.

Kyson swings open the door and leads me and my sister into the room. Only we're not alone.

"The fuck?" Kyson exclaims.

Camden stands up from the edge of the bed where he was sitting. He's wearing a suit that's wrinkled to the max, having seen far better days than this one. His normally beautifully styled hair is in a wild mess of waves around his face, as though he's been running his fingers through it all day.

"What are you doing here?" I ask and then hiccup. "Oh no." I frown and spin around to Evie. "I got the hiccum-ups. I hate the hiccum-ups."

Evie breaks out of Kyson's hold and takes a few tentative steps to me. She holds her hand up to her face in a shushing gesture and then points to our uninvited guest.

"Oh yeah, I forgot." I turn back around and stare at Cam,

opening and closing my eyes to make sure I'm not seeing a mirage in my drunken state. My imagination is awesome so I wouldn't put it past me.

Cam's face morphs into granite. "Are the two of you drunk?" he grates between clenched teeth. His fiery gaze goes to me, then Evie, and up to Kyson. "Did you get these women drunk in order to take advantage of them?" His voice borders on a yell.

I flail my hands and shake my head. "No, no, no! Me and Evie got drunk all by ourselves. Well, not by ourselves. We were hanging out with Kyson and Grumpy Face Lincoln at the sports bar, and the drinks were flowing and...huh." I drop my hands and stare at Cam while lifting a long hank of hair and curl it around my finger, then pull it across my mouth before letting it go. "I forgot what we were talking about."

Camden grunts and moves forward, cupping my face between his large hands.

I sigh and stare at his face. "You are the most beautiful man in the whole world," I say dreamily.

"What am I going to do with you?" He closes his eyes for a moment, cutting me off from their hazel glory.

I pout and then smile the moment he turns me around and hooks his arm around my waist, hauling my body to his side. Yummy. I wrap my arms around him and snuggle in, pressing my nose to his chest, inhaling the subtle hints of lemongrass, musk, and coffee.

"I asked you a question," Cam barks across the room where Kyson is holding up Evie.

"You got the wrong idea about me, man. And besides, you're the one who shouldn't be here. How the hell did you get in anyway?" Kyson keeps an arm around Evie. Her eyelids are starting to droop, but she's trying to stay awake. Probably doesn't want to miss the show.

Me? I want popcorn.

Oooh, popcorn sounds amazing!

I think about what's in my cupboards and whether or not I have popcorn until the chest I'm leaning against is bouncing up and down. I crinkle my nose and lift my very heavy head. Cam is hollering, but the words are garbled, not making any sense.

Kyson says something about taking Evie home since she's on the way to his house.

Before long, I start to lose my focus, and an intense need to sleep overwhelms me. I hear the door close, and my head feels incredibly heavy.

"Suda Kaye, baby, just stay with me. Let me get you to bed. Okay, sweets?" He shuffles my weaving body toward that area of my studio.

"Mmm, yes please," I say before a moment of clarity smacks me upside the head and sifts through the thick haze of alcohol pumping in my system. "Wait, um, no way. No bed for you, Mr. Engaged-to-Bimbo-Bitch-Barbie." I blink a few times, and the room spins. I'm caught up in the vortex and start to stumble.

Cam catches me and lifts me into his arms. "Shh. I'm not with her anymore. Broke it off earlier today for good."

His words settle deep into my heart, and I attempt to clap but fail miserably as my coordination is toast.

Eventually I'm settled on a cloud of comfy blankets. "Mmm, yummy." I snuggle into my covers and sigh contentedly.

Not long after, a heavy arm hooks around my waist and hauls me to an even more cozy spot. It feels like an electric blanket with the best heat in the world wraps itself around me.

I latch on to the warmth like my life depends on it. "So comfy," I mumble.

"Yeah, sweets, better than I remembered. Good night, Suda Kaye."

"Good night, Cam. Love you," I murmur before everything falls away into darkness.

The sound of the drill startles me awake. For a minute, I'm not sure where I am. The noise is familiar. The same irritating sounds I've been hearing for weeks. Grumpy Lincoln never lets up on starting the job promptly at 8:00 a.m. According to Kyson, if I'd let him, Lincoln would be on the job at six like he usually is, but since I live above the jobsite and he found out I like my sleep, he moved the start time to eight.

Kyson.

A warm hand skates up my side, over my bare shoulder to my long hair. I close my eyes and breathe deeply, trying to remember what the hell I did and who I did it with.

My head is groggy, but I've never been one to get a true bellyaching, head-pounding kind of hangover. This morning is no exception. Usually, I don't get so drunk that I forget who I bedded the night before. It's happened, but only with men I'd been dating regularly. I've never taken home a one-night stand and forgotten what I was doing with the man.

Only last night, Evie and I were hanging out with Kyson and his brother at a sports bar. We got plastered and became cheerleaders, rooting for the home team and spouting off boos and hisses when the opposing team scored.

The owner of the warm hand covers my body with his and nudges his nose against my ear and neck, inhaling audibly. His lips touch down just behind my ear, and I sigh. He moves his arms and runs a hand around my middle, pressing a sizable erection against my bum.

"Good morning, sweets," is said with a scruffy morning grumble I haven't heard in ages.

Camden.

Oh my God. *Oh my God.* Oh. My. God.

My entire body goes completely still. "Uh…what? Uh… Cam?" I'm at a complete loss for words as Cam rubs his impressive length against me in a *stellar* good morning hello that I would welcome willingly, if it were under different circumstances.

Camden rolls me onto my back, lifts up on a forearm and hovers over my torso. His hair is a wild mess of waves falling down around his face. He's not wearing a shirt and I mentally assess my own body.

Do I have clothes on? Yes, a sports bra and yoga pants. Thank God.

Is he fully naked? Um…maybe. I'm too afraid to wrap my arms around all that is the man of my dreams and find out for myself.

Without realizing it, I start to tremble.

Cam pushes my hair off my shoulders and tunnels his hand at the side of my neck until he can cup my head. "Suda baby, you're shaking like a leaf."

"Did, uh…did we have sex last night?" I ask with a tremor in my voice that's unmistakable.

He smiles, and that smile reaches his eyes and his entire face becomes so damned handsome I want nothing more than to wrap my arms around him and show him how very much that smile affects me.

"I know it's been a long while for us, but if we'd had sex last night, babe, you'd know it. You'd feel it in every pore, every nerve ending, and you'd definitely feel it when you tried to walk." He dips his head and brushes his lips over mine in a barely there kiss.

What. In. The. World. Is. Happening.

I squirm and attempt to move.

"Relax," he whispers in a hushed, sweet tone I remember from when we were just teenagers. His face is so close I can feel his breath against my skin.

I immediately follow his request, so out of sorts that I don't even know how to muster up my level of sass at being told what to do.

"No, we didn't have sex," he says with a hint of humor. "You came home drunk as a skunk, your sister no better. Maybe even worse."

I bite my lip and widen my eyes. "Is she okay? Where is she?"

"She's fine. You don't remember?" he asks gently.

I shake my head.

"What do you remember?" His eyes have turned a shade darker, more the mossy green I'm used to seeing when he's frustrated.

With a tad more effort than I would normally need, I think back to last night. "Belly dancing class. So much fun, by the way. Evie was awesome. As in *really* awesome. I'm going to make her take it with me more often."

Camden leans more of his body against mine, and his extreme warmth blankets my chest like a wall of fire. I don't mean to do it, but I moan a little trying to get closer. I can't help it. Cam is my dream man, and his naked torso is plastered against mine, his face so close I could kiss him. Really kiss him.

He brushes his soft lips against mine and I sigh into it.

Oh, my word. Cam kissed me. In my bed. No, it wasn't

one of those *I love you more than life itself, I need you back, I'm dying without you* type kisses, but it was a definite touch of lips.

"Why did you just kiss me?" I change the subject.

"Because you're cute. You've always been cute, but at that moment, your cute deserved a lip touch. Like you're earning one by being cute now."

I open my eyes wider, but it doesn't stop him from pressing his mouth against mine again, this time, adding a tongue sweep across my lips. My lips part automatically. I want Cam's tongue in my mouth more than my next breath, but it is a lost endeavor. Cam sucks on my bottom lip, running his tongue across the bit of flesh and letting it go.

"Continue. Belly dancing with Evie. What next?"

I frown and think back. "We went to the sports bar. Ran into Kyson and his brother, Lincoln. They invited us to join them for wings and beer. Turns out, I think we had more beer than wings."

"My guess is you'd be correct. Then what?"

"Um…he brought us home. We left Evie's car at the bar. He carried us both up the stairs like He-Man. It was really hot. And really cool."

Cam's expression becomes hard, and he kicks my leg out and to the side, centers his body between my spread thighs and settles down in a very territorial move.

"Too much info?" I bite into my bottom lip and gasp when Cam rubs his hard length right across my center in a delicious hip thrust.

I wrap my arms around his waist and run my hands up and down his bare, strong back. It's so much larger than it was before and packed with tight sinew and muscle.

"Yeah, sweets, too much information," he chuckles. "It's probably best not to talk about how good-looking another man is when you've got one hovering above you, hard as steel, and ready to fuck you into next week."

At that comment, I dig my fingers into his back, probably leaving little crescent-moon-shaped indents in my wake. "As much as I want this, you and me, together in this way… Cam… I don't know if that's a good idea. I don't want you to regret this."

"It's a great fucking idea and one I'd never in a million years regret. You're gonna finish your story so I can get to the good part where I fuck you and do it so hard that tool downstairs will hear your pleasure and know he is not getting in there. Ever."

This time, I smack his arm. "Seriously?" I narrow my gaze and growl.

He shakes his head. "This thing between us ends now, right here. From this moment on, it's me and you figuring out our shit, whatever that may be. And while we're figuring out, it's going to be me getting inside this sweetness." Cam accentuates his point by inserting his hand between us and cupping my sex.

An endless bout of desire rushes through my system at his crass and extremely hot dirty talk, making my clit throb and heat filter through my body. I thrust my hips against his hand, wanting so much more.

He grins at my automatic move. "Bet you're already wet for me. I wouldn't expect anything less. My girl used to run so hot, it would take everything inside me not to take what you offered until your eighteenth birthday. Wanted to do right by the only woman I ever loved. And then you left before we could ever experience more, all the good times we missed out on."

Anxiety swirls in the air around us but I have to say it. It's been ten years in the making. At the very least he deserves an apology. "Cam, I'm sorry… I had to. You won't understand."

He grips my center and rubs a sneaky thumb right over the tight knot begging for his touch, zeroing in on the perfect spot in a nanosecond. Like a dart right to the bull's-eye on the first throw.

"Try me." He brings his face so that his lips are against mine, not exactly kissing, but touching.

I grip his arms, digging my nails into his skin and circle my hips wanting more. "Not now. We shouldn't bed when we talk about this…"

He runs a hand down my chest and cups my breast, plumping it the way he used to, shattering any chance I might get my wits about me and get out from under him to neutral ground. Instead, I arch my back in offering. He moves his head and bites my nipple through the sports bra. I mewl when he unzips the front of the bra and flicks his warm tongue against the sensitive tip of my right breast.

"God, yes, Cam!" I continue to bow my back as much as possible, and he removes his hand from my center and cups my left breast, molding and plucking at the tip while he services the right fully. He alternates his mouth from one dusky-brown erect tip to the other, giving equal attention to both until I'm panting with the need to feel him inside of me.

Cam lifts his head from my breast, sucking deep until it falls from his lips with a soft plop. His eyes are now a fiery shamrock green, filled to the brim with lust I'm not sure will ever be quenched. If he's feeling anything close to what's running through my system, it's going to take a while to slake his need.

In the most beautiful move, Cam smiles, cups my jaw, and dips his head so his lips slant over mine. Nothing but beauty spills through my body like ribbons of electricity that have no way to get out, so the intensity hums under the surface as he takes my mouth in a blistering kiss. Cam's hand controls my head as he tips my face to the side and his tongue delves deep.

I rise up as best I can to get closer. His other hand strokes my waist and comes down to my ass where he grips and lifts, pressing me harder against his body and the large erection I can't wait to become reacquainted with.

It's a wild kiss of tongue, teeth, and lips. Both of us starving for the other's taste. It's the best kiss of my entire life. Better than when we were kids, better than any man after him.

Camden Bryant was not only made to kiss, he was made to kiss me.

For what feels like eternity but is probably a couple minutes, our mouths get to know one other again. He nips my bottom lip, while I nibble his top one. His tongue sinks deep, and I open wider. Call and response. Like we've done this a thousand times before, because we have, only it's been years.

I suck his lip and run my tongue along the plump surface teasingly. He growls, taking the kiss from sweet to ravenous and right to the point of no return. My body feels feverish, desire running thick through my veins, and all I can think about is how much I want him.

Want this.

Want his body, mouth, and hands, all over mine.

I need more. So much more. I push against his chest, he lifts up and watches while I shimmy out of my yoga pants. I take my underwear with them, shrug off the sports bra, and toss them both to the floor.

"Suda baby, you are so damn beautiful. Never met anyone as gorgeous as you." His words are pure honesty, and they sound as if they are being ripped from his soul.

I grin, lean back, and open my legs, unashamed, baring all for his lusty gaze.

He licks his lips, and his nostrils flare. I think he's going to lean back and pull off his slacks and boxer briefs, the only two things he's wearing. Instead, he blows my mind and falls down on my center like a starving, *desperate* man. He uses his arms and hands to hold my legs out wide as he dips his head and covers my entire sex with his mouth in one intensely satisfying lick.

Simultaneously, we both groan. I weave my fingers through his long locks and grip his hair tight when he covers the little knot of pleasure with his mouth and sucks…hard.

For a long time, Cam drinks deep from me. Sucking, flicking, licking, swirling, and nipping in all the ways I remember. Within minutes I'm moaning and trembling in ecstasy. The throbbing heat starts at my center and works its way up. Before long, my nipples are pinpricks of sizzling desire, erect and pointing straight up to the sky. I dip my head back and press one hand to the headboard so I can push down on his ravenous mouth while I use my other hand to force his head down harder between my legs.

This move makes Camden go nuts. He growls and wraps his hands around my legs and holds them down, locking them in place. I can't move, only take what he offers.

My orgasm explodes through my body, but I still can't move. He's relentless in his need, his yearning for more. He runs his hot tongue over and over the tight bundle of nerves until I'm panting so hard it feels like my lungs are going to burst with the force of air in and out of my chest.

"Baby, please, come inside," I beg.

Cam doesn't respond in words, nor does he listen to my request. Instead, he doubles down, bringing his fingers into the action. Two digits sink into me and I howl in delight as he sucks and licks me into oblivion, those talented fingers thrusting persistently.

"Cam, Cam, Cam," I chant until he thrusts those two fingers deep, sucks hard against my clit, and I lose my mind all over again, screaming his name, calling to God, to *anyone* who will save me from this endless pleasure.

"Damn, sweets, I forgot how loud you can get." He chuckles while kissing his way up my boneless body. His tongue circles around my navel and dips in teasingly.

A flicker of excitement has my center throbbing. Jeez Louise, my lady bits are greedy. Always wanting more.

I lock my arms and legs around Cam as he makes his way up my torso, kissing and nipping whatever he finds tantalizing. Instead of watching him, I just lie there, feeling everything he's doing, committing it to memory so that I have this to go back to when the true light of a new day dawns on the both of us.

Cam cups my breasts again. "They're a lot bigger than they used to be. Prettier, too." He swirls his tongue around one tip.

"I grew up," I utter throatily, running my fingers down his long muscular back and lats. "You did, too."

He smiles and dips his head so that he can kiss me wetly. I can taste the tang of me on his tongue, and it makes my slutty clit perk up even more. Traitor.

"Yeah, sweets, you did grow up. All of it insanely beautiful." He nudges me with his cock, and I whimper, wanting him inside of me so badly. "You on the pill?" he asks.

I grin, liking that he wants to protect me. "IUD. It lasts years. Just got a new one when I settled here in Pueblo along with a health screening. Everything's fresh as a daisy. Have you been checked since, uh…"

"Yeah, babe. I've been checked, and as she mentioned, we only had relations the one time, and I don't even remember it."

I close my eyes and frown, the moment of excitement leaving me at the mention of Miss Colorado and what she did him.

"Cam..." I try to say something but lose the words when he swoops in and steals my breath with an intense kiss, complete with tons of tongue action and even some teeth nibbling. Before he finishes it, I'm back to wanting him inside.

"You're safe," he says. "But before we do this, I need you to admit you want it to happen."

"I do."

He grins and lifts up on one hand, holding up the weight of his upper body. "You also have to admit this is the beginning."

"The beginning of what?" I run my fingers through his gorgeous hair and find that it's still soft as silk. A shiver ripples through my torso with the loss of his heat.

His gaze is scorching as he undoes his slacks. I help him shove them past his hips and thighs. In a series of shifts from left to right he removes both items and tosses them to the floor and dips his body back down, cradled between my thighs. He notches the crown of his cock right at my entrance. I moan and then hold my breath, waiting.

"The beginning of us." He nudges and just the wide head penetrates.

"Baby..." I sigh and thrust my hips, taking more of him in and loving every centimeter. "Come inside." I say the words he wants to hear without committing to what he wants between us. That conversation cannot be held now. This—whatever this is—is beyond logic.

"I never could say no to you." He growls and dips his head to capture my lips at the same time he eases home.

And that's exactly what it feels like, an overwhelming sense of home. While connected to Camden Bryant, my gut stops churning, the weird twisting ceases, and the emptiness that I've been fighting for years dissipates.

He eases back until just the tip is inside of me, then he slams forward. My teeth rattle and my heart swells with happiness.

He cups my cheek. "Open your eyes, Suda Kaye."

The exact words my mother said to me run through my mind, and at first, I fight it. Not wanting to see what's right before me. Afraid of it. Yet even though I'm afraid, I've never felt better, more content, than making love with Cam.

"Suda Kaye, open your eyes, baby," he says again, and I comply. His gaze is filled with desire, need, and something I hadn't anticipated I'd see in a million years...hope.

Cam rocks his hips in the most beautiful symphony of movement. I wrap one arm around his shoulders and cup his tight ass with my free hand, helping him grind into me until I'm a ball of incredible joy and never-ending lust.

"I've been waiting an eternity to be right here again. Look at us, sweets. We're beautiful together."

I follow his gaze and glance between our bodies. His length is thick, hard, and glistening with my essence. My legs are spread wide to accommodate his girth, and with every thrust, I watch my body accept him, holding on. I clench my internal muscles, and he cries out, starting to pound harder. It's magnificent to watch, to see him giving and receiving pleasure.

Once more, the heat starts up in my center again, spirals of pleasure splintering out through my body, seeming to encourage Cam along with it. His body drives into mine and we both clutch one another tight as our hips rock back and forth over and over.

Eventually, neither of us can hold out. The pleasure is

too great. It's too good. Together we fall over the edge, me clenching down tight and holding him like a vise with all four limbs. He buries his face against my neck, biting down painfully where my neck and shoulder meet as his entire form shakes and trembles. The results of his desire spill hotly, coating me with his essence from the inside out.

For a long time, we hold one another, not moving, locked in a moment we're not ready to give up.

Leisurely, Cam places kiss after kiss along my neck, clavicle, and up to my mouth. "You good?" He holds my chin in one hand and stares into my eyes, assessing me directly.

"Yeah. You?"

"Oh yeah." He grins.

I lick my lips as he snuggles against me, our bodies still connected.

"Give me ten minutes, and I'll be ready for round two," he murmurs against my skin. "I'm not as young as I used to be."

"Round two?" Seriously? He thinks he can best incredible, earth-shattering makeup sex in ten minutes?

"Uh, yeah, babe, round two. You think I'm going to finally get back in *there* and not stake my claim the way a man in my position should? Meaning, doing as I promised and banging the living daylights out of you. Besides, I'm looking forward to having your mouth again. Figure after you got three to my one, you need to work to even the score." He chuckles playfully against my skin.

"Are you seriously keeping score?"

He lifts his head. "What? You don't want to wrap your lips around my cock? You used to love doing that. Said it was your favorite thing to do in the bedroom aside from me going down on you. Did that change since we were last together?"

I pout and glance away. No, it is still one of my favorite sexual exchanges. I love having the power over a man's pleasure.

"Didn't think so," he murmurs.

"I'm hungry," I say flippantly.

He jerks his hips, and shocker of all shockers, he's semi-hard already.

"Not surprised. Only you're going to have to wait until after round two." He lifts up on his haunches, his cock slipping from me.

I mewl and he grins wickedly, obviously knowing that I didn't want to lose him.

My gaze zeroes in on his hardening cock and I'm absolutely fascinated at his ability to rise to the challenge so quickly after our first round. He lifts up on his knees and straddles my upper body. I stare at the wet tip of his manhood and find out that he's right. Damn him. I want that tip plowing in and touching the back of my throat. I want to kiss, lick, and drive Cam crazy like I used to when I gave him head.

"I see your hunger for food has changed. You got something else you want to taste?" He smirks.

I narrow my gaze and forcibly grip his hips. "You're an ass."

He chuckles.

"Now give me what I want." I lick my lips with anticipation.

"Always, baby. Always." He adjusts his hips and plants his hands on the headboard behind me, bringing his length into the perfect position directly in front of my face, the head practically nudging my lips.

I lick the tip, and he groans, dropping his head back with a hiss.

"When I'm done, you're feeding me scrambled eggs, bacon,

and toast." I suck the wide knobbed head and salivate at the familiar taste.

"You take it home, I'll make you breakfast, lunch, and dinner, baby."

I grin and place a kiss just on the tip, look up, and watch his eyes swirl with renewed heat. "Challenge accepted."

"Oh, fuck me."

"That's the plan," I retort and say nothing more because my mouth is busy.

In the end, I take it home and get mine twice more.

Challenge met.

13

"I like my bacon crispy!" I call out as I slip on a clean pair of yoga pants and a tank, sans underwear. I'm not sure if I'm intentionally baiting Camden by rockin' no undergarments, or just making things easy in the event we go for round three. Seeing as rounds one and two were phenomenal, the absolute best I've ever had—and I've gotten plenty in my day—I'm not opposed to another romp. Even if I don't believe it's the smart thing to do.

"Like I didn't know that," he responds briskly. Facing the stove, his bare muscular back is on full display. Cam is beautiful, in a suit or out of one. Sexy as sin in jeans and a T-shirt, but nothing compares to him standing in my kitchen in his dress slacks, with the top button undone, bare feet, and nothing else. I don't know what it is, but something about seeing a man, most specifically *this man*, a bit vulnerable… undone…is stunningly beautiful to me.

Making my way around the counter, I head to the coffeepot. "Well, ten years is a long time," I remind him.

"Yeah. I know that better than anyone," he grumbles while flipping the slices of bacon in the frying pan.

This isn't the first time he's mentioned our time apart in

a perturbed manner. I thought maybe with the addition of some stellar sex, we'd have moved past it a tiny bit. No such luck. I grind my teeth and set out two mugs, heat filling me as irritation prickles through my system.

"Are we going to have this conversation now? In all honesty, I'd rather not. We had a great time and I—"

Cam turns around with a pair of tongs in his hand. "No, I think we have some more pressing shit to discuss that's beyond the fact that ten years ago you shattered my heart."

I wince at his overt display of anger and fire back, "Yeah, like your newly ex-fiancée."

At the same time, he grates out, "Your contractor."

"Looks like we both have some concerns outside of our history to deal with." I grin and pour myself and him a cup of joe.

He maneuvers over to the fridge and pulls out the pumpkin creamer and the milk, setting them both next to the mugs. The creamer he obviously remembers is for me and I recall he takes milk and one sugar.

Once I've made our cups, I set his by the stove so he can easily reach it and lean against the counter, sipping my morning cup of gold. For a minute, I'm silent as I mull over what I want to say.

"Kyson is...hmm. A friend?" I finish with uncertainty as I let the concept of Kyson being my friend roll over my mind.

"You always kiss your friends?" He glares over his naked shoulder and lifts an eyebrow, then proceeds to remove the bacon from the pan and put it on a paper towel sitting on a plate next to the stove.

I take a deep breath and rub my lip along the edge of my monster-size coffee mug. I answer honestly, "Sometimes, yeah."

He huffs and starts to crack eggs into a separate sizzling hot frying pan. "You didn't used to."

"That's not fair, Cam. You were the first boy I kissed. The only boy I did anything sexual with in my entire adolescent years."

"And after?" He turns around and leans against the counter, crossing his long legs over one another at the ankle, doing the same with his arms over his bare chest. The tribal tattoo I'd only really glanced at spirals from his forearm up his biceps and around one shoulder. Like a weaving vine crawling up the side of a building. It is gorgeous and I want to inspect it more fully, but now is not the time.

I tip my head to the side and give him my full attention. "After, I did what I wanted when I wanted to do it."

"Fair enough." His jaw tightens, making his cheekbones and chiseled face seem hard. "Still you seemed pretty hot and bothered kissing Kyson this past week. Then you're having dinner and drinks to the point you get so drunk he has to take you and your sister home."

"Is that what he did? Drove Evie home?" I vaguely remember something about a conversation happening about this last night.

He frowns. "Of course. You think I'd let her drive inebriated?"

I shake my head instantly. "No. Just confirming how she got safely home."

"Yeah, apparently he lives in C-Springs. He was going to take her to get her car today, which I imagine he's already done since the work started a couple hours ago."

"Why didn't she come up?"

This gifted me a full Camden Bryant gleaming smile. "I

imagine she saw my car was still parked out front of the building and we weren't downstairs."

"Oh, right. She'd pick up on that."

He smirks.

"Anyway, Kyson's an attractive guy," I say. "It's not unusual to be attracted to a hot guy. Now that I'm—" I wave my hand between him and me, scared out of my mind to define this thing between us "—we're...whatever it is we are—"

"Exclusive," he states flatly, and I narrow my gaze.

"We haven't really discussed it, Cam."

"Yeah, we did." He lifts his chin toward the bed as if that's the only answer I need.

I set the coffee cup down on the counter and place a hand on my hip, my sassy attitude notching right into place now that I'm not distracted by my greedy lady bits. "Sex does not equal a relationship."

"You agreed, in that bed, that we were at the beginning of us. When you called out my name during the fourth orgasm I gave you, you sealed the deal. This is nonnegotiable, Suda Kaye. We're riding this wave until we figure out what it means."

"And what if I don't want to ride the wave? Surfing was never my strong suit." More like *doing* surfers was, but I keep that bit of info to myself.

Cam turns around and flips the eggs without breaking the yolk. Genius. On average, I break at least two out of four.

"Sweets, did you not just come harder than you have in your life right there in that bed not twenty minutes ago?"

I glare at him in answer.

"And did you not tell me you loved me last night before you fell asleep in my arms?"

At this revelation, my sassy attitude flies out the window

and I gasp while covering my mouth. An inexplicable wave of anxiety flushes my entire system, making me stagger, feeling unbalanced on my own feet. I hold on to the countertop and stare into his eyes.

"I did not," I whisper, even though loving Cam has been my best-kept secret for ten years. I never stopped loving him all the years I was away. And seeing the man he's become now, confident, strong, drop-dead gorgeous, leader of an entire empire, helping me set up my business, I've fallen harder. Even so, I've done everything in my power to push those frightening feelings to the back of my mind, safely locked in Pandora's box, never to be opened again.

"Babe, you did. Right before you fell asleep. I wrapped my arms around you, and you told me you loved me."

"I was three sheets to the wind. Drunk off my ass. That could have been anyone! I would have said it to Evie."

"But you didn't. You said it to *me*. Used *my name*, sweets. That meant something to me and regardless of the fact that, during the light of day, you may want to sweep it under the rug, I'm not going to let you. At least not forever."

I swallow down the fear and shake my head, whispering, "Cam, don't." It comes out as a plea.

He licks his lips and nods. "I can see that this morning has been a bit much for you. We both need some time to let all of this sink in. I promise I'm going to give it to you. However, while we're figuring all this out, I want your promise it's me and you. No one else."

"Are you going to promise the same?"

He offers a sexy lopsided grin. "Yeah, sweets. Wouldn't expect you to give it without being willing to give it myself. That means for you, no Kyson. No more flirting with every good-looking man that crosses your path."

Once more my irritation flares and my sass jumps to the forefront. "I do not flirt with every man I see, Cam."

He smiles and presses down the toast. "Babe, you do. Maybe you don't realize it, but alongside the fact that you have this hippie, flower child, daughter of Janis Joplin thing going on, your body is spectacular. Your hair is out of this world. Men want to sink their hands into it and give it a good tug. You've got the tightest ass and the absolute prettiest smile I've ever seen. You existing is flirting with every man that crosses your path."

Wow. That was an amazing thing to say. The fact that he believes it makes me want to say screw the food and screw something else entirely. Namely him. Right on the floor of my tiny kitchenette.

Instead, I let my sass win out. "It's not my fault men think with their penises. I'm just me."

"Yeah, you are. Always have been. And believe me when I say, the promise of you in their life, in their bed, means every hetero man you meet wants it or is wishing they could have it."

"That's not fair! I have no control over what men think," I interject, but he ignores me and continues with his rant.

"What I'm asking you to do is to try not to throw your sass at every man you see." He grabs the frying pan right as the toast pops up. He plates the eggs, then adds four slices of bacon to both of our plates. Once done, he grabs the toast, slathers a heaping dose of butter on each slice, and slaps them on top of the eggs and bacon.

Moving with the grace of a lion on the prowl, he puts my plate in front of me, leans forward, and kisses me soundly on the mouth. It wasn't his best kiss, but it was sweet and had a purpose. A purpose I didn't like much, because I figured it meant he wanted me to change.

"So now that we've had sex, you think you have the right to ask me to change who I am?" My voice is scratchy as the concern of what I'm saying really sinks in. He doesn't want me for me.

Cam sets down his plate, turns to me, and cages me in against the countertop. "Not at all what I'm saying." He lifts his hands and tunnels both of his into my hair, cupping my cheeks, and lifting my chin so he can look directly into my eyes. "What I'm trying to say to you, Suda Kaye, is that you are the whole package. I could think of ten men right now who would kill for a chance at the promise of what you could bring to their lives. I want you to let me be that man. Let this be the beginning."

The fact that, after ten years, we are back in this space and considering another go at a relationship has tears pricking the backs of my eyes. I've always wanted to be with Camden. He's the man I let go all those years ago, and right now, he's giving me another chance to have it again. Except, what he doesn't realize is we can't really start over. "It can never really be the beginning, Cam. We had years together."

He smiles so beautifully my heart stops, and I lose my breath. "Then meet me in the middle, sweets. Be in this with me. Commit to this new thing we're creating, together."

Meet him in the middle.

I absolutely love the sound of that.

"That I can do." I nod, and when the words really spiral through my mind, I like the concept more and more. Maybe this could work. Instead of starting at the beginning, we'll meet in the middle.

"Much obliged." He dips his face and kisses me. It's soft, sweet, and thorough. Almost a pact or a pinky promise.

When he's done kissing me, he turns and leads me to the stool. "Eat your eggs before they get too cold."

"Aye aye, Captain."

He chuckles. "You're such a nut. Guess some things never change."

"No, some things don't."

After breakfast, Cam and I take a long, productive shower together. This commences orgasms number five and six for me and number four for him. Even though we're not technically keeping score, I like scoring a whole lot, so I'm secretly keeping track.

As I stand in front of the vanity next to Cam, I glance over at him while brushing on my mascara. He's sliding some of my mousse into his hair and taming the waves.

"I love your hair." I wink at him and continue working on my lashes.

"I know. You make that pretty obvious, seeing as every time I get my mouth on you, your fingers are running through it or tugging on it."

"Does that bother you?" I stop brushing and ease back to look at him directly.

"Not even a little bit." He dips his head and steals a quick peck across my lips and then one on the side of my neck, where he inhales deeply. "Sweets, you smell so good. Fucking delicious."

"Thanks. Mom taught us how to make our own perfumes when we were younger, remember?"

"Yeah, Catori was a character. Loved her. Miss her."

My heart squeezes with thinking about Mom, but it doesn't

bring up the tears anymore. It took years, but eventually, I was able to think about Mom without crying or becoming depressed.

"So, uh…" I clear my throat. "We didn't exactly talk about what went down with Miss Colorado aside from you saying it was over."

His head jerks back and he tips it to the side to assess me more fully. Not wanting to hold his gaze so that I can get out what I need to, I go back to my makeup, grab my eyebrow pencil, and get to work filling them in.

"You called her Miss Colorado?"

"Mostly." I don't feel it prudent to share the other nicknames Evie and I had for her.

"Why?"

I frown at him through the mirror as he watches me do my thing. "Honey, she was picture-perfect, from her exquisitely styled platinum-blond hair to her expertly made-up face, super svelte body, and expensive threads."

He chuckles deep, and I feel instant relief that he doesn't think I was making fun of him. Truly I wasn't. She seemed perfect, even if she had a plastic fake vibe about her and obviously was a lying, scheming, manipulative bitch.

"Well, I wouldn't carry on with someone who didn't stir my interest, but when it came to Brittney, she caught me at a weird time. Mom and Dad had been riding my tail about getting married and having babies so that I could continue the legacy. This was right after I'd ended it with a woman I had been seeing exclusively for a year but stopped seeing because she wasn't *the one*." His shoulders drop, and I can tell what he's about to say next is hard for him.

"It happened to be our old anniversary, and I was just done. Brittney swooped in and, the next day, made her play for me, and I scraped her off. As you know, she came back a few weeks later, spouting the pregnancy lie. To be honest, babe, at that point, I was so desperate to have something of my very own, something that was mine, I just snapped."

"Explain?" I frown and lean against the sink and focus on him.

He runs his hand through his hair. "She was there at the right time with the right scenario. Figured our families liked one another. She wasn't hard on the eyes. Sure, she was spoiled and a bit annoying, but I figured a baby would mellow that out, and if that didn't, I would. At least my child would be raised in a good family knowing that he or she was loved. Stupid…"

He shakes his head, and I toss the eyebrow pencil into my makeup bag and take the couple steps in order to cage him against the wall. I put my hands on his waist and press my body to his.

"That is not stupid, Cam. That is beautiful. She used you. Took advantage of you at a moment when you were more vulnerable than usual. There's nothing wrong with wanting a family and wanting to give a child the best of everything, including two parents in the same household. It's commendable."

"You think so?"

I smile and place a kiss on his bare chest right above his heart. It's something I used to do all the time, and the memory of how it feels to have my lips against his skin has never left me in all these years. Having it in real life is magical. I sigh and run my hands up and down his sides soothingly. "Perhaps it's a bit old-fashioned but no less honorable. There's still one thing I'm wondering, even though it makes me seem a bit… bitchy." I run my hand down his chest over his heart.

"What?"

"Why did you stay with her even after she said she lost the baby?"

He purses his lips and clenches his jaw. For a few moments I just stand close, my hand on his kind heart waiting.

Eventually he sighs. "At the time, she was going on and on, crying so hard she started hyperventilating. Me, I felt like I'd been run over by a car. For three months I thought I was going to be a father. I had a purpose beyond running the family business. When that purpose was obliterated, the loss was intense. And with Brittney so convincingly sharing that loss, I finally felt close to her. We had something heavy, personal, and emotional tying us together. The loss of our baby."

I nodded and patted his chest over his heart. "I can see that."

Cam shrugs. "I wanted to do the right thing. Not only was I dealing with that loss, but I was dealing with a woman who wanted to be mine and wanted to build a family with me. At least I thought she did. You know that's something I've always wanted and I'm not getting any younger—"

"Shhh." I kiss him again over that wonderful heart and rest my head against his chest, listening to it beat. "I get it. You're an incredibly honorable man, Camden Bryant."

He wraps his arms around me and rests his hands clasped at the small of my back above my bum.

"What did you tell her after what you found out on Sunday?" I ask. "Oh, and I need to apologize. I really wanted to tell you what we found out in private, then everything just fell apart at the seams."

He rubs his hands up and down my back, this time him comforting me. "It's all right. My brothers and I don't have any secrets from one another. We learned to share and get advice as shit comes up so we're better able to deal."

I nod, wondering what his brothers did when I left him ten years ago. Rallied around him and told him how much I wasn't worth it probably. If the situation had been reversed, I'm certain that Evie would have done the same for me.

"What did you decide?"

He takes a deep breath. "Mom and Dad are beside themselves. They don't like the idea that I was manipulated into putting my ring on her finger or lying about a future grandchild in order to do it. From what I understand, they're meeting with her parents at the country club today to discuss the situation. I tried to get them to let it be, but they just can't. And at this point, I'm not going to protect her from her own parents. She could use a little tough love and some growing up."

"That's for sure." I smile. "Are you okay with it all?"

He shrugs. "Yeah, for the most part I am. Then again, being with you has made it a lot easier to be at peace with it."

"Oh. My. Goodness." I'm certain my eyes widen to the size of basketballs.

"What?" he says, his lips tight.

I slump against his form. "This sucks."

"What sucks?" he urges, his tone turning a bit harsh.

I press my head to the center of his chest, and he cups the back of my neck. "What sucks, baby?"

A little squawk slips past my lips as I pout and look up at him, resting my chin between his pecs. "I'm your rebound girl."

At my announcement, he wraps his arms tight around me, tips his head up to the ceiling and lets out a raucous bout of laughter. It bounces deep in his chest and runs through his entire body, shaking me along with it.

I playfully smack his chest. "Honey, I'm serious."

He chuckles, and his eyes are sparkling. "I know. That's even funnier."

"How do you figure?" I purse my lips.

"Suda Kaye, you have never, nor could you ever be, a rebound anything. You are my first choice. Believe that down to your pretty little toes."

I narrow my gaze and let his compliment take a few tumbles through my mind.

"And besides, if anything, every woman that has ever come after you is the rebound girl. You...you're right back where you're meant to be. In my arms. In the middle."

I smile wide. "In the middle, baby."

"Exactly. To end this completely, I didn't have any feelings toward Brittney that I haven't already worked through in a single day. And I mean that. We were going to raise a baby together. When she said she lost it, I suffered more dealing with that than anything else. To find out that it was never to be in the first place made me angry, embarrassed, and downright ready to move the fuck on."

A slither of unease slides up my spine. "Yeah, but she was your cookie. You must have felt something."

"She made up her own nickname and told me that's what she liked to be called. It was odd at first, but I didn't give a fuck. She was a decent person at first, and she was carrying my baby—I'd call her whatever she wanted. Then it became what I always called her. And let's not forget, she was pretty, doted on me, and looked good as someone who wanted part of a legacy family."

I lean back and sigh. "Yeah, I guess that's true. She's definitely perfect outside of her lying, cheating, and manipulation."

Cam chuckles and spins me around to face the vanity. "Finish doing your thing. We need to check on the job. We're getting close to the opening. Only a couple more weeks and Gypsy Soul goes live. Plus, I've got to get home, get a change of clothes, check in at work, plan a dinner out with my girl, and you've got a contractor to let down."

He walks out of the room, I'm assuming to put on his wrinkled suit. All of what he just said hits me. "Your girl?"

"Yes, sweets, my girl."

"I didn't agree to that," I fire off and add blush to my cheeks.

"You'll get used to it," he hollers from the other room.

"And I don't need to talk to Kyson," I blurt even though it's a complete, big, fat fib.

That brings Cam's face back into view in the mirror. "Don't even think about messing with me, sweets. You need to tell that contractor to stand down or I will." His words coupled with his gaze brook no argument.

The concept of him talking to Kyson brings up a vision of two hot gladiators, one light, one dark, dueling it out for the fair maiden. Me being the maiden, dressed up in an awesome velvet corseted gown, my boobs pressed up high, flowers in a ring around my head. Then the image of Cam striking Kyson with a giant shiny sword to the chest, blood spraying everywhere, obliterates that fantastical mini movie.

At the very least, it could go to blows and Kyson seems like the type that would instigate some physical bravado. And Cam? Well, he has three brothers. He is no stranger to taking or giving a punch.

"Okay, I'll talk to him," I offer, not wanting to see two

men I care about take shots at one another—physical or verbal. All three of us need to work together first and foremost.

See, this is why I shouldn't have ever kissed Kyson in the first place. Evie warned me not to mix business with pleasure, and she was right. Then again, I just spent the morning intimately intertwined in a variety of scrumptious sexual situations with Camden, who is also helping fund my business.

"Today," he insists.

I smirk, loving that he's being overprotective and blatantly jealous. But I'm also not enjoying the fact that I'm going to have to have a conversation with Kyson I don't really want to have. Not because I want to go there with him, but because it's awkward, knowing that he put himself out there for me and I didn't choose him. Technically, I chose Cam, even after I told him that Cam and I were just friends.

It's all so very confounding.

Cam looks me over from head to toe. I'm wearing a pair of bootcut jeans, a dark purple bra, and nothing else.

"You about ready?" he asks.

My grin is tinged with sass, and I place a hand on my hip. His lips twitch with mirth at my move.

"Yeah, I'm going to go down there just like this."

He loops his arm around my shoulder and nudges me all the way to my wardrobe. "Put a shirt on and stop giving me shit."

"But you're so easy!"

"Hmm. That's not what you were saying in the shower. I believe it went something like, 'Harder, Cam, harder.'"

I grip a cute, long-sleeved, V-neck tee and allow my mouth to drop open. "You are so bad!"

He chuckles. "Again, that's not what you were saying—"

This time I bum-rush him and cover his mouth. "Shush.

I'm getting dressed. As a matter of fact, why don't you just be on your way and pick me up for dinner as you mentioned."

He shakes his head. "Suda Kaye, if you think I'm walking down there without you on my arm, making it very clear who was up here with you all night and all morning, you'd be wrong."

I slip the shirt over my head and grab my kick-butt wide brown leather belt with the awesome turquoise stone surrounded by silver at the buckle and run it through the loops before clasping it. Within seconds I've put on a pair of suede booties that match the belt perfectly.

"Fine! I'm ready. Let's go shove your win in Kyson's face."

Cam hooks me around the waist and dips his face for a quick, heartfelt kiss. I've got my eyes closed when he runs his bearded jaw along my chin and toward my ear where he kisses me again and says, "I'm glad you see it my way."

Before the sass can come back out, he kisses me again, grabs my hand, and we're heading down the stairs to my shop.

14

Cam is overtly obvious about holding my hand all the way downstairs and through the shop until we get to where Kyson and Lincoln are putting up the shelving units. I glance around the space, surprised once more that all of this is mine.

From the incredible window unit to the different unique displays, the amazing bar-style cashier section, to all the little nooks and crannies we've put into making Gypsy Soul unique. In a couple days, we'll be painting the entire room a deep eggplant that beautifully pairs with the soft gray fabric draping we decided to run across the open ceiling. I'd thought about leaving the warehouse-like exposed look, but it just didn't fit the cozy, eclectic sensuality I was going for.

Cam clears his throat. "Kyson."

Lincoln turns around first, looking Camden up and down, his gaze flitting from Camden to our intertwined fingers and finally to me with a sour expression. "Hey, Turbo. Finally let her out of bed, I see. Surprised she can still walk in her slutty shoes after the drilling you gave her." His tone is one of disgust and filled with rage.

I can't hold back the shocked gasp that leaves my throat or the unease that ripples through me. Cam, however, takes a step forward and an angry electric intensity fills the air. It flows from Cam toward Lincoln, who's clearly in more of a mood this morning than he normally is.

Lincoln squares his shoulders, ready to take whatever Cam wants to dole out, but Kyson extends an arm out across his brother's chest, keeping him in his place. "I've got this. Not your fight, and what you said was inappropriate, especially to Suda Kaye. Apologize." His tone is serious and uncompromising.

Properly chastised, Lincoln moves his focus to me. "Sorry, Suda Kaye. That was crass. But the next time you want to hang out with my brother like you did last night, falling all over his words with flirty winks and casual touches…how about you just don't."

I step back away from the men as though I've been physically slapped.

"Bro, un-fucking-cool. Suda Kaye doesn't owe me shit. Definitely not an explanation or an apology if that's what you're gearing up for," Kyson snaps.

Lincoln shakes his head and turns his dark gaze my way, his lips pulled back much like a rottweiler does when it's about to strike an intruder. "Women like you, all the same. Always out to hurt the good guy. Trading up for a bigger payout."

My mouth drops open and tears fill my eyes as my throat goes completely dry.

Before I can say anything, Cam pushes past Kyson and steps face-to-face with Lincoln. "You are out of line. You work for Suda Kaye; have some respect." His voice brooks no argument. Cam scowls and glances briefly at Kyson. "You, too. It would be best if you remember your place."

Lincoln scoffs but doesn't respond.

"You're right. I'll take care of this. He doesn't understand."

Kyson places a hand on Cam's shoulder, which speaks more of solidarity than retribution even though it's Kyson's brother that Cam is facing off with.

"I want him gone. Now," Camden grates through his teeth. "A man shouldn't ever talk to a woman like that, and you most certainly don't talk to *my* woman like that, nor your employer. Are we clear?" Cam's anger is white-hot, sizzling around his form in energetic waves of heat.

"Whatever, man," Lincoln sneers.

"Not helping, bro," Kyson laments.

Cam's jaw firms and his hands at his side curl into fists. "I'm serious. I don't want to see you here again. Get your shit and get out. If we have to, we'll hire another crew."

I enter into the huddle and place my hand on Camden's arm and give it a reassuring squeeze. "Cam, it's okay. Seriously, I'm fine. A total misunderstanding..." I attempt but Lincoln huffs and tosses his tools on top of his box.

He lifts his chin and smirks. "Like I said, whatever, man." He bends down, grabs his toolbox, slaps a baseball cap over his hair, and walks toward the door. As he holds open the door to leave, he nails me with a parting shot. "She's all yours. Good luck with that."

I gasp at his words and lower my head, my skin feeling hot and flushed.

"Don't let the door hit you in the ass!" Camden hollers before placing his hands on his waist. His jaw is tight, his lips are a snarling angry white twist of flesh when he faces Kyson. "Give me one good reason not to fire your ass right now," Cam demands.

Kyson takes a deep breath and lets it out in a long stream of air. "I can't give you a good reason. What he said was so far outta line, it demolished it. The only thing I can say is that my brother is protective of me. I…uh…was severely fucked over by a woman. One we all thought was good, but that's not the point." He runs a hand over the back of his neck and looks down at his work boots. "Apparently, Lincoln got the wrong idea about Suda Kaye and me while working on this project and seeing us interact, not to mention hanging out last night. Then we…uh…heard some of the festivities, then see you both happily bouncing down the stairs, and Lincoln mixes up what me and Suda Kaye have. Which is not much—"

"Nothing now," Camden scoffs.

Kyson licks his lips and looks over at me. "I wouldn't call it nothing, but I get that the two of you breached whatever divide was between you. Straight up, I never offered anything serious. Not that I didn't hit on her. Brown eyes, you understood the score, right?"

Finally, I get to talk. "Yes! Oh, my word, a thousand yeses. We're birds of a feather. No strings. All about friendship and pleasure—"

"You *were* about that. Now you're not." Camden's voice is a finely sharpened blade, cutting through all three of us.

I swallow down the nerves and nod. "Yeah. Cam and I are working through something right now," I attempt to explain, not knowing how to begin, but I'm happily interrupted when Kyson waves his hands up in front of him.

"Say no more. It's all good. I'm happy for you guys. Finding one another. Working toward something you both want. I get it. I just don't want that for myself. Still, what my brother said was beyond the pale. Totally uncalled for and I will be going over it with him. In great detail. I have no problem getting in another guy or two to work here. I'm just sorry for what he said. If you're willing to put this aside, I'd like to finish the job."

His blue eyes are soft, his features filled with frustration and a hint of sadness. He's feeling something about what his brother is going through at the same time wanting to make it right between us.

"As long as he doesn't come back," Cam says, "and you understand your 'brown eyes' is actually *my* 'brown eyes,' we'll be just fine."

Kyson grins and holds out his hand. Cam purses his lips and stares the man down, but Kyson doesn't give up. Definitely a man of strong integrity and grit.

Eventually, even Cam can't blow off a man trying to do right and make amends. He shakes his hand and Kyson keeps grinning but looks at me.

I'm floored when he says, "Your man is a suit-wearing hard-ass. I like this for you."

I look heavenward and declare to God and my mother, "Seriously...men are crazy."

Both Kyson and Camden share a laugh.

"I'm going to go back to work and make some calls about getting more help. Again, really sorry for the outburst. Nothing like that will happen again," Kyson promises.

"I'll take your word on that. Thank you." Camden holds out his hand to me. "Walk me to my car?"

"Sure." I take his hand and follow him outside.

Once there, he presses me up against his shiny black Range Rover and wraps his arms around me. He places his forehead against mine. "You okay?"

I lift my head and chuckle lightly. "Me? You were the one losing your mind in there."

He frowns and rubs his nose along mine. "I will not tolerate any man disrespecting you, Suda Kaye. Not ever. He went too far."

"You do realize that I can take care of myself. Have been doing so for over ten years. Once the shock and burn of what he said wore off I would have nailed him to the wall myself." I hook a thumb toward the scene of our drama. "Besides, that back there was nothing. I've experienced much worse."

Cam lets out a long breath that tickles the skin of my face. "But now you don't have to. You've got me at your back."

A flurry of warmth fills my chest, and I wrap my arms tighter around him, plunge my hands into his hair, and bring his mouth to mine. I kiss him hard, tasting a hint of coffee and mint, and my favorite flavor… Camden.

He dips his tongue inside, chasing mine, then sucks on my bottom lip. For a long time, we kiss, me pressed between him and his car, letting it all hang out in the Colorado sunshine. I don't care who sees it, and since we're out on Main Street during a busy time of day, pretty much everyone out right now is seeing this.

Once we both have gotten our fill for now, I pull back and stare into his mesmerizing eyes. "This is going to be weird and hard for me. I haven't had a boyfriend since you. I'm not really sure how to be with a guy officially."

He frowns. "How the hell is that even possible?"

I shrug. "What I said earlier was honest. Honey, after you, I never committed to anyone for any length of time. If I had a man in my life it was for a time, a season maybe. Then the desire to leave would start deep in my gut. I'd feel the twisting like a blade, and my feet would itch. The only answer was to move on. Start the next adventure."

Cam cups my cheek. "Sweets, you're gonna have to fight that feeling if it comes up again." His expression turns to stone, but his eyes are still soft and hopeful.

He wants to trust me.

I want to be worthy of that trust.

Shaking my head, I let out a sigh. "It's weird, I don't really understand why, but I've been here months and that feeling hasn't resurfaced. Not once. Usually, I'd get warnings. Start to feel unsettled or lost wherever I was. I'd pray about it, talk to Mom about it, and then I'd open her book and point to a page. Then—poof—I'd be on the road, a plane, or a boat, and off to my next destination."

"Her book?" Cam tightens his hold on me.

Crap. That is not something I meant to share.

I try to change the subject. "Doesn't matter."

"What book, Suda Kaye?" Cam presses, but I continue to shake my head.

"Another time."

"That's three things we're avoiding talking about," he warns.

I narrow my gaze and scrunch up my nose in uncertainty.

Cam runs the bridge of his nose along mine. "Sweets, the first being why you left the way you did all those years ago and for how long. The second being you telling me you loved me before falling asleep last night."

"Drunk! Hello. I think you are forgetting that little tidbit," I insist, desperate to get him past that slipup.

He ignores my squabble. "The third thing is this mysterious book. I don't like secrets, and I definitely don't want a storm cloud hovering over us when I haven't brought an umbrella. You feel me?"

I nod quickly, fear and anxiety pushing me to move away from this line of discussion and step into more pleasant territory.

It's not the right time.

It may never be.

Cam doesn't say a word, but his gaze is all over my face, piercing right through me, trying to dig for answers I'm not ready to give him. A melancholy comes over him, and he firms his jaw and nods. "Okay, another time. For now, only the good."

This makes me smile huge, and that melancholy I saw slip over Cam's features disappears at the sight of me happy.

"Dinner tonight. Taking you to Twenty-One Steak."

"Fancy?"

He grins. "A sexy dress would not go unappreciated. Now kiss me again before I go home to change and head to the office."

I pull him close and lay one on him. Again, it turns into a mini make-out session.

When he pulls away, he sucks in a harsh breath. "Damn. Missed this in my life, baby."

"Missed what, honey?"

"That feeling of never wanting to leave my girl. Having the fire inside me that always wants her in my arms, heart pressed to mine. Never had that before you. Never had it after. Pleased I've got it back."

This time, I'm incapable of holding back the tears, so I let them fall down my cheeks. He wipes them away with his thumbs, kisses me softly, and then steps away.

"Go to work," he says grouchily as though it's my fault he has to leave when I would have been happy never leaving my little apartment...or the bed for that matter.

"Okay, honey."

"Stay, Suda Kaye," he says softly and walks around to the driver's side door of his shiny boxy Ranger Rover.

I frown as his words penetrate my consciousness. "What do you mean?"

He smiles, one arm resting over the top of his SUV, the other holding the door open. His golden-blond waves are blowing in the breeze, giving his handsome face a much softer, less rugged, and more *GQ* appeal. The sun is shining, and he squints as he gifts me the sexiest grin.

"Just stay," he repeats.

"Stay." I shake my head and smile at him.

"Yeah, sweets, just stay...stay forever." He taps the top of his car.

Without further comment, he gets into his car, shuts the door, starts the engine, and is off to his home to change and then go to work.

I cross my fingers and watch as his car disappears into traffic and down the street. I send up a silent prayer to my mother, to God, to whoever will listen that I'm capable of granting that wish.

Just stay.

"You're back together?" Evie screeches through my cell phone.

I pull the phone back to save my eardrum and set it on the wooden surface on speaker mode. I pick up the leather punch and center the tool over the wide band of camel-colored leather and make the first of many circular cuts in the hide. This belt, along with the fifteen others in different colored leather I've already attacked, is going to be badass and perfect for most sizes. Since I'm stamping the entire belt with the holes, then burning the leather with whatever design suits my fancy, the customer can pick from many of the cool belt buckles to attach. Technically, they are mix-and-match, so if they want to go whole hog and buy two, three, or more belt buckles, they are completely interchangeable.

"I'm not exactly sure how to best answer that," I say. "Yes, seems too simple. I mean, two nights ago, he had a fiancée, albeit one that used and abused his trust, and someone he was nowhere near in love with, but then again, I've been gone ten years."

"And…" Evie urges me to continue, but it's hard. I'm still working it out in my own mind.

I sigh deeply and set aside the leather tool and run my hand through my hair. "It's scary, Evie. I don't want to mess this up, but I didn't think I would last time, either."

"Mom's not here to mess it up this time," she says, her tone filled with malice.

"Evie…" I gasp. "Mom is not the reason I broke it off with Cam."

She snorts and laughs in a manner that I know is fake and very telling about how she feels about that time years ago. "Whatever you say."

"That's the second time I've heard that today, and you know what? I don't need to hear it from you. Mom's letter may have been the catalyst all those years ago, but it wouldn't have mattered if that need to go wasn't already living inside me. So now, what the heck do I do with it? That thing, that feeling, is always going to be there. I just, I don't know what to do. Ev, I can't hurt him again."

Evie's tone changes immediately to the supportive sister I know. "*Huutsuu*, you won't. You're not eighteen anymore."

"What does that have to do with anything?"

"Kaye, you have different priorities now. You're older, more mature. Look at all you've done in the short months you've been here. You're two weeks away from opening your own boutique. That's an achievement you need to be proud of as well as realize that committing to the business means you're settling. You're making a place you can call your own. A home. Finally."

I let her words sink deep into that place inside where my uncertainty lives. "Do you think it will be enough?"

She takes a full breath, and I wait, my heart pounding, to hear her thoughts.

"Only you can be the judge of that, sissy, but I think having Gypsy Soul, me, *Toko*, and now Camden back in your life…" She pauses for a long moment. "I have to believe it will be enough, otherwise we'll all be lost."

We'll all be lost.

Even me.

She didn't say it but that's what she meant.

"You know you're the smartest woman I've ever known, right?" I say.

"Uh, yeah?" Her haughty laughter fills my heart with the lightness I need right now. "So, what's the next step in the Camden and Suda Kaye part deux?"

"You mean besides boinking the hell out of him?"

Evie groans and singsongs, "La, la, la, la, laaaaaa."

"Like you don't want to know if we had sex last night."

Another pause…and…

Three.

Two.

One.

"Okay, fine. I wanna know. Did you two do it last night?"

"No," I state flatly, which technically, isn't a lie. We didn't have sex *last night*.

"You didn't sleep together? His car was still there when Kyson dropped me off at the bar and I drove right over to chat with you but saw his Range Rover and didn't want to intrude."

"I didn't say we didn't sleep together."

She whines, clearly annoyed, and I laugh out loud. I love messing with her.

"We slept, as in only spent time sleeping next to one another last night."

"Oh." She sounds downright bummed. "That's all you've got?"

"What more were you expecting?"

In a rushed breath, she says, "I don't know. Something else, like wild monkey sex that had you screaming the walls down in ecstasy."

Hearing my straitlaced sister use the term *wild monkey sex* and *screaming the walls down* is basically almost as good as someone handing me a perfectly made chocolate cupcake fresh from the oven, piled high with ganache.

"No, we did that this morning. Actually, so loud that Mr. Fix It and his grumpy brother heard it."

"Good God…"

"After all of that, when we went downstairs, Lincoln basically referred to me as a hoochie who was taking advantage of his brother."

"He said what?"

"This, of course, did not go well with Cam who lost his mind and made him apologize."

"No way!"

"Mmm-hmm, then Camden fired Lincoln and threatened to fire Kyson, too."

"Holy crap!"

"Right? Kyson apologized profusely. They worked it out and now Cam is taking me to Twenty-One Steaks for dinner but he made it clear before he left for work that he wants me to stay forever."

"Whoa, whoa, whoa, back up. First of all, are you okay after what Lincoln said?"

I shrugged even though my sis couldn't see it and grabbed the leather tool, suddenly wanting to punch some more holes into something. "Yeah, it is what it is. People are going to judge me regardless of what I say or do. It's a fact of life. I learned that a long time ago. And besides, Cam handled it."

"Yes, it sounds like he very much handled it. Exactly like a man who's in love with his woman and won't stand for her being treated poorly," Evie says a bit dreamily.

"Don't go there, Ev. We've had sex, technically, three times. He's thrown down in a manner between me and my contractor and my contractor's brother. He's taking me to dinner. We have a history. I'm trying to focus on the good and live in the moment. You with me?"

"Live in the moment. Got it. Totally with you." She reminisces on a breath of whimsy, "You know, Mom used to say that. 'Live in the moment, my darlings, you never know when it will be your last.'"

I smile, remembering a time when Mom said that to us. "Yeah, she always knew what to say and when to say it."

"Yeah. Well, I'm looking forward to hearing more about this. Call me tomorrow after your date?"

"Definitely." I change the subject. "Now how's *Toko*?"

"You'd know if you'd call him yourself, which he has decided will be a precursor to another visit, but I've talked him into coming to the grand opening."

"No!" I gasp, not believing my ears. "He's going to step off the rez?"

Evie chuckles. "Yep. He says he even has someone to drive him up and take him home. He's going to stay with me, but he says he's very much looking forward to seeing his bird take flight in a new business venture. Something that lets her fly but doesn't hold her down."

Lets me fly but doesn't hold me down. So *Toko*. My grandfather is wisdom personified.

"Again, you'd know all of this if you had called him," Ev says. "Can you do that?"

"Yeah, I need to get in the habit. And Dad? What's he up to?"

When we were young girls, my stepfather was gone more than he was around. The military had him on what seemed like endless deployment. Though when he was home, it was the best because Mom would *always* be home during those leaves. Two or three times a year, we'd have the perfect family life. He'd get deployed and shortly thereafter Evie and I would be dropped off at the rez with *Toko* while she fled on one of her adventures. If I was being honest, until the cancer kept her home when we were in high school, we spent more time with our grandfather than either of our parents.

Evie clears her throat and groans softly. "I don't know. It's kind of freaking me out. He hasn't returned my last two emails. I know he was leaving Poland to lead some stealthy undercover branch somewhere in the Middle East, but he hasn't reached out."

"How long has it been?" I think back to the last email I got from Dad. For me, it's been months. We usually touch base on birthdays, mine, his, Mom's for sure, the anniversary of her death, and a couple random ones in between. I haven't actually spoken to my stepfather in the better part of a year. Sadness sweeps over me, realizing how selfish and despondent both of us have been.

"Couple weeks."

"Oh, honey, that's not much time at all. If he's deep in,

he may not respond for a month. Give it a little more time. Yeah?" I urge, not wanting her to worry about our military dad. He's always been able to take care of himself.

"Yeah. Okay. I'm off to work. Call me tomorrow morning?"

"Miss me?" I say softly.

"Miss me more!"

"Always, sissy. Always. Love you."

"Love you back."

15

"Suda Kaye, you are a vision." Cam's voice is a deep, appreciative rumble as he takes his fill, looking me up and down.

I grin and hold the door open with a hand on my hip. "This dressy enough for you, honey?" I stand, holding the door and curving my body in a way I know best shows off the slip dress.

For our first evening out as a couple, or whatever it is we are, I chose a dramatic look. Lotsa skin, lotsa sex appeal. The dress has the tiniest straps holding up the cowl neckline that gives a tad more than a healthy dose of cleavage. The dress is a dark blood orange ombre satin number that falls to a point on one side and rides high up on the other side in a sexy diagonal swath of shimmery fabric. I've paired it with a raspberry peep-toe wedge that shows off my long legs. Ensuring maximum appeal, I've let my hair fall in big waves, painted my toes and fingers with a matching dark burgundy, and shined up my skin with a body scrub and complementing lotion so that every bit of me is sparkly in a subtle and classy way. I add some flare for my funky side with a big oval gold ring on my first finger and a pair of gold chandelier earrings.

Camden stares for a full minute, his hands fisted at his sides. His longish hair is pulled back into a sleek small bun at the base of his neck. His handsome form is so becoming in a pristine dark navy suit that I want to unwrap him like a present.

Apparently, Cam has the same idea because, before I can string a few intelligent words together, he's pushing me into my home and slamming the door.

"Honey, what in the world?" I gasp when he loops his arms around me and lifts me from under my bum so that I have to wrap my arms around his shoulders. He carries me standing straight up until he reaches my bed. Once there, he lets my body slide down his body delectably.

His voice is a wicked growl tinged with unquenched lust. "Turn around."

I lick my lips. "Cam, we have a reservation," I remind him.

"Turn around. Now." He uses his caveman *you woman, me man* tone that shouldn't make me hot but does on so many levels.

"Oh boy." My skin starts to tingle and my heart pounds out an erratic beat. Doing as he says, I spin around on my platforms. The moment I face the foot of my bed, his hands are trailing up the backs of my legs.

"Bend over, Suda Kaye. Show me what's hiding under that slip of a dress."

I can barely pull in a breath as I tip forward at the waist and rest my hands on the edge of my mattress. He smooths the silky fabric over my now heated skin until it's bunched up around my waist.

"Tsk, tsk, tsk, my woman is being a bad girl." Cam grips one hip tight, digging his fingers into the soft skin there while the other hand roams over my bare ass.

When he dips his hand between my legs and finds me wet and waiting, I squirm in my heels. "Hon…eeeyy."

"Did you think I wouldn't notice, sweets? That I'd get

within a ten-foot radius of you and not be able to tell that my girl is wearing absolutely nothing underneath this slip of fabric?" He pinches my ass and the pain smarts, making me jerk forward, but his hand at my hip is unrelenting, not letting me move even an inch.

He tsks again. "Now, if I were a different man, I might ask you to change into something else. Since I like my woman to be happy and confident, I'll just have to stake my claim in another way. I'm thinking you wearing that dress with a just-fucked look will do the trick. What do you say? Hmmm, Suda Kaye?" He plunges two fingers deep within my heat.

"Oh, Cam. Please." I push back against his fingers as he works me over.

"Would you like that, sweets? Would you like me to fuck you good and hard right now so that all night long you can still feel me between your legs long after the entrée is served?" He twists his fingers and scissors them until I'm thrusting my hips against the intrusion.

"God, yes! Cam. Anything, baby, just hurry."

Shortly, I feel his fingers slide out of me and can hear the sound of his belt buckle tinkling and a zipper going down. Every second is like a full hour of anticipation skittering through my system. I circle my hips in the cool air as he prepares himself to take me. It's so hot knowing he's going to plow into me at any moment, I can barely keep my arms straight without trembling as I teeter in the position he wants me.

Within moments, his hands trail up and down my back, and I swoon at his heat when he plasters himself against me, creating incredible warmth that eases down my legs and over my back. Cam leans over me, running his hands up my arms, shifting my hair to one side so his lips can trail down my neck, over my bunched-up dress and down my spine.

"Gonna take you hard. Brace, baby," he warns two seconds before he notches the wide head at my entrance and tunnels inside.

Instinctually I go up on my toes to take as much of his driving length as possible. He grips one of my hips and one of my shoulders to do exactly as he said he would. Ride. Me. Hard.

Every molecule within me is hyper focused on Camden.

His length pulsing inside.

His body heat wrapping around me protectively, even as he takes me rough.

His scent invading the space with lemongrass and earth notes.

His breath as he pants and brings extreme effort into his task, using his entire body.

Before long, he stretches an arm around my front, slides his hand under the plunging neckline, and wraps his fingers around my breast. He squeezes delicately at first before realizing I need a much firmer touch. He pinches my nipple, elongating and tugging it mercilessly as I buck and rock my hips back into him.

"I want what's mine, Suda Kaye. Give it to me. Now, honey." He growls close to my ear and plants his body over mine, squeezes my breast, pinches my overly sensitive nipple, and pounds his hips even harder.

That's all it takes. His words in my ear, demanding what he wants of me, have me shooting off like a star in the night sky. I tip my head back and cry out as the orgasm ravishes me from the inside out. It starts huge, working its way through my entire body until I'm a bundle of exposed nerves, feeling like I'm on a never-ending pleasure cycle.

While I'm still coming, Cam lets go of my breast, stands fully, and hammers me from behind, stretching out my release into one of the longest I've ever experienced. I can't stop panting and pushing back against his body so hard my earrings are smacking my cheeks and my knuckles have turned completely white.

"Enough, baby!" I roar, clenching my teeth and my sex so tightly Camden's forceful gyrations stop all together, and his entire body slams one last time against me as he turns to stone, groaning out long and deep into the otherwise quiet room.

Once he's spent and his length softens inside of me, he runs his hand up and down my back. He slips out of me and I mewl in protest, never wanting him to leave. Within a second, his body is just barely hovering over mine where he places a line of kisses from my bum up my spine to my neck.

"Relax, sweets. I'm going to get a cloth."

"Okay." I inhale and exhale several times, trying to get my bearings after the wildest bout of sex we've had so far.

While I stand there submissively, hands to the bed, the fact that Camden just pushed me inside, acted like a Neanderthal, fucked me standing, fully clothed, really hits me, and I can't stifle my laughter.

When Cam comes out of the bathroom with a wet warm cloth, I'm in full guffaws.

"What's so funny?" he says sweetly as he wipes the fluid from between my thighs before placing a kiss on my butt cheek, then grabbing my dress and sliding it over my hips to cover me again.

"You." I stand up and fluff my hair before setting my boobs in the dress correctly, so the cowl doesn't show too much of the girls.

He chuffs and takes the cloth back to the bathroom where I can hear him turn the water on. "How is me fucking you funny?" He returns, wiping his hands on a towel.

I smile and move over to him and wrap my arms around his neck. "Baby, you didn't even kiss me first." I giggle like a schoolgirl who's finally gotten the boy she wanted.

He grins and cups my face. "You. That dress. Your curves. Hair flowing everywhere. Sexiest smile on the most beautiful woman I've ever known." He shrugs. "I reacted."

"You reacted?" I look at him with raised eyebrows.

"Yeah," he says, not offering any more.

"You react like that a lot?" I tip my head and focus on his dark green, sated gaze.

"Never with anyone but you, Suda Kaye."

I grin. "Feel free to 'react' any time."

This time, he chuckles deep in his chest, and I feel his laughter through his body. It fills another empty hole with beauty and light.

"If the mood suits and I want to 'react,' knowing you're all in for it is sweet, baby. I'll keep that in mind for future... *reactions.*"

I lean forward and hover my lips just over his. "You do that. Now, will you please kiss me, then feed me?"

"Not a hardship, but watch out—I'm thirsty, baby," he warns only a scant half second before he kisses me hard and deep.

We end up twenty minutes late for our dinner reservation but after Camden has a chat with the manager, we are accommodated within ten minutes of our arrival.

Once we're settled in our seat, we order the charcuterie board containing a variety of local meat, cheeses, nuts, jam, and more. We also both order steaks as our entrées right away so we'll not be interrupted too much by the staff.

I slather a slice of toasted baguette with the green chili

spread, place a piece of meat on the bread, then coat the top with the cherry-date jam before taking a scrumptious bite.

"Mmm, this is delicious."

Cam's gaze is on my mouth as I lick my lips to catch any potential crumbs from the crunchy bread. One of his eyebrows rises. "I've missed this," he remarks cryptically.

I chew and swallow my bite and finish it off with a swish of the fabulous red wine Cam picked out. "What do you miss?"

He picks up his own piece of bread, then places a slice of salami on it followed by a chunk of a nutty cheese and a gherkin pickle. He holds the perfectly layered appetizer aloft as he replies, "Watching you eat. Hell, watching you do just about anything."

"That's a nice thing to say, Cam."

He plops the entire piece in his mouth and chews thoughtfully for a moment while I make my second mini masterpiece of meat and cheese.

"It's true, though. The way you approach things, *anything* is special. Food, clothing, people." His eyes darken to a mossy green. "Sex." He grins and a blush steals across my cheeks.

"You live, Suda Kaye. Every moment, every experience is exciting. You could be taking your clothes to the laundromat and you'd strike up a conversation with a person, find out their entire life's story, and then be invited to their next family barbecue. And you'd likely attend and have a blast."

"Sure, why not?"

He lifts his wine and takes a hearty sip. "Not everyone looks at a new day as an opportunity to be had. Too many wake up on the wrong side of the bed, go to jobs they hate, working for people they despise, and go home to cook food they don't like, in a house they are breaking their back to afford."

"Unfortunately, this is often true," I admit.

"Not you. Not my Suda Kaye."

I love being called his Suda Kaye, but he isn't done laying out what he intends to say. So far, all of it is interesting and extremely insightful. My skin warms as Cam sits back and gives me more honesty.

"Sweets, you rally against the societal norms, and in doing that, you live. Truly live. I think you're phenomenal and your mom would be proud of you. I know I am."

The air around us turns electric, and my heart pounds as his words sink in. "You think all of that about me?"

"Yeah, I do."

"Even after I left."

He extends his hand and interlaces our fingers. "You're here now. We're in the middle, remember? We have to be able to speak about our time apart, about what we had, and move on from it. We're different people, but, honey, the important parts, our morals, how much we enjoy being with one another, that gravitational pull we feel any time we're together, that hasn't changed. At least it hasn't for me..."

"For me, either." The words are a whisper I know he hears, because he smiles huge in reply.

"Good. Then we're on the same page. Now let's start with our time apart. Tell me something you did or experienced. Perhaps something you'd like to show me one day?" He grins and sips his wine while squeezing my fingers.

I tighten my hold on him and stare into his handsome face. "I'd love to take you to Oslo. You've always had an incredible appreciation for the earth and its beauty. There are these mountain roads you can take that lead you up to this quaint little eatery about twenty or thirty minutes outside of the city proper. There, you can look out over the fjords where some of the larger mountains split and water spills down the center. When I first saw it, I had a delicious latte and a scone, and I just sat there and stared out over the cliffside view. I'd love for you to see that."

"Sounds right up my alley. I'm game." He lets go of my hand to pick up another piece of bread, and I realize I wish he hadn't. Being here with him like this, so comfortable, enjoying great food and even better wine, I want to be closer to him, not farther away.

"Your turn," I say. "Tell me something new that I don't know about you."

He rubs his hand over his cropped beard and purses his lips. "Okay. About two or three years back, Porter conned me into doing a bike and beer tasting tour." I'm certain my eyes light up because Cam laughs and shakes his head. "Don't get any ideas just yet."

"Already sounds like fun." I grin but wave my hand as I crunch on a tiny pickle.

"It actually was, but when I agreed to the tour, I didn't know the thing was for five days."

I cover my mouth and start giggling. "That's a lot of biking."

He nods. "More so than that, it was a lot of beer tasting. So basically, we drove down to Fort Collins where the tour begins. We took our own bikes. I actually had to buy one before the trip."

"Oh no! Don't tell me this was an advanced level tour?" I chug back a gulp of jammy goodness and lean forward to hear more.

"Nah, he's not that cruel. It was fine for beginners, but when you haven't ridden a bicycle in years, it wasn't easy on the ass or the nuts. I'll put that out there right now."

Imagining Cam shimmying his tight butt on the seat of a

bike while trying to find a comfortable spot has me laughing so hard I have to cover my mouth with my napkin so I don't embarrass myself or draw the attention of the other patrons.

Cam chuckles. "Yeah, that part sucked."

"What did you do?"

He shrugs. "What else could I do? I got drunk daily to get through it. Started that plan on day two, which means the tour was awesome."

I snicker and wipe my mouth on the napkin. "Is that when Porter decided he wanted to go into the beer business?"

Cam tips his head from side to side with an uncertain expression. "Nah, he'd already been learning how to brew beer under a master brewer for a couple years. The tour was just a good way for him to make new contacts in the Colorado area and taste even more beer. We did three to five tastings and facility tours a day."

"Wow. Sounds like a blast to me. I'd be in." I grab a hunk of dry salami and pop it in my mouth.

"Of course, you would," he grouses playfully.

Before long, our entrées come out and I'm cutting into the most tender filet I've had in a long time.

"Your turn," Cam says before taking a bite of his own steak.

"Hmm, there's always France. I love Paris, and it's definitely a place for lovers."

"Meaning you had a man while you were visiting." His gaze zeroes in on mine, but there is no hint of concern or jealousy there. Just intrigue.

"Um, kinda…" I shove a bite of potato puree into my mouth and look out the window.

His hand lands on mine warmly. "Remember, we both had a past. Eventually, I'm going to have to tell you about Val."

"Val?" This must be the woman before Brittney.

"Continue. It's your turn." He smirks, and I roll my eyes.

For a minute, we eat while I think of a place he'd enjoy. Eventually, it comes to me. "I think I'd take you to Lisbon." I jerkily nod. "Yep."

"Why? What's cool in Lisbon?"

"So many things, but for one, there's this bookstore. It's the oldest bookstore in the world. It's called Livraria Bertrand. The entire outside, like most of the city, is decorated in mosaic square tiles about three inches wide. Inside, it's actually really quite simple. Deep inset bookcases from floor to ceiling, tables with stacked books."

He chews on a bite of his steak and then takes a sip of his wine before speaking. "What about the city itself?"

I finish my own mouthful and continue. "The city itself is quite lovely. The sidewalks are crafted with small stones that are set with gravel. They mostly use black-and-white and create intricate designs throughout the city. You could be walking down the street and all of a sudden you're walking on giant black-stone circles or painstakingly placed smaller stones that have been placed in a complex design that ends up being a woman's face."

"I'd like to see that."

"And we could take a ride in a tuk tuk. It's a small three- or four-seater golf cart type thing. They're usually driven by a guide, and they'll zip you through small busy streets and show you around. It's awesome."

"Sign me up. Wherever you want to go, I'd be happy to go along with you. I would have ten years ago… I would now." His features are soft when he smiles sweetly.

Unfortunately, his statement hits my gut, and it starts twisting and churning. My breath catches in my throat when I scratch out, "What did you say?"

"Sweets, I'd be happy to go anywhere you want to go. Then and now."

Heat suffuses my entire body in a fiery flush. My brow prickles with sweat as a sour taste makes me salivate, the telltale sign that I'm about to be sick. I stand so abruptly my chair topples to the wooden floor with a crash. Cam stands and makes it to my side to pick up the chair.

I rush away from the table like evil dogs are nipping at my heels and head straight to the bathroom. I slam the stall door shut and place my forehead against the cool tile wall and attempt to breathe. Panic slithers up and down my spine setting off gooseflesh in its wake. My vision goes in and out, turning black with small pinpricks of light. I can't hear much of anything as it seems like I'm being pushed underwater. Before long, I am shaking violently.

"Suda Kaye, let me in!" I hear his words as if they are far away though they can't be.

I plaster my body against the wall and breathe as best I can.

"Unlock the door, baby. Just reach over and unlatch it."

I can hear him speak, but I can't move.

"Fuck this, I'm climbing over," he calls out, but his words sound warped and discombobulated to my ears.

After a couple of staggered breaths, my forehead still planted against the tile wall and tears streaming down my face, he's there. His front is plastered against my back, caging me in.

"I'm here, baby, I'm right here. You're okay." One of his strong arms slides around my belly and he holds on. I move one of my hands to his and grip it as if my life depended on it. He moves my hair away from my face and plants his own against my neck so I can feel him invading the darkness that is trying to consume me.

"Suda Kaye, I'm right here. You're safe. Breathe with me, baby. In for four, out for four." He audibly inhales and exhales.

Eventually, I follow his breaths until the shaking subsides and my heart doesn't feel like it's going to pound right out of my chest. He must feel the change because he pulls me from my spot against the wall and turns me in his arms. I burrow against him, placing my arms inside his suit jacket and around to his back. He cups my head and runs his hands down my hair in a soothing gesture. "You're okay. I've got you, sweets. I've got you."

When the scary feeling finally disappears, I feel completely destroyed, emotionally, physically, and everything in between.

"You ready to get out of here?" he asks softly against the crown of my head.

I nod against his chest and wipe at my tearstained cheeks. Camden leads me to the sink where I splash some water on my face and wipe away the running mascara. He's right there with me, handing me a paper towel and curling an arm back around my shoulders. The overwhelming feeling of being right where I'm supposed to be, my cheek to his chest, is staggering, but he's there. Holding me up. Keeping me close.

He leads me out of the women's bathroom, and the manager is there, pacing the hallway. "Thank goodness. Madam, are you okay? Do you need medical attention?"

I don't answer but Cam does. "She's fine. Thank you for your concern," he says before pulling a business card out of his pocket. "Call this number and my assistant will pay for our meal. I apologize for any inconvenience."

"Not a problem. Would you prefer privacy for you and the lady and exit out the back entrance?" He offers his hand toward a door that's not far away. Thank God.

"Greatly appreciated. Thank you." Camden guides me toward the exit.

"Sorry," I mumble, not leaving the warmth or safety of Camden's arms as I try to figure out what the heck just happened to me.

The moment I feel the fresh air, I inhale fully. Camden walks us swiftly to his Rover, stops at the passenger side, takes off his coat, and wraps me in it before helping me into the car and buckling my seat belt.

Once I'm settled, he hurries around to the front and gets in. "You're staying at my place tonight. I want you near me."

I nod without saying a word. I'm not exactly sure what to say, although there's one thing that keeps running through my mind on repeat.

Sweets, I'd be happy to go anywhere you want to go. Then and now.

I feel the tears at the backs of my eyes and lean my head to the side and stare out the window as I allow them to fall.

He'd go anywhere I wanted to go. Which means he wouldn't have held me in Pueblo all those years ago. He wouldn't have clipped my wings with the obligation of his family legacy.

Maybe, had I not acted so rashly, we could have made it work. Somehow. Someway.

A tremor takes over my body as I silently cry a river.

Cam reaches out and tugs my hand. He lifts it to his mouth and kisses the center of my palm, my wrist, and then every one of my fingers. I glance his way, and he takes in my tearstained, blotchy face.

"I'm going to take care of you. We'll work through whatever just happened in there. Together, okay?"

"I'm sorry." I swallow down the emotion about to drown me in a tsunami of guilt and grief. "I'm so, so sorry."

"What are you sorry for, baby? I don't understand." His jaw is tight as he maneuvers through the traffic but still keeps an eye on me.

I close my eyes and let the tears fall.

On a tortured, shaky breath, I let it out. "I'm sorry for leaving. I'm sorry for everything."

16

Cam drives his Rover down a long asphalt road shrouded in trees. The branches of the trees are so wide they meet in the center, creating a curving catacomb. Briefly, I imagine how beautiful driving through this canopy would be on a sunny day. The cropping of mature trees eventually leads to a sprawling one-story, raised ranch home with a giant wrap-around porch.

Once Cam parks, he jumps out and comes to my side of the vehicle. He undoes my seat belt and hooks one arm under both of my bent knees and around my back, hauls me out of the car, and shuts the door with his foot.

"You don't need to carry me. I'm okay. I can walk," I say just slightly above a whisper. My throat is raw, my voice sounding as though it's been through a cheese grater.

"Sweets, you *could* walk, but you're not going to. Just shush and let me take care of you."

I sigh but try for a smile as I wrap my arms around his neck and press my face into the warmth of his skin there.

He shuffles me around, opens a door, and flicks on a dim light. I try to lift my head to look around, but I find that I'm completely drained. From head to toe, I don't have the energy to lift my head, let alone take in the environment and assess his home the way I would normally.

Without any delay, he walks me through a series of rooms until I'm laid on a bed with a comforter that I swear is softer than a cloud. For a moment, he leaves me to sit on the side of the bed. My shoulders are hunched over, and I can't bother with caring. I'm a total mess.

My heart is breaking, grieving for all the lost time we could have had.

My mind is replaying his words like a song stuck on repeat.

My emotions are headed to hell in a handbasket.

And I'm beyond tired.

Cam moves around the room, coming over to me after flicking on a lamp on the side table nearest me. Its glow sheds a soft halo of light across Camden's face. His expression is one of intense worry, and his brow is furrowed deep with what seems to be concern. I hate that my actions put that there.

"I'm always hurting you, aren't I?" I bite down on my bottom lip so hard I worry it will bleed.

Cam's shoulders drop as he pulls something out of a tall dresser about ten feet from where I'm sitting restlessly.

"Suda Kaye, I don't know what's going on or what made you have a panic attack... I just know that, for now, I want you to relax and get some rest. You scared the hell out of me. Now hold up your hands." He walks over to me with a gray T-shirt in his hands.

I hold up my arms and he bends forward, takes hold of the satin at my thighs, and lifts it. I rise up enough so he can remove the dress. Quickly he places my arms in the T-shirt and then lifts it over my head. After he's done, he pulls back the squishy comforter.

I turn to the side and crawl on all fours to the top of the

bed.. He covers me completely before tucking me in and kissing the top of my forehead.

I grab his wrist before he can leave me. "Where are you going?"

He smiles. "Gotta feed my cat and make sure the house is closed down for the night. I won't be long."

"You have a cat?" My mood lightens at the thought that this rugged man of the world, leader of an empire, has a cat. I have imagined him more as a dog person. Then again, a cat is a lot easier to maintain when you're a busy CEO.

"I do." He grins. "When you're feeling better, I'll introduce you. He's pretty social, so you may end up meeting him sooner rather than later."

I smile, and I swear a dark shadow leaves his gaze and his features lighten. He bends at the waist and kisses my lips softly. "Sleep. I'll be in soon."

"Mmm-kay," I answer, snuggling into the cloud of comfort. Before he makes it back, I'm dead asleep.

Sometime in the night I wake to extreme warmth at my back, a heavy arm around my middle, and the sound of an engine running right by my face. Moving my head, I blink open makeup-and-tear-encrusted eyes to find a pair of startling green cat's eyes attached to a pitch-black furry face. The noise is not an engine but Camden's cat, purring loudly. It's nestled its body against my chest with its face lying only a few inches from my own on the pillow.

I lift my hand and run my fingers along the cat's head. "Hello, new friend," I whisper.

The cat presses its head to mine and nuzzles his face along my cheek.

"Aren't you the friendliest fur baby in the world?" I keep petting the cat until the arm around my waist tightens and

I feel Camden's body shift and feel his scruffy beard against my neck and shoulder.

"Hey, Buddy." Cam reaches out his hand and scratches the cat's head and the side of his face.

"What's his name?" I ask while running my hand down the cat's soft body.

"Buddy."

Wait a minute. I shake my head a little, thinking I might have misunderstood in my hazy sleepy brain. "Did you just say your cat's name is Buddy?"

"Yeah." His voice is the deep sexy rumble of a man just woken in the middle of the night.

I can't suppress a bout of laughter. The cat meows in response, probably in irritation because I've disturbed his peaceful petting session.

"You named your cat Buddy?"

"Yeah." He hugs me closer and kisses my cheek.

"Why?"

"He's friendly. Overly so, as can be seen by the fact that you're a stranger, and he crawled right into your arms, laid against your chest, and fell asleep. This also proves my cat has impeccable taste." He chuckles against my back, and I can feel his movements all the way down to my toes.

I press back and turn in his arms so that I'm lying flat. He's still got an arm curved around my belly, but he's now up on his elbow, his head resting in his hand.

"Yeah, I guess it does fit him. He's everyone's buddy."

"Exactly." He shifts his head down and kisses me sweetly.

Before he can get into any real kissing action, he releases me, hooks a pillow, and shoves it under his head. "You ready to talk to me about what happened tonight?"

I groan and cover my eyes with my arm. He grabs for my hand, brings it to his lips, and kisses my fingers. It's something he didn't used to do in the past, which makes it more power-ful that he's done it more than once now. It's as if we're learn-ing one another all over again and discovering new things to appreciate and love about one another.

For a few minutes, we lie in the dark, comfortable in one another's space until, finally, I get up the nerve to share.

"I'm not exactly sure what happened tonight. It's just some-thing sank in my gut and twisted, and I worried I was going to throw up."

"Suda Kaye, what you experienced was not a round of simple nausea, so if you were going to try to play it off like that, I'm not buying it. You had a full-blown panic attack."

I nod and turn to my side so that I can focus on his hand-some face. Even though it's dark in the room, there is enough light from the moon through the windows to cast shadows, leaving it bright enough to see most of his strong features.

"Something spooked you, and I want to know what it was."

I lick my lips and take a breath. "It was something you said. It just hit me, and I don't know, I lost it. I've never had that experience before. Ever. It scared me, too. I thought I was either going to pass out or throw up or both."

He nods and runs his fingers through my hair, lightly at my temple before sliding along the back of my head. "What was the catalyst?"

It's now or never.

Right here, I'm safe. In Camden's bed, there's nothing to get in the way of being honest with him. Nothing but me and my own fears and anxiety. And for some reason, right now, at this age, in this body, having had all the experiences I've had to date, I'm more capable of dealing with the fallout.

"You saying that you would be happy to go anywhere with me then and now," I state simply.

He stops running his fingers through my hair and rests his

hand on the side of my face. "I'm going to need a little bit more to go on, baby."

"Cam, I left to experience the world."

"You left me," he states on a grated timber.

I shake my head and lift up enough to cup his cheeks. "It wasn't you I left. That's why it was so hard, and why I freaked out tonight. I… I…" The words slip away, and suddenly, I'm back to that night ten years ago when I turned eighteen and read the first letter my mother left Evie and me.

Evie handed me the stack of letters our grandfather gave to us when our mother died. We'd kept them in a box in the living room. We were to read the first letter on my eighteenth birthday, which, incidentally, was Evie's twentieth. I sat with my back against my padded headboard, untied the satin string, and reached for the first pink envelope.

In her beautiful penmanship, the front of the first letter said Suda Kaye—Eighteenth Birthday, and that's it. I flipped the letter over and noted it was sealed with the imprint of a pair of lipstick-stained lips.

Sealed with a kiss.

I closed my eyes, slid the envelope open, and pulled out the pink parchment. When I read the salutation, I choked back a sob, but I controlled the emotion, knowing my sister was across the room, sitting on her bed, reading her own words from our mother. I didn't want to make this moment all about me.

Once I got a lock on my sorrow, I held the letter up once more and started to read.

Suda Kaye, my little huutsuu,
I'm off on my last grand adventure. Yes, it's far sooner than I would have liked, but even still, I lived a good life filled with

nothing but beauty. Leaving my girls behind this final time is the hardest thing I'll ever have to do.

In the past, I always knew I was coming home to my beauty queens. My wildflowers. My little bird and my sunshine. You would have grown but so would I. We'd share in both our experiences and spend the next set of weeks, living our lives and talking of the things we missed.

I appreciated every experience.

I lived for every moment.

I loved you every minute of every day.

You and Evie were my greatest achievements. And I hope you understand, huutsuu, that my need for adventure all these years was not because I wasn't happy being your mother. It was because I wanted to be able to give you and your sister more. I tried to be a good mother, and I hope in some small part, I achieved that. More, though, I wanted to be the kind of mother you were proud of. One who had done something worthy in her life.

No, I wasn't the best at the traditional things many of your friends' moms were, but I shared the world. Dancing. Art. Music. My experiences.

This is something I want for you most, Suda Kaye. I want you to travel the world. Experience everything there is to offer that you'll not be able to find in your own backyard.

I know you are in love with Camden. He's a fine young man and will likely be an excellent husband and father to your future children. He will work at his father's company and do well, his feet firmly planted in Colorado soil. Huutsuu, you have to decide…is that what you truly want for your life, right now, in this moment?

Do your feet not feel the earth moving beneath you?

Do your eyes not wish to see the magnificence beyond your home?

Do your fingers not itch to reach for new experiences around every corner?

There is so much out there for you. Don't live your life with regrets. If I've learned anything in my short time, it's to decide what you want and go after it with purpose. If you're not sure what it is you want, chase after something. Experience everything you can until you find what's right for you.

I've left you and your sister an inheritance. It is my dying wish that you use that money to travel the world, my darling. Experience anything and everything while you can. Until you're done. You'll know when to stop. Live like your mama did.

Don't let your feet be still when your wings can offer you flight.

The world is waiting for you.

Fly free.

"Just tell me. I've been waiting ten long years, thinking it was me—us having sex for the first time—that made you leave. You have no idea what that did to me, not only losing the woman I loved, but doing so after the first time we'd consummated our relationship. I thought I'd hurt you. Irreparably."

I widen my gaze and sit up abruptly, pushing my hair out of my face. "No! My goodness no. Cam, you were everything I could have ever dreamed of. You made that night incredible for me. It was by far the best and worst night of my life."

He sits up and pushes with his strong legs, moving his body until his back is against the headboard. His chest is bare, and he settles the blanket over his lap. He runs his fingers through his loose waves and rests the back of his head against the headboard. "Then why, Suda Kaye? You changed both of our lives with that one choice."

I close my eyes and fiddle with my fingers in my lap. "Because I knew if I'd stayed even one more day, I never would have left. You were my everything. All I had in the world besides Evie, my stepdad, and *Toko*. I was consumed with you."

He shakes his head. "That's not answering my question and makes no sense as to why you would have left if that were the case. Tell me," he urges more forcefully.

"Okay. Mother wrote Evie and me letters while she was sick during those last six months. Our grandfather gave them to us when she passed. The first one was supposed to be opened on our birthdays. My eighteenth, Evie's twentieth."

"I'm following, but I'm not sure how this explains anything about us." His voice is rather terse, but at the very least, he's entitled to his anger. Frankly he's handling this conversation a lot better than I would have expected, considering what I did.

I take a deep breath and let it out. "Just bear with me."

He nods.

"When we were given the letters, we were given an inheritance and the remains of her life insurance policy. At the time, it was around a quarter of a million dollars each."

"Jesus, I had no idea."

"I didn't either until *Toko* gave us those letters and the trust information. Mom didn't want us to have to wait to have what she left us, so we got it right away. And she encouraged me to use my inheritance to travel the world. To experience all the things I'd always dreamed of. You have to understand, my entire life my mother filled my mind with all these fantastical places she'd been, the amazing things she'd done, and I was enamored with each and every story. I wanted nothing more than to do exactly what she did, see those things, and experience every one of them for myself."

"Fuck," he sighs and cocks a knee.

Even knowing he's not happy, I continue on. "When I was presented with my mother's dying wish for me to go out and experience the world, I was faced with letting down my mother whom I'd just lost and spent my entire life wanting to emulate, or leave the man I loved who wanted to provide me a different life. A much safer, more settled life here in Pueblo. Not to mention you had a legacy to fulfill, working for your family's empire. I couldn't make you choose. I wouldn't put you in that position."

Cam reaches out in a flash, grabs me around the waist, and pulls me across the bed until I'm straddling his lap and we're face-to-face. "Suda Kaye, I would have gone anywhere, spent any amount of money, given up my entire family legacy if I could have had the option to be with you."

Tears fill my eyes and spill down my cheeks. "And I didn't want you to have to make that choice."

"You should have given it to me. I was devastated when you left. Visited Evie every day, who was also hurting, not only having lost your mom six months before but then losing you shortly after. I wish you would have talked to me. Told me the truth. Let me be a part of your future in the way we'd always dreamed." Tears filled his eyes but didn't fall.

I cupped his cheeks and stared into those beautiful, soulful orbs.

"Christ, we're a pair."

I nod.

"It could have been so different," he says. "We could have found a way to make it work so that you had your wings but didn't lose your roots to the earth. You could have had it all. Maybe we could have worked out a system where we traveled every couple months to a new place on that money while, in between, I worked with my father in the family business."

The tears keep going. "I couldn't have known you would have wanted that," I say. "You never ever talked about traveling. You saw my mom leave time and time again, and you hated it for me and Evie. Told me all the time how selfish it was for her to leave and chase after her dreams."

"Yeah, because teenage girls need their mother around. In the end, it was too late."

I cup Camden's beautiful face. "I had what she could give, and, baby, it was enough."

He shakes his head. "Don't you see? It wasn't or you never would have left the way you did. It was cowardly and changed both of our lives. I didn't get a choice to lose you. I didn't get a choice to even fight for you. Do you understand how messed up that is? You disappeared in the middle of the night after I made love to you the first time. Why did you do that?"

I sob, and my shoulders and chest shake with it. "Because I wanted to experience your love fully at least once. One time so that I could have that memory of us forever, and through all these years, it's the best memory I have."

"Sweets..." His voice is filled to the brim with sadness as he tugs me against his chest, pushing my face into the hollow of his neck and shoulder. He wraps me tightly in his arms. "So tonight, you realized that you could have had me and your adventures, and the truth of that was too much to handle, wasn't it?" he surmises.

I nod against him and the sobbing turns into big, heaving, monumental outbursts of years' worth of sadness and regret.

Camden holds on as I cry. He holds on as I heave. He holds on as I tremble and shake letting it all out. He just holds on.

After a solid twenty or thirty minutes, I finally calm down enough that the tears fill my eyes and slip down my cheeks, but I'm no longer distraught. Right now, we're both quiet and reflective.

"You get a lock on that, sweets?" His voice is so deep it rumbles through my chest.

I nod and take a breath.

"Look at me, baby."

I swallow down the fear and hurt and focus my gaze on his.

"I loved you then. I loved you when you were gone. And I still love you now. The love we have is not something that easily goes away. It may have gone into hiding for a decade, but it's back out now, shining as bright as the sun. And, baby—" he cups my cheeks "—it's not going away again. I understand why you did what you did now, but I still wish with my entire being that you would have confided in me. Giving me the chance to be a part of it all. But we can't go back, we can only move forward. The heart wants what the heart wants and my heart wants you. We'll get past this."

The tears still fall, and he wipes them with his thumbs. "But...but...we could have already been married," I say, "and had kids, and..." The list goes on and on of what we could have already been.

He grips my face and brings my forehead to his. "Suda, you're twenty-eight, not forty-eight. We have time to get married, have all those babies we talked about having, and we have the rest of our lives to do it. We lived ten years apart, experiencing and doing what we both needed to do. If I'm being honest, I very well could have crushed your need to see the world for my own selfish needs to be the man my father wanted me to be. I can't sit here and let you take all the pain of our jagged past. You became the woman your mom wanted you to be. Like I said, she'd be proud of you. Hell, I'm proud of you. Even though I didn't get to be a part of it, I get to now. Besides, we're older, smarter, more mature, and have the money to do whatever the hell we want when we want to do it."

I snort-laugh because he's cracking jokes even though he

should be screaming the house down and making me feel like dirt for what I did when I left him.

"Now that I know why you left, I'm no longer mad."

I jerk my head back. "You're not?"

He shakes his head. "No. I'm sad. I'm sad you didn't talk to me about what you were dealing with when you got those letters from your mother. Had I known, we would have had a very different conversation, and I would have taken care of you through that time. You were eighteen. Your mother told you her dying wish for you was to take off and travel the world the way she did. I can't blame you or be mad at you for doing it. If I was in the same position, I'm not sure what I would have done.

"I'm hurt you didn't feel you could share it all with me. The entire truth. I'm sad that we missed out on ten amazing years together, but who knows what would have happened in those years? Now we're both adults. We have responsibilities. We have family. We have each other. We don't have anything more hanging over our heads. We both know exactly what we want in life."

"When you put it all like that, it seems so simple. To just be able to move on."

"Because it is."

I swallow and wipe at the renewing tears. "I hurt you and I ruined everything."

He places his hand around the back of my neck so I'm forced to focus on his face. "No, baby, you made a choice. And yeah, it hurt at the time. Really bad. I loved you. Told you that. Still do. We can't change anything that came before. We can only focus on what we do with today. Right here. Right now. In this bed. Together we make a decision."

"And what decision is that?"

"That we don't waste any more time. We don't allow any-one or anything to get in the way of us being happy together. That we enjoy the middle and all it has to offer us. We be honest with one another about our needs, desires, and dreams. Then we work toward them as a team."

"You make it sound so easy."

"Being with you is easy. Wanting to spend the rest of my life with you is easy. Loving you is easy. As long as I have you... I'm good."

"And everything that came before is left behind us." My breath shudders out of me as if I've been holding on to it for a year.

He nods. "For the most part, yeah, you've got the right idea. I think we have to talk about it all, but we just make the deci-sion right here and now that it's not going to break us. It's not going to change the easy we have. We're just going to accept it as who we were then and not let it define who we are now."

I blurt out, "I've never loved any man besides you. You've always owned my entire heart and soul. Always, Cam."

He smiles wide, wraps an arm around my form, and slides his other hand down to my bare bottom where he gives it a healthy squeeze. "I'll take that gift of your heart and soul and hand you mine for safekeeping."

He tunnels his fingers in my hair, squeezes my behind, and grinds his hardening length against my center.

"I'll keep it safe this time," I say. "I promise."

His lips hover over mine, and I squirm in his lap, ready to take everything this man is offering and give him every-thing in return.

"I trust you," he says before he covers my mouth with his and seals our promises with a kiss.

17

A week later, and I'm fluttering around my almost-complete boutique. The shelves are up. Displays are ready to be loaded, walls are painted, and running down the length of all the free wall space are boxes filled with product to be displayed.

"Thank you so much, sissy, for taking a couple days off work to help me get this set up." I pass Evie, who's digging through a box of silk kimonos in a wild array of colors and sizes. She adds a dark forest green one with a burst of cherry blossoms crawling up the back and across each arm. Evie hooks it on the black velvet padded hanger and sets it on a circular rack.

"I told you I'd be here to help you out, just not with all the business aspects. Though I will say I'm thrilled Cam is working with you."

I nod and open up a small box of studded leather bracelets designed to appeal to the biker babes who roll through town as they often do in this area. The goal for my shop is to have a bit of something for everyone, including plenty of one-of-a-kind items.

Once I've displayed the bracelets on a circular black velvet display, I open another box and pull out some kick-ass rings

I scored from a designer out of Arizona. She works primarily in silver and gold and natural stone. In the box are twenty different rings with silver, moonstone, labradorite, and more. I even found a wicked-cool artisan who creates geode and crystal bookends that I'm going to display with other unique household things like vases and statuesque art pieces.

"Yeah, he's been amazing, though this week he's bombed at work. Not that he'd be any good at displaying things he considers 'girlie' anyway."

Evie chuckles while adding the last kimono to the rack. "What else goes on this one?"

I point to a box I've already opened. "Those tanks over there. They'll go perfectly with the kimonos. On the first one, I want you to add one over the tank, then wrap one of my specialty belts around it. Maybe the brown one with the turquoise in the center."

"That's a great idea, Kaye. Totally fashion forward but still Colorado chic."

"Thanks! Now have you heard anything from Muscular Milo?"

Evie's back goes ramrod straight, and for a moment, she doesn't move. I can tell by her body language she's unhappy, but I also know my sister. The moment she adjusts her shoulders and lifts her chin, I know she's about to sugarcoat something. At the very least, I can tell whatever she's about to share is something she doesn't like.

"Actually, I ran into him at a restaurant in C-Springs. I was taking a client to lunch and he was…"

"He was…" I rotate my hand in a circular motion to get her to speak.

She swallows and firms her jaw. Not good. "He was out to lunch with his wife," she says with her lips curled into a snarl.

Wife?

"Excuse me? What the—"

Evie holds up a hand to stop me in my tracks so I don't get too far into losing my mind.

"My client and I approached, and Milo looked incredibly uncomfortable."

"Did he introduce you to her? Oh my god! This is awful."

She shakes her head. "No. The petite blonde stood up, all bouncing curly hair and bodacious body, and introduced herself as his wife, Kimberly."

"I can't believe it. How did we not know he was married?"

Evie chuffs and pushes her long bangs out of her eyes and to the side behind her ear. "And the weirdest part, he looked angry that she introduced herself. He sized up my client as though I was on a date, and here he is out to lunch with his wife!"

"Sissy, I'm sorry. That had to be a blow—"

"No, no, no. It's not. I may have had a crush on him for the last bazillion years, but I had no basis for it. He never hit on me. He never so much as gave me the hint that he was interested in me for more than just a friend. And now I know he never will be."

"Umm, I don't think so. He definitely gave me the impression that he was very into you. He even calls you *nizhóní*. Hasn't he always called you that?"

She laughs dryly. "Yeah, he didn't call me that when he was sitting in front of his Heather-Locklear-at-twenty-five look-alike wife."

I wince. "Oooh, he definitely has a type."

Evie spins around, her icy gaze set straight to freezer burn, and places her hands on her hips.

I lift both of my hands in a submissive, calming gesture.

"Sorry, sissy, but you said his wife looks like a young Heather Locklear."

"And…"

Rolling my eyes, I make a face and say, "Is it lost on you that you look almost exactly like Blake Lively?"

She purses her lips. "I've been told that many times, but what does that have to do with Milo and his freaking gorgeous wife?"

"Um, maybe because Heather Locklear could play Blake Lively's mother in a future Lifetime movie?" She stares at me, dumfounded. I groan. "Sissy, the man has a type. Blond, blue-eyed babes."

"Except she was petite and had a body like Jessica Rabbit."

I shrug. "So, what? You're every man's wet dream. Tall, svelte, small breasts but you work them, with legs long enough to wrap around a man's waist twice. And your hair is to die for. Long, perfect, natural waves, thick. You'll never be bald."

"Gee thanks, sissy. Great compliment. You might not have much in the boob department, but you're tall and you won't go bald."

Her interpretation of what I said leaves us both snickering and laughing.

When we become quiet, I walk over to her and put my arm around her shoulders. "I'm really sorry about Milo."

She frowns and nods. "Me, too. Guess it's the end of an era."

"Guess that means it's finally time to get you out on the town trolling for sexy men!" I bump her hip with mine.

"You already have a man, and I doubt he'll be fine with you going out and being my wingwoman."

I make a face. "He'll get over it. Besides, we can go to Porter's brew house. Men love beer. We love beer. And we love men. That also means I can use that as a safe way to be your wingwoman."

She frowns. "I don't know. Not sure I much feel up to it."

"Too late. I've already got the perfect dress picked out for you. And it's smokin' hot." I give her a sly grin and a wink.

Evie shakes her head. "Oh no. No way. I draw the line at you dressing me."

I stop where I stand and hold my arms out wide. "Um, I'm kinda good at that, seeing as I'm opening a freaking boutique. And besides, I have these brand-new slinky silk dresses that just came in. I wore the orange-and-raspberry one to dinner with Cam last week, and it was the impetus to us clearing the air and working through our past."

"Really?"

I nod. "Plus, the second he saw me in the dress he pushed me inside my apartment, lifted me up, set me down in front of my bed, spun me around, and banged me from behind. Fully clothed."

"Jeez Louise…" Evie fans herself. "You need to warn a girl before sharing that kind of thing."

"Hot, right?" I think back to how that moment felt, and my blood starts to heat, and my heart rate rises.

Evie licks her bottom lip and bites down, nodding. "Yeah. What other colors does it come in?"

I grin huge. "That's my *taabe*. The sun on a dark day."

"Love you being home, Kaye," she admits suddenly.

"And I love being home. I don't know, Ev, this feels right. Being here, opening this store, being back with Cam, having you in my world all the time." I inhale fully and let it out. "It's what my heart wants and where I'm meant to be." I use the phrase that Camden said to me that continues to resonate within my entire being.

Evie bites the inside of her cheek and nods. The telltale sign that she's holding something back.

"What?" I prompt. "No secrets now. We promised, remember? We're letting it all hang out."

"What if it was always where you were meant to be, and you never should have left in the first place?"

A shiver of doubt rushes through my system, making me feel cold. I cross my arms over my chest and rub at my upper arms to ward off the chill the feelings spur. "I'll never know that for sure. All I know is that it feels right now."

Before I can move on or change the subject, Evie pushes. "And what if it doesn't feel right a year from now? What then?"

I shake my head. "Evie, we never know what life is going to throw our way. There's no reason to live in fear or worry about something that may or may not happen down the road. It's useless. Looking for things to worry about today is only going to take away the beauty I've got now. Besides, Camden and I have agreed to live in the moment. Enjoy this phase of our lives together."

"Which means you're not planning for the future."

"My future is in my commitment to this store, to choosing to be in your life, to loving Cam and wanting to be with him. I can't tell you what tomorrow will bring, and I'm not going to stress over it. I'm going to do what I can today to make today amazing. That doesn't mean I won't hope tomorrow is badass. I just won't worry that it may not be. Fretting over things that haven't happened yet is a waste of time. I prefer to use that time experiencing today."

She nods and walks over to another box, lifts it, and takes it over to the section she was working on.

"Are you gonna be okay?" I ask. "You know, with this Milo thing?"

Evie smiles softly and it's absolutely beautiful and heart-breaking at the same time. "Of course. It's just disappointing," she whispers.

"I'm here for you."

She gifts me a big smile. "And that I'm thankful for. Now let's blast some tunes and get this store set up!"

"You got it." I grin and head over to the intricate cashier area and maneuver around it to the stereo system. "What do you want to hear?" I call out.

"Just play something funky to keep us motivated."

"Wine would keep us motivated."

She laughs as I smile and think that's the best idea I've had all day. As I'm picking a station, I'm cataloging the contents of my fridge and realize that there's a bottle of champagne we haven't popped. I turn the radio on a soft rock station that's currently playing Sheryl Crow's "Soak Up the Sun" and turn it up loud enough to jam out.

Time for booze and some sister solidarity.

"Jesus, you're energetic…fuck me!" Camden growls down my throat as I slam my hips down harder on his length, stars exploding behind my eyes. I cry out and let the orgasm flow through my body while Camden sinks his teeth into the ball of my shoulder, his own body tightening and letting go inside me.

We're both a sweaty, tangled heap against my headboard, breathing roughly, coming down off the sweetest high.

After a few minutes of sucking on and kissing the expanse of his corded neck and jaw, I get a lock on my body through the booze and sex haze and tip my head back.

Camden's eyes are half-mast, and his body is languid against the headboard. "Getting you drunk more often, sweets. Never had that with you before. Like it. Want it again. Soon."

I grin and dip forward, give him a wet kiss, and nibble on his bottom then his top lip before letting go. "Mmm, that can be arranged."

"Damn, you're a wildcat with a few drinks in you. Love this side to you, baby."

I chuckle and give him a quick peck on the lips. "I'm going to go clean up."

I take care of my lady business, tinkle, and then slip on a pale pink nighty hanging on the hook in the bathroom.

When I saunter back, I find that he's no longer in bed. Scanning the room, I find the fridge door open and the light showcasing his nearly naked body. He put on his dark navy boxer briefs, which means I get to unwrap him a second time.

I make my way over to him, wrap my arms around his middle, and run my fingers up and down his defined abs and hard pecs. I kiss a line from the dip in his back up his spine and across one sexy shoulder where his tattoo wraps. He bites into a strawberry and grabs another handful.

"When did you get your tattoo?" I mumble against his warm skin and trace the design with one finger.

"After I graduated college with my business degree. Spent the entire summer in Hawaii visiting every island. I knew I was going to dedicate my life to the family business and wanted to make sure I had a summer that was all for me. Got it there to represent the change in my life, where I was, where I planned to go, and what I left behind."

I attempt to hold back the tears and win. "I should have been with you." I rest my forehead against his shoulder, wishing for time I'll never get back, even though we've found a happy medium in the middle.

"You were."

I frown and stare up at him, my voice a little tacky with emotion when I ask, "How?"

"You're in the tattoo."

I step back and pull his arm out and run my fingers over the intricate black designs. "Where?"

He smiles and opens his arm. On the bicep mixed into the tribal design is a Native American bird totally different than the Polynesian tribal design but in the same rich black ink. The bird's wings are outstretched, its head turned to the side with designs across its body. The tail feathers end in four blocky points, and each point contains two stacked letters. Read horizontally, they spell out S–U–D–A on top and K–A–Y–E on the bottom.

Tears fill my eyes, and I have no hope of stopping them from falling down as I lean close to his arm and rest my lips over the design. "You've kept me with you."

"Right by my heart. See, when I lift my arm or cross it over my chest, the bird lies directly over my heart. It also can't be seen unless someone is staring at my inner bicep, because this tat, my little bird, is just for me."

"Jesus, Cam." I lift up on my toes, wrap my arms around his shoulders, and kiss him with everything I have. It's a kiss of love lost and love found, a kiss meant to soothe and sate, a kiss of regret and commitment. "I'll never let you go again. I promise."

"I'm going to hold you to that promise, sweets."

Before he can kiss me again, a shrieking noise fills the room. Both of us spin around and look at the empty darkness.

"What the hell is that?" I ask.

"It's the alarm. Someone's tripped it."

"Oh my god! Is someone breaking in?"

"Baby, I don't know. Call the police. I'm going down there." He rushes over to the bed and pulls on the dress slacks he wore to work, the same ones I stripped him of the minute he walked into my apartment where I was drunkenly doing the dishes from the pizza and booze Evie and I had demolished.

"Please don't. We'll call the police and wait for them." I holler over the alarm.

"Takes too long. I'll be okay." He wraps his fingers around my neck and kisses me swiftly.

"Wait!" I rush over to my bed and dig under it to find a baseball bat. "Here!" I shove it into his hand.

"Why do you have a baseball bat under your bed?"

"In case of a break-in. Woman lives alone, she has to have some kind of weapon."

He inhales but takes hold of the bat and opens the door. Quickly he dips his head down the staircase and back, shaking it. "Call the police."

I dash over to my nightstand to grab my phone and press 9-1-1. Immediately I've got an operator.

"Yes, my name is Suda Kaye Ross, and I live above Gypsy Soul on Main Street. My boyfriend and I think someone is trying to break in. The alarm just went off."

The operator confirms the address and tells me that units are on their way and will be there in four minutes.

"Please hurry." I rush over to the hallway and, quick as lightning, look down the staircase but don't see anything. "Shit, shit, shit."

Suddenly the alarm goes silent and my heart stops.

"Suda Kaye, it's okay! Come down here!" Cam calls from somewhere in my shop.

I race down the stairs like a bat out of hell and come to a screeching stop when I notice he has the front door open and is outside on the sidewalk. His expression is murderous as he stares at my giant display window.

Without delay, I maneuver around the remaining boxes and dash over to his side. He's holding the bat loosely between his fingers with the tip resting against the concrete. His entire body is wired, his face set in a deep, frightening scowl, nostrils flaring, and jaw clenched. I scan the window and finally see what has him so upset.

It takes me a moment to understand, but when I do, my heart drops, and my body starts to shake. Only it's not with fear; it's with anger. The window looks as though someone took a crowbar to it; cracks spiderweb all over the double-paned glass, but it's the rest that fuels my ire.

Painted in big, bold, red letters someone has left me a message:

PAYBACK IS A BITCH LIKE YOU

There's only one person in town that could possibly hate me enough to act out in this manner.

Brittney.

"I'll kill her." Camden grates through his teeth. "She thinks my parents talking to her parents is bad. This is war. I'll destroy her."

I nod but can't even believe what I'm seeing. All the work I've put in, gone in a flash of paint and broken glass. I come to the only conclusion I can. "How am I gonna fix this in time? We'll have to push the opening."

"No way in hell. I'll call on any resource, pay any amount of money to get this fixed immediately. Don't worry, baby, I've got you." Cam wraps his arms around me and holds me close.

"Honey, it's a custom window…"

He holds me tighter. "I've got you."

The wind picks up the sound of the sirens barreling down the street until the flashing lights and cars stop right in front of my shop. I'm in a pink nightie with bare feet. Cam is in his dress slacks, barefooted and bare chested. Even with this setback, I squeeze Camden around the waist and press my face to his chest, burrowing into the only thing that's real.

His words filter through the air, and I'm not sure if it's me repeating them in my mind or him whispering them at the crown of my head. All I can hear is the one thing I have to hold on to right now.

I've got you.

18

Once we've dealt with the police and given our statements, Cam drags me upstairs in order to get dressed.

"Pack a bag."

I shove my arms through the V-neck sweater I'm pulling on and glance at him as he buttons up his dress shirt.

"Why? We should be trying to go back to sleep, not that I could at this point." I sigh and run my fingers through my hair, pushing it out of my face.

He finishes the last button on his shirt and folds up the sleeves. "Exactly. You're not staying here. Not for a while. Maybe not ever, if I have anything to say about it."

"Whoa, whoa, whoa." I hold up my hands and stand a few feet in front of him. "We know what this is. It's a sad, dejected gold digger who got her hands slapped for being a bad girl. She's acting out. Thankfully, my business benefactor has connections and can help me deal with this situation, but I'm not afraid of her, Cam."

Cam's jaw tightens, and a muscle in his cheek visibly twitches. "We don't really know her, Suda Kaye. Vandalism could be the start. The last thing we need is for you to be up here alone with God knows what she could be planning. If the woman is sick and twisted enough to attempt to trap me into marriage by faking a pregnancy, she's capable of anything. Frankly, I'm not willing to risk your safety."

I step closer and place both of my hands on his chest, running them up and down. "I'm fine. Nothing's going to happen to me."

He loops his arms around my waist and rests them at my lower back. "I know, because I'm going to make sure of it. Now, please, pack a bag."

I shake my head, about to reject his request more forcefully until he locks me in place, curves one of his hands around my jaw and dips his head so that we're face-to-face, gaze-to-gaze.

"I just got you back. I'm not going to let *anything* get in the way of our happiness or your safety. Please, sweets, humor me." His voice is breathy and tortured.

At war with myself, I realize he's truly not asking much. Cupping his jaw, I nod. "Fine. For now. I make no promises, but I'll stay with you at least until we get this situation with Brittney figured out."

Camden sighs before laying a sweet kiss on me. "Thank you, baby."

"Well, you've got to let me go in order for me to pack a bag," I tease, and he drops his arms.

He grins. "Pack a big one."

I roll my eyes and huff loudly. "In the meantime, what are we going to do about the window? We can't have that mess visible when tourists and the other business owners get up in the morning."

He frowns and pulls out his phone. "You're right. I've got an idea. You deal with the bag, I'll deal with the window."

As I open my wardrobe, I hear Camden making a call. "Hey, Kyson, it's Camden Bryant. Sorry it's so late. Gypsy

Soul has been vandalized...yeah, the window smashed and painted with profanity. Either way, I need to get that window replaced ASAP. Do you have any contacts?"

A few moments go by of Kyson responding before Cam says, "It would be a great help. Thank you. And, Kyson, I'll owe you one."

I chew on Camden being willing to owe Kyson anything while I shove in jeans, dresses, sandals, and tanks as well as underwear and all of my essentials into my big trusty suitcase.

I wonder what the heck I'm going to do about this Brittney situation. Is this just a onetime payback or is she gearing up for something worse? Technically I'm the one who ruined her plan as well as hooked up with her meal ticket. I imagine she's pretty pissed her little masquerade didn't go as planned and I scored the big fish she was trying to catch.

I told Cam nothing was going to happen to me, but now I'm beginning to wonder if this will be the end of Brittney's tirade. Having known women like that in the past, I doubt it.

While mulling over the situation and how to best proceed, I hear Camden end his call.

"Kyson actually knows the window maker that put in all of these windows. He's going to call him first thing this morning to get them working on a window right away. He says he'll pull in every favor, plus he's coming down here now to take a look at the damage and see what he can do to make it more presentable to the public for now."

I let out a deep sigh of relief. "Thank you."

"Don't thank me. If what he says is true and he can spring a miracle with the window maker, we'll be in debt to your contractor." His tone is dry and humorless.

"You hate this, don't you?"

He nods curtly.

"Then why did you call him?"

He crosses his arms over his chest. "There is no length I won't go, no discomfort I wouldn't endure to ensure your safety and happiness. He knows the building best and is a well-known contractor in the area. Regardless of my personal feelings toward the man, or the fact that he threw his hat in the ring for your affections, he is the best resource we have at the moment. He's also the most willing."

I drop the sweater I'm holding on top of the pile in my suitcase, walk over to Cam, and wrap my arms around him. "I love you."

He inhales deeply against my neck and hairline. "God, I hate how much I needed to hear that, sweets. And I love you. Come home with me, Suda Kaye. Let's get some rest. We're going to have a lot to deal with later on today."

Camden was not kidding last night, I think to myself while staring at the shattered window that now boasts a huge tarp taped to the entire storefront.

Kyson appears at the door with a roll of duct tape in his hand. "Hey." He quicksteps over to me and pulls me into his arms. "Jesus, I'm glad you're okay, brown eyes." He hugs me tightly, and for a moment, I rest in his easy warmth.

Cam clears his throat from behind us.

I smile and step back. "Thank you, Kyson." I glance at the window. "For everything."

He nods. "I'm just glad you're okay."

"Any news on the window repair?" Camden steps forward, hooks his arm around my shoulders, and forces me to lean against his side. Staking a claim if I ever saw one. Doesn't upset me, though. I've been missing this for ten years. At this point, I'd do just about anything to stay wrapped up in his arms forever.

Kyson clocks Cam's move and smiles cheekily. "Yeah, actually. Had the guy out first thing. He's already measured and is working on the replacement. Luckily, he was called by the building owner across the street and was already working on new windows that are close to a perfect match for these. He's got time on the builder across the way, but I swayed him to knock out the new window for Gypsy Soul. It's going to cost a pretty penny."

Camden nods. "Whatever it takes. Did he say he could have it done before the opening this weekend?"

"Yeah. It will be done in two days tops."

"Two days!" I squeal and jump up and down with my hands in the air. "Woo-hoo! This is awesome." I shimmy around in a circle as both men watch, matching grins on their faces.

Of course, that doesn't stop the black Porsche that screeches to a stop at the curb behind Camden's Rover, which brings my victory dance to a sudden halt.

Evie dashes out of the car at a dead run, her golden locks flying in the wind as she plows into me. Her arms wrap around me, and she squeezes me tight. "Oh my goodness, Kaye! Are you okay?" She holds me to her in a vise lock, arms clinging, nails digging into the flesh of my back through my clothing.

"Sis…sis…can't breathe," I choke out until she lets me go.

I suck in air and hold her a full arm's length away from me. I notice that she's in her pajamas, face free of makeup, and slippers on her feet. "Jeez Louise! I'm fine. What in the world is wrong with you?" I gasp and focus on her wild eyes and face. "Better yet, you look like you've been awoken from a nightmare. What's going on?"

Evie's eyes are completely wild with fear as she runs her hands up and down my arms until I hold her hands still. "I—I got a text with the picture of your window."

"A text? I didn't send anything. Cam?"

He shakes his head.

"Kyson?"

"Brown eyes, I don't have your sister's phone number."

"Well then, how the heck did she get a text? Where's your phone, Ev?"

Tears fill her eyes. "In the car. I thought you might be hurt. I just got you back and…and… I was so scared," she croaks, her expression tormented.

I pull her into my arms and hold her close. "Go check her car, Cam."

He lifts his chin and heads toward Evie's Cayenne. I pet my sister's hair and whisper words of comfort into her ear, promising her that I'm fine, nothing's wrong or going to happen to me. Eventually, her erratic breathing slows down to a normal rhythm, and she sniffs and lets me go.

"Password for the phone?" Cam calls out.

"M-I-L-O, uh… I mean, 6456."

I loop my arm around Evie's waist. "Your password is *Milo*. Seriously?"

"Shut up," Evie huffs and then crosses her arms over her chest protectively.

Cam focuses his attention on Evie's phone. His entire posture changes as he reviews the text she received. His hands tighten into fists, his jaw locks as though he's grinding his teeth, and a wave of fury rolls off him so hot I step back, bringing Evie with me.

"What, baby?" I swallow, not wanting to know but needing to anyway. "What does it say?"

"Below the picture, it says, 'You are next, bitch.'"

My entire body instantly sizzles with a heat so intense I feel like I could throw fireballs from my hands like one of those superheroes in the comic books. "Are you telling me she threatened my sister?" I growl as though the very hounds of hell are nipping at my heels and amplifying my ire.

Camden lifts his hands. "Sweets..." he warns.

I take the few steps necessary to snatch the phone from Camden's hands and review the text. There's a picture of my destroyed shop window in all its mutilated glory. Just like Cam said, underneath the picture is the threat against Evie. Seeing those four words directed at my kind, loving, sweet-as-pie, would-never-hurt-a-fly, beautiful sister sparks a rage the likes of which I've never felt before simmering through my veins.

"I'll kill her," I yell, my fury so intense I can hardly contain it. "Where does she live?" I fist my hands, ready to do whatever I have to in order to get my sister out of this vile woman's crosshairs. "She wants to take a shot at me, then bring it on!" I scream, letting the anger out where I stand in the middle of the sidewalk in front of my store.

Camden cups my neck on either side and brings us nose-to-nose. "You will do no such thing. We're bringing this new development to the police. In the meantime, we'll ensure that Evie is safe with us. I have plenty of bedrooms on the ranch. For now, let's get her inside and into some clothes. We'll have some coffee and call the police. Okay? Let's take a minute to settle down. We will get justice, and Brittney will pay. I promise you that."

His words register, and I glance over my shoulder to find Evie's arms crossed over her chest, looking more vulnerable than I've ever seen her.

"Your sister needs you right now, baby. Go take care of her. I've got this."

I lock my teeth, take a slow breath through my nose, and go comfort my sister.

"Mom, Dad, what in the world are you doing here?" Camden says while I place another handwoven scarf over the rack I'm assembling.

Patty Bryant bustles inside the store and pulls me into a hug. "Kaye, sweetheart, I'm so glad you're okay."

I hug Patty, allowing her motherly warmth and concern to filter through all the negative and bring some peace to my soul. "Hi, Patty."

"Oh, stop that Patty business. You used to call me Mom and now that you and my boy are back together, all is right with the world once again. Isn't that right, Coltrane?" Patty grins and looks over her shoulder.

Coltrane maneuvers around his son, opens his arms, and pulls me into them. "Darlin' girl, I'm so sorry you were vandalized by that spoiled brat. When Porter contacted us after driving by the place this morning, we knew we had to hustle down and be here for moral support."

I lean against Coltrane's side and soak up his fatherly concern. My own stepdad and I have never had as easy a relationship as I've had with Cam's father.

"And your brothers will be here shortly."

"Call them off. Seriously. I've got the situation under control—" Camden attempts before his father cuts him off.

"Now, son, you know when family is dealing with a situation, we all pitch in."

"Exactly. Sister! Bring it in!" Preston stands at the cusp of the door to my shop, both hands up and his fingers waving for me to come to him. I smile and run over to him, and he scoops me up into a big bear hug.

God, I missed this family.

Preston shakes me silly while holding me tight, then lets my feet touch the ground. "You need me to knock some sense into someone for you?"

I laugh heartily and shake my head. "Missed you, bro."

He hooks an arm around my shoulder and tucks me to his side before lifting his chin up toward Cam. "What's the sitch, brother?"

Camden sighs loudly and runs his fingers through his hair like he's done for the millionth time today. "We've got the police dealing with this."

"What can we do?" Porter says from behind us.

Preston and I spin around.

"Are you all right, Suda Kaye?" Porter's voice dips gently, and he reaches out a hand to squeeze my arm.

"Yeah, Port, I'm fine. Thank you for coming. Thank you all for coming, but you didn't need to—"

"That's what families do for one another." CJ ambles up to Porter's side, hands in his pockets, a surly expression marring his otherwise handsome face. Briefly I wonder if I'll ever win over CJ, though him being here does say a lot about how he feels about me.

Camden groans and looks up at the sky. "Guess the gang's all here."

I giggle and let go of Preston to get my guy to relax. I place my hands on his chest and look up at his handsome face, waiting for him to focus on me. When he looks down, I smile. "Baby, you have an amazing family and they care about your happiness—"

"And yours, my dear. No woman has ever been right for

my boy besides you. We're just all so thrilled you're back," Patty announces sweetly. "We're here for you and my son."

"Thanks, Mom." I smile and give her a wink before bringing my attention back to Camden. I run my hands up and down his chest. "It's okay. The more the merrier, right?"

He chuckles and wraps his arms around me. "You're right. Let's start with you telling us what we can help with to finish up the store. You can work on your special pieces until the detectives on your case have an update."

"Well, to start, I imagine we're going to have to remove everything from the window display in front and set them off to the side until the window can be repaired." I point to two stacks of boxes along the far wall. "All of these boxes need to be unloaded, some product displayed, and others put in the storage room in the back. And then there's Evie—"

"What about Evie?" Porter's voice lifts in volume and grit.

I lick my lips and widen my eyes at Cam. "You didn't tell them about the threat?"

"Who's threatening Evie?" Preston's muscular chest puffs out, reminding me of a dragon inhaling just before it obliterates an enemy with a blast of fire.

Cam's head drops down, his chin toward his chest. "Hell, the last thing we need is my brothers vying to protect Evie—"

"What do you mean, protect her?" Porter chimes in. "What are you not telling us?"

"Evie got a threatening message from whoever did this, which we are assuming is Brittney. The message basically said Evie was next," Camden fills in.

Preston edges me aside and grips the lapels of Camden's suit jacket. "And you neglected to tell us this?"

Camden shoves Preston's hands off him. "Back off. I didn't neglect to tell you anything. None of this is any of your business. Like I said, the police are dealing with both threats. Evie is upstairs right now, working."

Within seconds, Porter and Preston are dashing up the stairs.

Cam lifts his arms and intertwines his fingers at the back of his head. "Jesus…"

I grin. "Right! Who knew that Preston and Porter had a thing for Evie?" I clap. "This could be good, especially since Milo's married and out of the picture."

"Who the hell is Milo?" He narrows his gaze and a bit of a sinister look flashes across his eyes. "You mean the guy that was helping you? Native American guy. Long black hair. He's into Evie?" Cam places his hands on his waist and waits for me to respond.

"I told you that a long time ago. He's actually friends with one of your brothers. He worked with another tribe member to get the foundation's help years ago."

For a moment, Camden looks at me like I'm wearing a multicolored clown wig until he apparently works it out. "Oh shit. *Milo*…" He closes his eyes. "Milo Chavis is CJ's friend from college? Hell, I didn't put the two together before because I was so focused on thinking you were dating the guy. I don't recall being part of the project he worked on before. Evie's into him?"

"Uh, *yeah*, only been half in love with him since we were kids."

"Wow, that's gonna be awkward for Porter. He's always had a thing for Evie."

"Not really. Last week, Evie ran into Milo and his *wife*. He's definitely out of the picture now."

"Guess so."

"Then why is Preston rushing to check on Evie?" I frown,

worried that my sister is about to get in the middle of a Bryant brotherly battle for the damsel in distress.

"Because he loves you both like sisters. He's fiercely protective of his family. He won't intrude on Porter finally making his play for Evie."

I blow out a breath and pull my hair into a messy bun on top of my head, using the scrunchie I have on my wrist. "This has been quite a day. Broken windows. Police. Your family stepping in to help. Porter finally getting a chance to make his move on Ev. Jeez, tomorrow is going to be utterly boring."

Camden chuckles and pulls me into a hug. "We can only hope."

I frown and let a small niggle of fear surface. "Do you think she's really capable of hurting my sister?"

He shakes his head. "No, I don't. I think she's upset and acting out. That doesn't make her dangerous physically, but it's obvious her mental status is not healthy. The woman needs to be dealt with, though I assume it's nothing a little community service and one helluva shrink can't fix. You and Evie are going to be just fine."

"Thanks, for being here, for being you. I'm sorry that she hurt you, but I'm not sorry it led us here, to one another."

He grins and runs his nose along mine. "Now *that* we both can agree on. Come on, let's get this place ready. Mom's already got boxes open and is bossing Dad around. If you want things your way, you're going to have to direct the show."

I chuckle. "I'd rather check on Evie. Make sure the Bryant brothers aren't freaking her out."

He nods. "Good idea. I'll get Mom and Dad on getting us all some food. How's that sound?"

"Wonderful."

"Wonderful is what you are, Suda Kaye. You get hit with all

of this craziness and you take it all in stride. A lot of women would be cowering in the corner, crying. Not you. You're pulling up your bootstraps and getting to work to fix what was broken. I adore that about you."

I tip my head to the side and smile. "Couldn't do any of it without you."

"That's what I'm counting on, sweets. You never having to do anything without me again." He kisses me swiftly and lets me go, heading to have a chat with his mother.

I make my way to the stairs, and once I get to the first step, I look over my shoulder and see his parents nodding and putting on their coats. Camden's father pats his son on the back, and his mother kisses his cheek. As they walk toward the front entrance, they wave at me. I wave back, but my eyes don't leave the man I love.

That's when it hits me. I don't want to do anything without this man in my life. Ever again.

With the knowledge that I'm exactly where I'm supposed to be, I head upstairs to check on my sister.

19

Camden presses his head back into the pillow, his corded neck stretched, the muscles bulging as he moans. I run my tongue up his length and spin a circle around the bulbous, weeping tip.

"Jesus, sweets." Camden's fingers tunnel into my hair, and he grips so tight it pulls at the roots.

The pleasure ripples from my scalp down my spine to land hotly between my thighs where I'm desperate for attention, but not until I've made him lose his mind. I suck hard at the tip, flatten my tongue, and lave at the sensitive underside until his hips are powering up as I descend, taking his length as deep as I can. Once the knobbed head bumps the back of my throat, I hum, knowing the exact reaction I'm going to get.

Camden presses my head down, his cock plunging down my throat where I swallow, giving him exactly what he needs.

"Holy hell, I'm going to come." He grips the sides of my face as I hollow out my cheeks and suck hard, bobbing up and down until his entire form is squirming and he's gritting his teeth, his eyes shut and those beautiful hands digging into my skin. "Want to come inside you, Suda. Need it. Now!" he growls and yanks me up off his length and flips me to my back.

He spreads my thighs, grips my ass, centers his cock, and plows inside. This time, I'm the one moaning, stretching my back and pushing my hips up to get more of him. Always more.

"Want deeper," he grates between his clenched teeth.

"Take what you want, baby." I pant against his ear as his length pounds me into the mattress.

After a few more glorious thrusts, Cam reaches for my knees, slides his hands under them, and presses me in half as he gets up on his knees to take me deeper. His length drills inside of me, touching places I didn't even know he could, dragging along the sensitive, swollen walls, sending waves of intense pleasure careening through my body. His gaze leaves mine as his head falls forward to watch his cock enter and retreat.

"You're so beautiful. Us together is pure beauty, Suda Kaye. Open your eyes, baby, and look. Watch me take you." His voice is dripping with carnal lust, and his eyes are wildly focused between my thighs.

As best I can, I lift my head and watch him take me. It's ridiculously hot and mind-melting at the same time. "Too much, baby, too much," I gasp as his he twists his hips and his cock rubs along something sending a surge of electricity through my body.

I cry out, right on the fringe of pure bliss.

"Never too much, never enough," he roars, picking up his pace, shifting my legs to wrap around his back. I squeeze his ribs with my thighs as I hold on for the ride of my life.

Cam doesn't disappoint.

Within moments, my center throbs, heats, and explodes outward as my entire body locks around Camden.

"Fuck yeah!" he thunders, one hand holding my ass in place, the other under my back and tugging on my shoulder where he can maneuver me the way he likes.

My orgasm is finally petering out while his body is the exact opposite, working like a finely tuned machine, muscles bulging, and skin misty with the effort he's exerting. Then, all at once, he buries his face against my neck, until he gifts one final deep thrust where he plants himself, shooting off hotly inside me. His release sets off tingles of excitement through my sated body.

I close my eyes no longer seeing his rather masculine bedroom and soak up his sounds, the feel of his body lying in my arms after our lovemaking. He's vulnerable and soft against me. His breathing is labored, but it doesn't stop him from placing tiny kisses along my neck, jaw, and clavicle. "Love you, Suda Kaye. Always."

"Love you always, Cam." I slide my hands up and down his slick back.

Camden lifts his head and kisses me for a long while, shifting his hips so that he's lying at my side. He strokes his fingertips up and down the front of my naked body, circling a nipple and watching it pucker before moving down to my ribs where he traces each one.

I sigh and turn to my side so that I can snuggle Camden's warm body. "I never knew sex could be like this."

"Like what? Insanely good? Provocative? Hot as hell?" He kisses my forehead and combs his fingers through my hair.

I giggle and kiss his chest, then stroke his defined abs and perfect pecs. "No. I just… It's hard to explain. It's different with you."

His body tightens in my arms, and for a second, I worry that he won't like this line of sharing. With him being so protective as well as walking a pretty thin line of being jealous of any man that looks at me, it's probably not the best conversation to have.

"Why do you think it's different?" he asks.

"Isn't it for you?"

He looks down and grins. "Yeah, sweets, it's different for me because it's you. The woman I want to spend the rest of my life with."

I smile and lift up onto my forearm. "Sure, but I mean, what we have is so…intimate. I've never felt like this before."

He waggles his eyebrows playfully, then his face takes on a more serious expression. "Sweets, I don't know about you, but I've never slept with anyone I was in love with besides you. I imagine that's the difference for both of us."

"Hmm, I think you might be right. It's not just about the pleasure—it's about the connection. Wanting to please the other, make them as happy and fulfilled as they are making you."

"Oh, you pleasured the hell out of me. You definitely have not lost your head-giving skills."

I snort-laugh and smack his arm lightly as I sit up. I lean over and kiss him softly. "I'm going to go clean up."

"Okay, come right back. I'm not done with you."

I bite down on my bottom lip and get out of bed. "Perfect reason to hurry." I dash forward and trip over my exploding suitcase on the floor between the closet and his bathroom, banging my big toe in the process.

"Ouch! Crapola, that hurt!" I jump around naked, grabbing for my foot, my boyfriend's release leaking down my thigh. "Ugh…" I hop over to the vanity and into the bathroom.

Camden has flicked on the lights and enters the bathroom naked as the day he was born. "You okay?"

I pout and hop over to the toilet where I sit down. "Yes, but turn around for a sec." I suddenly feel embarrassed. I tinkle, then wipe away the mess he made of me. "Can you grab me a nightie?" I ask.

He laughs and uses his toe to poke around the clothes spilling out of my suitcase. "How do you expect me to find anything in this mess? Baby, you need to hang your clothes in the closet. There's the entire right side of the closet for all your stuff. I've even cleared out three drawers in that dresser for your unmentionables that I'd like to mention are absolutely inspiring."

I hold my sore toe and inspect it, barely taking in what he's going on about. No blood or true damage, just a little chip on the nail of my big toe, which royally sucks. "What are you saying?" I call out, still checking out my nail.

Camden appears in the doorframe. "Sweets, you need to move in. You cannot live out of your suitcase, such as it is."

I huff and run my hand through my hair. "Honey, I've always lived out of a suitcase. It's really all I know. Even when I stayed at Evie's, I never unpacked, and I was there months."

He crosses his yummy arms over one another, muscles protruding in a delectable way that makes me want to sink my teeth into an expanse of skin and mark him as mine. He still hasn't put on anything, and I adore how comfortable he is in his own skin, especially in front of me. There's a separate type of intimacy in that act alone. It's familiar and warming. Something couples who have been together a long time aren't afraid of. Kinda like sitting on a toilet clearing away your sex mess and inspecting your busted toe.

A chuckle slips out of my mouth. "It's really not a big deal. Soon, I'll just be moving back into my apartment anyway, right?" I shrug and wash my hands before pushing past him to paw through my belongings until I find a royal blue night-gown that has deep slits up the sides. It's flashy, the entire thing a soft satin material that looks amazing against my skin.

Once I've got my gown on, he hooks me around the waist and presses me to him. "I don't want you to leave. I want you to put your clothes away in the closet, your panties and nightgowns in the wardrobe, and then I want you to go to your apartment, pack up all your other belongings, and then bring those here and put those away, too."

I frown and cup his neck on either side. "Are you asking me to move in with you...permanently?" My heart starts beating erratically against my chest, but I ignore it.

He chuckles and nuzzles his nose against mine. "Isn't it obvious? We're playing catch-up, and we've got ten years to make up for. I'm not getting any younger. Neither are you. We have our work, family, and most important, each other. Why spend any of our free time not sleeping next to one an-other or sharing a meal, talking about our day, you know... being settled in our relationship?"

"Settled." I mull over that one word, and for some reason, it doesn't taste as sweet as it once did when I was discussing something similar with Evie. "Let me see if I have this right. You want me to prove that I'm not going to leave you again by moving in with you?"

My heart sinks until he grins one of his beatific smiles that could cure any concern.

"Not a bad idea, but I hadn't really thought about it that way. Definitely wasn't my motivation in asking you to move in. Mostly I just want you in my life as often as I can get you. That means stepping over your clothes, dealing with your hippie-dippy-trippy aesthetic in my home, and knowing that my woman put it there. It means waking up to your beautiful face every day. Making love to you every night. Fighting over which way the toilet paper roll should face—"

"People fight over that?" I cringe, not comprehending why that would be something anyone would worry about. It's just toilet paper.

He chuckles and wraps his arms around me and rests his forehead on mine. "Not us apparently, if that's not one of your quirks."

"It's not."

"Good, me neither. Baby, I just want to be with you. You moving in will absolutely give me a sense of commitment that you weren't capable of giving me in the past. It's not exactly something I need from you, more something I want. And it's certainly not something I've ever given anyone else in my life."

"What about that Val woman you mentioned? You hinted you were in a long-term relationship with her."

Cam leans back and nods. "We were together for a year. She wanted to move in, take our relationship to the next step. I didn't want her here. The thought of having her in my space day in and day out was enough of a reason for me to break it off with her." He sighs and it seems like it's a heavy burden sitting on his chest. "I just couldn't see forever with her and it wasn't right to string her along when she felt the exact opposite."

I frown and run my hand over his chest soothingly. "I'm sorry. Did you...uh, did you love her?"

He shakes his head. "No. I cared for her. Deeply. Liked spending time with her, but not enough to want to do it forever. Ultimately, sweets, when it came to discussing our future, I didn't see her in it."

"Why not?"

He smiles and cups my jaw, his thumb sliding across my cheek. "Baby, she wasn't you. I never got over you. And I'm glad I didn't, or we wouldn't be here right now, talking about moving forward in our future together."

I lean into his hand, close my eyes, and rub my cheek against his palm. Moving forward in our future together sounds way better than being settled does. "I'll move in with you."

His fingers tighten against my hip and face, forcing me to open my eyes and pay attention. "Just like that?"

I smile and nod. "Just like that. It's always been you for me, too, Cam. This is right. Me. You. The family. Evie. My store. Your empire. Everything feels...right."

"Couldn't agree more." He dips his head and slants his mouth over mine. Our tongues tangle and dance until he's lifting me up by my ass and bringing me to his bed.

Technically...*our* bed.

The next morning, I wake to Camden kissing down the length of my arm. He lifts it and kisses each one of my fingers. "Good morning," he says from where he's sitting cross-legged in bed, a pair of pajama bottoms on, ones he didn't have on when we finally went to bed last night.

"Morning," I mumble, still fighting off the sandman.

"I have something for you. I was going to wait until tomorrow at the grand opening, but I decided this is a moment I should keep between us."

"Well, you know I love presents, so lay it on me." I lift up and push with my legs until my back hits the headboard. I settle the blanket across my chest and body, keeping the naked bits covered.

He rolls over to the side of the bed where the end table is and opens the drawer. He pulls out a long box, maybe the size

282 • AUDREY CARLAN

for a monogrammed pen. He shuts the drawer, crawls over to where I'm sitting, and hands me the box.

I take it from him and smile. "Thank you. I'm sure whatever it is, I'll love it."

He chuckles. "You haven't even opened it yet."

I shrug. "Yeah, but it's from you."

"Just open it, sweets."

I smile and lift off the top. Lying on black velvet is a thin gold chain. At the end of that chain is a small ring. Removing the chain from the little clasps, I hold it up. The small gold circle catches the light, and instantly, I lose my breath. My heart pounds so hard I place my other hand over it.

"Breathe, baby," Camden warns, putting his warm hand on my thigh with encouragement.

Tears fill my eyes and fall down my cheeks as I bring the small circle closer to my face. I know exactly what it is, though I haven't seen it in ten long years.

"Cam..." I choke out, gripping the ring in my fist and holding it against my heart. "I can't believe you kept it. After... after everything I did." I sob, closing my eyes tight, incapable of dealing with the rush of memories pounding against my body.

Camden pulls me into his arms, and I straddle his lap, locking my four limbs around his body tightly while I lose myself to the tears.

"Hey, hey, none of that. This gift was not meant to upset you." His tone is filled to the brim with concern and regret.

I swallow around the giant lump of grief lodged in my throat. "H-how c-can it not? You k-kept it all this t-time," I stutter against his shoulder while he rocks me.

"Sweets, look at me." His voice is stern and demanding, but I ignore it.

I shake my head and cry harder, hating myself, hating what I did to him ten years ago, hating every moment I didn't spend by his side. Hating leaving.

"Suda Kaye, look at me, baby." He curls his fingers under my chin and eases my chin up until I open my eyes.

"I hurt you." The three words feel like a knife striking straight through my bleeding heart.

He purses his lips, and his jaw tightens. "You made a choice. Yes, it hurt me. It also hurt you." He runs his hand along my hair until his palm rests against my neck. "Since having you back and finding out why you left, I've come to realize that, sometimes in life, we have to make tough choices that invariably hurt others and ourselves. It doesn't make that choice wrong, it just makes it part of life."

I shake my head, and he wipes at my tears. "We could have been together the whole time." I barely get the words out, the power of that truth bursting from my soul in a wave of sadness.

"We already went over this. Maybe. Maybe not. As much as I believe I would have gone anywhere with you as you traveled the world, you were right about my family legacy. I couldn't completely leave it. Not for long. And besides, back then, I wouldn't have wanted to." His eyes are a dark mossy green while he lays out the truth. "The more I've thought about it, the more it became clearer that you, Suda Kaye, you had the entire world at your feet. Your mother set a path for you, one you wanted more than anything before us. Did it hurt? Fuck yes."

A sob tears through my throat. He cups my cheeks and stares into my eyes. "Ultimately, that path has brought you back to me. We're different, stronger than we were before. We get the beauty of learning about one another all over again, while still knowing the love we had survived it all."

I swallow as he wipes away my tears, letting his words pierce through the pain.

"And we've agreed to move past all that came before. You're moving in. We're together again. This ring, this promise I made to love you forever back when we were just kids is still true. Until I replace it with an engagement ring, I'd like for it to be back where it's meant to be."

I hold the necklace out and let the gold strand fall through my fingers like silky ribbons. "Why, um, why is it on a necklace?"

He smiles softly and takes a breath. "I've been wearing it around my neck for years. I even lied to Val and Brittney, telling them it was my grandmother's who passed, and it made me feel closer to her." He looks completely chagrined but still honest and...vulnerable.

Shockingly, his admission has me snorting and giggling at the same time. "You didn't."

He shrugs one shoulder. "Wanted you close," he says in answer as if it makes complete and total sense.

"But you had the tattoo already."

"Wanted you closer. Suda Kaye, you could never be close enough to me. Taking our time, getting to know one another before I put a big diamond on that finger is going to be torture as it is."

I take a full breath of my own, letting the light in and the darkness out as I wrap my arms around his neck. "We sure are a pair, aren't we?"

"Yes, and I wouldn't have it any other way." He grins and nips at my lips.

I hold up the promise ring he gave me years ago, unlatch

the chain, and let the ring fall into my palm. I place it on my left ring finger.

"Still fits," he says smugly.

I laugh and stare at the ring. "Thank you, for giving this back to me. For not hating me. For loving me anyway."

"What'd I tell you, sweets? Loving you is easy."

20

"Today's the day! Are you excited or what?" Evie singsongs her way through the door and spins in a flirty circle, showing off the ice-blue satin slip dress that turns into a dark ombre green at the bottom. The sexy dress falls to a couple inches above her knees with a slit up the side that shows off her long, tanned and toned legs. She's wearing a saucy pair of banana-yellow peep-toes and a long, multilayered gold chain necklace that falls right between her perky boobs. She's as golden and radiant as the sun.

"You. Look. Amazing!" I squeal and open my arms until she dashes into them and squeezes me. We both jump up and down like little girls getting to attend their first real dress-up party.

"Sunshine! You've outdone yourself," Camden declares as he comes down the stairs from my soon-to-be ex-apartment, carrying two more bottles of champagne.

Evie backs out of my arms and spins slowly for his perusal. "You like?"

He grins wide. "Not as much as my brother will," he chuckles.

"Huh? What are you talking about?" She tips her head to

the side, pondering his comment as if she genuinely has no idea what he's talking about. Probably because my sister is absolutely clueless when it comes to men finding her attractive. My theory is she's dateless because her normal business exterior is pretty icy and aloof to the attentions of the opposite sex.

Camden shakes his head. "Never mind. It will be more fun to watch that play out."

This is true.

She shrugs. "Whatever. Let me help with the champagne." She takes the two bottles and heads over to the long cashier bar where we've had the caterers set up tons of hors d'oeuvres, white and red wine, as well as champagne.

I interlace my fingers and putter around my store on my super-sweet new hot-pink suede wedges I scored for a song at the store down the street. I'm rocking a skintight pair of leather pants, one of my black studded belts, a multicolored silver bustier that has thread woven through in wild splashes of color and the skinniest straps at the shoulders to hold up the girls. On one wrist is a double layer of slinky bangles, on the other, a one-of-a-kind leather bracelet I made, and on each hand, I'm wearing some silver and gemstone rings. Everything I'm wearing aside from the shoes is available for sale in my shop.

As I'm fixing one of the displays, touching up the placement here and there, Camden comes up from behind and wraps his arms around me. "Don't be nervous," he says against my ear. "You've done an amazing job here. It's beautiful, has tons of unique items that people are going to lose their minds over. You may even have to restock all the shelves after just this party."

I grin, turn around in his arms, and look up into his gorgeous face. "Thank you for believing in me, for taking a chance on all of this."

He kisses my nose and presses his forehead to mine. "You're worth any risk, Suda Kaye. I really think you're going to do great. Just give it a chance. Take a breath and relax."

I nod just as the door opens and Kyson enters.

"Wow, who are you, and what did you do with my contractor?" I chuckle and turn to the side so I can stand next to Cam instead of in his arms.

Kyson grins and walks in wearing a pair of black dress slacks and a burgundy long-sleeved dress shirt. On his wrist is the one-inch etched black leather bracelet I gave him after I noticed him admiring it in the display case. His shirt is unbuttoned at the collar with no tie or suit jacket, but he still looks good enough to eat. His thick dark hair is swept back away from his face and shows a dusting of curls I hadn't noticed before.

"Brown eyes, the place looks smokin' hot. Almost as good as you do." He winks at Camden, who groans and curses under his breath.

I leave Cam's arms to hug Kyson tight. He returns the gesture but lets go quickly since I'm certain Cam is behind my back, shooting daggers his way.

"Truly, Suda Kaye, I'm honored I got to help make your vision come to life. It's really quite something." He squeezes my hand and reaches forward to shake hands with Camden.

Camden lifts an eyebrow and then smiles when he takes Kyson's hand, giving it a hearty shake. "You do good work, Kyson. Thank you for taking care of my girl. I'd like to chat with you next week about a few other builds my company needs."

Kyson blinks a few times, his facial expression one of surprise. "Really?"

"Yeah, really. You're thorough, stick within budget, and don't waste time pussyfooting around when there's a job that needs to be done." Camden glances at me. "And you have stellar taste in women, but know when to bow out gracefully. I can't say the same for your brother."

"He's moved on to the administrative side of the business. He's always been good with numbers, so we put him in charge of the office staff and running the operations side of things. He won't be on the jobs, but he will be in the office, which means if you have more work, I can't avoid the two of you crossing paths." Kyson shrugs and runs his hand over the back of his neck. "He's really sorry, feels like an ass, but he's working through some things, and I really feel like he's got a handle on his penchant for outbursts."

Camden claps Kyson on the shoulder. "I trust your judgment. I'm happy to work with him, provided he has no further connection with Suda Kaye."

Kyson grins. "Now that I can promise."

"Good man." Cam slaps his arm again. "Get yourself a drink, I see the mayor just arrived."

I spin around and see Mayor Browning with two other women, one of them in a suit, probably her assistant, and the other a tall teenager. The young girl is all legs and tiny jean shorts, hair in a ponytail, wearing a very stylish, slouchy, off-the-shoulder top, and a pair of cowboy boots.

"Oh my God, Mom! This store is so cool!" The gangly girl rushes over to a leather purse that I just stamped and applied the multicolored fringe to yesterday. "I have to have this purse." She picks up the item and wraps it around her small frame. "It's soooooo me!" She turns around and shows her mom. "Can I get it?"

The mayor chuckles. "Your budget is one hundred and fifty bucks. That purse looks like it might cost your entire shopping spree, if not more. Be thoughtful about your choices."

The girl's body sags but then something else catches her attention across the store and she sprints over to it.

The mayor approaches me. "That—" she points to the teen-ager "—is my sixteen-year-old daughter, Addison."

"Addy, Mom!" she hollers from another rack where she's trying on a super trendy patchwork jean jacket and checking herself out in the mirror. It looks killer on her.

"Excuse me, *Addy*." Mayor Browning rolls her blue eyes. "God, she needs a job. She hates sports, so no after-school activities to keep her busy. She's a straight-A student, but the only thing that interests her is fashion. Anyway, the store looks amazing, my dear," she says, looking around the shop.

"Thank you, Mayor Browning. I'm pretty happy with how it turned out, too. And you know, I actually do need help. Of course it would only be for maybe fifteen to twenty hours a week and only minimum wage."

The mayor's eyes widen. "Seriously? It wouldn't be a problem to hire my daughter?"

I shake my head and laugh. "Why would it?"

She sighs. "You wouldn't believe the number of places she's interviewed for. Once they find out she's the mayor's daughter, somehow someone else always gets hired. It's confounding and breaking my baby's heart."

"Well, why don't you have her come in next week, and we can chat about the opportunity?"

"What opportunity?" Addy comes up wearing the patch-work coat, the stamped leather purse over her shoulder, and a handful of bracelets in her hands. "Mom, check these out. So lit. My friends would love them!"

I lift my hand and hold back the laughter. The girl is ab-solutely adorable with a bright and shimmery personality.

Customers start coming in, and I can see that Evie is welcom-ing them, pointing to the food and other things to check out.

Addy watches two women, probably in their twenties,

checking out a purse display. We lose her attention when she frowns and moves to the women. "Oh no, ladies. I have the perfect thing for you over here." Addy bails on us and drags the two women over to another display, and immediately, one holds a handbag against her outfit that Addy picked. I note it does match really well.

"Perfection," Addy compliments. "But you really should pair it with this necklace over here." She points in the opposite direction and the women follow the teenager eagerly.

"She's hired. You can't beat exuberance like that. Once she knows all the products, she'll be dressing half the town."

The mayor tugs me into a warm bear hug. "You've made my year. My baby is going to be so happy. Thank you, Suda Kaye. Now I'll leave you to it and get some shopping in before the press arrives."

"Have fun. We're closed Mondays, but tell Addy to come after school on Tuesday."

"Will do. And thanks again."

I scan the growing crowd, watch the people milling around, and suddenly I realize I'm not sure where Camden is. I eventually find him chatting up customers behind the counter and taking their money.

"Wow, you put yourself to work already?"

He grins. "Absolutely. No rest for the wicked." He cashes out a woman, and I head over to Addy, who's talking another set of older women into a few scarfs and some statement pashminas.

"Hey, Addy."

She smiles at the ladies and turns to me, all big blue eyes and freckles sprinkled across her button nose. "I love your store. It's the best store in Pueblo by far!"

"Well, it's good you feel that way because I've told your

mother I want to hire you to work here two or three hours a day after school and one day on the weekend. How does that sound?"

"Are you freakin' serious?" she practically screams, and I laugh out loud.

"Yeah, sweetheart. But if you want the job, you need to go help out my boyfriend who's also part owner. See him over there?" I gesture to the cash register and the line forming. "Do you think you can do that while your mom is here?"

"Definitely! And in between, I can help people find things and make new sales."

"Since we haven't made this official yet, how about you do that, and we'll settle up with you getting that purse you wanted so bad that's outside of your budget? Hmm?"

"Holy crap, that would be AH-MAZE-ING!" Her eyes widen and she jumps up and down. "I work at Gypsy Soul. My friends are going to DIE!"

"Let's hope not...future customers." I wink. "You better get to work. Camden has a line of people." I point to the cash register once more.

Without another word, she beelines over to where Camden is working and inserts herself right into the job. Eventually, I see him show her how to work the computer and credit card machine.

Happily, I move around my store and chat with all the new patrons, discussing where they're from, what they are interested in, and so forth. As I'm discussing the benefits of a pair of leather pants with a silk blouse to a local lawyer who wants to amp up her own style but still stay professional, I feel a tap to my shoulder.

When I turn around, I'm face-to-face with the stunningly

attractive Milo Chavis. I smile. "Excuse me," I say to the woman, who nods and goes back to comparing leather skirts.

"Milo." I pull him into a hug and his leather-and-smoke scent filters through my senses. "It's so good to see you. Thank you for coming."

He dips his head. "Wouldn't miss it. I didn't come alone." He steps aside, and I figure this is when I'm going to meet his wife Evie mentioned, but when he moves, I find I'm staring into the face of the one man I lift above all others. My grandfather.

"*Toko!*" My eyes fill with tears and I bow my head until he runs his hand over my hair to cup my nape and pull me against his wide-barreled chest. I sniff against the warmth of his poncho and let the tears fall. "You're here." I smile and nuzzle against him.

"*Huutsuu*, I would not miss your opening for all the stars in the sky." He pats my back. "Now hush. Just because an old man rarely leaves his home does not mean it is worth your tears. Save them for a true sadness."

I chuckle and pull back so I can look at his beautiful face. It's richly tanned and lined with the years he's spent in the sun. His long black hair is tied back with a string of leather. Though it's his dark eyes, so like my mother's, that steal my breath. They are shining so bright they could rival the sun. And all I see is pride.

"My little bird has found her nest." He cups my cheek and gifts me the tiniest lift of his lips. Camden takes this moment to enter the small huddle we have going on.

"Tahsuda, sir, it's an honor to finally meet you after all these years." Camden lifts his hand in greeting.

Toko gazes at me, then at Camden's hand before he places

his wrinkled one in Cam's. "And you've found your mate, I see." One perfectly arched eyebrow rises in assessment.

I smile so wide I probably look like a lunatic as I nod vigorously.

Camden puts his arm around my shoulders. "Everyone is having a great time, and you've already sold a few thousand dollars' worth of product. That young woman you hired..." He mock-glares at me, making the point that I hired someone without telling him. Not that I have to, but since his foundation is technically a partner, I probably should have mentioned it. "A natural saleswoman. And she seems to know a lot about fashion. I just saw her upsell a fifty-dollar scarf because she told the woman an outfit was incomplete without it. Anyhow, Tahsuda, I look forward to a family dinner soon. It would be our honor to host you."

Toko silently watches Camden but doesn't miss a beat in deducing our relationship status. "Do you have an address change to inform me of, *huutsuu*?"

Shoot. Forgot to mention that. "Um, yeah, about that... Kinda moved in with my boyfriend, Camden." I hook a thumb to my guy.

"I see." *Toko* lifts his chin in dismay, his lips flattening into a thin line, and he nails Camden with a whopper I wasn't expecting. "And do you find that living with my granddaughter before marriage or any avowal of commitment is acceptable?"

"*Toko*..." I attempt, but Cam holds up his hand for me to stand down.

"Suda Kaye, I got this." He turns his attention back to my grandfather. "Actually, no, I don't because she's worth more. However, I wanted her out of the tiny apartment above the shop, and your granddaughter is pretty stubborn and set in her ways. It was hard enough to get her to move in as quickly as I did. My intention is to marry your granddaughter very soon, sir."

I hold up my hand with the promise ring. "He gave me this ten years ago, and then again recently. This ring comes with the promise to love me for eternity."

"Eternity." *Toko*'s coal-black eyes narrow as he assesses Camden for what feels like a full minute and then me. "Yes, I do see eternity in your future. I shall pray with the elders about this union."

My mouth drops open and I shimmy a little and give a mini cheer. "Yay!"

Camden frowns and leans over to whisper in my ear. "Is that good news?"

"Oh yeah. If he's involving the elders, that means he sees a future for us. Otherwise, he wouldn't waste time praying with the elders. It's a pretty big deal," I whisper. "*Toko*, why don't you and Milo go get something to eat? I believe Evie is over there somewhere."

"Evie?" Milo finally steps forward from his stoic position, standing respectfully behind elder Tahsuda.

"Hey, man, how are you?" Cam holds out his hand and they shake. "Did you bring your wife? I'd love to meet her."

I scowl but try to remain impassive at the mention of Milo's wife.

Milo's expression is confused at first, then turns hard. "My *ex-wife*? Why would you assume I'd bring her?"

"Did you say ex-wife?" I ask. "As in previously married but not married now?"

Milo inhales and adjusts the cuffs of his pristine suit. "I do not like to discuss that time in my life, but yes, Kimberly and I are no longer married."

Toko harrumphs and crosses his arms as if he's not thrilled with this admission. It's pretty well-known that our culture prefers to mate for life, even though in today's society that can be very unrealistic.

"But... Evie says she saw you a couple weeks ago, and a woman named Kimberly introduced herself as your wife."

Milo sighs. "That was unfortunate and a situation I'd rather not get into—" he looks around the busy room "—at this time."

"Oh yeah, sure. Well, if you'd like to talk to Evie, she's over there. If I were you, I'd lead with the fact that you are no longer married."

He frowns. "And why would I do that?"

I shrug. "Women's intuition?"

Camden bumps my shoulder. "Stay out of it, sweets. This is none of your business."

"My sister's love life is totally my business. And furthermore—"

"Love life?" Milo interrupts.

"Jesus, you can't help yourself, can you?" Camden shakes his head and crosses his arms.

"Are you suggesting that Evie is interested in me in a romantic capacity?" Milo asks bluntly.

Toko sighs wearily. "Star-crossed match. This, too, I will discuss with the elders."

I grin at *Toko* and nod wildly at Milo but say, "Maybe you should ask her yourself?"

"She's given me no indication..." He frowns.

"Pssshhhaaawww!" I interject as though I'm letting all the air out of my lungs at once.

"Look, I'm sorry. On top of that, I'll apologize for my woman's loose lips. Evie is over there. Perhaps you can continue this conversation with her?" Camden offers.

Milo straightens his jacket and nods curtly. "Agreed." He leaves our huddle and walks confidently toward Evie.

"Wonder how that is going to go?" I smile and put my hands together in a prayer position sending up a quick "pretty please" to the Big Guy on Evie's behalf.

"You should stay out of your sister's romantic affairs. No good will come of this," *Toko* advises wisely.

I frown and nod. "Fine. Oh, I know! We need booze! *Toko?*"

"Do you have the—"

"Native American wine that you love? Yes. Evie told me you might come, so I bought a bottle just for you and hid it in the back." I beam and hook my elbow through my grandfather's. He pats my hand sweetly.

"Gratitude, my *huutsuu.*"

"I love that you're here, *Toko*. It's almost like Mom was." The words are true, but the realization behind them that she'll never be able to participate in the important moments of my life is heartbreaking.

Toko stops and places his hand over mine and waits for me to look into his dark eyes. "My Catori, your mother, would be bursting with joy over your achievement. She only ever wanted you girls to be happy. To live life as she did. Loving everything and everyone in it."

I smile. "I do love my life. Everything and everyone in it."

He dips his head and kisses my temple. "You are your mother's daughter."

"Yes, I am."

21

"Why didn't you warn me that Milo was here?" Evie grumbles in a whisper from where she stands behind me, her head dipped over my shoulder.

I grin and avoid turning around by viewing my party in full swing. "Camden says I'm not supposed to get involved in your love life."

"I'm sorry. Who are you, and where the hell is my overbearing, nosy, bear-poking sister when I need her? Did you hear me? Milo. Is. Here."

I chuckle and watch as the door opens, and the rest of the Bryant clan arrives. "And so is Porter."

"Porter? What does he have to do with anything?" Evie grips my upper arm and spins me around. Her lips are pursed, and her eyes are wild with worry.

A sigh I can't hold back leaves my lips. "Sissy, how can you not know that these guys are both into you?"

She rolls her eyes. "Stop it. Porter is a family friend. That's it. Almost family by association. And Milo…"

I lean forward. "Milo is what? Hot. Muscular. Can take out any man here aside from maybe Preston. Oh, and did I mention insanely hot?"

Evie growls and clenches her jaw. "He just asked me if I'd be interested in dinner. Says he has an opportunity to talk with me about?"

I clap just my fingertips. "Yay! That's awesome. When are you going?"

She shakes her head. "I said I was very busy and not interested."

"You *what*?" I say this so loud the few people milling around us stop what they are doing and look our way. I smile, grab Evie, and push her farther into the corner. "Did you just say you're not going to dinner with him? Why in the world not? You've been in love with him since the beginning of time. This is your chance."

Evie lifts her hair off her neck and flicks it behind her. "You're not paying attention. I can't get involved with a married man."

"You obviously didn't talk to him because I just found out a half hour ago that was his ex-wife. Emphasis on the ex part. Meaning no Kimberly. Meaning yes to Evie."

Evie frowns and her nose crinkles in that cute way. "Then why would she introduce herself as his wife?"

I raise and drop my hands dramatically. "How the heck would I know? Perhaps you should ask Milo?"

Evie flattens her lips and firms her jaw. "Nope. That's it. End of discussion. I don't care what opportunity he wants to discuss. I need to get away from him and bury that crush I've had for…hell, for forever it seems like. I'm done."

I groan out loud. "This is ridiculous. Happiness could be at your fingertips!"

"And so could sorrow. I don't have time for a broken heart, and that man has broken heart written all over his sexy, chiseled face."

"Forget it." I hold up my hands. "How about we go say hi to the Bryants? Porter is looking rather dashing this evening." I point to where he's standing with Camden and the rest of his brothers. He's wearing a Bryant Brews polo and a pair of black pants. His hands are in his pockets, and he looks perfectly comfortable in his own skin. Damn fine skin, if I do say so myself. He's like the dark horse standing next to my hot blond. I scan over CJ, Preston, Camden, and Porter. "Good God, the genes in that family are stellar."

Evie finally grins and locks elbows with me. "You are not wrong, sister."

We make our way over to the Bryants and Patty engulfs us both in a maternal hug. "My goodness, girls, this place is magnificent. Kaye, darling, you must have magic at your fingertips. Everywhere I look there seems to be something new and interesting to see. I love it." She pulls back and takes my hand in both of hers. "I'm so proud of you, darling. And Catori would be beside herself if she were here today."

I pat her hand. "Thank you, Patty. You all being here means a lot."

"Well, I can't wait to shop. First though, I think I'll start with the bubbly. Coltrane?"

He eases by my side and kisses the crown of my head. "Great job, darlin' girl. I'm going to go get my Patty Cakes a drink. Would you like one?"

"Definitely. I'll have champagne, too."

"Evie?" Coltrane asks.

"Oh, I'll get it for her, Dad," Porter speaks up. He hugs me briefly. "Incredible store, Suda Kaye. Evie, would you like to get a drink with me?"

I nudge her shoulder, and she glares at me, then turns and smiles at Porter. "Sure."

The four of them head toward the food and drink, and before I can say anything, Preston is squeezing the life out of me.

"Bro, lay off," Camden says. "Jesus. Let my woman breathe."

"Damn proud of you, sister. This is the shit!" He jiggles me from side to side, and I end up laughing heartily until he releases me.

CJ points up at a picture hanging on the wall. It's of a woman standing behind sheer curtains facing out toward an open balcony. Her form is a silhouette mostly, but some of her skin can be seen through the sheer curtain. Mostly it's just an amazing and seductive image of a woman gazing out at the horizon.

"I need to own that. How much?" CJ asks.

"For you...free," I say at the same time Camden says, "A thousand dollars."

"Done. Who do I pay?" CJ says without taking his eyes off the photograph.

"Hey now, that photographer listed the image at five hundred bucks, Cam. You're overcharging."

Camden chuckles. "Baby, you're underselling. That's a damn fine piece of art."

"One of a kind? I mean, only one copy of that available in original format?" CJ queries, still not taking his eyes off it.

"Of course. All the art is, and that's a local photographer. She's the model, too." I grin when CJ's gaze shoots to me.

"Really?" His question is filled with awe. Makes me wonder if it's the woman or the image that's getting to him. Maybe a little of both.

I shrug. "I asked the same things. Something about setting up the camera on a delay, then poses, and whammo? Art?"

"Fucking brilliant. I want it tonight..."

Camden claps a hand to CJ's shoulder. "Cool your jets, brother. How about we get past the grand opening before you start making demands?"

CJ's gaze changes, and he blinks a few times as if he's breaking out of a daze. "Wow, sorry, Cam, Suda Kaye. I was just—"

"Taken by her beauty? Wait until you see the one I have in the back to replace that one. It has her face in it."

"I'm ready now," he insists without any hint of humor.

Cam squeezes his brother's shoulder once again. "Dude, chill. The pictures aren't going anywhere. Go get a drink, pay for the picture. And don't even think of skimping. A thousand bucks. You got me?"

CJ finally grins a megawatt, Bryant, pearly-white smile. I relax a little at the sight. "Any bourbon?"

Camden's lips purse and he narrows his gaze. "You get what you get, and no, there isn't any bourbon. This isn't a bar—it's a party for my girl." He shoves his brother toward the drink area.

"That was weird." I focus on the image of Jasmine Quinn, my new photographer friend. She really is stunning and an excellent photographer.

"A lot of things are weird about my brothers."

"Did I tell you that Jazz asked if she could photograph me nude, too, for a new show she's putting together?"

His eyebrows shoot right into his hairline and he clears his throat. "And, uh…what did you tell her?" His voice is tight, but I can tell he's holding back his desire to respond with something overly alpha and cavemanlike.

I wrap my arms around his neck and nuzzle the skin at his jaw, planting my body against his. "What do you think I told her?"

"Sign me up?" He chuckles but slides his hand down my

back and settles the palm against my bum, giving it a little squeeze in emphasis.

"Actually, I told her I'd have to talk to my man."

His smile is one I'll never forget. Beaming with pride and humor. "Excellent. Then no. I'd prefer to be the only man to see your…treasures."

I grin and tip my head back. "Figured."

Right as I'm about to steal a kiss from my man, I hear a strange splat sound against the big display window.

Camden and I both turn around and head toward the door. Before I can even open it, a series of projectiles hits the door and display window. Yellow sludge and white flecks slide down the clean glass.

"What the heck is this?"

Another few splats hit the glass as Camden races out the door, Preston, CJ, and Porter hot on his heels.

I follow but hold out my hand. "Everyone just stay inside, please. Evie, call the cops."

Milo, who's standing next to *Toko*, shifts me aside without saying a word and bounds out the door.

"Crap!" I race out the door to find Preston holding a Latino man by his collar and the waist of the man's jeans against the wall of a shop across the street from mine.

"You egging my sister's fuckin' store, man? Are you insane? Give me an egg." He holds out his hand, and Camden promptly places one in his hand without question.

I look around and notice a white landscaping truck, and in the bed, dozens and dozens of eggs.

"You like your eggs so much, how does this feel?" Preston smashes the egg right against the guy's chest. "Feel good?" he barks as he rubs it in, yellow oozing from between his fingers.

"Back off, man! She deserves worse!" this man I've never

met in my life spits out, kicking his legs wildly. I'm sure he got Preston's shins a few times, but Pres doesn't let him go.

"Screw you! Suda Kaye is a woman trying to make something of herself, starting a business, and this is how you treat her?"

"She ruined my life!" he hollers, and Preston holds out his hand for another egg.

Instead, Camden gives him another but pushes him out of the way. Preston drops the man to his feet, and he immediately bends over and gasps for air. Camden doesn't give him much time, yanking him up and slamming him back against the wall, putting his much larger form in front of him.

"Speak. Now," he grates through his teeth. "And you better have a good reason to be egging my woman's store."

"Your woman! That's rich! Weeks ago, you were with *my woman*!" he roars, spittle dripping out his lips and over his chin.

Camden rears back. "Is that what this is about? Fucking Brittney? The gold-digging *liar* that got me drunk, slept with me, and then pretended to be pregnant with my damn child? That's your woman?"

"She's gone and it's all your woman's fault!" The man's head drops forward, his chin to his chest. "Brittney left town. Ran off with some old guy from her parents' country club."

Ah, I realize the connection now. This is Alejandro. The lover Brittney talked about.

"So that's reason for you to shatter my woman's window, paint profanity, and egg her store on her opening night? What the hell did you think you could gain from doing this?" Camden lets the guy go and steps back right as sirens can be heard coming up the street.

"I loved her. Wanted to build a life with her. Give her

everything I could. I was even willing to be her man on the side just to have her in my life. A beautiful, perfect woman like that, coming from her family, wouldn't normally look twice at a man like me. Immigrated from Mexico, got my citizenship, and started my own business. We've done well but I'll never make the money she's used to. But I know in my heart we were in love. I know she loved me." He lifts his chin and firms his jaw with a bravado I'm surprised he still has at this moment.

Right when I think Camden Bryant couldn't possibly be a better man, he places both his hands on the man's shoulders and closes in. "You may have loved her. She may have loved you, but sometimes love isn't enough. She worshipped the mighty buck, man, was trained by it from the moment she took her first steps. You don't need that in your life."

Alejandro's gaze turns from sorrow to icy cold. "You didn't know her like I do."

"You got that right, but now look what it's done. I can probably talk Suda Kaye out of pressing charges, but you're paying for that window replacement, and if you've done any more damage tonight, you're paying to fix that, too."

At this point, the two cops enter the fray. "We've got it from here. Even if she doesn't press charges, you've disturbed the peace and vandalized a business. The owner may have other opinions on his version of justice. Come with us."

As Alejandro is led to the back of a police car, Camden puts his arm around me and tugs me close to his body.

"Hey, Alejandro!" I call out and the man turns around. "How did you get my sister's phone number?"

His shoulders sag and he looks down at his egg-coated sneakers. "Her business cell phone is available online."

Crap. My sister needs to change that immediately.

"Come on, baby," Cam says. "Let's get back to your party. I'm sure there are a lot of people that want to hear what happened."

"Yeah, at least I know now that it wasn't Brittney and that Alejandro is being taken care of. I don't want to press charges, and I'll have a talk with the property owner. The guy's a sad, sad man who lost the woman he loves. Regardless of how horrible she was to us, he loved her, and that has to count for something."

He rubs my arm soothingly. "It does, sweets. Love counts for everything when it's with the right person."

"Thanks, guys." I glance at CJ, Porter, Preston, and Milo.

"You should have let me hit him," Preston mumbles sourly as he kicks a rock.

I snort-laugh. "Come on, drinks on me." I chuckle at my own stupid joke.

When I make it back to the store, Evie, Addy, and Patty are wiping down the egg mess. My sister hands a bottle of Windex to Addy. "You okay, sissy?"

I nod. "Yeah, it was just a really sad guy with a broken heart."

Evie grins. "See, I told you. Broken hearts are the devil's playground."

"Why would you say that?" Milo questions from a few steps behind us.

Evie's eyes widen and she licks her lips. "Um, no reason. Anyway, let's get back to the party! The mayor says the press she called are on their way, and she wants to do a ribbon cutting."

"Ribbon cutting?" I squeal and do a little cheer. "Fun!"

Camden laughs and pulls me into his arms before we can enter my store. "Nothing ever gets you down, does it?"

I smile and shrug. "Why would I be down? When I was young, I wished on a star with my mother and sister, and my wish came true. I traveled the world for ten years, seeing everything I could have ever desired. I came home and opened up the most kick-ass business ever, sharing all that I am with the people I care about most. My sister is healthy, happy, and in my life daily. The only man I ever loved forgave me for leaving him and wants to marry me someday soon. I'm pretty sure when it comes to the dreams lottery, I won...big time!"

Camden cups my cheeks, and his bright hazel eyes sear into my brown ones. "Well, I also wished on stars. Every day for ten years, just like my love taught me to when we were teenagers. And finally, right here, right now, you in my arms, planning to spend your life with me...my wish came true."

I run my fingers through his golden waves, emotion filling my heart. "Camden." I stare into his eyes, my chest ready to burst with the love I feel for this man. "What did you wish for?"

"Suda Kaye, my sweets, I wished for you to come home to me."

EPILOGUE

Six months later

"What? Huh? What's going on?" I feel my sister shaking me awake from a dead sleep.

"Shhh, you might wake everyone. Come on." It's dark in the room with twin beds that Evie and I are sharing at the Bryant ranch, but she's got the door open, and the night-light in the hall makes her dark form more visible.

I groan. "Evie, I'm supposed to be getting married tomorrow. I don't want to look like death warmed over because I didn't get a good night's sleep."

She reaches for my hand and tugs until I push out of the covers and stand next to her. I'm wearing nothing but bootie shorts with the word *Bride* printed across the cheeks in gold script letters and a matching white cotton camisole.

Evie hands me the Bride robe she got to go with my outfit. She's already wearing her Maid of Honor-inscribed pajama set and matching robe. Hers are far more demure.

I slip my arms through the robe and tie it at the waist, then push my messy hair out of my face. "Are you okay?"

"Yeah, yeah. I just... We have to do something." She sets

my sparkly Bride flip-flops on the floor, and I push my feet into them.

She grabs my hand, hooks the afghan that was at the end of my bed over her shoulder, and grabs a bottle of champagne and two glasses she had sitting on the dresser. "Just follow me, and I'll explain when we get there."

Always one for an adventure, I don't ask any more questions and squeeze her hand and follow her blindly. I'd follow my sister just about anywhere she asked me to go.

We tiptoe quietly down the stairs, make our way through the family room, out the sliding door and down the stairs to the open pasture that's already set up with a hundred white chairs and a gorgeous, flowered awning chock-full of sunflowers and daisies. A dance floor has been set up in front of the barn I love so much; it'll be part of the background when I have my first dance with my man as husband and wife. The Bryant brothers strung up tons of twinkly lights all over it to give it a nighttime hoedown feel.

I can't wait until late afternoon when I get to say *I do* to the man of my dreams once and for all.

Evie leads me toward the barn. We walk across the wooden dance floor and into the dark cavernous space of the barn. I can still see because the big, second-story barn door is completely open and the moonlight is shining in, giving us plenty of light.

"Here, take one of these. I can't hold both." She hands me one of the champagne flutes and then gestures to the ladder that goes up to the loft. The same loft where I lost my virginity to Cam. I can't recall ever telling her that's where it went down, but it's pretty funny that, the night before my wedding, I'm trekking up the same ladder where I gave Camden my body and my heart.

Once we both make it to the top, she spreads the afghan over the wooden boards, slips off her sandals, and settles right in front of the open window. She even lets her legs fall over the sill, as though she's bathing in the moonlight. Her hair glows a golden halo as she pats the space next to her. "Come on, sit down, sissy."

I kick off my shoes and crawl to where she is. I get myself situated with just my legs over the edge, the backs of my knees touching the sill just like hers. I swing my legs in the open breeze, lean back, open my robe, and let the moonlight kiss my skin.

Evie pops the cork on the champagne, fills my glass and then one of her own.

"Now that you have me up here, are you going to tell me what this is about?" I'm super curious as to her intention. Evie never does crazy rash things.

She licks her lips and nods. "Well, it's gonna sound weird coming from me but… Mom came to me in a dream…"

I gasp. "What?"

"I know, I know. It sounds crazy but I swear, she came to me. It was like… I could feel her and hear her. We were sitting just like this, me and you." She pats the foot of space between our bodies. "Mom was in between us. The three of us had champagne glasses. Her arm came around us both and she kissed each of our temples."

"What did she say?" Emotions fill my heart and squeeze like a vise, the need to feel my mother right now more powerful than anything.

A tear slips down Evie's cheek and her lips quiver. "She said, 'Look up at the stars, my darlings. I am always there, watching, wishing, and loving you every moment.'"

I scoot closer to my sister, filling the empty space. A wave of

pure love surrounds me like a cloak, sending butterflies flutter-
ing in my stomach, my heart pounding and my skin tingling.
I close my eyes and wrap my free arm around Evie's shoulder.
She mirrors my move and wraps her arm around my waist.

"Did you feel that?" I whisper.

She blinks, matching tears falling down both cheeks.

"Mom's here." I smile and look up at the moon and stars,
glorying in the moment.

Then, holding my sister and her holding me, I could swear
I hear my mother's voice as a whisper on the breeze.

All I ever wished was for my girls to be happy.

Wishes do come true.

Keep wishing, my darlings.

And then it's gone.

Evie lifts up her glass to the open sky. "We miss you."

"We love you." I lift my own glass.

"Thank you for this." Evie turns her head and looks at me.
"Thank you for giving me Suda Kaye."

I let the tears fall unchecked down my cheeks. I stare into
my sister's gorgeous blue gaze and thank my mother out loud.
"Thank you for giving me my Evie. The best big sister a girl
could ever have."

We both giggle and sip our champagne.

"Evie?"

Evie tips her head to the side and kicks her legs against the
wall of the barn. Her gaze flicks to me, then back up at the sky.

"I don't think I could have made it to this point in my
life without your support," I say. "Taking care of me when
Mom died. Checking in with me regularly when I traveled.
Dropping everything to visit me. Bringing me home. Helping me get the store going. Making me see that all I wanted
and needed was here. You've always believed in me...and I..."

Evie puts her hand over mine and squeezes. "And I always will. I know it's scary to commit to one person, but Cam loves you more than anything in this world. If you told him you wanted the moon, he'd try to find a way to lasso it and give it to you."

I chuckle and nod.

"Allow yourself to enjoy every moment of tomorrow and your life together. He'll never hold you back. He'll let you fly free when you need to. The odds are he'll be the one booking your flights. Camden will be the man who sits next to you when you feel the need for adventure. You're no longer alone. I've always wanted that for you because I could never be that person."

I hold her hand. "You know, I want that for you, too."

She gifts me a sad, small smile. "Not sure the perfect man is in my cards, but I'll keep an eye out." She nudges my shoulder with her own.

Now that I'm back home for good, I'm going to find a way to help my sister get her own happily-ever-after.

Evie holds up her glass and then clinks it with mine. "To a beautiful life with the man of your dreams."

"I'll drink to that." I lift my glass and drain the entire thing in one go. "Fill 'er up!"

She chuckles, knocks back her own champagne, and then refills both of ours.

We spend the next hour giggling and sharing secrets like we used to when we were just young schoolgirls. It will forever be one of my most cherished memories with my sister.

A knock on the door startles me as I peruse my reflection from top to toe. Simple, white-lace, floor-length gown. A ruffled bunch of fabric and lace from the back of my knees spreads out into a small train that's still manageable when I walk.

Evie opens the door and my grandfather enters. *Toko*'s long black hair is parted down the center, each side braided with leather ribbons and secured at the end with turquoise beads. A chest-plate-size necklace lies against the front of his pitch-black leather poncho. The chevron shape is made from a series of long, ivory beads, each one the size of a green bean, and bordered by small yellow and turquoise ones. Strands of dove-gray leather fringe dangle off each of the ivory beads. It is a beautiful piece, and the only other time I've ever seen him wear it was in a picture of my mother and stepfather on their wedding day.

I turn around fully and tip my head in respect. *Toko*'s warm hand cups the back of my head, then shifts to my face where he grasps my chin and lifts my face up toward him. I look into his coal-black eyes, and they are shining like glass marbles.

He speaks in Comanche. "You are prettier than the sunset over the mountains of our home. More beautiful than my old eyes can grasp for too long."

"*Toko*..." My voice shakes.

He presses his lips to my forehead. I wrap my arms around his waist.

"She would be so happy today. My Catori. So proud of the woman you have become."

Tears prick the backs of my eyes, and I breathe deeply to stave them off.

"I have a gift from her."

I swallow and step back, surprise and shock likely plastered across my face. *Toko* lifts an intricately designed golden box about eight inches long, a few inches wide, and maybe two inches deep. It is stunning all by itself.

He hands me the box, and I hold it between my hands. It is warm to the touch, as though this is a living token of my mother's essence.

Evie steps up behind me and places her hands on my shoulders. I'm not sure if she is doing it for emotional support or because I honestly feel as though the rug has been pulled out from beneath my designer wedge sandals.

Toko dips his chin toward the beautiful box. "Catori gave me this to give to you on your wedding day and not a day sooner."

"H-how would Mom have known I'd even get married or find love?" I sniff and clutch the box to my chest, wishing it was my actual mom pressed heart-to-heart.

Toko holds his hands together in front of his poncho. "Catori was a dreamer. And she lived them. My daughter believed in our destiny. In the end, she believed this was yours." He smiles and nods again at the box. "She was right."

"Toko…" I swallow the emotions threatening to crush me into a million pieces.

"I shall leave you in peace. Spend the time you need with your mother and your sister. I will wait outside to walk you to your eternity." And with that, he slowly leaves the bridal room and shuts the door behind him.

"Open it, Kaye," Evie urges.

"I'm afraid to."

She smiles softly and runs her hands down the sides of my arms soothingly. "It's from Mom. It's a gift from beyond the grave."

I nod, inhale fully, and let my breath out in a long slow gust. "Okay."

I slide the little latch to the side and open the ornate box. Inside is a gold bracelet on top of one of her pink envelopes.

I pick up the charm bracelet and recognize it instantly. I was obsessed with her charm bracelet as a child. When she passed, Evie and I looked for it everywhere but could never find it among her things. It had a charm from all her favorite places she'd visited around the world. I clutch it against my chest and the tears fall like a river down my cheeks.

Evie can't hold hers in, either, a sob tearing through her as she places her hand over her mouth. I've wanted that bracelet on my wrist for as long as I can remember.

"Read the letter," she urges, but I can't see through my tears. I stumble to the chair next to the vanity and practically slump into it.

I hand the letter to my sister and shake my head. "I can't. You read it to me."

"But it's yours. It's private…" she attempts.

"Evie, there is nothing that Mom could ever say to me that would need to be kept a secret from you. Please, I can barely breathe…" I pat my chest over my heart where it is pounding so hard against my breastbone, I fear it will crack a rib.

"Okay, okay." Evie wipes her eyes with a sweep of her fingers along each tearstained cheek. She clears her throat and removes the letter from the envelope. Unfolding it, she takes a full breath and reads aloud.

"My dearest *huutsuu*." She swallows once more, shakes her head, and continues with a strength I admire but have never had myself.

"Today, above all days is one I dearly miss. Today you will commit for eternity to your one true love… Camden Bryant."

Evie's mouth drops open, and I gasp and cover my own mouth in absolute shock. How could Mom have known I'd end up marrying Camden even after she encouraged me to leave him all those years ago?

Evie fans her face with the letter, lifts her head to the sky, and takes a couple breaths. "This is so crazy, Suda Kaye. It's like she's here…like last night."

I get up and stand next to Evie and put my arm around her waist. "We've got this. Me and you. Sisters. Together forever, no matter where we go in life, no matter who we commit to. It's gonna be us in each other's lives forever, Ev. Now keep reading."

"You will have ups and downs, feel an enormous amount of happiness and sadness, but I believe the two of you are meant for one another. When you find the person you are meant to be with, something just clicks in the universe. No matter who they are, where they go, when you find them, they are yours.

"It's why I knew that suggesting you experience the world wouldn't change a thing. I believed with my whole heart that he was your other half and would be regardless of how much time you spent apart. If you are reading this, I was right. I love being right."

Both Evie and I laugh because Mom really did love being right.

"Today, Suda Kaye, know that you are so loved. Even though I'm not there in the physical sense, I will always be with you and your sister. All you must do is think of me and I'm there. Whether it be a memory, a soft breeze, a ray of sunlight on your face, or a familiar feeling that comes over you. That will be me, forever close, loving you."

Evie wipes her eyes, swallows, and clears her throat again.

"I'm proud of you, my darling *huutsuu*. You've spread your wings, experienced the world, and now know more than ever before that where you are is where you're supposed to be. Not all who wander are lost because you always know where your home is. Now your home is beside the man who worships you and a sister who adores you."

The tears come back and drip onto the page that Evie holds between us.

"Be happy. It's all I've ever wished for. On every star in the night sky, I wished for my girls to be happy in their lives. Be happy with Camden. Share your soul. Start a family. Live like there is no tomorrow. All my love to my girls on this grand day, Mom."

I inhale, grab the letter, press my lips against it, and I'm instantly invaded by my mother's scent. Citrus, patchouli, and a musky, earthy smell. I close my eyes, take a few deep breaths, fold up the letter, put it back into the envelope and then the box.

"Are you okay?" Evie asks.

I nod and go to the vanity to fix my makeup. I reapply my mascara and spread some foundation under my red eyes. Once complete, I hold my arm aloft, hand stretched out, clutching the charm bracelet.

"Something old," I whisper, and Evie smiles sadly and fastens it on my wrist. The golden charms shimmer wildly as they dangle, spreading sparkles of light to reflect across the floor in gleaming rays.

"Something new." Evie hands me the gorgeous earrings that Camden's mother has gifted me. They are a pair of simple teardrop pearls that go perfectly with the sweetheart neckline and simple lace gown.

"Something borrowed." She pulls off the birthstone ring our mother gave her when she turned eighteen and slides it on my right ring finger. It fits perfectly.

"Something blue." She places the circular halo of blue wildflowers on my head and fluffs my long, curled hair all around my shoulders.

"You're the most beautiful thing I've ever seen," she croaks and we both laugh, letting the sad emotions fall away and the light fill up all the space surrounding us. "What now?" She takes in my appearance from head to toe.

"Now I marry the man I wished for." I hold out my arm, crooked at the elbow, and my sister laces her arm through mine. "Lead the way."

And with Evie leading the way in a sunny yellow dress, and my grandfather at my side, I take the steps on a petal-covered path to my happily-ever-after.

★ ★ ★ ★ ★

AUDREY CARLAN TITLES

Biker Beauties
Biker Babe
Biker Beloved
Biker Brit
Biker Boss

International Guy Series
Paris
New York
Copenhagen
Milan
San Francisco
Montreal
London
Berlin
Washington, D.C.
Madrid
Rio
Los Angeles

Lotus House Series

Resisting Roots

Sacred Serenity

Divine Desire

Limitless Love

Silent Sins

Intimate Intuition

Enlightened End

Trinity Trilogy

Body

Mind

Soul

Life

Fate

Calendar Girl

January

February

March

April

May

June

July

August

September

October

November

December

Falling Series
Angel Falling
London Falling
Justice Falling

ACKNOWLEDGMENTS

To my husband, Eric, for showing me what true love looks like every single day. Twenty-two years and counting...

To the world's greatest PA, Jeananna Goodall, I hope I did your mother's memory justice. This book has meant more to me than any that came before it because I wanted to make it beautiful. For you. I wanted you to feel the sister solidarity between us and your mom and her sisters. Even though it was all made up, with hints of the past here and there, her essence was alive in full force. I thank you for allowing me the honor of sharing her with the world. I think there's a lot of your mother in you and I know with my whole heart that she'd be incredibly proud of the woman you are today.

To Amy Tannenbaum for finding the perfect home in HQN for this romantic, family tale.

To Ekatarina Sayanova with Red Quill Editing, for doing the developmental edit and helping me find the right mix of sweet and heat.

To Susan Swinwood, lead editor, for taking a chance on a new type of women's fiction and romantic tale and helping me form this story into one I truly believe will resonate with women across the globe. I feel incredibly blessed to work with you and look forward to the next stories on the horizon.

To my alpha beta team, Tracey Wilson-Vuolo, Tammy Hamilton-Green, Gabby McEachern, this was a difficult story that took months! Sending a chapter and then waiting weeks for the next had to be brutal but you three stuck by me, challenged me, and cheered me, every step of the way. Thank you for being such an incredible support system.

To HQN for choosing to take on a racy romantic women's fiction story, I thank you. Sometimes all a person needs is someone they respect believing in them. I endeavor to rise to the challenge in this new genre and am thrilled to be doing so with your commitment and support. Dreams definitely come true. I'm a Harlequin author!!! I think I'll have to say that a hundred time over to truly believe it.

To the readers, I hope you connect to Suda Kaye's journey with Evie, Cam, Kyson, the Bryants, Milo, and of course elder Tahsuda. Thank you for trying out something new. When you make the choice to pick up a book, it doesn't have to be one of mine. I appreciate you giving me your time. Now pick up a bottle of wine or champagne or something fruity, whatever it is, sit back and call your sister, or your soul sister or your book sister or anyone that makes you feel whole. Tell them you love them and maybe tell them about this great book you read about sisters...wink!

Madlove!

ABOUT AUDREY CARLAN

Audrey Carlan is a No. 1 *New York Times*, *USA Today*, and *Wall Street Journal* best-selling author. She writes stories that help the reader find themselves while falling in love. Some of her works include the worldwide phenomenon Calendar Girl serial, Trinity series and the International Guy series. Her books have been translated into over thirty languages across the globe.

She lives in the California Valley, where she enjoys her two children and the love of her life. When she's not writing, you can find her teaching yoga, sipping wine with her "soul sisters," or with her nose stuck in a sexy romance novel.

NEWSLETTER

For new release updates and giveaway news, sign up for Audrey's newsletter: https://audreycarlan.com/sign-up

SOCIAL MEDIA

Audrey loves communicating with her readers. You can follow or contact her on any of the following:

Website: www.audreycarlan.com

Email: audrey.carlanpa@gmail.com

Facebook: https://www.facebook.com/AudreyCarlan/

Twitter: https://www.twitter.com/AudreyCarlan

Pinterest: https://www.pinterest.com/audreycarlan1/

Instagram: https://www.instagram.com/audreycarlan/

Readers Group: https://www.facebook.com/groups/Audrey-CarlanWickedHotReaders/

BookBub: https://www.bookbub.com/authors/audrey-carlan

Goodreads: https://www.goodreads.com/author/show/7831156.Audrey_Carlan

Amazon: https://www.amazon.com/Audrey-Carlan/e/B00JAVVG8U/

HELLO NEW FRIENDS,

I wanted to connect with you personally to share how much joy and excitement I have that you've read *What the Heart Wants*. I developed the idea for this story after my dear friend and longtime personal assistant Jeananna told me her family history. Her mother is the real-life Suda Kaye Ross. Although she has left this world, she left her mark deeply. Through Jeananna's account of her mother's rich history, and her family line extending through the Comanche and Wichita Native American lines, I couldn't help but come up with my own story of what life could be like for a woman who grew up on and off a Native American reservation.

Much of what I've included here is the result of hours of research, including a great deal of focus on the Comanche and Navajo language in order to be as accurate as possible with the few words I've used. Jeananna also shared some of her mother's personal experiences, which allowed me to spin a fictional tale I'm very proud of.

Still, as a fiction writer I took a lot of liberties and would never wish to offend anyone. I know how rich and diverse the Native American culture and tribes are, and I'm thrilled to have been able to shed a little bit of light on such beautiful people.

Like Suda Kaye, I'm very much a traveler and adore getting lost wherever my travels take me. Because of the success of my stories internationally, I have traveled to many of the places that Suda Kaye has mentioned in her journey and am constantly fascinated by different places, cultures, food, clothing, customs and everything in between. I hope in my fictional world you find a little bit of wanderlust and seek out an adventure of your own.

As for sisters, well, I have three biological sisters and a couple soul sisters. I come from a very large Italian family where your sisters are always a part of every facet of your life, very similar to the way that Suda Kaye and Evie are with one another.

My goal with this book was to show that not all who wander are lost. Reading should be a beautiful escape. It should give you something to think about long after you see the words *The End*. My greatest hope is that a small piece of Suda Kaye's, Camden's, Evie's, Milo's or any of the characters' experiences resonate with you, and you finish this story having taken something away with you. Maybe it's the lesson that you can always go home. Which I wholeheartedly believe. Or perhaps it's realizing that you've been so grounded in the day-to-day you haven't given yourself a chance to really live for you. Maybe it's that you need to reach out to your sister, cousin or friend and rekindle that relationship—as those connections can often fall away as life takes over. Whatever it is, my heart wants your heart to find what it wants.

Madlove,
Audrey

If you loved reading about Suda Kaye,
you'll want to know Evie's story, too!

Enjoy this sneak peek at the next novel
in Audrey Carlan's Wish series,

To
Catch
a
Dream

Coming soon from HQN Books

PROLOGUE

Ten years ago…

Tears track down my face as Tahsuda, my *Toko*, which is the Comanche word for "grandfather," hands me a large stack of pink envelopes tied with a ribbon, my mother's beautiful handwriting on the top. He hands another stack to my eighteen-year-old sister, Suda Kaye.

"From my Catori, for her *taabe* and *huutsuu*," he begins, using the Comanche nicknames my mother gave us. "To have a piece of her on their birthdays. One for today, one for each birthday and important moment in your life to come. I shall leave you to your peace, but know I am here for you, forevermore." Tahsuda puts his hands together under his worn red-and-black poncho and dips his head forward. His long, black, silky hair gleams a dark midnight blue in the rays of the sun's light streaking through our bedroom window. His hair is so much like my mother's I have to swallow down the sob that aches to come out in a flood of misery and grief.

Misery because I'm so angry at her for all the time we could have had together. Grief because she left this world six months ago, and today, on my twentieth birthday and Suda Kaye's eighteenth, we are facing a full life without her. This isn't one of her many adventures where she'd skip around the house, packing her battered suitcase and telling us all about what she hoped to see and do on her travels, while we stayed behind and went to school. Dropped off at the reservation where our grandfather lived as she fluttered around the globe for an undetermined amount of time only to reenter our lives months later with a smile on her face and a song in her heart as though she'd never even left.

At least she'd come back.

As much as I hated the fact that our mother left us for her adventures, I always knew eventually she'd find her way home. Her weary feet would be tired, and she'd come dancing into *Toko's* home with grand tales about a world I didn't ever care to see. Not if it was so great it kept taking her away. I didn't want to go anywhere that made me up and leave my family for months on end. Them always wondering where I was, who I was with and whether or not I was okay.

No way. That was not me. And it never would be.

I finger the ribbon on the stack of envelopes and take mine to the papasan chair in the corner of our shared room. Suda goes to her twin bed and stretches out.

We live in a two-bedroom apartment in Pueblo, where Suda Kaye has just graduated high school. I'd started at the local community college in order to be close to my dying mother and sister still in high school.

The one thing Catori Ross never imagined could happen to her was illness. In all her grand plans to travel the globe, to experience absolutely everything she could, she didn't factor in the time to get regular checkups. Since she didn't tend to get sick, Mom hadn't been to a doctor in a solid decade before she started to feel unwell. Her first round of tests after

TO CATCH A DREAM • 333

three solid months of lethargy and depression, two things our mother never had, gave us the first blow.

Cancer.

Stage four.

She believed with her whole heart that she could beat it, but as *Toko* says, cancer took his wife and his daughter. He says it was written in the stars. The same reason he never gave Mom hell about her traveling and leaving us with him. He'd always said a person must do what their heart wants. Dreams are not only for the sleeping. They are meant to be chased and caught.

Our mother lived. Chased every dream with a hunger that could never be quenched. I feared my sister would do the same.

Suda Kaye sits against her headboard as I cuddle into the chair. I untie the ribbon and then set all but the top letter to the side. The first envelope has today's date on it and her nickname for me. *Taabe*, which means "sun" in Comanche.

Mom called me her sun because I was light everywhere she and my sister were dark. Mom was full-blooded Native American like *Toko*. Suda Kaye and I are half, with different fathers. I got a lot of my coloring from my father, Adam Ross. Like Dad, my hair is a golden blond and I have his icy-blue eyes. Though the structure of my high cheekbones, eye shape and full lips are my mother. Suda Kaye has dark, espresso-colored hair, amber eyes, and will one day have a knockout figure. She's already growing into the womanly hourglass shape with the full bosom, long legs and rounded hips. Me, I have the tall, lengthy, athletic build. Still, there is no denying our heritage even with the play on light and dark in our coloring.

We are Catori's daughters, a vibrant mix of her and our different biological fathers. Though Suda Kaye and I don't know much about her real dad. We just know what Mom told us much later in life—that she had made a mistake. She and her husband, my father, Adam, were going through a rough time and separated for a year. In that year she'd gone on an adventure and come back pregnant with my sister. I was only two when she was born, so it never mattered to me one way or the other. My father treated Suda Kaye mostly the same, which also didn't matter because he wasn't around much either, always being on deployment.

I thumb the envelope and run my fingers across her pretty handwriting.

I miss you, Mom.

Taking a full deep breath, I ease back in the chair and open the first letter.

Evie, my golden taabe,
Never in a million years did I think I'd be in this situation. Gone from you and your sister's lives in a way that I cannot come back from. I know you've always hated my need to wander, as it took me away from you and Suda Kaye, but you were never far from my mind or my heart. Never unloved.

I had to chase my dreams, taabe. One day, you'll understand.

My greatest hope is that you know my love for you transcends any reality, location or final destination. It is as the sun, shining brightly each day. Never ending, always warm, forever shedding light onto you and your sister.

With me gone, without the burden of having to take care of me and Suda Kaye, I want you to think long and hard about what it is you want in life. Just you. Think big. Live out loud.

What is still out there to explore?

Where in the world do you see yourself visiting?

What new journey have you wished to undertake?

Think of all the beauty I've shared through my stories and photos over the years. Those experiences are a huge part of me. And I'm so grateful I had them. It gave me the ability to open your eyes to the fact that anything in life is possible.

My only regret was having to leave you and your sister behind. Though I hope now you will take time out for yourself.

Evie, you are so grounded. Your feet firmly rooted to God's green Earth. Pull those roots, my lovely girl. Break away from all that keeps you still and give yourself an experience unlike any other. Perhaps then you will understand my need to go, to feel the wind in my hair, the sand between my toes, the gravel under my boots. I lived every moment to the fullest and I want that for you so deeply.

Please take the inheritance I left you and use it to live.

See the world, my precious girl.

With all my love,

Mom

I grind down on my teeth and wipe my nose with the back of my hand. I fold my letter into thirds and stuff it back into the envelope. Clearing my throat, I flatten my hand along the front before lifting it to my nose and inhaling the familiar scent of citrus and a hint of patchouli.

"Smells like her." I clear my throat as a traitorous tear slides down my cheek.

Suda Kaye sniffs her letter and smiles sadly. "Mom always said if you're going to smell like anything, let it be natural. Fruit and spice."

"And everything nice!" I chuckle, then sigh as the weight of everything in my letter festers in my heart and soul, mixing with the layer of intense sorrow I haven't removed in the six months since she passed.

"I miss her. Sometimes I pretend she's just gone off on another one of her adventures, you know? Then I can be pissed off and plan out all the catty things I'm going to say to her when she finally returns with a suitcase full of dirty clothes and presents to smooth over the hurt of her absence."

My sister gasps and her stunning amber eyes fill with more tears. "Evie, she didn't want to leave…"

I grind down on my teeth, rekindling the anger that never seems to disappear when I think of all the years we lost with her. "Not this time, Kaye, but what about all the other times? Years and years of time lost. And for what?" I huff and stand, pacing our small room with mom's letters plastered to my chest like a well-loved teddy bear. "Fun. Wild experiences. *Adventures!* It killed her. This need to see the greener grass on the other side."

Scowling, I point at myself. "Well, that won't be me. No way. No how. I've got my feet firmly planted on terra firma. I'm going to finish school, get my bachelor's in finance, then my master's, and make something of myself. And I'm going to be happy!"

How I'm going to be happy without my mother in my life, I don't know. I never knew how to fill the hole she left with each adventure she took. It just seemed that the void got bigger and bigger, but my mother, she was such a glorious woman, an incredible presence when she was there, she could easily fill up that gaping wound that I call my heart each and every time she came back.

Finding that the pacing isn't doing much, I toss my stack of letters onto the chair and drop onto the bed next to Kaye, face planted dramatically in the crook of my arms, my nose touching the mattress as I breathe deeply and try my best not to break down in front of my baby sister.

Slowly, she strokes my hair in long soothing sweeps of her

hand. Once I've gotten myself under control emotionally, for now that is, I turn over.

"What did your letter say?" I ask.

Kaye licks her lips and glances to the side. We don't have any secrets from one another, but I can tell this is one she'd rather keep from me. Eventually she caves and hands me her letter. Pulling myself up, I sit cross-legged and read out loud.

"'Suda Kaye, my little *huutsuu*.'" I cover my mouth and close my eyes. Mom called Suda Kaye *huutsuu*, which in Comanche meant "little bird," to my *taabe*. My sister has always been the one up for a grand adventure. She could make going grocery shopping the highlight of anyone's week with her dramatic flair and interest in all things. Same goes for a laundromat, a car wash, a walk around the neighborhood. Always something to experience, to see, hear, sense. My sister soaks up life like a sponge until she's wrung out, and then starts all over again. That apple did not fall far from the tree, much to my dismay.

She smiles wide. "Always and forever, *taabe*," she responds.

Not wanting to make Suda Kaye get more emotional, I quickly read her letter. With every sentence my heart sinks. Basically, Mom tells my sister to leave home. To get in her car and travel the world, starting with the States. To leave *me* in order to allow me to find *my* own calling, without the worry of my baby sister there to hold me back. My stomach churns and acid creeps up my throat as I read the last couple sentences that tell her that if Camden, her longtime boyfriend, truly loves her, he will set her free.

My hands shake as I pass it back to her, my entire body stiff as a board. I feel as though I've been staked through the heart and left for dead.

My mother wants my sister, my best friend, to leave me.

To go away for as long as it takes to find herself.

"You're not going to do it, are you?" I ask, the fear clear in my tone.

She bites down on the side of her cheek and nods.

"Kaye...you can't do that. What about Camden? He won't understand. A guy like that...the life he wants to give you. No way. You just..." I let out a breath, grab my sister's hands and squeeze, trying to transfer all the worry and fear I'll experience with her leaving me behind. And yet I don't say a word. In this moment she has to make the choice that's right for her.

I swallow down the lump of emotion swelling in my throat and whisper, "What are you going to do?"

She stares into my eyes, right through to my soul, and says the five words I never wanted to hear from her.

"I'm going to fly free."

I close my eyes, lean forward and kiss her forehead. "I love you, Suda Kaye." It's the only thing I can say. It's raw, honest and life changing.

"You know, you could come with me." Her voice fills with hope, but the last thing she needs is me tying her down, trying to run her life for her. Mom made that very clear in her letter. Heck, she made it clear in mine.

Shaking my head, I cup her soft cheek. "You have to make your own choices."

She nods, folds up her letter and puts it back in the envelope, then ties up the stack together once more.

My sister, not being one to let grass grow under her feet, pulls out a big suitcase from under her bed that Mom had ordered for her graduation and sets it on the comforter. Methodically, without saying a word, I help my sister pack up her things. The last item she puts on top of her clothes is a picture of me, Mom and her last year before Mom became too sick. It had been a good day and we'd taken a picnic to the park. Laughing, snacking, and listening to our mother share one story after another.

I knew then that those good days would be few and far between, so I encouraged her storytelling, while Suda Kaye ate up every ounce as though it were her very favorite dish.

Holding hands, I walk my sister to her car and put her suitcase in the trunk.

"Do you know where you'll go after you see Camden?" I ask, knowing she wouldn't leave without seeing him first.

She smiles and shrugs. "We're in the middle of the country. I'm going to pick a direction and just keep driving until I get too tired. Then I'll stop and decide where I'm meant to be next."

"You call me. I'll come get you anywhere, anyplace. No matter wh-what." My voice shakes as I pull her into my arms and inhale her cherry shampoo and lotion. I allow the scent to imprint on my memory bank for I know I'll need it in the lonely months, maybe even years, to come.

Suda Kaye walks around her car and opens the driver's side door. "Miss me," she says, and the deluge of tears falls from my eyes like a waterfall.

"Miss me more," I whisper and hold up my hand.

She mimics the gesture, placing her palm against mine. "Always."

Then I watch for a long time as my sister's taillights eventually fade and disappear into the black night. Before long, I look up into the open sky and the wealth of sparkling stars blanketing the sky like diamonds over black velvet.

I pick a star and make the same wish I've been making since I was a child.

"One of these days, I wish someone I love would stay."

1

Present day…

"I cannot believe you talked me into this, Kaye." I grumble through clenched teeth as I adjust the fitted hip belt with dangling cold coins around my body. It jangles and tinkles while I tie it in a knot. The *bedlah* I'm wearing is a stunning teal color, encrusted with gold beading all through the bra-style top. The skirt is made of a gorgeous tulle matching the top but flowing out in swaths of fabric that are designed to accentuate the curves and highlight the body to the max.

As I stare at myself in the mirror, it's definitely highlighting my half-naked body instead of hindering anything.

Suda Kaye stands next to me, sharing the mirror while putting a platinum-colored headband in her long brown locks. Her outfit is a deep crimson with silver accents. She looks like the perfect version of a belly dancer. Not that I look bad. It's just not as common to see a blond-haired, blue-eyed dancer in the traditional garments.

"You look amazing. And you've been belly dancing since you were a child. This is a corporate event. If you drop a hip roll on the wrong beat, no one is going to know. I swear. You're really doing my dance group a solid filling in tonight."

I roll my eyes and sigh. If my sister hadn't given me the sob story of the woman who was supposed to be wearing this getup tonight, I'd have never agreed. Alas, a child facing leukemia treatments tugged on every last one of my heartstrings. The boy's mother uses the belly dancing crew as her one small getaway from all the trauma of caring for a sick child. Unfortunately, the boy took a bit of a turn for the worse and she couldn't make this evening's show, hence me becoming a substitute.

Our mother was an amazing belly dancer and taught both of us at a very young age how to dance. One of our first presents that I can recall her bringing back from her travels were the pretty little finger cymbals called zills, often used in the dance. Suda and I had entertained ourselves endlessly playing with those cymbals and dancing all over the reservation where we spent most of our childhood growing up.

"Here, let me help you." My sister places an ornate gold headband strategically in my hair on the crown of my head. It's incredibly pretty and I do feel a little like a Turkish princess in the full getup.

Suda Kaye's eyes light up at the sight of both of us. She shimmies her hips and the coins vibrate against one another, creating a lovely sound that gets my heart pumping and my excitement up. I follow her movements and together we create a beautiful harmony.

Watching us both in the mirror, we are two opposites attracting magically. One light, one dark. My sister jumps up and down and pulls me into her arms for a hug. "Tonight is going to be so much fun! Just like old times."

I snuggle my girl and swing her body from left to right.

"You're just saying that because your husband is in the audience. You love showing off!"

She pulls away and grins wide. "Ab-so-freakin'-lutely. Any chance I get to shimmy and shake all sexified in front of Cam is a good day. He's been working god-awful hours on some new project his foundation invested in." She pouts. "It's time to give my man a little relief."

I chuckle and check my lipstick in the mirror. A glossy sheen of pink suits the outfit and my naturally golden light brown skin tone and blond hair. My entire abdomen is exposed, which sets a few flutters of nerves to skim down my form. I rest my hands against my belly and breathe.

"Are you nervous?" Suda Kaye frowns.

I bug out my eyes. "When was the last time you saw me this revealed? I mean, I'm cool with showing a lot of leg, but not so used to wearing what is essentially a bikini with a sarong and shaking my booty in front of a room filled with strange men."

Suda Kaye waves her hand in the air as though it isn't even a slight bother. "Puh-leese. You're going to have each and every one of those men salivating."

"Kaye, I'm not interested in any of those men."

"Not true. I know for a fact you're interested in one of them." She grins manically and my heart about drops out of my chest.

"No..."

Her face lights up as though the sun is shining straight through her. "Yes."

"You did not tell me he'd be here. Kaye, I can't do this." I gesture to my half-naked body. "Not in front of *him*."

Kaye laughs heartily, turns me around and leads me toward the other dancers lining up. "You can, and you *will*, because some sick little boy's momma needs you to take one for the sisterhood, and I know you. My Evie would never let down the sisterhood due to a few jitters over seeing her childhood crush."

I grit my teeth and clench my hands into fists. "I hate you."

She snorts. "You love me so much you'd die for me! Now trust your baby sis. I've got you. Girl, I've *so* got you." She waggles her eyebrows and shakes her sexy hips until the coins rattle musically.

The dance troop leader comes through and hands each of us two pairs of finger cymbals. I place the loops around the appropriate fingers and press them together a few times to ensure they are in the right position.

"All right, ladies, as practiced, we flow through the tables, stopping strategically where you see a small black X taped on the ground."

I bump Kaye in the shoulder and whisper under my breath, "I wasn't here for the practice round. I don't know where to stop."

"Don't worry. You'll stay behind me about six to ten feet. When I stop, you stop. I'll make sure you're in the right place."

"Okay." I nod and start deep breathing, calming my racing heart.

I can't even think about the fact that somewhere in the ballroom is my childhood crush. The man I've been avoiding for months since he reentered our lives. He helped my sister with the financing to open her boutique, Gypsy Soul, which ultimately put her back in touch with Camden Bryant, the boy she'd loved and then left for ten years. One crazy event after another, and here we are just over half a year later and my sister is newly married to the man of her dreams and finally living in the same state as me.

I'd be lying if I didn't say I was ecstatic to have my sister back. Her presence fills a small bit of the hole inside of me, but there's still a big gaping wound the size of the Grand Canyon that has never healed all these years. I've gotten used to the emptiness, the feeling of never being full. Suda Kaye helps enormously. Having her in my life on a daily basis slowly started stitching the edges up of that void, but not entirely. I'd lost hope of feeling complete a long time ago.

The music starts and the double doors open into the huge hotel ballroom. The first dancers flow into the room one after another, leaving the appropriate amount of space between them. Closing my eyes for a moment, I allow the music to filter through my subconscious and ease away any nervousness or fear. I open my eyes and watch as my sister's arms flow out to the side. I mimic her position and follow behind her.

Every so often we spin, swaying our arms, skirts, and making exaggerated hip movements along with the music. Suda Kaye leads me to the right side of the room, toward the front where I can see her zeroing in on a table where a man with long dirty-blond hair has eyes only for her. I glance down at the floor to ensure I haven't hit my mark yet and follow until she stops right in front of Camden's table. She nods subtly and I stop on the X, wedged in between a grouping of four tables.

The music changes and I watch as Suda Kaye lifts her arms and starts the routine I've had memorized since I was a child. It's one we were taught by our mother. It comes to me on autopilot and I get into the music, dropping my hips, using the cymbals to accentuate the beats and flow.

I'm having a blast until I do a series of hip rolls while spinning around to face the other two tables and stare right into the coal-black eyes of the only man I've ever wanted more than my next breath.

Milo Chavis.

Swallowing down the surprise, I keep up the dance. Only this time, I feel as though I'm dancing for an audience of one.

His dark gaze leaves mine only when it's slowly tracking up and down my body, from beaded sandaled feet, along my bare legs, gyrating hips, working abdominal muscles, rolling shoulders where I arch my back, thrusting my chest forward as I arch back and forth.

Since I know this routine so well, I can take in every inch of his masculine form as I dance. He has pitch-black hair parted down the center and tied tight at the nape of his neck. His jaw and cheekbones could have been chiseled from stone by Rodin himself, they're that defined. His eyebrows are black slashes above his dark eyes and his skin tone is a toasted brown that reminds me of the desert hills on the reservation when they're shaded from the sun at dusk. He's wearing a black suit with a crisp white dress shirt underneath. At his neck is an intricate bolo tie made of black leather, twisted rope strings hanging down his massive chest, an etched medallion at the throat that has a thumbprint-sized turquoise stone in the center.

One hundred percent Native American.

One hundred percent all man.

One hundred percent beautiful.

One hundred percent everything I could ever wish for in a man.

One hundred percent never meant to be mine.

Not wanting to torture myself any longer, I spin around and face the other direction, following along with the crew and glancing over at Suda Kaye. She smiles and nods her head, gesturing to Milo as though she's handed me a gift.

I close my eyes and continue the dance until the music

changes, ramping up to the big finale right before the part where we're supposed to wrap it up.

Thank God.

I spin around and around, the finger cymbals clapping together for our dramatic ending, and stop only a few feet away from Milo as though my body gravitated right toward him.

His jaw is still hard but twitches as I stare into his beautiful face. I can't help it. The man is magnificent, everything I could ever wish for in a man, and I've been in love with him since I was eight years old.

Only, he doesn't see me in a romantic light, and I doubt he ever would. He's never so much as given me a hint that he's interested in anything more than friendship. With the four-year age difference between us, he's always seen me as a child when we lived on the reservation. The awkward, skinny, gangly, little blonde girl he had to save from a group of bullies when we were kids.

Tahsuda's granddaughter. Catori's daughter. Suda Kaye's sister.

That's all I'd ever been to him, and even though he's been emailing and calling my office to schedule an appointment for some business matter he wants to discuss, I haven't had the courage to call him back.

After running into him several months ago while he was at lunch with his picture-perfect wife, or supposed ex-wife, I was reminded what I was, and would always be to him. Just a friend. I no longer would covet Milo Chavis.

He was not the man for me.

It was a newer resolution, but one I was planning to stick to until I found a nice-looking, hardworking man who wanted to be with me for me. Warts and all. Well, I didn't have any warts, but I did have a lot of hang-ups, ones I've been recently discussing with a therapist.

We stare at one another for so long the music changes and I am bumped into action by Suda Kaye. "Go, go, go," she urges me forward.

I dance my way back to the open doors where all the dancers are spilling through like rainbow confetti bursting through a pop gun.

Immediately my sister leads me over to a quiet corner away from the other dancers. "Okay, tell me *everything*. Was he drooling over you or what!" Her voice drips with innuendo and excitement.

I purse my lips and shake my head. "You should have told me he'd be here."

Her expression twists into a knowing look. "No way. Nuh-uh, you'd have never come if I did."

I groan and tip my head to the ceiling. "Lord, please save me from my well-meaning sister before I've run out of patience."

"He was staring at you the entire time," she gushes. "Not even so much as a glance at the other dancers. All his focus was on you."

"Because I was standing right in front of him, thanks to you!" I snarl.

"Sissy, you have got to talk to him. He's been hounding you for months. Just give in and listen to the man..." Her voice trails off.

"That sounds like a good, logical idea. You should listen to your younger sister, *nizhóní*," came a deep male voice from directly behind our huddle.

Nizhóní. Navajo for "beautiful." I closed my eyes at the compliment. I don't remember when he'd taken to calling me that, but I always thought it was sweet. Unfortunately, it also filled my head full of ideas. Making me believe he could feel for me a little of what I felt for him all these years.

Suda Kaye's eyes bulged and a huge smile split across her face. "Milo, so good to see you, you big hunk of hotness. We were just talking about you." She positively beams.

I glare at my sister and then plaster on a smile as I turn around and back up a few steps, clasping my hands in front of me, the cymbals clanging stupidly.

Milo stands with his hands in his pockets, his large presence making the hallway feel smaller.

"I'm just gonna go find Cam." Suda Kaye grips my shoulders and kisses my hair before dashing off like the free bird she is.

I bite down on my bottom lip and wait for him to address me.

"You've been avoiding me." His voice is stern and straight-forward.

"Well, I wouldn't exactly call it *avoiding*." Even though it absolutely was, I still wasn't about to admit it.

"You've ignored my calls."

"I've just been busy. You know how it is in finance—never a dull moment," I lie. There are a ton of dull moments being a financial adviser. A lot of them are spent watching the market trends and following up on leads.

"Evie, why?" His voice is the low thunderous warning before a storm really hits.

"You've got your life, I've got mine," I make up lamely, trying to avoid the real reason.

He doesn't let me off the hook. He crosses his arms over his wide chest and the fabric tightens around large biceps. What I wouldn't give to see them free of clothing. I used to see him running around bare-chested all the time on the reservation, but we were children. Me eight, him twelve. He hadn't really transitioned into this mammoth of a man back then. After he went through puberty, I watched with avid fascination as he grew more manly, but then he went off to college at eighteen and Mom moved us to Pueblo when I was fourteen so we could go to a public high school. We kept in touch via email and Facebook once we were both out of college and realized we were in the same field, but nothing more.

"That's not an answer," he calls me out on my bull.

My shoulders drop as if separated from my body. "Look, I don't answer to you, nor do I have to" is my unusual and rather uncharacteristic response.

"You're attracted to me."

I go still. Everything around me warps and disappears as I allow the truth to seep into my conscious self.

"What?" I half gasp.

"That's why you are avoiding me. You are attracted to me."

"I am not!" I jerk back and lie through my teeth. "How dare you." More fake indignation.

"I'm not offended. I'm rather pleased, as I have always been fond of you."

Fond of me.

I blink stupidly, trying to wrap my head around having the man of my every fantasy tell me he's fond of me. *Fond.*

I shake my head and hold up my hand. "I'm outta here." I move to dash around him, but his long arm darts out and captures me at the waist, tugging me toward him and plastering me to his solid wall of a chest.

Being in his arms makes me dizzy and I place both of my palms against his chest. He holds me close around the waist and back as I tip my head to look up and up. I'm tall at five foot nine, but he's at least six foot four and I'm not wearing heels.

"Let me rephrase. I'm *deeply* attracted to you, Evie Ross." His words filter straight through my brain, slither down my spine and settle hotly between my thighs.

My heart pounds and my cheeks flush. "You are?" I let the honesty fall from my lips as my body relaxes in his arms.

"Yes. Although my romantic interest in you is not why I'm here. That is for another time. I have a business proposition for you to consider."

I frown and find my feet beneath me, taking on more of my own weight. "A business proposition?"

"I believe we have the same interests, and combined together, we could be a dynamic team and a force to be reckoned with in the finance world."

Him bringing up my business acumen while I stand half-naked in his arms has me stepping away from his warmth. Suddenly I'm cold, and the heat I felt before dissipates instantly.

"Of course. You want to do business with me." I huff.

He nods. "You are a shrewd businesswoman. The best financial adviser I've seen in the area, and we have common interests."

"Common interests?" I shake my head as if this is a dream and I'm about to wake up at any moment. *Please wake up.*

"Yes, our people. Your business is far larger, but I carry the trust of all the tribes in the area that could easily span to the surrounding states. I'd like to meet with you to discuss a merging of our businesses. Together I believe we could make ten times our yearly profits and help Native Americans across the US."

I close my eyes, cross my arms and rub up and down them,

feeling chilled to the bone. "I'm not sure I'm interested in expanding at this time." Another lie. I'd already assessed that I needed more offices farther out of state, maybe even in Kansas or Utah.

"Allow me to plead my case over dinner." His dark gaze heats and he reaches across the space to finger a long blond wave of my hair.

Is he using my attraction to him to get me in bed with him, or to get me in bed with him in the business sense? My stomach plummets as I realize this is simply a ruse. He's a man who sees an opportunity to make more money and uses his good looks and the longtime attraction of a stupid girl to meet his needs.

I shake my head. "No, no, I can't do this. I've got to go. Have a nice life, Milo."

With tears of embarrassment in my eyes, I run, literally run down the hall to the series of rooms that the dance group changed in. I don't even bother changing, just grab my bag and head for the door.

"Evie!" Suda Kaye calls after me, but I don't stop until I'm in the safety of my Cayenne and racing home.